HEADS OR TAILS

23 Stories

F.W. Watt

FriesenPress

Suite 300 - 990 Fort St
Victoria, BC, Canada, V8V 3K2
www.friesenpress.com

Copyright © 2014 by F.W. Watt
First Edition — 2014

Front Cover photo: lithograph by Joel Sibisi

Some of these stories have appeared in *The Canadian Forum, Quarry, Chatelaine, Queen's Quarterly, The Malahat Review, Fiddlehead, 82 Best Canadian Stories.*

All rights reserved. No part of this publication may be reproduced in any form, or by any means, electronic or mechanical, including photocopying, recording, or any information browsing, storage, or retrieval system, without permission in writing from the publisher.

ISBN
978-1-4602-4425-8 (Hardcover)
978-1-4602-4426-5 (Paperback)
978-1-4602-4427-2 (eBook)

1. Fiction, Short Stories (single author)

Distributed to the trade by The Ingram Book Company

Table of Contents

Author's Preface and Owner's Manual v
Nolan and Son, Farriers 1
I Am Dying, Egypt 16
Death of a Star 29
Revenge 43
The House Cats 56
Book Of The Duchess 63
Bayley And I 84
Dans le restaurant 92
Paddy the Horseman 103
An Oxford Anecdote 117
Frenchmaid and the New Sci-Fi Age 128
A Jar In Tennessee 140
The Offering 151
Old Friends Of Farmer Smith's 161
The Jumbo Special 175
Prospects of Employment 185
The Mare 194
A Very Special Tuesday 208
The Last Ride Together 226
Winter Wheat 234
The Birthday Present 246
A Shaggy Dog Story 260
Desolation 284
About the Author 306

Author's Preface and Owner's Manual

The author had the good fortune to live, learn, and work for years in a rich variety of rural and urban settings. Born in Saskatchewan. Grew up in Vancouver, British Columbia. Four years in Oxford as a Rhodes Scholar. A couple of decades in Toronto, and more in the burgeoning towns and countryside nearby. Here, in Ontario, he still witnesses the sprawl of big city development encountering the shrinking world of agriculture, horses and cattle, hay fields and pastures, historic homes.

The people captured in the stories are just as varied. A small town lawyer reluctantly enmeshed in the lives of his clients. A burly blacksmith weakened by his troublesome son. An assorted handful of university professors proving that higher education is no guarantee life will be sedate. A star high school quarterback enduring a dreary future, and his former team-mate who doesn't enjoy a grownup meeting with him. An ambitious politician, before his race to become Prime Minister of Canada, revisiting the Oxford of an earlier stage in his life. An Irish stable hand whose dedication to booze and his horses draws him surprisingly close to their animal nature. An urbane Toronto husband and father struggling with his guilt over leaving his grieving wife. An expatriate writer of best selling romances who is smitten by the intrusion of a real life love from his Canadian past. A middle-aged couple who ride horses together but don't live out their relationship quite as publicly as Antony and Cleopatra. An old guy who frequents a fast-food outlet, where he recognizes a stranger's unwelcome face. A high-school graduate who looks back at his school day friends and measures their maturity against his own. A city lawyer writing his memoirs, whose search for the meaning of Youth leads him into an unlikely encounter. And — well, too many more to list here and now.

How should this book be read? Different stories may appeal to different readers. Here is the manufacturer's recommended procedure.

1. Select two stories at random.

2. Name one Heads.

3. Name the other Tails.

4. Toss a coin.

5. Read them both — in the order dictated by the coin toss.

6. Repeat the process until you have finished the book, or had enough.

Good luck.

HEADS OR TAILS
23 Stories

Nolan and Son, Farriers

"Reggie Nolan is the best damned blacksmith in the country."
"I'm sure you're right."
"Good blacksmiths are as scarce as hens' teeth."
"I know that as well as you do."
"We're lucky to get him."
"No doubt."

I can be stubborn too, when I want to be. Attempts to brush me aside as a silly old dodderer especially get my dander up. Neither Reggie Nolan, the best damned blacksmith in the country, nor his ardent but not entirely disinterested supporter Fred Pitts (in my opinion, incidentally, one of the worst stable managers in the country) could keep me from being at the Hunt Club when my own horses were being shod.

Pitts didn't enjoy his part in this conversation, which took place last Sunday morning. At that point he found a half-smoked cigarette behind his ear, pulled a wooden match from his old tweed jacket pocket, lit up, and tried another tack with me. His ingratiating tone is even more detestable than his feeble attempts to be overbearing.

"George Reade, you know, brought over by Colonel Sifton after the First War, he learned Reggie the trade, the proper way, the way they do it in the Old Country," Pitts said, telling the oft-told tale again. Fixing me with his watery eyes, smiling weakly with his thin unshaven lips. "Seventy, if he was a day, crippled with the arthritis. Used to take a stool and sit himself down straight behind the horse. The fellows that worked for him had to trim and shape the hoof and fit the shoes right — all hot shoeing then, of course — nail, clench and rasp, every step of the way, that crusty old devil ready to chew them up if they made a single mistake, and if they did they didn't do it a second time. Never missed a thing. All the good old-time blacksmiths in these parts passed through his hands. That's the kind of blacksmithing school Reggie Nolan went to."

"He's very good, I know."

I didn't say anything more, just stood by the mounting block outside the open stable doors, seeming to enjoy the thin October Sunday morning sunlight, tapping my dusty riding boot with my crop. I let Pitts pretend I'd forgotten what I'd approached him about, or that I'd changed my mind, if that's the way he wanted it. He snuffed out his butt with a thumb and tucked it back behind his ear, under his battered grey felt hat. He turned his sallow face up to the sky as if to gauge the time by the position of the sun, his country-wise pose.

"Well," he drawled, "must see how the boys are doing with the mucking-out."

"Surely," I said, still not moving off to my car in the parking lot, after my morning ride, giving him a last chance to capitulate before I put an end to his obsequious evasions.

"Hunting next Wednesday, Mr. Martin?" he asked, half-turned towards the stable doors, not quite daring to try to break off without conceding to me or saying something to indicate that he refused.

Now, the time had come. I summoned up my energies.

"I shall hunt on Wednesday," I said, emphasizing my words with an extra firm smack of the crop against my boot, "if my horse is ready and fit to ride, and if you will be so kind as to tell me what time Tuesday morning I may come by and personally give my shoeing instructions to the farrier."

A flush struggled up into Fred Pitts' scrawny cheeks.

"I'll ask him to do your horses right off. Eight o'clock in the morning," he said in a rush, all pretenses gone. He darted through the doors like a weasel at his hole when threatened by a stick.

I've reached a stage in life when I will do a good deal to avoid conflict. People sense that in you. They try to take advantage of you, especially when you begin to show your years. I couldn't help savoring a certain satisfaction at a small victory, as I drove back to my apartment in Aurora. Pitts was, I'm sure, experiencing the opposite sensations, which I understand very well. It's not the first time we've tested each other in trivial disagreements of this sort. I don't always win. The sick churning in the stomach, the helpless exasperation, probably the beginnings of real apprehension, worm-like creature that he is, at the prospect of the kind of scene he imagines I will make when I arrive to see the blacksmith. But I plan to use more subtle methods.

Not that I really blame Pitts for trying to fob me off. It was worth the attempt. But he should know by now how strongly I mistrust changes in stable routine. A good stable establishes a routine and sticks to it. The horses like it that way, the grooms like it, the boarders like it. Pitts has chosen to replace the regular blacksmith, who was doing a perfectly competent job, because he's got into some problem, no doubt something to do with trying to get a kick-back on the blacksmithing bills. Personally I have no interest in Pitts' petty swindles, as long as they don't affect the care of my horses and my peace of mind.

Well, enough of that. Already my own stomach begins to churn as I rehearse these ridiculous arguments in my head. Besides, the situation has changed somewhat since my Sunday morning conversation with Pitts. A telephone call Monday afternoon from Reggie Nolan's son-and-heir Reginald Junior has added a certain interest to my meeting with Reginald Senior and has made it highly unlikely that he will be uncooperative with me, of all people.

Despite myself the silly affair preoccupies me on this Tuesday morning early, as I get dressed. I look in the full-length mirror in the hallway before leaving. It's an old court-room lawyer's reflex, no doubt. At Osgoode Hall, fifty years ago, we were taught in all seriousness that judges could be swayed by the cut of a suit or the breadth and color of a tie. I retired from my law partnership in the City before these rakish modern fashions for men set in. Out here in the Newmarket-Aurora area conservatism comes so naturally to me, and to the judges I occasionally appear before, that I hardly know if to be conservative in dress would be a conscious choice on my part. In any case, it's not an appearance before a judge that I'm making first thing this morning. A dark three-piece suit will serve me on a typical Tuesday morning in my law office in Aurora, and it will serve for a brief preliminary visit to the Hunt Club stables.

Reggie Nolan is just tying on his leather apron, standing beside the open back of his truck, which is parked at the south doors of the stable, as I pull into the parking lot. Despite the nippy air drifting in from the empty grass paddocks and rolling hills around, he has taken off his plaid sweater-coat and is wearing only a dark T-shirt that shows his massive shoulders and biceps. He pushes his cap back to scratch his head as I approach, and I realize that his hair has thinned and he has aged considerably in the half-dozen years or so it must be since I last remember seeing him.

"Morning," he says gruffly, evidently not really focusing on me, just using the tone he offers everybody coming near him as he's about to begin his day's work. He never was much inclined to make small talk. He strikes me as having become even dourer with time.

"Good morning, Reg," I say, stationing myself beside his portable forge as he stokes the charcoal before throwing in a match. He operates the bellows and soon is producing more flame than smoke, a pleasant sight and feel in the crisp air.

Fred Pitts is just opening the double doors at this end of the stable aisle, and I see now that he has already backed my bay gelding into position between the cross-ties, the horse still blanketed because of the chilly draft in the doorway. The floor is level there, and there's lots of light. The blacksmith always works in that location.

"I missed having a word with you when you came here for the first time last month," I say, as Nolan continues to sort out his tools at the back of the truck. He looks around and down at me enquiringly, perhaps a little warily. I have this bizarre image of how a grizzly bear might react if you tapped him on his shoulder to get his attention.

"Oh yes," he says, taking his wooden tool box by the handle and walking into the stable aisle. He remembers who I am and is beginning to get the picture. A gesture with his blackened thumb: "This your hunter?"

I walk in behind him, avoiding the horse-droppings with my trouser cuffs and polished shoes, and place a hand on the horse's rump as he stoops to pick up a front foot.

"Yes it is," I say. "That's my chestnut mare, too," I add, gesturing down the aisle. I have no complaints about his shoeing of her, however, so that's a little beside the point. It's just that Nolan is not making it particularly easy to get to the point.

He has already loosened the first shoe, and with a quick twist of his big hairy wrists he flips it off, drops it on the cement floor with a clang, and goes on to the next. His whole manner is of someone in a hurry, knowing exactly what he wants to do and has to do, set unshakably in his routine. I try to control the testiness I always feel rising when people want to brush me aside as if I were some fussy old fool not worth noticing.

"The first time you shod this horse," I say, deliberately pausing, deliberately waiting for him to straighten up, look at me unsmilingly with that big, square, sullen, early-morning face, the face of a strong animal that has never been afraid of a human being, "Fred Pitts forgot to ask you to correct a little problem I have with him."

"A little problem," Nolan says, tapping the jaws of his pincers impatiently in the palm of his broad hand before bending to the third shoe.

"Yes," I say, undaunted, calmly and clearly, "this horse forges badly, he forges badly unless he's trimmed off very short behind and is angled in front to turn over easily."

Two more shoes clatter onto the floor before Nolan looks up or says anything. He picks the four shoes from the floor and walks out of the doorway to his truck. I was expecting to make slow progress. I follow him and repeat what I have to say, indicating the angles I have in mind with my fingers in the air. He taps the old nails out of the shoes as I talk. He might be a rock-cliff hanging over me, or a giant deaf-mute for the way he responds, expressionless face under heavy brows, furrowed forehead bearing the mark of his cap's head-band. Now I see Fred Pitts out of the corner of my eye. He has been watching us from farther inside the stable, no doubt. He has left his mucking-out crew, and is now hovering in the doorway, thin and miserable and pale-looking in his seedy old jacket and soiled baggy trousers, fishing a cigarette from behind his ear.

"I was explaining to Reg," I say, in a louder voice, forcing Pitts to acknowledge that he's listening and to come closer, "that my bay hunter forges badly unless he's specially trimmed."

Pitts coughs out some smoke, looks at Nolan's dour face, and mutters an answer he hopes will walk the line between antagonists.

"Well, I reckon nobody knows any more about shoeing horses than Reggie Nolan here."

He nods his grey fedora sagely towards Nolan, a crooked grin touching his unshaven lips. Nolan turns back to the horse, ignoring us both. But he walks right around the animal with a kind of slow swagger, as if seeing him for the first time, till he's at the head again, and looks almost threateningly back along his sides to Pitts and me, two men half his height and weight, behind him in the doorway. The bay swishes his tail. He doesn't appreciate being taken away from his hay and being given all this attention. He lifts a foot as if he'd like to kick, if he weren't so aware of his manners.

Nolan pushes his cap back and scratches his balding head. His expression is grim, the look of a man with his own depths of troubles quite enough to occupy his attention without other people making demands. He has been known, as Pitts reminded me on Sunday morning in some alarm, to throw his tools into his truck and drive away from a stable and a horse half-shod, when provoked by clients or stable managers telling him how to do his job. I come forward and stand beside him, sharing his view of the horse, tactfulness itself.

"Well, the way he's built, there's nothing much you can do," Nolan says sourly, leaving me to decide how much insult to my horse's quality and conformation he means.

I don't feel it's a matter requiring me to take offence. My horse is not for sale.

"True," I say, "but we have found over the years that with corrective shoeing he moves quite passably."

"In fact," I add, perhaps despite myself bridling just a little at his attitude, "he's a rather pleasant ride, though you might not know it by looking at him."

Nolan jams the cap back on his head and stoops with his trimming knife to a front hoof.

"Well, I'll do the best I can," he says.

As far as he's concerned, the subject is now closed. I say nothing, but stand watching as he picks up the foot. Fred Pitts moves away. Obviously he thinks the matter has been settled without an explosion, though he must be as uncertain as I am as to what Reggie Nolan will really do with the horse. However, I'm not finished yet.

"Your son was in to see me yesterday," I say to the stained top of Nolan's cap.

His huge shoulders tense and ripple as the knife in his fist slices the horn white and the horse shifts his weight restlessly on three legs, leaning on Nolan's powerful body with some part of his three-quarter's of a ton. Before Nolan can possibly have finished trimming it, he lets the foot slip from between his leather-aproned legs, and he straightens up, in a slow, stiff way, to look directly down at me by his side.

"What's the boy done this time?" he says quietly, sucking breath and spittle between clenched smoke-stained teeth.

The jaw is as square and set as before, but I realize the force of my thrust. There's a sick wavering expression in his pale-blue eyes.

"He hasn't said anything to you?"

I'm delaying, of course. It seems to me unlikely that the boy, an only child, who left his father's trade and home in some sort of senseless rebellion a year or two ago, would go back to his parents at a moment of disgrace.

"Nothing. He hasn't been near the house for a couple of months."

Nolan puts an arm on my horse's side. He almost leans, as if too weary to hold up his own massive frame any longer, strong and almost as big as a horse though it is. As he slumps his head forward a little, looking at me and waiting for the bad news, his body seems to slacken. What was all muscle and sinew shows a softness, a heaviness, a fold here, a roll there, and the impression of deep weariness grows. The weariness of a life of hard manual labor going sour. The knife is still clenched in his big fist. He's grinding his jaws.

"Well, perhaps I shouldn't say anything then."

"You might as well. Sooner or later he comes running home. The wife keeps asking about him."

The bitterness in that voice. His eyes are dull and watery. My mind goes back to…what would it be? Five, seven years ago? The young Nolan standing beside his father. At the Aurora Horse Show, that's where it was. I was still listed in the program as a Director then, though it was years since I'd done much of anything for them. Nolan was there as official farrier for the show. At the ring-side with his blacksmith's truck. I remember it particularly because you could see the freshly-painted "& Son" on its side. The two of them bare-armed, the teenage boy staring out across the hunter course, almost as tall as his father, with the same big shoulders and biceps and wrists already. Downy hair, the beginnings of a beard and moustache sprouting on a fresh, cheerful, boyish face.

They seemed happy enough then, buoyant even. The son perhaps just now for the first time fully acknowledged as carrying on in his father's footsteps, a solid trade and business to grow into. Everybody knew old Reggie Nolan. People would stop and talk with him and the boy, who had left school at fourteen to serve his apprenticeship in a much-needed, thriving occupation. Now and then an exhibitor would bring a horse over to have a clench tightened or a shoe reset. Usually, though, the official farrier has very little to do at a horse show, except to watch good horse flesh in action, and all those expensive people who use it to fill up their leisure time.

I imagine that's the kind of situation that led Nolan's son to get ideas above himself. Those groomed and braided horses, the polished riding boots and tailored jackets and tightly stretched britches both the men and the women wear nowadays. Drinks flowing in the Exhibitors' Bar. The idle rich at play. It must have looked attractive to an impressionable teenage boy — I'm not sure I would let children of mine, if I had any, grow up in that environment — especially when he got a chance to mix a little with the socialites as Reggie Nolan established a small stable and began to breed and show a few horses himself, and his son was able to enter the show ring in front of the judges and the crowd and collect a ribbon from time to time. No doubt he liked the excitement and attention, and who can blame him? Besides, it would take a more sensitive and perceptive and sophisticated young man than Reggie Nolan's son has ever given signs of being to realize that in the horsey set, if he was noticed at all, he would always be labeled with amused tolerance as 'the blacksmith's boy'. Or even if he did have some inkling, he could never appreciate the exact qualities associated with that identification in the minds of those who would use it.

Reggie Nolan himself isn't vulnerable in that way, and never has been. He's made of simpler and tougher stuff than his son. I remember seeing him often enough at the Aurora Horse Show Association dinners years and years ago, when I used to attend. He wasn't ever seated at the head-table of course, but at one of those set aside for some of the minor officials. Shoulders and thick neck and biceps threatening to split the seams of his Sunday-best dark suit. Sweat beading his dour heavy-weight boxer's face. Once the speeches and trophy-giving were over and the dancing and socializing began he would likely leave.

He stopped going regularly, even before I did. I can quite imagine him saying, 'I don't have time for that crap anymore,' or some suitably proud and independent rejection, if anybody asked. In the old days, people used to say of him, he's his own man. Today of course no one would even know what that description meant.

Reggie Nolan is still silent, towering over me, waiting for me to speak. To say what I have to say about his son, whom he has almost given up on, but can't escape feeling involved with, whom no doubt he wishes would just go away, far away, forever, if he won't come home for good. Nolan looks as though he'll stand here beside my horse all morning brooding and waiting. I see over his shoulder that Fred Pitts is creeping closer again, pretending to wield a broom as a help to his mucking–out crew, who are working their way to the other end of the stable. I make a gesture of my head and eyes up to Nolan. It's one thing to talk to him alone about his son's problems. It's another to give a snoop like Fred Pitts something to retail with embellishments to every ear he meets that's as idle as his tongue.

"It's not quite proper for me to discuss the matter with you," I say quietly to Nolan, as we stand side by side looking into the back of his truck. He fidgets with his forge out of nervousness or habit. "Your son has come to me for legal advice."

Nolan slams the tongs angrily onto the tailgate. My introducing the delicacies of legal ethics at this stage is altogether too much for his patience. There is anguish in his voice.

"For Christ's sake, he's my kid."

"Yes, yes, I understand," I say, raising a hand to calm him, "that's why I'm talking to you….You weren't at the Aurora Horse Shows Association dinner Saturday night?"

"Christ no."

"Neither was I. But your son was."

Nolan's mind is moving along the right path. He has no doubt observed his son on social occasions of that sort often enough in recent years. They bring out the worst in him. The boy sporting his maturing moustache and side-burns, and bright-colored tie, red-faced from too much drink, laughing too loud, barging into other people's conversations, making a spectacle of himself with his bulging young muscles stretching his flashy blazer to the limit. The good natured flamboyance easily turning to hurt aggressiveness. A child's mind and feelings in a strong man's body.

"Well, what did he do? What did he do?"

I mustn't hold off giving Nolan the facts any longer. He looks as if he could straighten the horseshoe he's holding with his bare hands. I quickly sketch in the main outlines of the story as I have put it together.

His son got up from his table when the band began to play and asked Colonel Rivers' daughter, Judy, for a dance. She's a conceited, silly, pretty creature a few years older than the boy. I know her from the hunt field, to which her father, who has been Deputy Master of the Foxhounds, introduced her as a mere child, riding a well-mannered grey Welsh pony, if I remember rightly. Young Nolan went up to her where she was sitting with her fiancé, Geoffrey Biggin, eldest son of the Biggin of Biggin and Floyd, the Toronto investment firm. There was a party of a dozen or so with them, celebrating the girl's twenty-first birthday with champagne. In fact, they had just finished a noisy singing of Happy Birthday, which I suppose is what attracted young Nolan's attention.

It wasn't so much that the boy asked and was refused by the girl. It was the way he asked, and the manner of the refusal. My legal secretary, Mrs.Hodgins, who comes in four afternoons a week and a fifth if my work gets ahead of her, has been on the Women's Committee of the Horse Show for years. She was at the dinner. She was at the next table. She heard every word. I have her account verbatim in my file, describing every detail in her usual meticulous way. It greatly supplements but pretty well corroborates what young Nolan remembers. Something for Geoffrey Biggin's counsel to consider, if necessary, at any future date.

Biggin was obviously in a festive mood. He usually is on these occasions, I understand — a standard type of young person in that set, a tall, gangling, dark-haired, good-looking young fool in his late twenties with too much money in his pocket and too little to do to keep him out of bad habits. He led the joking as Nolan's son appeared and stood at their table uninvited. Biggin and his friends all in formal dress. 'Look who's come to visit. Anybody lost a shoe? Keep your feet under the table, everybody. Oh, he wants to dance! Well, then, why doesn't he dance? Hey, dance, dance, dance!' People started clapping in unison. Harmless enough joking, I guess, if taken in the right way, though they were clearly laughing at, not with, young Nolan in front of them, shifting from one burly ham to another, big wrists showing, face beet-red, now-splendid moustache bristling, grinning no doubt in that sheepish, idiotic way he always used to have when trying to please. He couldn't retreat, he couldn't advance — but he did, even so. He stepped forward and reached for Judy's hand. She was startled. Didn't like the look on young Nolan's heavy jowls, probably. Maybe the boy lurched a little towards her, over her, it's not entirely clear. She drew back, in any case, laughing nervously. Geoffrey Biggin stood up, a foot taller than the boy but a hundred pounds lighter, and — this much is certain — gave him a little push, saying, "The lady doesn't want to dance with you, stupid."

And then the coup de grace — I got this from Mrs. Hodgins, not from the boy — Judy's high-pitched laughing call, as young Nolan took a half-step back to get his balance.

"Oh Geoff, darling. Just what I wanted for my birthday, how did you ever guess?"

Apparently everybody roared as she pretended to open her arms to receive her gift into them, and Geoffrey, laughing too, continued to push or poke at the lad's shoulder. It wasn't really a fight. Young Nolan simply lifted one huge hand in a kind of clumsy swipe, rather like a bear paw, connected with a thud on the side of Geoffrey's face, and downed him as if he were a tree struck by lightning. The boy then turned around and walked off in a daze, probably not even quite sure what he'd done, leaving those farther away from the scene to wonder why people were crowded around the prone dinner-jacketed figure which, when he had his wits about him, was Geoffrey Biggin.

That was Saturday night at 11.15 p.m. The Horse Show Association officials of course tried the best they could to control the aftermath. Luckily Biggin came-to almost immediately, was taken off to the York County Hospital in Newmarket, where all he needed was half a dozen stitches, some pain killer, and a certain amount of reassurance that his beauty wasn't marred forever. It's pretty hard to stop rumors from spreading in a closely-knit group like the horsey set, but I imagine they probably will have managed to keep any sordid little stories out of this coming Wednesday's *Aurora Banner*. The big question was, what would Biggin do when he sobered up and recovered from his hang-over?

Well, like the spoiled young ass that he is (or perhaps it was his fiancée or his friends who persuaded him), he decided to lay charges, which he did yesterday, Monday, at York Regional Headquarters in Richmond Hill. Late yesterday afternoon young Nolan telephoned me from Toronto to say that the pals he is currently living with — a lot no better than himself, in some disreputable farmhouse outside of King

City — warned him not to come home Monday. The police had been in already looking for him. Nolan was obviously bewildered, if not frightened. What should he do? Of course I told him to drive out to Aurora at once, to talk to me at my office where I went specially to meet him, and then to go home to his friends and go to bed. The York Regional Police are hardly likely to pursue him all through the night like a bank robber or a murderer, even if it was a Biggin whose head he cracked open.

Reggie Nolan's face has gone white and green and red, and white again, as I give him as much of a description of the state of affairs as I think is useful or that he can endure. He's biting his lips in exasperation and sucking air and spittle through his clenched teeth by the time I'm finished.

"The damned fool, the damned fool," he groans. "I told him where the drinking would end up. Biggin. Why did it have to be Biggin? They'll throw the book at him for something like that, won't they? He'll go to jail this time for sure, won't he?"

"He could," I say, judiciously. "We'll know better at ten o'clock this morning."

Nolan looks at me enquiringly. A faint hopefulness begins to cross his dazed face as he watches my expression.

"Your son is coming to my office at nine-thirty. I have invited Geoffrey Biggin to see me at ten. At that time I hope to have a realistic discussion among the three of us that will ensure that Geoffrey Biggin withdraws his charges."

Nolan says nothing. It sounds too good to be true. I feel I must add the qualification.

"Of course I don't know that Biggin will accept my advice. The Biggins have always thought well of themselves, and the lad has his pride to consider."

In fact, Biggin Senior is a notoriously self-important ass of a man much involved in horse show activities and in the social life of that set. Nothing else I could say would be likely to hit Nolan so hard. Even so, his reaction is stronger than I expected. He turns to me, spluttering, almost incoherent in his rage.

"Now look, Mr. Martin, you tell that son-of-a-bitch Biggin …..Don't do us any favors. If he's going to make trouble, I'll set him straight myself. Whatever my boy did, I know he's in the wrong, OK, there's no way around it. I'll foot the bill. But I want you to make sure he gets a fair shake, as good a deal as anybody else, I don't care how many Biggins there are, they got no right to do more than what the law allows."

He goes on in a steady rant, glaring at me as if it were my fault, but appealing to me all the same, appealing to my professional skills. Baffled, frustrated, helpless for all his strength. Feeling the worse for being so strong, no doubt. I let him run down and then I answer.

"I think, Reggie, I think I can assure you that your son will get all the protection before the courts that the law can provide. But I should say that I feel pretty confident that it won't come to that. The charges will probably be withdrawn."

Nolan wipes his hand on a rag and silently puts it out to me. My fingers crumple like dry twigs in his big hot paw. I turn to leave and he goes back to my horse. My last glimpse of him is of a ponderous, tired hulk of a man bending wearily for what must be his millionth horse's hoof. Surely it was different for him when he had his son working beside him, growing into the trade, ready to take over when his back finally gives out, or his hernias, occupational hazard of blacksmithing, can't be operated on again. He must know better than anyone that the boy is most unlikely to follow in his father's footsteps, or take up any serious trade. He's a spoiled apple. The father's labors must seem more and more pointless — to both father and son.

However, he's doing the job now. He's going to finish the trimming of my horse's hooves, the way I want it done, the way it really should be done. I could have been more reassuring, I should have said more. Told him that his son's affair is more or less settled already. That at least I know exactly the extent of the paternal feeling of the other father in the case.

Biggin Senior and I, after a telephone call from me, had a night-cap and a long chat at the Aurora Golf and Country Club lounge late last night. I still know a little about how to get things done in this part of the world. And I haven't been a lawyer for fifty years not to treat the courts as only the last resort. In the course of that chat Biggin assured me that he would tell his son 'not to be such a blasted fool' and to 'jog down to Richmond Hill and withdraw the charges first thing in the morning,' that is, this morning. I assume he's doing just that. I in turn undertook to have the blacksmith's boy meet with Biggin Junior afterwards in my office. To apologize. Which he will surely do, mortifying as it must be for him, and for his father as well. What other choice has he?

But if I explained all this to Nolan, I might have passed on the reason to him as well, the main reason for the old man's cooperation and his annoyance at his own son. I might have been tempted just to tell him what Biggin actually said to me.

"The blacksmith's boy is a gorilla, and deserves to be put in jail. But I simply can't afford to have any trouble with our old friend Reggie Nolan. You have to handle a chap like that with kid gloves at the best of times. He's a dying breed. You know as well as I do, he's the best damned blacksmith in the country, and he shoes all my horses, has done for years. Couldn't do without the fellow."

The whole business, I reflect, as I drive out the lane leaving Nolan, head down, concentrated on the job, and his tradesman's truck with '& Son' still faintly visible under the covering paint, the whole business demonstrates one of the important facts of life. There's precious little guarantee of respect from your fellow man at the best of times in this world. None at all, unless you have something to offer that other people can't do without. I fear that's a lesson the blacksmith's boy will have to learn the hard way.

I Am Dying, Egypt

(Antony to Cleopatra Act 4 Scene 15)

I had no intentions of getting involved with Robert Smith and Felicia Edwards. I've had enough troubles of my own to last me a lifetime, without taking on their problems. Which have always seemed ridiculous to me in any case. But there I found myself, cooling my heels in the second floor waiting-room of Newmarket's York County Hospital, looking up at the clock that already said ten-thirty, cursing about the undone work still ahead of me before I had the afternoon to myself and my reading, hoping for a chance to sneak in to see Mrs. Edwards without having to stay around until Visiting Hours began at eleven. To add to my annoyance, half the second floor is given up to maternity cases. Every time I got up to pace the hall or peek down towards Room 240 I passed the Delivery Room. Some condescending nurse or orderly was bound to go by smiling encouragingly at my grey hair, as if I were an aging husband or expectant grandfather nervously awaiting a blessed event.

I'm just a casual visitor, I felt like saying. I'm not the slightest bit worried or personally concerned. I'm childless and have been wifeless for more than twenty years, and I'm just here to do a good turn for a couple of people I'm mildly acquainted with. One's in the hospital for a suspected broken neck, dear old Felicia Edwards. The other, Robert Smith, can't come to see how she is but is dying to know, though he's so bottled up about it he can't say so out loud, even to me. I'm a self-appointed messenger going between two middle-aged romantics who will hardly admit that there's anything serious to pass between them. Perhaps there isn't. How, I ask myself, how did I ever get into this?

Mrs. Edwards' bay mare came back to the riding stable by herself about noon last Sunday. She was waiting patiently at the gate into the north paddock, stirrups hanging, but the reins still intact over her neck. Somewhere along the way she'd had a good run, judging by the dried sweat on her shoulders and quarters. But now she was just grazing quietly, glad to be home. Of course the search began, but nobody was too worried. People from the stable do come off from time to time, and get away with a bruise or two, especially some of Mrs. Clive's, the owner's, young pony clubbers.

I had been foxhunting on Saturday and my big chestnut needed to stretch his legs anyway, so I saddled up and set out through the fields to the north. Not too hopefully, since there are hundreds of acres of riding country all around. I had no idea where Bob Smith and Felicia Edwards went for their weekend rides, because I always steered clear of their paths apart from a wave or a good-morning, coming or going. When I want to ride in company I go foxhunting. Otherwise a good horse is all I need to keep me happy. I'm probably only ten years older than Smith, but thank God I've got to the stage where I no longer blunder into that kind of futile emotion-draining human entanglement. What an ass he makes of himself, bouncing off up the lane on his ugly Roman-nosed grey gelding, as fat and wheezy as he is, trying to keep up with a lady whose hair has as much middle age in it as his, riding a horse just as common and ugly though a decent enough old mare, and bouncing in the saddle just as precariously. I remember them going off together last Sunday like that, more or less as they have every Sunday for the past ten years, or whenever it was that they graduated from Mrs. Clive's beginners' classes, bought their own horses, and started to go out unaccompanied. They have been astonishingly regular, except for a couple of periods when Mrs. Edwards' equestrian career was threatened by her health problems and her husband's lack of enthusiasm for it. It always seems to me they're taking their lives in their hands, but surprisingly they usually come back together and in one piece. However, this was really no joking matter at Mrs. Edwards' age. I kept my eyes open at every turning and path crossing.

I was almost out to the Second Concession when I thought I heard hoof-beats. I halted and listened, and there was no doubt about it. I trotted ahead to the wicket gate that leads out onto the gravel road. By the time I'd shut it behind me and turned around, there was Bob Smith, in clear sight, coming right down the middle of the road from the north, clomping along at the fat grey's fastest pace, which luckily for Bob is really no more than a hand canter. His elbows and knees were flapping as if he were about to take off from the back of the horse and make his own way home to the stable. He started yanking on the reins as soon as he saw me waiting on the verge for him to arrive. The grey was only too glad to stop, but just as a matter of habit he threw up his head and skittered a little, almost shaking the rider off.

Bob Smith's round face was brick-red under his black riding cap which on the run got tipped forward over his eyes. He was chewing ferociously at his little grey moustaches. He sputtered a moment or two before he could get the story out. Mrs. Edwards had had a terrible fall, her horse had evidently stepped in a ground-hog hole at the gallop and come down. They had been up at Scadding's place, and fortunately Scadding and his man had been working on a fence only thirty yards from the accident. The ambulance had come out from Newmarket in twenty minutes and taken Felicia away, conscious but in pain and still not quite sure where she was.

"Well then," I said, putting a hand on Bob's knee to try to settle him, "let's you and I turn in here and go back to the stable together. There's no use haring all the way. She's in good hands and there's nothing you can do."

I led him back through the gate, opening and shutting it myself, because his grey was so unruly after the excitement that Smith couldn't get him near it. We jogged along more or less together most of the way back. Bob never stopped talking. I think you would have to say that he was hysterical. I wish I could forget that turgid flow of words, phrases, half-sentences. Bob would be far more embarrassed than I, but the irony is that I'm sure he can't really remember what he said to me, or the tone of his voice, or he would never look me in the eye again. I imagine he's blotted out the whole conversation with me. Silly old fool. If there's anything I detest its lack of restraint, self-control, particularly about matters as personal as the feeling a man has for a woman.

I suppose in fact it served to calm him. By the time he'd described the accident to me in the fourth or fifth version it was beginning to sound coherent. Dear Felicia, an artist at heart, wanted to see the autumn colors beginning in Scadding's woods. They got off to pick a few leaves, no other reason, Bob Smith unnecessarily assured me. As if I cared to scrutinize their absurd relationship. They had got a little late, Mrs. Edwards was due in the City to receive afternoon guests with her husband. And so they set off at a brisk pace for the stable. Bob, cantering on ahead of Felicia, was just waving at Scadding when he saw Scadding straighten up from the fence he was wiring, and start to wave him down, his arms high, and run towards them. Bob looked over his shoulder and saw to his horror the four legs of Mrs. Edwards' horse kicking in the air.

"My God, my God," he kept saying to me or to himself as he remembered the shock of it.

By the time he got there, Scadding and his hired hand running up behind, the horse had picked herself up and was starting to gallop off down the road. Scadding caught at the reins but missed, so they let her go. The hired man took hold of Bob Smith's horse, as Bob jumped off and knelt beside the body stretched straight out on the ground, face down.

Afterwards, this part still brought moisture to Bob's eyes as he talked about it. Felicia, when he eased her over on her back, was black with earth gouged out by her face, her mouth was full of grassy dirt, her eyes were blind with gobs of moist earth, and she was gasping faintly for air. Scadding ran off at once to his house to call the ambulance. His man walked Bob's grey, frantic to follow the bay mare down the road, in wide circles, trying to watch and make encouraging suggestions, while Bob lifted Felicia in his arms as if she were a corpse freshly excavated from the grave, and attempted to clean out her mouth and eyes. Blood began dribbling from her nose.

The description became so familiar to me that by the time we came through the gate into the north paddock I really felt I had been there myself, I could see the scene so clearly. The sight of Smith's pudgy face emitting that flow of anguished words about another middle-aged creature's fleshly injuries and suffering quite repulsed me, but there was nothing I could do to shut the poor man up. And that wasn't the worst part of it. No, the worst part was to have to listen to him talking about his relationship with the woman, his long troubled non-affair with her. His feelings, yes, his wretched feelings about her. That was really too much. Why should he imagine anyone else would be interested to know that they met only here at the stable to ride together, and nowhere else. That his wife, who was a semi-invalid, and her husband, an old man with a weak heart, would die if they knew about the relationship. That neither she Felicia nor he Bob could bear to hurt their spouses and yet they wanted so much to be able to marry each other. A serious, deep commitment, no trivial sordid amour, indeed true love — Romeo, Antony (I am dying, Egypt, sweet queen), the Duke of Windsor, God knows who else, all rolled up together no doubt. What endless rubbish he talked. On and on. And his worries about what would happen now, and how he wouldn't be able to see her or comfort her or help her, not even know how she was, once her husband learned of the accident, as he probably would immediately, and came from the City to take charge of her.

"Well," I found myself saying, "It really doesn't sound too serious. They'll probably just examine her, make sure she's broken nothing, and send her home. You'll see her out riding next Sunday. In any case, somebody from the stable will no doubt drop by at the Hospital and see how things are going. If she's not let go immediately."

He hardly heard me, but perhaps the tone got through to him. Certainly as we led our horses into the stable he appeared much more composed. He had to be, because word had spread already as it usually does in such cases, and he found himself having to tell the whole story of the accident to Joan Clive, the stable owner, and several riders and neighbors who had come by. I slipped away while he was going through it all again, surrounded like a hero fresh from battle by concerned faces. My last glimpse was of his short round shape, pudgy jowls, and agitated little moustaches in constant motion.

I was late and in a hurry. I don't like to waste time, especially on Sundays. Theoretically I'm semi-retired now, and I do try to keep my law office open only in the mornings. But after practicing for almost forty years in the Aurora and Newmarket area, I'm usually busier than I want to be. My remaining hours are precious to me. The fact is, to put it bluntly, poor Mrs. Edwards dropped right out of my mind as soon as I left the stable.

My Sunday routine is to change at my apartment after my morning hack, go over to the Golf Club for Sunday dinner, my one big meal of the week, and then to settle down at home again to a long afternoon's and evening's reading. Occasionally I share my table with an old acquaintance, perhaps a grass widower from the town or another divorced man or a bachelor client, but of course we never talk business. Although I have never been a drinker, I enjoy a half bottle of wine with my dinner to put me in the right mood for the afternoon. Others may think such a Sunday prospect too quiet for their tastes. But I can assure you that my adventures in reading take me quite as far into space and time as I could wish to go. And for companionship I have the finest minds civilization has produced. No wonder poor Bob Smith and unhappy Felicia Edwards faded so quickly from my conscious thoughts.

I was particularly delighted to have recently made the acquaintance of the work of the renowned German archaeologist Dr. Karl Richard Schliemann. Earlier I had read with complete absorption his account (in two volumes) of the excavations that brought the legendary kingdoms of Assyria, Babylonia and Sumeria into the compass of human history. Literally dug them out of the dark shadows and deep sands of the mythical past. Perhaps the average reader might find that sort of writing a little technical and dull at times. But I've made quite a study of the subject over the years, and have developed almost a professional interest. Of course I've had no first-hand experience of archeological work, as I carefully explained to the Aurora Ladies' Literary, Cultural and Historical Society when they invited me to give them a talk, my first public appearance as an amateur archeologist, some ten or twelve years ago, it must be now. Not that that bunch of ridiculous old women could tell the difference anyway. I managed to put together what was generally acknowledged, even by my wife if I may say so, to be a thoroughly successful lecture and slide show out of mere bookish enthusiasm. Since then my reading has gone on apace. On the Sunday afternoon of Mrs. Edwards' mishap I was lucky enough to be able to immerse myself in a third volume by Dr. Schliemann, dealing with ancient Egypt and especially the discoveries centering on the tomb of the Pharaoh Tutankhamen, which dates back to approximately fifteen hundred years before the birth of Christ.

Mummies and pyramids have always fascinated me. Schliemann's dry prose seems remarkably appropriate to his subject, because he lets the subject speak for itself. By which I mean that I find it more deeply engaging than any deliberate appeal to one's sense of the macabre and the strange could ever be. Of course Tutankhamen's tomb is a great temptation to play on popular feelings. The handsome young ruler died at eighteen. His loving young wife pictured in that ancient funereal bas-relief, grieving. Her actual parting gift of simple spring flowers left in the tomb still astonishingly identifiable, despite the passing of the centuries — almost as if they were picked the day before. Real flowers more eloquent in sorrow than the whole extravagant display around. All that gold and jewelry and the idols and protective angels and all the other lavish preparations of the body for a fleshly resurrection, the miracle they seemed to expect, the miracle that three thousand or four thousand years later had in any case certainly not taken place. Because the body was still there, undeniably dead. And now with the sacrilegious breaking of the seals by unbelieving Egyptian workmen and European scientists the possibility of such a miracle was gone forever.

I must say, for all that expenditure of love and hope and fear and reverence, those ancient Egyptians had a most preposterous self-contradictory way of dealing with human flesh. Could they really believe they were preserving that comely young prince's body when they felt they had to do such awful things to it? Pull the soft matter of the brain out through the nostrils with a metal hook. Cut into the visceral cavity with their stone knives and take out the shapeless guts (or perhaps in this case drag the innards out through the anal aperture). Put the organs in a large vase. Pickle the remains in brine. Plug up all the orifices with balls of linen. And then, and only then, dress and lay out the corpse in state. How could they think that it was really Tutankhamen they were winding in the linen cloths and the jeweled wrappings? Even more so, how could the beautiful young woman depicted in the bas-relief drop her flowers with her tears over such a revolting relic?

Well, there has to be an explanation, though Schliemann is too good of a scientist to pretend he fully penetrates the mysteries of the ancients. Perhaps they weren't so strange after all. Perhaps the vast labors and craftsmanship and wealth that went into the tombs and pyramids of the pharaohs were really just a public cry of anguish. Anguish at the intolerable fact of human transience. Everything that can be done must be done, they may have felt, to counterbalance the enormity of the passing of the vessel of human life. Even though in the end nothing avails. Absolutely nothing, however grand, however ridiculous.

When I get reading a Schliemann or an Evans or a Ceram or any of the other great archaeological writers, present time disappears and these are the kinds of thoughts that begin to course through my mind. No doubt it's my equivalent of alcohol or drugs. I devour an author. I live on his words, afternoon and evening. Rush through my morning's work with the utmost impatience. Everything else seems flat and lifeless by comparison. Only one other activity is absorbing enough to take my attention away and hold it: foxhunting, with its curious mixture of ritual and raw excitement. I've hunted for forty years or more. In any case, small wonder that it was Wednesday, yesterday, before I thought again about Robert Smith and poor Felicia Edwards' accident.

Of course I assumed that by then she would be out of the Hospital and safely back, however reluctantly, in the bosom of her family in the City. To my astonishment, as I was sitting in my office in the old town hall building in Aurora I got a telephone call, a most confused, sputtering, virtually incoherent telephone call, from Bob Smith. Ostensibly asking me about some legal matter he claimed to have mentioned to me a week or two ago. Well, in a few minutes it dawned on me that he must have some ulterior motive, and then it only took a moment to discover what it was. Evidently he hadn't got his usual mid-week signal from Felicia, whatever it was, to indicate that she would or would not ride on the weekend. For all he knew she was still in some hospital, or dead. At any rate these were the impressions I pieced together from Bob's incoherent chatter. Finally I cut across the nonsense and said, "Look, Bob, would you like me to make a few enquiries about Felicia and get back to you?"

The conversation came to a rather rapid end with that. Bob almost scuttled for cover like a fat frightened rabbit. He was horrified at such directness. He was dismayed to think that in making almost an open reference to it I might be assuming a public character to his relationship with the lady in question. I found myself having to pass off my suggestion as an idle remark motivated more by my own interest than his, or at least a mutual casual concern. Nevertheless his need was obviously so great that he wanted something done and had risked greatly in his hints to me, and he ended by indicating that he would be in touch with me again about the legal matter he had originally raised with me. By the time he had hung up I was alternately laughing and fuming at his idiocy and my involvement.

Something clearly was required, however. Kindness to dumb animals. I picked up the phone and rang York County Hospital. Yes, indeed, they had admitted a Mrs. Felicia Edwards on Sunday. And, again to my astonishment, yes, she was there still, having X-rays, examinations and treatments. Feeling a little chagrined at my earlier casualness, though God knows I hardly know the woman except to chat with, I decided to slip into the Hospital and see for myself what the state of affairs was. I happened to be visiting Newmarket Family Court first thing in the morning in any case. Much as I detest the whole atmosphere of hospitals, that's exactly what I did, going right to the Patient Information wicket without bothering to check on visiting hours.

"Are you a member of the family?"

"No, no, just a friend."

"Visiting Hours start at eleven. You can go up to the second-floor waiting-room if you wish."

Of course I had no desire to wait about. I went straight to her room. A sharp-eyed nurse was just coming out the door.

"Mrs. Edwards is downstairs having X-rays taken. You can wait along the hall in that alcove if you wish."

I immediately took the stairway down to the X-ray Department. Though I hadn't been in the Hospital for years and it's grown, I knew my way around. The corridor was lined with decrepit, broken, or simply watchful, sorrowing, worrying human bodies, on crutches, in wheel-chairs, leaning against the walls, pacing up and down. I could feel the miseries of the human race seeping into my bones. I stepped around the corner and glanced through the short hallway into the Department. There was an empty wheelchair, an orderly standing to read his instruction notes, a filing clerk coming out with a sheaf of records. Then another orderly appeared wheeling a bed-stretcher backwards out of the X-ray Room. On it was a body covered to the face by a white sheet.

Despite myself it was rather a shock. I'd never seen Felicia's face except with the usual touches of feminine adornment and normally under a riding cap. The flesh was as white as the sheets on the stretcher, except for a small strip of brown tape over the enlarged nose. The eyes were shut, the skin bluish under them, the drooping cheeks immobile as wax, the thick pale lips half-open showing a dark hole. I suppose in fact she was dozing in a perfectly relaxed way, knowing from her various experiences how to conserve your strength and spirits in a hospital. She looked like a corpse. I quickly stepped around the corner and walked back up to the second floor.

The nurse had said she would let me know when Mrs. Edwards was ready to see me, and I knew it wouldn't be long now. I felt I had to speak to her, though my already small appetite for it was diminished by the sight of her stretched out, motionless in those white wrappings. Looking for all the world like a body just prepared for entombment thousands of years ago, preserved against all physical change but oblivious to the attentions that were lavished on it. Already inhabiting some never-never land, not human, not natural, not heavenly, trapped in a perpetual limbo. I was trying to shake off the macabre associations, and steady my darting fancy, so I would be ready to see an actual living Mrs. Felicia Edwards, when the nurse came for me.

I should perhaps have told her to announce to Felicia that it was Mr. Martin, a friend, come to see her. I didn't think of it until I was entering the room and approaching the bed. Then of course I realized that poor Felicia must have had wild hopes, as well no doubt as fears, that her visitor would turn out to be her hero, her other man, Robert Smith, stealing in to see her before Visiting Hours, driven to all the dreadful risks those two so scrupulously avoided over the years. How else can I explain the transformation, the erect shape supported by a protective collar against the stacked pillows, the flounced hair, the hectic cheeks, the shining eyes, the breathless smiling lips? A corpse revived by the miracle of romance, the loved one resurrected into intense life, a vital happy human being, if only for an instant. I was embarrassed.

"Why it's Mr. Martin, how unexpected. You're too kind."

Of course the face paled again under the newly applied cosmetics. Of course the light died in the eyes. But Mrs. Edwards is nothing if not courteous and friendly. She rose to the occasion, however different from the one she had hoped for and dreaded. How I hate these faces full of half-controlled feelings, especially these soft, lined faces, these tired middle-aged faces. Why can't people keep hold of themselves? I chatted on as best I could, and naturally I interwove references to Bob Smith into the talk as fully as seemed decorous. There was little I could say, especially when I realized she was countering every such reference with an allusion to her husband. As though she were feverishly battening down the respectable coverings over her secure way of life, fending off the threats of storm. Good God, woman, I felt like saying, relax, I have no intention of giving your dismal little affair away, even if there is anything to give away. Never was a go-between so discreet. Never, I may say, so unrewarded. My temper is not the best. People, I know, are inclined to think of me as testy. I could feel my impatience rising. But then Felicia let the conversation die for a moment, and I noticed, though of course I turned away to look out the window, that moisture was threatening to spill over her eyelids and that her lips were quivering. God, I thought, she's going to cry. It was mortifying.

"Perhaps," she said, in a changed voice which she was obviously trying to keep on an even keel, "you might mention to … to Bob, Bob Smith, that … that he will have to ride without me for at least two weekends. Yes, the doctor says for at least two weekends."

Then her face composed itself into its mask of cheerfulness.

"After that," she concluded with determined gaiety, "we shall just have to see."

At this point a business-like nurse came in briskly, flashing me a professional smile. I looked to her as a drowning man might catch a glimpse of a lifeguard.

"I'm afraid I'll have to ask your husband to leave for a little while, Mrs. Edwards," she said, stepping to Felicia's bedside.

Your husband. I almost choked. I opened my mouth to disabuse the woman of her bizarre misapprehension, when I caught Felicia's eye. She was obviously startled too, and had her lips parted to speak. But women are so unpredictable. What did she do? Suddenly, so sad a moment before, she laughed like a girl of eighteen. And despite her obvious stiffness and pain, she reached a hand out to squeeze mine. The softness and warmth of her skin surprised me.

"Goodbye," she said, "and thank you."

"Not at all," I answered as I turned to go, finding it impossible not to bow and smile back at the silly woman. "Not at all, it was the least I could do."

On my way to the parking lot, I began already to frame words and phrases and sentences delicate and discreet enough to render a comforting telephone message to her waiting lover. That is, if at least in the privacy of my thoughts I may presume to think of that absurd pair as *lovers*. For I knew that only after speaking to him would I be able to free myself from this unexpectedly demanding personal involvement. To settle down once again to the deep fascination of studying the strange and mysterious funerary practices of the ancient Egyptians, in peaceful solitude.

Death of a Star

I have not seen Mr. Tim in person since he retired into his private Observatory, once and for all, five years ago. I have not seen a meteor (or a supernova, if such an amazing phenomenon can ever be identified with the naked eye) since I was a boy fifty years ago, lying on my back in a hayfield on my father's farm a couple of miles from this office — trying to count the stars, until I grew frightened and ran for home. I have seen that family farm and my client's horse, Mr. Tim's old grey gelding, Milky Way, which is turned out to grass there, only once since I left my wife twelve years ago and came to live in town. Why I should be sitting here brooding on these three things — the man, the stars, and the horse named after the stars — is hard to explain, even to myself. It's not sensible. It's not healthy. I must be getting as eccentric as Mr. Tim to be harboring such unrelated thoughts and trying to make sense of them.

The immediate cause is of course simple enough, and I have to do something about it: Mr. Tim's letter. It came as a shock, and puzzles and troubles me still. Most unsettling. That spidery hand of his, familiar enough but grown ghostly, skeletal, over the years. What a graphologist could do with it! Signs of premature senility, though in fact the man is only my age, in the quavering where once there was immaculate precision. But the strange, private, in-turned quality of the script. The repression, the icy control. The dreadful despondency, cramping and narrowing and paring those pen marks to an almost invisible thinness ... but is all that really there, or am I imagining it?

Perhaps you would have to know Mr. Tim as well as I do to see any of those things in his writing. And to know him that well you would have to have been acquainted with him for a life-time, as I have. Even then, you could hardly claim to understand such an odd little man.

But the letter itself is clear enough. Mr. Tim's instructions to me have always been a model of simplicity and clarity. I wish all my clients were as sure of what they expected and didn't expect a lawyer to do for them. No doubt it's more true of small town practice than of city practice ... but I get very weary of trying to be priest, philosopher, politician or doctor of medicine to old ladies of both sexes and all ages who don't know what to do with their property or their affairs until you suggest something sensible they can disagree with ....

I didn't mean to indulge my bad temper and get off the track. I've got more important things to think about. You fall into these habitual reactions as you get older. Your mind and feelings lose their freshness, and you find yourself grinding out the same few dreary tunes, whatever the specific occasion. You get to hate the sound of your own droning. Enough.

Mr. Tim's letter, as I say, is simple and clear. He wants me to have his old hunter, Milky Way, put down. Now, at once. Straight off the spring grass. After all these years. He will leave the arrangements to me, with the understanding that the manner be painless and dignified. Particularly, I am to make sure that the Italian specialists in equine butchering are kept out of it. Milky Way is not to end up in cans of dog food or strung up in fleshy lumps in a Toronto ethnic meat market.

The old grey is well over thirty, an incredible age for a horse. Still relatively healthy, it seems, though certainly he couldn't any longer be sound of wind, limb, eye and heart. He's been retired for fifteen years, ever since Mr. Tim suddenly stopped fox-hunting, which by then was the last of the man's more or less normal social activities. Well, his decision is hardly one to be quarrelled with. Nothing seems more sensible than to have the useless old horse put down. Unless you begin to wonder why Mr. Tim has waited fifteen years to do it. Why is he acting *now*? Why has he left the horse at grass on my family farm, in my care, and then in my wife's, only to dispose of him arbitrarily after all this time? With maybe a phone call once a year in spring or fall, followed by a five-minute visit to the stable in his chauffeur-driven Bentley, a look in the stall or across the paddock, an ear for hurried assurances about the animal's health and happiness from the farm manager or my wife, and a faint smile and nod before he drove down the lane in a cloud of dust. An unchanging pattern. It was never even clear whether he was really very interested or cared. All the bills of course paid promptly and without question. For fifteen years. And so, *why now?*

In the first two or three years, when I was still there at the farm, before my spouse and I finally separated, I tried to be present for his visits. But he really didn't want to be seen or to talk to anyone, though I'm sure he was more comfortable with me than with most people. I doubt if he has ever been close with anyone. He was a solitary fish back as far as our schooldays together at Upper Canada College, running off every chance he got to play with his telescopes. But being born into such a wealthy and prominent family as the McLeans of Toronto, he was always placed in such a supportive social situation, as a boy and youth, that he wasn't allowed to seem all that odd. If he just drifted along, he automatically got to be at the right places with the right people at the right time. But then he grew up, and had to begin to make more and more of his own situation, his own choices, and his own way of life. After that legendary patriarch Donald C. McLean died, much of the family's coherence and sense of direction simply vanished, though of course not the money. That keeps multiplying. When I was at Osgoode Hall completing my law degree he had dropped out of university and was being tried in various roles in the family commercial and financial empire. But I gather he was pretty much a disaster. They couldn't even manage to marry him off, though I saw in the social pages that he was put together with the right pretty and expensive faces often enough. I suppose he was no more cut out for married life than I, and discovered the fact for himself a good deal earlier.

To my knowledge the only thing he really wanted to do was to develop his private Observatory on the country estate north of Aurora that Donald C. left him in his will — significantly it was that place that was left to him, I suppose, since the main properties of the McLeans are those over Oakville way. Perhaps his family should have pushed him into science instead of commerce. He might have become a genuine astronomer. But I think it's unlikely. He was never that bright academically, and in any case he was probably too queer to make his way along a professional route. My own experience as a lawyer in training and in practice has given me a good sense of the kind of difficulties you have to face, the conventional hurdles you have to jump, whatever the profession.

When I moved my family out of Toronto to my father's old farm, and set up a small office in nearby Aurora, after some nervous problems which I don't need to go into now, Mr. Tim was already a kind of local oddity among the people in the neighborhood. Timothy C. having become Mr. Tim to distinguish him from that more important, substantial and dignified gentleman, his father, who was never reduced from Mr. Donald C. McLean. He brought me his local legal business from the day I opened my office, partly, I suspect, because he knew from our schooldays that I wasn't the type of person to invade his privacy. I like to keep to myself as much as he does most of the time. Of course I was well qualified as an old resident of this township, with many family connections still, to handle all the small annoying problems an owner of a big country place can get into with the by-laws and the tradesmen and the neighbors. Especially if you want to build something on the property as peculiar as an astronomical observatory whose dome was to be seen (as anyone who travels north on Highway 11 will know) for miles around. The difficulties we got into over that conspicuous but completely innocuous installation!

Mr. Tim was grateful to me in his own quiet way for smoothing away those difficulties, and well he should have been. I take particular credit for wooing the Aurora Ladies' Literary, Scientific and Historical Society. Though in fact this was the part of the whole business which, strangely enough, I think Mr. Tim himself came closest to enjoying.

It was I who first persuaded the Society to invite him to address them as a guest lecturer. It was I who got him to realize how a talk to the Society on his pet subject, astronomy, would encourage those snobbish and culturally pretentious ladies to swallow any number of McLean Observatories, and what they swallowed their husbands on the Council would have to stomach, so to speak. I wasn't worried about Mr. Tim, odd private character that he is, not being able to give a performance up the Society's standards. Even at Upper Canada, Teasie (our descriptive schoolboy version of T.C.) was always able to talk confidently, knowledgeably, even interestingly though we might not admit it, about the stars, however red-faced, tongue-tied and awkward he could be at other times. I knew the interest had grown over the years. He even got into the papers several times that I know of. Once, I remember, when he wrote to correct some error of the Toronto Globe and Mail's science reporter on the climatic influence of sun-spots. Once in a rather cranky way joining in correspondence about flying saucers and the possibilities of extra-terrestrial life which humans might visit on other heavenly bodies or which might visit Earth in the future. I wasn't sure what specifically he would do for the Society. But I was confident that, by their parochial standards, it would be magnificent.

So apparently it was, in a way. I have both my wife's reactions as I got them at the time (she was — no doubt still is — a Patron of the Society) and the excerpts printed in the *Aurora Banner* Fall Supplement to go by. I gather the talk lived up to its title, "How and When Will the World End?" Everybody had such a good time, despite the lugubrious bent of the subject, that for two or three years after Mr. Tim was invited back annually and he accepted and elaborated on the topic. Then, following the deepening pattern of his life, he just cut the good ladies off and withdrew. As with all the other social ties, one by one.

The only connection left with the rest of the world, as far as I could see, was his weekly ride during the foxhunting season — he came out for the Wednesday hunts — with the Aurora Hunt Club. In fact for some years his McLean estate was on the Club fixture card for the first

Wednesday in November. And he hosted the Hunt Breakfast there, in person, silently but in grand style. Later, at first occasionally and then habitually, he absented himself, leaving the responsibilities to his butler or domestic bursar or other appropriate employee. It was still a fine occasion. I never missed the McLean hunt when I was still active. Great country, maple woods, sandy soil, rolling pasture land, all cedar-rail fenced with splendid coops and panels well kept up. We always turned out a field of fifty or more horses and riders and the full pack of hounds. To top it off, despite the rabies epidemic, there always seemed to be fox in the McLean country. Then the hunts, too, came to an end. And now the only sign of life you are likely to see on Mr. Tim's estate is the changing direction of the white Observatory dome as those hidden eyes look skywards and try to decipher, I suppose, how and when the world will end.

Today when I think of Mr. Tim, the man conjured up by his letter dominates my other images. That little round grey-haired, grey-eyed, grey-faced person, with his grey words and grey silences, who evidently has never had to and never felt the need to do anything in particular with his life. The smaller, flustered, nervous, blushing school-mate grew into that man. Somewhere in between was the Mr. Tim I used to glimpse in the hunt field. Beautifully turned out, of course, in hunting pinks on his big immaculately groomed grey Irish thoroughbred with that rather descriptive but somewhat high-flown name, Milky Way, a mount his father had presented him with on his thirtieth birthday. Mr. Tim looked a bit of a peanut, admittedly, at full gallop along the concession roads of King Township on that bold, long-striding horse. But he stayed with him, sitting quietly, and they made an acceptable picture of control and good manners, though always close behind the Master, however difficult the country, and in at the kill, at least as far as I could see whenever I myself was there on my big reliable half-Clyde gelding.

Members of the Hunt Club were baffled when Mr. Tim stopped hunting and then withdrew his estate from the fixture card. Colonel Seivers, the Master of the Fox Hounds, even asked me whether there was any possibility that Mr. Tim had been offended or somehow put off by anyone. After all, the McLeans were an old riding and hunting family, great supporters of the sport, personally and financially. Donald C. had been M.F.H. at the Aurora Hunt Club in earlier years, and rode with the Hamilton Hunt almost to the day of his death, a grand old horseman.

I had a personal explanation but it was so simple that I couldn't possibly give it. The man was then approaching fifty, a bachelor, with virtually no contacts with people outside of his own domestic staff and some amateur astronomer pen-pals around the world. And now the horse he had hunted for most of his adult years with the Club was showing signs of navicular disease in both front feet, aggravated no doubt by the hard pounding over gravel roads and clay-baked or frozen fields. Our hunt season is cruel to horses, particularly those of the lighter thoroughbred type. A more normal man would have had them give old Milky Way a dose of Butazolidin or some such drug on Tuesday night, hunted him on Wednesday, and meanwhile would have got another suitable mount started or bought one already fully 'made', for when the Bute didn't work anymore. After all, money was no object. And it wouldn't have been necessary to import a horse. I myself could have named half-a-dozen stables with good-looking well-mannered high-quality hunters in the ten or fifteen thousand range, appropriate to a man of his substance.

The thought never seriously entered Mr. Tim's mind, I would imagine. I think I understand why. He would no more team up with a new horse at fifty than he would with a new acquaintance. His universe was shrinking, not expanding. He simply brought that phase of his evolution to an end. I suppose he just hung up his hunting pinks in one of those enormous dark walk-in cupboards I once saw in the bedrooms on my only tour of that old-fashioned oak-paneled bachelor's mansion. On a certain day, before cub-hunting began again, one of his clear, simple notes arrived at my office. He wanted to find a suitable place where Milky Way could be turned out to grass. Could I make the arrangements: check out the quality and reliability of the farm, make the decision, and have the horse shipped from the Hunt Club stables where he was now, and let him know when it was all done? Well, since I had a couple of my father's retired hunters at grass I offered to keep the old horse myself. At the going rate, certainly, but least of all for the money. It was a small help in a difficult situation.

I haven't given the matter serious thought for years. But this morning, after opening the mail and finding, along with Mr. Tim's disturbing letter, a piece of business calling me up to the county court in Newmarket, I took a little detour along Wellington Street West and drove north on the Third Concession, a route I have meticulously avoided since I moved into town. The rather unworthy idea occurred to me that Milky might have died years ago, and my wife might have just gone on collecting Mr. Tim's cheques. Or perhaps found another old grey to take his place, thinking the owner wouldn't visit any more, or was too senile to tell the difference in any case. She's always been quite sharp about money matters, an aspect of that stubborn ability to survive which I may mock from time to time but for which I truly envy her.

I pulled up at the cedar-rail fence and got out to look across the green fields towards the house and stable, hidden in the trees, trees which my father and his father and I after them planted. There was a nice breeze so early in the morning. The dew was still on the rich spring grass. The horses were already out, three or four of them. My old Clyde wasn't there. He had to be put down ten years ago …. Yes, one was a grey. I tried my low-pitched whistle. Heads lifted from the grass. The group began to straggle across in my direction out of curiosity. Then, as if to put on a performance worthy of my unusual visit, a couple of frisky chestnuts I didn't know lit off towards me, one of them nipping at the old grey in passing. It was Milky Way, alright. I watched with amazement and delight as the grand old man lifted his quarters in a cross between a kick and cavort, and set off in a stately canter towards me after the others. I can hardly say he shed his thirty-odd years. But there was a thrust and verve in his uneven gait that showed how happy he was to be alive, at least on this day, despite his aches and pains, and despite whatever dreadful effects of senility he might be enduring but could never complain about.

They settled to graze along the fence-line once they discovered there were just a dusty old car and a quiet man in a business suit standing at the roadside to watch them. Milky Way turned his splotched grey rump towards me, his sides heaving a little from exertion. The once-strong back has sagged to show his hips and withers prominently, but he is in good flesh without being grass-bellied, and is muscled enough for what he has to do. Most of all I liked the calm, alert, steady eye that watched me, the handsome head slanted a little in my direction. Mr. Tim has definitely been getting his money's worth in horse care, I give my wife credit for that.

Well, there was hardly any point in telling Milky Way my bad news. With luck, the truth will penetrate his thick skull and primitive brain quickly and painlessly enough for him not to have to wonder why. I turned away, leaving him to what his old teeth could make of the knee-high grass, and got back in the car.

After a morning in Newmarket, I'm back at my desk. I've cleared up all my immediate business. There's nothing to stop me from dealing with Mr. Tim's instructions. What's required is a brief impersonal note to my wife — we keep our communications on a strictly business level — a phone call to Dr. Kelty, the veterinarian, who will give the fatal needle, and the selection of a firm date and time to be passed on to the Animal Carcass Removal outfit in Bradford. This last is particularly important in view of the warm weather we've been having. I have Mr. Tim's whole file, the correspondence, the accounts, contracts, newspaper clippings, everything, in front of me now. Astonishing to think that he's paid out over thirty thousand dollars in cheques I have forwarded to my wife to keep that old horse alive in the years since retiring him... But why, why should he bring the whole history to a halt now? That's the puzzle.

I spread the twenty-year old *Aurora Banner Supplement* out on the desk. Prominent New Resident Addresses Ladies' Literary, Scientific and Historical Society: "How and When Will the World End?" What a bizarre occasion. I don't have to have been there to see that little round grey man — he was greying by the time he was thirty — standing beside the projector screen in Colonel Seivers' wife's drawing room.

With that bevy of Aurora and district matrons beaming up at him (I've addressed the Society myself, God knows), trying to follow him on his conducted tour through the starry heavens and the vast reaches of cosmic space and time, which he knew better than the geography of King Township.

I had forgotten what heavy stuff he had to offer. I think even with the help of Mr. Tim's lecture notes the Banner lady reporter was somewhat at a loss. First, it seems, Mr. Tim presented the proposition that there could be life — intelligent life, not just vegetation — on billions of other planets circling the stars which form the system of the Milky Way. Was that a heart-warming hypothesis? Did Mr. Tim therefore think that the universe is a rather pleasantly crowded social scene? Evidently not. For, and here was his second less debatable proposition, evolutionary time in other parts of the system stretches millions of years before and after life on Earth. That is to say, other possible places for intelligent life have been in existence longer, already, than our Earth itself is going to last. Therefore, according to Mr. Tim's chilling conclusion, if interstellar spaceship communications were at all possible in the nature of things, the inhabitants of the most highly evolved and advanced worlds, worlds already much older than ours will ever be, should by now *already* have developed them and come to visit us here on our backward planet. Since they have not, it follows logically that the people on Earth will *never* be able to travel to the stars. After all, the time remaining to us in our system is only a mere five billion years, and that's a period for evolution and scientific progress long surpassed in other regions of the Milky Way. So it looks as if, basically, we're stuck with what we are and what we have right now. If there is intelligent life elsewhere, then like human life on Earth, it is dwarfed and prisoned by the immensities of space and time. Earth remains an isolated and lonely speck of consciousness in cosmic night.

There's more. Mr. Tim's long wooden pointer touches one of his pictures projected on the screen. He is showing us the end of even the limited existence of our world. The end of time as we know it. There. See? *Supernova.* A lovely word for an awesome unimaginable phenomenon. A star, like our Sun, but at a later stage of evolution. Demonstrating where we are heading, how it will be for us.

What is going to happen, asks Mr. Tim, when our Father, the Sun, five billion or so years from now, goes through the last agonies of stellar death, as it surely must? Incredible heat developing from nuclear explosions like magnificent fireworks from the Sun's core will reach out into surrounding space. Gaseous flames will lick at the nearby planets which have lived as peaceful neighbors to the Sun for ten billion years. And the planets, including Earth, will melt. Streams of hot gases emanating from the exploding Sun will probably hurl the molten planets clear out of the solar system. When the force of the explosion is finally exhausted, what is left of the Sun and planets will gradually cool to the temperature of the surrounding limbo of interstellar space, which, in contrast to the fantastic heats of the earlier inferno, is hundreds of degrees below freezing. Extremes beyond the limit of human imagination. Yes, truly an awesome spectacle. Pity that no human eye will see it.

What did those comfortable wealthy ladies make of it all? My wife said that they found Mr. Tim fascinating, eloquent, but a trifle pessimistic. She has a knack for sarcastic understatement. She added that all the tea and cakes they could offer didn't seem to cheer up Mr. Tim himself. And he left as soon as courtesy would allow.

Well, what have the stars revealed to Mr. Tim in the years since that talk? I don't have any real clues. But I imagine him getting up evening after evening from a solitary dinner served by his silent butler at the huge oak table of his bachelor's dining hall, passing through the long covered arcade that leads to the Observatory, and reclining under his great telescope all night long. Travelling like the captain of a crewless ship wherever in the heavens the winds blow him, whichever way the wheels of his giant dome turn him. Maybe sometimes before he goes there he enters the huge lined closet of his bedroom to change into his smoking jacket. And he runs his hand down the arm of his hunting pinks that are hung there unused, useless, for all their brightness. The most worldly of worldly things, they would seem to him. I've done the same thing with mine, occasionally, where they hang pushed to the end of the rack in the biggest closet of my Aurora apartment. There, perhaps, he thinks of his old mount Milky Way, wonders how he is, wonders …. Wonders why the horse with which in their prime he shared the exhilaration of the hunt should be left to run out his time into disease, weakness, injury, and very likely a slow, painful and meaningless death. For what purpose? Why delay? Then, as Mr. Tim lies back and surveys the endless stretches of blackness marked here and there by unspeakably distant points of lights, the planets and the stars, he gradually makes up his mind. Mr. Tim finds decisions difficult at the best of times. I'm well aware of that. Much of his life has been a matter of cosmic drift. It has just worked out that way, I know the feeling. Now he will be decisive, as he has rarely been. Perhaps he will be more decisive than he has ever been before.

Yes, I think I can see it now. I understand Mr. Tim's sense of the Milky Way stretching across the sky and those billions of years before and after any particular moment in time, and that inhuman heat and cold ahead. All those intimations that the poor *Aurora Banner* reporter tried to catch in her report of his lecture twenty years ago. He must sit down and write his letter to me. Give me the minor matters to take care of, the practical things, as he has done so often in the past. He is sure I will do what he asks without questioning him, without interfering. He may even sense in me, from schooldays and the occasional crossing of our orbits in later years, a certain parallel if distant life, a comparable understanding of the way things are.

There is the vet to be called, and the Animal Carcass Removal people in Bradford. But I can't inform Mr. Tim of one useless fact. There is no chance of keeping Milky Way out of the dog meat cans or the garbage. That's how these things are done. Neither the horse nor the owner need ever know. The death of an animal can be painless, perhaps, but never dignified. That's an illusion, a comforting lie. A transfer of values from the realm of man to the realm of nature. I'm frankly a little surprised that Mr. Tim seems to cherish that remnant of human weakness.

It's the other matter that's the real quandary. For now it's obvious to me why Mr. Tim has written me that note. What that note signifies, beyond what it says. The truth has come to me with persuasive certainty, as if I knew it all along …. Is it to be a clear night tonight? Will the Milky Way be spread millions of miles across the skies for Mr. Tim to see? I have a feeling that this night, or the next, or the one after that, he will leave that terrible, splendid vision after a while, perhaps earlier than usual. Sometime in the middle of the night, saying to himself that now he has seen enough, he will go back along the arcade and into his room. A man who lives alone has special feelings about the room where he sleeps and dreams or lies awake night after night. I know I have. He will go into the pitch-black high-ceilinged cupboard where his clothes hang from the heavy rod. But he will not reach down his pajamas and dressing-gown. He will rummage for the last time among his hunting pinks and his white stock ties. He will take a handful of those stock ties, traditionally worn on the hunt field because they are strong enough to use for splints, slings, or a tourniquet for a bleeding rider or horse. He will knot them together into a rope and a loop. Slip his grey head inside. Climb the footstool. Feel for the high hook. Kick over the stool, and without a cry drop into the dark.

Yes, it's quite a manageable method. I'm sure that's the way it will be. That or something very like it. All the more sure as I run my eye again and again over the faded yellow *Banner* Supplement and savor Mr. Tim's bleak vision as he expressed it so long ago, and no doubt lived with it darkening night by night over the years.

It is naïve and foolish, he said, to believe that Homo Sapiens, who is after all less than a mere 100,000 years old, will survive as a species for the approximately five billion years of life remaining in our solar system. It is virtually certain that the place of Homo Sapiens will be taken in due course by some other intelligent species, which may develop, say, from some rodent or even from an insect. We do not know. We will never know. We must live out our lives to their individual conclusions in ignorance of what the stars have in store for the human race.

But enough of this. What am I to do? I suppose it boils down to the question of whether existence, brief flicker of color and light that it is for each of us, whether existence is really worth the trouble that goes on adding up the longer you live. Worth watching out, that is, to the last second that nature allows. Whether it ought to be so watched out.

Tonight I think I'm going to leave my indoor privacy for a few hours, my apartment, the telephone at my bedside which could, if I had the desire or the right to intrude, put me in touch with Mr. Tim in a moment. I'll take a long walk past the outskirts of the town of Aurora. In the fields I knew as a child I'll stop, look up at the night skies, see what can be seen with the naked eye, and count the stars as I tried to do when I was a boy.

I trust that an old man, with really no place to hide, at least won't be so frightened as to panic and run home. To observe the stars, as the saying goes, you have to lift up your head. Although I don't consider myself a sentimental person, I may then choose to say my farewells to Milky Way, to commit his spirit to the heavenly bodies after which he was named.

As for Mr. Tim…. Should I try to speak to him? Show him I understand? Call him? Or not intervene? He's a man, after all, a rational being. Privileged to make his own celestial calculations and come to his own conclusions, just like the rest of us, whether we choose to do so consciously or not, just as I have to do this very night. There's no necessity for him, for anyone, to accept a particular given place and time in the universe — as if he were a dumb animal or, on the other hand, one of those bright observable fixtures in the heavens that seem so permanent, so everlasting, to human eyes.

Revenge

The first thing you notice about her is her lipstick. Young women don't seem to wear lipstick at all nowadays, but older women still do, as they all did when I was young, either from habits formed years ago or in the ludicrous assumption that it distracts attention from their wrinkled and sagging flesh. Mrs. Howell is at least fifty. I find myself always thinking of her as older than I, in fact, though of course she isn't. She could be fifty-five. Her pink lipstick is a dreadful slash across a face that looks like the dried oatmeal porridge in the bottom of my breakfast pot. She's been the same for at least the last fifteen years. Imagine my astonishment when she came into my office on Saturday morning to give it the weekly clean-up as usual and said:

"Well, this will be my last week, I guess. I'm getting married."

If she had just said she was quitting, my first thoughts would have been entirely selfish. I would never be able to find anyone else in town to take her place. Awful as she is, detestable in so many of her habits, heaping any files or letters I leave on my desk into arbitrary mountains, shapely but senseless, unplugging all the lamps to plug in the vacuum cleaner, never cleaning the toilet bowl in the little washroom, showing her meticulousness in dusting by tilting every frame on the walls to a conspicuous angle, especially my legal diploma which somehow she probably identifies, even though I have good reason to believe she can't read English, let alone Latin. Nevertheless, I say to myself every Saturday morning as I get up to leave the place to her tender care, nevertheless, I say on Saturday afternoon or evening, when I slip in on my way home from the Hunt Club riding stables to correct her faults and repair the damage, nevertheless: she is a pearl beyond price. And the only one of her kind in the whole town of Aurora. Without her I would drown in dust, trekked-in snow or mud, cigarette butts and coffee spills. No self-respecting client would continue to bring his business to me. Besides, the last thing in the world I want is tension, or the ugliness of an argument, or unpleasant scenes of any kind. So I smile, and take Mrs. Howell's repellent features along with the good.

"You're getting married!"

I tried to keep the amazement out of my voice, but it was impossible. I could see I embarrassed the poor woman. A darker color showed through the corrugated brown of her cheeks. The red slash parted horizontally in the middle to show her small even tobacco-stained teeth and her prominent pink gums. Not that I mock those teeth. I only wish I still had as good a set. But if I had hers, believe me, I would smile in public as little as I do now.

Mrs. Howell turned to the washroom door in which there is the cupboard for the cleaning equipment. With one hand on the doorknob she seemed to feel safer. Fifteen years ago when she first started cleaning for me, she conducted any brief morning chat with me in that position. My impression is that at first she thought I represented a threat to her chastity. A divorced man of private, perhaps eccentric ways, whose solitary life was, I know, cause for comment in town. My being in the office so early every Saturday morning could probably only be understood by the theory, more alarming to me than to her, surely, that I was lying in wait for her. The fact that I'm smaller, lighter, older and no doubt weaker than she, wouldn't cool an imagination like hers. Over the years she has relaxed a little, knowing now at least that I always work strange Saturday hours, from five a.m. to nine a.m., except during the foxhunting season. But in any case she likes to get right down to work, thank goodness, and usually has the vacuum roaring before I've got my hat and coat and am out the door.

This morning her news was startling enough for me to delay my departure a few minutes and for her to need the security of the doorhandle. She stood looking down at her ankle-length socks and old sandals bulging with bunioned and be-corned toes. I found myself staring afresh at the bride to be. Her ink-black mop of tightly curled hair, dyed of course, the watery nervous black eyes, the brown lined face, the painted lips moving as she explained. With a certain reluctance I let my eyes run down her body. Yes, for a woman of her age she was still possessed of attributes which might have had sexual connotations in another setting. Her waist was slim and there were quite appropriate protuberances above and below it, her tight-fitting short white slacks and purple sweater worn open at the porridge skin of her throat presenting all the main physical features clearly to any interested observer. I had a slightly queasy vision for a second of this aging femininity clothed in the satiny veiling of a formal white wedding such as I myself endured some thirty-five years ago. But I knew that if I could concentrate on what she was saying the prospect would turn out to be otherwise.

"He's been down to the Town Clerk, and there's nothing to stop us getting it done in the Town Office next Saturday. My sister and her husband from Bradford will be the witnesses. There has to be two."

She looked up from the floor and laughed almost girlishly at this, realizing perhaps that she didn't need to explain the legalities of a marriage to me, of all people. Finally I screwed up enough courage to ask the obvious question. I was sure she hadn't deliberately kept me in the dark. It's just that her mind doesn't operate sequentially. Or perhaps a natural modesty made her feel that anything her mind contained must already be within my range of knowledge.

"And who, may I ask, is the lucky man?"

"Oh dear," she said, looking open-eyed straight at me, a hand half-covering her blazing mouth, "Didn't I say? Bullie. Bull Rivard. You know Bull."

Of course I know Bull. Of course she knew that I knew Bullie Boy Rivard. Whatever else she might not be aware of in the relation between the prospective groom and me. Everybody in this neighborhood knows him, if not personally, by reputation. But she felt obliged to keep talking to fill up the silence. I was at a loss what to say. Oh God, no, I can't believe it, was the closest I could have come to putting my reaction into words. In the circumstances, she did very well. Telling me how many years she has known Bull. Telling me how she never considered marrying again after finally divorcing her drunken old scoundrel of a husband, Sammy Howell, ten years ago. I did that job for her, but she has never been able to collect alimony, with Howell continually drinking himself in and out of welfare and jail and hospital. Telling me how she went dancing and drinking with Bull Rivard at the Princess Hotel in Bradford last year several times. How last month Bull popped the question when he was drunk and she refused. At my age, she said. But finally, when he was sober and asked her again:

"I figured, why shouldn't I? Ten years is a long time. I'm tired of living all by myself."

What could I say, with her suddenly defiantly silent, looking at me out of those watery black eyes, about to bolt through the door?

"Surely, Mrs. Howell, surely. Why not? I wish you all the luck in the world."

The news of this macabre coupling — quite apart from anything else, the bride is at least fifteen years older than the groom, though he is hardly in the first flush of youth — would need digesting at leisure. Meantime my own problem came to the front of my mind. I realized, now that Rivard's name was out, what the answer was likely to be, but I asked anyway, let's say, out of a taste for the grotesque. Perhaps I was curious to know whether Rivard had discussed me in particular with her.

"But won't you want to keep on some of your old jobs? Even if it were only every second week, for example?"

Mrs. Howell had the door half-opened. At this she turned with another parody of the feminine flutter of hands and eyelids, giggling and coloring at my failure to appreciate the new delicacy of her situation.

"Oh, Mr. Martin, Bullie says he won't have me cleaning up for other people any more. He says he's going to give me enough work to keep me busy hisself."

As she finished, she discovered she had made a remark which might be construed as a double entendre. By this time the bizarre farce of it all and more seriously the considerable inconvenience it would mean for me had made me lose patience.

"Oh I'm sure he will, Mrs. Howell, I'm sure he will," I snapped at her, before she could disappear out of earshot into the cupboard in the washroom.

I was on my way down to the Hunt Club, which is only a couple of minutes' drive south of Aurora. When my wife and I were divorced many years ago I moved my two hunters in there from the farm, and I ride Wednesdays and Saturdays, at the minimum, whether it's foxhunting season or not. I must have a quiet, steady routine. Bull Rivard wasn't working in the Hunt Club stables at the moment, but he had been, off and on, over the years. So I had additional reason for thinking of him as I left Mrs. Howell to clean up the mess of the week for possibly the last time. I say possibly, out of a twenty year acquaintance with Rivard and a pretty good knowledge of his ways. As a matter of fact, whether or not Mrs. Howell knows, or even Bull Rivard for certain, I was primarily responsible for getting him fired from the Hunt Club the last time, two or three years ago. Frankly, it didn't especially please me to have to think about him at all, let alone in connection (of whatever kind) with Mrs. Howell.

Freddie Pitts, the stable manager ever since old Harry Jarvis died, kept Bull on for years, despite interruptions for weekend drunks, days in court, jail terms and so forth, because — so Freddie claimed — Bull was good with the hounds and a good man around horses, and 'good stable help is always hard to find.'

"But isn't he rough with the horses?" I remember asking early on, on the basis partly of a few glimpses I had of Bull at work, and partly from a natural deduction knowing how he behaved with people in the hotels in Bradford, Newmarket, Aurora and Richmond Hill.

Pitts isn't a man you can make much headway with if you want him to do anything he doesn't want to do. He is a small man, about my size, skinny, weasel-faced and no doubt weasel-hearted, the kind who will bite when cornered perhaps, will certainly snarl at the weak, but who for the most part tries to blend ingratiatingly into the environment.

Which is why he has survived so long, in a business where ignorance is dangerous, and negligence a crime.

"Well, yes," Pitts answers, "he can be rough at times, I reckon. Course more trouble is caused in a stable by being too soft than being too tough. By Gee, I recall once when I was working at Colonel Baker's as a boy, there was a fellow…."

Pitts pauses to light a limp hand-rolled cigarette that he has kept ready behind his right ear for just this occasion, and we are launched on a diversionary story of real roughness. However strongly I may feel I never like to press matters, it's not my way. The subject of Bull Rivard's behavior is forgotten. The truth is, I suppose, that Bull suited Freddie, despite their apparent differences.

Twenty years ago when he arrived out of the backwoods of Manitoba or wherever it was, Bull Rivard was sleek and swarthy, brown of face and arm, broad enough in chest and shoulder to justify his nick-name. A big, nosy, aggressive man, black hair always greased to a shine, sleeves rolled above his big biceps, teeth flashing in a leer at every girl in sight, full of loud, sexy, bullying talk, especially when he had a few drinks in him, often enough. He must be in his forties now, probably his late forties. There's no glow under the brown skin any more. The bright teeth are obviously false. There's a lot of loose skin around the eyes and neck. The big chest seems to be caving in as if some of the air is leaking from his lungs. When did all this start happening to him? Although I've probably seen him every year since he arrived in this part of the world, except for the eighteen months he was in the penitentiary, I couldn't put a date to the changes. No doubt when you're not so young yourself you're reluctant to notice these things.

To me until recently he was still the Bull Rivard of the hay bale in each hand, or the wheel-barrow heaped higher than his head with manure as a joke and show of strength, or the tight chain shank threatening a rearing horse, or the empty squashed beer can dropped from a big fist, reaching for another in the circle of stable-hands on the hill-side behind the barn after work. The Bull Rivard who was always called for when a job of heavy lifting or pushing had to be done, when rain threatened the haying, and loading or unloading had to be finished in a hurry, when a difficult horse had to be shipped and wouldn't go on the van. If you got within fifty feet you could hear his voice. Bragging about what he'd done on his day off, in the most disgusting language. The rich woman who bought him drinks at the Princess Hotel, and begged him to go along with her to the Bradford Motor Inn in her car. Tits as big as watermelons. Waist you could put your hands around. Ass like a couple of big balloons. Jesus, did she want it. I gave it to her six times, and by Christ, she'd had enough by then. So I give her one more, right up her …. The flashing grin. The waving descriptive hands. I find that kind of sexual crudity and bravado particularly distasteful. There are other people besides myself who thought Bull Rivard didn't do much for the tone of the Hunt Club. They were usually those like me who were around at odd times of the day and saw more than the ordinary member.

No doubt they sighed with relief when Bull disappeared for the weekend or got drunk and sick during haying and was fired, or when he was sent to jail for car theft and drunken driving. But they must have groaned too when he kept returning and getting re-hired by Freddie Pitts as if nothing had happened. Good stable help is hard to find. Once again you would hear Bull's voice echoing down the aisles while the crew mucked out, telling grander and grander stories about his adventures in copulation and brawling. Freddie Pitts, with his sallow thin face sagging into a weak grin, would lean against the stable office door, hands in pockets, old felt hat tipped back, and listen. If his little sunken eyes shone you knew the stories were specially lewd or violent, but otherwise he remained a shadow. Later Pitts would, in some moods, give his own embellished versions in which Bull Rivard became an even more virile and potent figure than he was in his own presentation.

Pitts especially licked his lips over the visit of the Ontario Provincial Police to the Hunt Club three or four years ago, and their interrogation of Rivard, if it can be called that. The police always kept an eye on Rivard after car thefts or minor burglary or that sort of thing. This was a rape-murder case. Two teenage girls, knifed, mutilated, bodies left in a gravel pit near Schomberg. As usual the papers gave the crime lurid coverage. Pitts was driving Rivard into Aurora after work a few days later — Bull's license had been taken away again, a regular occurrence — when they were met in the lane by an O.P.P. cruiser with two officers in it. There was a word exchanged between Freddie and the driver and then the police car backed off the lane and Pitts' half-ton truck pulled over on the verge in front of it. The four men all got out. They stood in a group beside Pitts' pick-up truck in full view of the Hunt Club and passersby on Highway 11. They must have talked for at least half an hour and then the two policemen got into their car and drove off.

Freddie Pitts made a good deal out of such modest material, which I suppose is the mark of someone who gets more satisfaction out of thinking and talking than out of doing. He was helped by the fact that, uncharacteristically, for a while at least Bull Rivard kept his mouth shut, and even might have seemed a little subdued, if you wanted to interpret his behavior that way. The climax of Pitts' version of this story was always when, using one of his limp hand-rolled cigarettes to demonstrate, he showed how the cops at a certain point in the questioning offered Bull a smoke and lit it for him. Then after Bull had taken a few drags one policeman quietly reached over, took the cigarette out of Bull's mouth, stubbed it out, and slipped the butt into an envelope. Pitts liked to hold out the spitty end of his cigarette for you to see at this point.

"Saliver, you see. For the saliver test."

The impression that Pitts was licking his wet lips with relish was unavoidable, and the effect was enhanced by the fact that at no time did he let on whether or not he personally thought that this might have been the incriminating piece of evidence that would link Bull Rivard with the raped and murdered girls. The vulgar sexual aura that surrounded Bull thickened for the next few weeks as he went around leering and boasting and bullying and showing off his muscles more and more in the usual way. Gradually interest cooled. But the rapist, whoever he was, was never caught and brought to court. Presumably he's still around somewhere.

I suppose Bull Rivard took the interest of the O.P.P. as a compliment to his notorious virility. A man given to absurd verbal fantasies of sexual prowess in which disgust and contempt for the female appear disguised as lusty appetite has, certainly, some of the attributes of the rapist. Add to them a history of drunkenness, social irresponsibility, and petty violence and you have a likely suspect. Personally however I think it most improbable, mainly because Bull is too quick to use the safety valve of talk. The one actual rapist I defended in court a few years back — I try to avoid the more garish sorts of legal business — was a very silent innocuous-looking teenager.

After leaving my office to Mrs. Howell's customary tact and skills, I first drove round to my apartment on Slater Street. It has always seemed odd to Mrs. Howell, that I need her to clean my office but not my apartment. I'm sure she is convinced I have some terrible secret hidden there. The truth is that I do not want her in my apartment, or any other woman. It is my exclusive retreat: my two rooms where I keep the curtains drawn, read my books for pleasure, listen to my music, eat an occasional simple meal of my own devising, and do a little meditating or whatever else I choose to do. My office is more or less public property. My apartment is entirely private. Like Mrs. Howell, I find living alone not without its difficulties. But if I must live alone it will be absolutely so, with no compromises.

I changed into my riding-clothes and set off for the Hunt Club. As I passed the Liquor Store on the outskirts of town, just before Highway 11 enters open agricultural country, I glanced at the rows of cars waiting to be loaded with Saturday night alcohol. It was just a glimpse, but there he was, at the wheel of a cab from the Aurora Taxi service, a bare arm resting on the open window, hair slicked back, face a little sallow from lack of accustomed sun, eyes staring off in a dead sort of way across the parking lot and into the distant fields. Bull Rivard, groom-to-be, former stableman at the Hunt Club, former tough guy, strong man, dark violent hero, bragging center of attention, here a solitary figure, driving a cab in Aurora, waiting meekly for his fare to buy a somewhat happier Saturday, I felt, than Bull and Mrs. Howell were likely to enjoy this week or next.

With that same flash view of Rivard come a series of images from the past that fitted the present better than I would have expected. How often, now that I thought of it, did you really see Bull using those vaunted muscles and that much-advertised virile potency? Actually working, lifting, pushing, sweating, fighting, let alone copulating? No, it was the typical picture, dwindling shoulders slumped over a steering-wheel. The hands starting a tractor, the face growing paler and thinner peering out of Pitt's truck, sitting at the fork lift or the manure spreader, or the snow-blower, or at the wheel of any one of a dozen old wrecks of cars that he picked up fifth hand and soon ruined. He was no more the vital natural man than … than I am myself. He was a twisted, hunched up, worn out machine man. As sedentary as me, really, perhaps even more so. Everything else was probably just talk. The details of how he came to fall into Mrs. Howell's arms, so to speak, were mercifully hidden. But the fact seemed less astonishing, as I updated the image. The power of the man was no doubt illusion, probably always was, and it was the real weakness that led him to that grotesquely logical fate. As for Mrs. Howell, God knows, perhaps she saw something quite different in it all. I felt oddly relieved to get a better perspective on the man.

I was held up at the stop-light briefly, during which time I reflected that Rivard had less reason to like me than I him. He knew, or at least should have had a pretty fair idea, that it was I who got him fired from the Hunt Club and forced him off to drive a cab. When my two horses first came to the Hunt Club stables, I was distressed to see how they were cared for. Of course they were used to the very good stable I always kept at the farm. Pitts, though he had enough weasel-cunning to have won a reputation as a fine old Ontario horseman among the amateur horsemen who knew least, was really a lazy, weak, ignorant fellow, full of bluff and pretense, dependent on the fact that, except indirectly, horses can't tell you what people do to them. Stable help did more or less what they liked, which in the case of Bull Rivard could be especially unsatisfactory. I was anxious to fit in and certainly had no desire to cause trouble. But neither kindness nor bribery could get consistent feeding and watering, or handling which was even humane, let alone capable. My horses and I were glad for those times when Bull was not around.

Then the moment came when I thought I had a chance to deal with Rivard once and for all, with the minimum of unpleasantness, get rid of this admittedly minor by constantly recurring annoyance. He hated the Master of the Fox Hounds, Colonel Seivers, for having been ordered by that emphatic old-fashioned gentleman not to swear in front of Club members. The Colonel could certainly be crusty and ferocious in the traditional military way. I gather he gave Rivard a splendid dressing-down. Because I was around the stable at unusual hours, and rather blended into the surroundings, I suppose, my nature being what it is, I was able to discover that Bull was getting his revenge on the Colonel in a somewhat unexpected way. Not only the occasional kick or poke with the pitch-fork at the Master's three horses in their stalls, which was hard to prove or do anything about. But the feeding! Bull's ideas of revenge must have flowered. He must have had visions of the Master being magnificently humiliated in public: run away with or bucked-off in front of the Hunt field, or at the very least suffering the indignity of over-fresh horses kicking out disgracefully at those around him or, worst sin of all, at the hounds. Bull began to stoke those horses outrageously, hard Western oats by the gallon, and all the supplements he could cram into them. Pitts was so lazy that usually he left Bull to do that most delicate and important of a horseman's jobs, the judgment and measuring of individual feeds. Bull had no one to restrain him. In any case, all ill-intentions aside, he no doubt knew as much about the job as Pitts. Now, Colonel Seivers was of course getting on, my age or older, and hardly the athletic rider he was when he rode for the Canadian Equestrian Team in the thirties. He might have been badly hurt or even killed by an unruly mount.

My intention was to prove malicious intent, for such there was indeed. I by-passed Pitts. Once I had prepared the ground by a discreet telephone call, overcoming Colonel Seivers' incredulity and distaste for such a sordid business, it was a simple matter to persuade him to carry out a couple of quick unobserved inspections at feeding time.

"Wonder the cursed blighter hasn't foundered all my mounts," Colonel Seivers raged. It would have been the firing squad for Bull Rivard in another context. Instead he was sent down the road at once, with a week's pay and a warning never to come on Hunt Club property again. Pitts and he meet in Aurora from time to time, I know, and I'm sure that long ago they put two and two together and figured out my part in the matter.

I was held up again making a left turn across on-coming highway traffic. The turn into the Hunt Club is always a bit hazardous, but I pride myself on being a careful driver. My thoughts were preoccupied to the extent that I may have been a little late, I admit, in putting on my turning signal. On the one hand, I was thinking, it pleased me in a repugnant sort of way to see Bull Rivard crown his long manly career by wedding himself to the beauteous Mrs. Howell, with her lived-in skin and ever-renewed lips. I imagined her in later years becoming an aunty, if not a motherly, figure to him. On the other hand I was wracking my brains to decide how I could manage without my cleaning lady. A person who lives alone is upset by disruptions in routine. At any rate, it hardly seemed necessary, even if my thoughts were straying for a brief moment, for the car behind to honk its horn quite so aggressively.

Then I looked in the rear-view mirror and I realized that Bull Rivard's cab had caught up to me. His fare, a large fat man, was reading a newspaper in the back seat, oblivious to anything around him. Bull was head and one shoulder out the window, a hand on the horn. Just as I recognized Bull, he saw that it was I who was delaying his progress down Highway 11. He reached a long bare arm out the window and straight forward in my direction. He glared ahead at my face framed in the mirror, helplessly watching him. And then, without the slightest provocation of movement or expression on my part I can assure you, he made that thoroughly disgusting, aggressive, obscene, upward-thrusting public gesture of the fingers which I have always considered especially abhorrent. In broad daylight. In slow motion. The blood surged to my face. However there was simply nothing I could do. Nothing. I turned into the Hunt Club driveway at the next break in the traffic (I feel fairly confident no one there saw the incident) and let the man sail on past me down the road, grinning like an insane creature from ear to ear, with his wagging arm stretched crazily full-length out the window, still sending me that revolting message.

I must confess the whole unpleasant business made me feel rebuked, deflated, old and tired, sick of myself, full of a sense of the difficulties of life. I must have sat slumped in my car for fully five minutes. But then, as if the tide were turning, irresistibly I began to revive a little, with an unexpected access of energy — I could even call it zest — of a kind I have not felt for years. Life goes on in its ridiculous and unpredictable ways. Sooner or later, no doubt, we all get what we deserve, all of us. And then I found myself, with I think uncharacteristic fervor and sincerity, suddenly laughing out loud, sitting there in the car all by myself, laughing out loud, and wishing Mrs. Howell and Bull Rivard a long and close marriage.

The House Cats

Is it worse to be a man or an animal in pain? For the man, there's the question, why? Why me? Why this? There's the wife at bedside, the family, the doctors and nurses. The knowledge that if it gets too bad drugs may take the pain away. Or maybe not. For the animal, there's ignorance, blind fear, no sense of an end or relief to the suffering. It's such a responsibility, having creatures around that rely on you, whether they are aware that you care or not.

Sitting by her husband at the hospital, Mrs. Dawson was remembering how Timmy, their orange cat at home, lay under the bed in the spare room where he rarely stayed, tail arched a little, big eyes peering straight into hers, when she eased herself down on her arthritic knees, raised the coverlet, and looked into the half-darkness to find him there.

Their other cat, Tammy, Timmy's black-and-white girlfriend, was rubbing against the legs of the bed. That's how Mrs. Dawson realized where Timmy was hiding. Timmy paid no attention to the other cat, to anything, except the pain that kept him rigid.

Mrs. Dawson was full of regrets. Why hadn't she understood sooner? Hadn't she heard the cries from the basement litter-box? Hadn't she seen the straining, the licking of private parts, and the spotting of puddles from a cat that, like Tammy, for five years living day and night in the house, had never made a mistake?

Well, she certainly never neglected their two house cats. Just the opposite. For the last difficult six weeks she had put out food and water in the bowls on the kitchen floor every morning before her daughter-in-law came to drive her to the hospital. There, often the first thing her husband John asked her, when he was aware she was there, was, "How're my little 'tats' doing today?"

When he put his dairy farming days behind him, he'd had a lifetime of nameless barn-cats, coming and going as they pleased, a dozen more or less, all of them wild, the number depending on how smart they were to steer clear of the coyotes. It was his idea to choose two kittens and keep them in the house, always — to domesticate them. At home, he would regularly spend a few minutes laughing at the antics of Tammy and Timmy, before heading out for his daily walk.

Now of course everything was different. Especially Sundays. Their son jokingly called Sunday his mother's day off. She didn't go to the hospital. She slept in — meaning she lay in bed alone wide awake and watched the sun rise over the hills to the east, then gradually slant its wash of summer light across the scattered houses and still empty two-acre lots that surrounded their retirement house. And she tried to imagine life without John Dawson.

At ten o'clock their fifteen-year-old grandson would arrive on his bicycle from Schomberg, dusty from the concession roads. He was a quiet, tanned, square-shouldered lad who looked more like his farmer grandfather than his father, the son who ran the Schomberg service station that John had used some of the money from the farm's sale to set up for him.

Mrs. Dawson would supervise the boy's day of chores. She liked to be sure that he mowed the boundary between their lawn and the still-vacant lots on each side of them in a straight enough line to satisfy John Dawson's farmer instinct for tidiness. John would have been pleased. As the summer progressed, and the grasses and weeds grew higher in the wilderness around them, their mown lawn was more and more like an island of order in the two or three foot high seas of chaotic greenery in their half-developed part of the new sub-division.

It was hard for her to leave the house and go into the sights and smells of the city hospital, especially when John's arms and nostrils were taped with tubes and his efforts to talk lasted for a shorter and shorter period each visit.

"My 'tats'," he would grunt, his lips a grey line, his eyes half-closed, a squeeze from his hand maybe about all the sign he could give to show that he really knew she was even there. She would just talk on, knowing that his mind could be pushed down certain corridors of memory or reverie by the right words, until the rising pain brought him back to the present, and the nurses came in to drug him again.

She wasn't sure. He might be thinking of nights they used to sit in front of the TV, content just to be together, Tammy or Timmy on his lap. Or he might be thinking of that day twenty years ago when he was bounced off the top of the loaded hay-wagon by his half-drunk hired man, who hit a rock with the tractor's front wheel. John fell hard. Had to be brought in from the field flat on his back on an empty wagon. Now in his hospital bed wishing, no doubt, that the new pain that started to come deep in his back half a year ago really was, as he thought it was at first, a return of that old injury that put him in hospital for the first time in his life.

Instead, it was something different. Something with a common label everybody talked about in hushed tones, an affliction so terrible, yet so ordinary and familiar, that he chose never to refer to it by name. Even after the doctors tried to cut it out of his body and then put him on the harshest program of radiation treatments.

Or maybe his mind was running back through much earlier days, when he was courting the girl who milked the cows and fed the chickens over on the 17th Sideroad. That was the time they both liked to remember, when he was first farming his father's land by himself. Long before they retired and sold up to the developer from Toronto, keeping only the corner lot for themselves to live in and enjoy, in their old age, after their own son left the farm to follow another way of life.

Sometimes Mrs. Dawson still felt exactly like that twenty-year-old farmer's daughter, with her strong hands and long brown hair, and quick laugh. But she knew the thin, stiff-jointed, white-topped lady in the bedside chair was nothing like her. Except maybe for the laugh.

"Do you know what Andy said to me yesterday?" she asked John one day, looking into the grey face against the pillows — Andy was their grandson — "he said, why don't Tammy and Timmy ever have any babies?"

She gave that laugh, taking the flicker of John Dawson's eyelids for an answer.

"And him fifteen years old! These town kids! I guess they just aren't around animals enough to learn the facts of life."

And then, as if she were speaking the words John himself might use: "They wouldn't know a steer or a gelding if it flicked a tail in their face."

At that point Mrs. Dawson changed the subject. She remembered that she hadn't yet told John about Timmy. It was partly because Timmy was a gelding — well, a neutered male — that he got sick. Or so the vet said. Apparently neutered male cats were the ones who had those urinary problems, the crystals forming in the urinary tract, the blockage, the pain, and the possible damage to their kidneys. Usually they could put a catheter in, flush out the bladder, give some drugs, and send the creature home again in a day or two. But not Timmy.

That was not a story to tell John now.

Timmy had sat still on her lap all the way to the clinic. Maybe he knew when people were trying to help him. She wanted to think so. At the clinic, the young girl assistant in the blue pullover and jeans held him against her breast and soothed him. But the last Mrs. Dawson saw of Timmy was his big yellow eyes staring at her as the girl took him to the cages hidden away in the back of the building. It was her daughter-in-law who gave the go-ahead for euthanasia when they heard by phone that the internal damage was too much for Timmy to survive any of the options to cure him and end his pain.

Since then every night Tammy slept at the foot of the bed. She seemed happy enough while Mrs. Dawson was at home. After breakfast, she sat on the window sill while Mrs. Dawson washed the dishes, just as she and Timmy always did. She stared out at the fields around, at the trees stirring in the wind, flashing her black tail with its white tip when the birds flew close. But now when Mrs. Dawson left for the hospital Tammy was at the door — she would never, of course, expect to go out, having lived her entire adult life indoors — and she was there again when Mrs. Dawson came back. Once, as Mrs. Dawson waited outside on the porch for a minute, she thought she could hear howls on the other side of the door. So on Sundays, her days off, she always produced something special for Tammy's bowl — some fresh pork liver, or a little canned fish — and made an extra fuss over her, regardless of her own state of mind.

But on this last Sunday, she was going to leave Tammy all by herself for a long time. In fact, she would be gone for the day and evening too. Her son and daughter-in-law had it planned. They were insisting that she shouldn't come back here and stay on in the house by herself that day. They were going to take her to their home in Schomberg for lunch and for the night. Then a few days from now her grandson, and her twenty-year-old granddaughter just back from a trip to Europe, would move into her house for a month, until school and college started. In the fall, or so they all expected, she would sell the house and go live with them in Schomberg.

Mrs. Dawson looked into the bathroom mirror as she adjusted her black hat and tried the little veil over her eyes. She pushed the hat to one side and the other. It looked silly on her white head. John and she hardly ever went to church, except for weddings and funerals. She felt no more easy in formal black than he did in his dark three-piece suit that she had helped him buy in Toronto twenty years ago for their son's wedding. And that looked so big on his bony frame, even when he was at rest trying to seem comfortable.

"Leave the damned thing off. That's what John would tell me, I'm sure," she said out loud to her image in the mirror.

She gave the hat a last push and turned away to collect her gloves and purse from the hall table. Tammy rubbed her black-and-white sides against her legs as she tugged the gloves over her fingers. For a moment she eased herself down on the chair in the hallway.

"Tammy," she said, tugging on the cat's ears gently as John always did, until the creature squirmed in purring ecstasy, "What are we going to do? Do you want to come with me and live in town in a new house with me and the family?"

She looked around at the familiar walls, covered with photos of all the generations. Tammy had lived inside this house all her life. But she was strong and healthy, could run and climb. John was never able to teach them not to claw their way up the drapes and jump from chair to table to chair. Most people wouldn't put up with that. And God help the occasional mouse that strayed into the house. But lately all she did was eat and sleep. That's why the daughter-in-law, who was no cat lover anyway, felt it was alright for Tammy to be let alone for a few days, with the grandson biking over to put the cat food in the bowl on the kitchen floor, and clean the litter box. Mrs. Dawson was too confused at the moment to know what was best.

She went into the kitchen to make sure there was enough water. Tammy followed and jumped up on the window sill. Around their lot the verge of tall grass and weeds, lush in the early morning sunshine of mid-August, was waving in the breeze. She stepped over and stood looking out, stroking Tammy's back.

The ground sloped off to the north. Despite the scattering of houses in the distance, some still under construction, owned mostly by newcomers who expected to commute to the city, it was still the same land that John had ploughed and planted, grazed and cropped, for forty years. Nothing of their own was growing there now, but the memories were alive.

Suddenly Mrs. Dawson felt a surge of certainty. There really was nowhere else she wanted to live. It would be difficult, maybe even risky at her age, but she had to stay. And after all, there was only herself to worry about now. Except, of course, Tammy.

She lifted Tammy into her arms off the window sill and walked straight to the kitchen door. She put the purring cat on the floor, and opened the door wide. Tammy sat looking up at her in the doorway.

"It's alright, Tammy. Go ahead. Try it. Go out. It will be all new and exciting out there."

She stood over her until Tammy carefully set her paws as far as she had ever gone before. Onto the threshold. Mrs. Dawson eased past her outside the door, and stood there encouragingly, as if the black-and-white shape, so low on the porch floor looking up at her, needed her full permission. The cat began to glide along the outside wall of the house towards the steps. Mrs. Dawson stood perfectly still and watched. The cat moved more fluently now, still close to the floor, tail swishing, head turning here and there. She half slid down the three steps and onto the grass. She nosed and poked it for a moment, and then began to walk across it with high-stepping delicate paces. A neighbor's dog barked in the far distance. Instantly the cat froze to the ground, head swiveling to all sides. In another moment she continued away, edging now directly towards the verge of high grass and weeds that surrounded their patch of safe civilized lawn.

Mrs. Dawson turned back to the kitchen, looked out a last time, and softly closed the door behind her. Inside, she picked up Tammy's bowls and put them in the kitchen sink. Then she went to the window and stood there to watch Tammy reach the edge of their lawn. Now, tail switching fiercely, the long black-and-white shape began to follow the boundary line, eyes and ears turning as if to penetrate the dense growth.

Then she stopped, and crouched for a long while with one front paw lifting, hind legs moving silently on the spot as if to gain a foothold. Suddenly she arched boldly high into the air and plunged out of sight into the unknown.

"There," Mrs. Dawson breathed to herself, "you can manage on your own out there if you have to, can't you, Tammy?"

She was still standing at the window, her heart beating fast and strong, looking at the spot where Tammy disappeared, even though behind her she could hear the car coming into the driveway, and her front door opening.

"Mother? Are you ready?"

Her son's deep, cheerful voice.

He found her at the kitchen door, where he put an arm around her shoulders and hugged her.

"Come on, Mother. Dad will be awful mad at you, if you're late for his funeral."

Book Of The Duchess

For the better part of a week the same question had been creeping into his mind, disturbing his sleep, even interrupting his work. Was it ever really possible to say, "I'm sorry?"

Of course, since one may hear oneself glibly saying "I'm sorry" almost every day, the question has to be put more rigorously: Is it ever possible to say "I'm sorry" and *mean* it? — mean it enough to act differently if history permitted one a second chance?

Despite his deep interest in history, he didn't usually choose to dwell on his personal past. His own life stretched away behind him like a trail of flotsam and jetsam left by a travelling ship, discarded, ignored, and virtually forgotten. A ship that was crossing an uncharted, seemingly endless ocean, through (on the whole) more sunshine than storm. A rudderless ship. Or, perhaps, not so much rudderless as one without any chosen destination out of the many possible — whether in fact its navigator had ever actually been capable of mapping a route and aiming at a specific harbor. A ship whose purpose was solely to travel, never in any significant way to depart or to arrive.

That simile, however, has overtones of danger and adventure which he realized were not especially relevant. A train would perhaps be more appropriate to his sense of himself, an existentialist train of the kind Sartre describes, laying its own tracks ahead of it as it rolls along through the desert.

"I'm sorry," he said, experimentally, to the reflection in his bathroom mirror. "I'm sorry." Savoring the words on his tongue and lips, silently, as he gazed at the familiar, worn, middle-aged face with its deepening creases around the mouth that appeared to have smiled too often for too little reason. "I'm sorry," as the recessed, pouched, and now saddened blue eyes gradually watered until the vision blurred.

He could have been saying these words for many reasons to many people. After all, he had been alive for fifty years, yes, and a full half-century. He could have been saying them simply to himself. But in fact, on this belatedly lush spring morning, in the seclusion and quiet of North Oxford, in the year of our Lord nineteen hundred and sixty-nine, it was not himself he was addressing. He was staring down from the second floor bathroom window of the tall brick house which was his (leasehold from Merton College for eighty-three more years) into the long, narrow, walled garden, where the grass almost perceptibly rose towards him from the moist earth. The twigs and branches that yesterday, or so it seemed, were still brittle skeletons, had become lithe green streamers in the mild southerly breeze. On this quite unremarkable, unhistorical but distinctly April-like morning, he heard his own repeated bleak utterance in front of the mirror, so inappropriate to the season — and knew that it was actually directed at another person. A person, whom he thought of rarely and, certainly, had not addressed directly in over a quarter of a century. A woman, of course.

"I'm sorry, my dear, I'm sorry."

The mirrored face swam in waves as the tears swelled up over the eyelids and trickled down the impassive, freshly-shaven cheeks. Then abruptly a sob shook the absorbed concentration of the viewer and he pulled himself away from the private spectacle of remorse he had staged so unexpectedly, so uncharacteristically, with so little apparent justification. He pulled his black silk dressing gown from the back of the bathroom door, drew it around his shoulders, and walked along the carpeted hallway lined with its familiar drawings and watercolors. Entering his windowless study, he sat at the large cluttered table that ran the length of one wall. Elbows placed on the sheets of foolscap covered with his own scribblings, he buried his wet face in his hands.

Melancholia, that's what it must be. A fit of melancholy. A mood, a vice all too well understood by the ancients. To be shunned, to be dreaded. Indeed, one of the deadliest of sins. A medieval vice at that, rising like a poisonous mist straight from his deep studies of the past few months.

"I've been too long at my desk, that's it," he said, raising his face from his hands and looking at the large reproduction from the Ashmolean Collection on the wall in front of him, a scene from the Roman de la Rose depicting a Knight mourning for his Lady. On each side were the tools of his trade, books: books half-read, open, face-down, books closed with strips of paper marking places for easy reference.

"An occupational hazard," he said, taking up the pile of manuscript pages in front of him, representing yesterday's work, and tidying the edges with both hands. The Book of the Duchess Blanche, An Historical Romance. This is what should have been occupying his attention for the several hours since his first morning cup of tea. His working title. He never settled on a title once and for all until a book was completed. It was too confining to name the whole before it had taken shape fully and finally. For a young writer, an apprentice, that naming was all right, perhaps even a necessary piece of self-encouragement. But now, at this stage in his mastery of his craft, he could let his historical imagination meander through the inert facts and documentation of research, and select and shape more spontaneously, allowing himself the privileges and pleasures of the unexpected direction and emphasis, the unpredictable discovery, the wayward-seeming or even whimsical impulse that might bring more excitement to the act of writing than anything deliberately planned. Without that freedom, the pastness of history might by now, a full twelve historical novels into his career, begin to seem intolerably limiting and depressing.

"God knows," he would sometimes chaff his publisher on his annual or semi-annual visits to London, "it's about time I took more cognizance of the present, or even the future, instead of dwelling always on the distant past. How would you like me to bring you something in the Science Fiction line next year?"

However, his publisher of more than twenty years' standing, Lord Ragelly, had the comfortable knowledge that Edwin St. Cyr was as addicted to historical romance as an opium eater to his opiate, or as any one of his several million faithful and trusting readers. His compulsion had never been to conquer the modern world, but rather to escape from it, to provide an escape from it for others. When Lord Ragelly drove St. Cyr to Paddington in his Humber Snipe and saw the author's portly, tweed-jacketed, balding shape safely aboard the last train to Oxford — a man who conceded a need to expose himself to the realities of present time to the extent of a first-class carriage trip home, instead of a chauffeured limousine ride — both men recognized that a year or a year and a half hence the bundle of typescript under the arm of the returning author would be nothing to disturb legitimate, long-established commercial and literary expectations.

At times, when a book was not going well, as was certainly the case now — hence perhaps his discordant feelings — he did genuinely contemplate a change of subject or form, a radical change. Something from the real world of the present, something from his own direct experience, even. In the end, nothing but history, in particular British history from the Middle Ages to the Eighteenth Century, truly stimulated his fiction. And sooner or later, at least so far, he had always managed to work through whatever artistic problems may have temporarily set him back and discouraged him.

This time his difficulty was, he was beginning to suspect, quite possibly an essential feature of the very task he had settled on. Not the Duchess Blanche herself. She was a splendid subject. And he was still half in love with her, as he always was with a heroine until he completed the book enshrining her life. Blanche's delicate, fresh, generous-hearted beauty was famous enough among the English nobility in the 1360's even without — even before — Geoffrey Chaucer's posthumous celebration of it in his elegy, *The Book of the Duchess*. Her grace, purity, perfected by the cruel finality of her early death (one could say), haunted St. Cyr's dreams as though he were privileged to be a creature of her time, a secret admirer in her household, an unacknowledged, unrequited courtly lover, pining and wasting away in hopeless adoration of her, simultaneously nourished and tortured by the merest glimpse of the Lady White at the side of her great lord. He, the Duke of Lancaster, destined after her death to become the most powerful man in England, royal blood in his veins, though never himself a king.

There, indeed, was the crux of the problem. Blanche was after all only the first of the three wives of John of Gaunt. By the time he came virtually to control the monarchy in Richard the Second's reign, was Blanche more than a faded dream to him — though the human warmth and power she once possessed could even now fire St. Cyr's imagination? Was she only a forgotten early contributor, through her dowry the Duchy of Lancaster, to John's secular triumph? The Duke lived on for another thirty years, almost long enough to see his son, Henry Bolingbrooke, ascend the throne of England. What evidence was there that his first wife Blanche mattered in the slightest to that powerful nobleman and great patriot (if one believes Shakespeare, which as an historian one certainly shouldn't, of course) during the longest period of his worldly success? How good it would be for the novelist's purposes if he could show that the passion and grief of the young widower, the Man in Black, stayed in his blood — even though he recovered sufficiently to re-marry three years later, and a third time in his maturity. That a whole destiny was overshadowed by the beautiful lady's untimely death. That kind of thing, certainly, is the stuff of romance. However, St. Cyr had built his reputation by paying more than lip service to the truths of history. In that way he retained the tolerance if not the respect of historians. Neither he nor his critics nor his general readers would accept flagrant distortions of the facts. There was, after all, a basic discipline to his craft which to date he had never disregarded.

So there it was. Disproportion in the very foundations of his edifice. The Blanche Book was not rising steadily and gracefully, not even like a medieval cathedral, with its own kind of order and coherence, let alone a classical simplicity and symmetry. It was going nowhere. It was a set of sporadic excavations, surrounded by a pile of stones and marble.

He had several alternatives, tried methods of getting out of impasses of this kind. He could go back to school, so to speak. Call his former tutor and advisor, the distinguished historian Sir John Neale, still active though semi-retired now. Or his occasional sparring partner through the review columns and at dinner parties, Professor A.L. Rowse. Or perhaps one of the younger history dons come to the University more recently, from Red Brick, from the Colonies, or even from America. Or some fresh young face and mind straight from Oxford Schools. He needn't of course expose his current embarrassment, the temporary freezing of his notoriously facile and fluent pen. But it was amazing how often a lively conversation with one or two intellectually brilliant dons could touch off a spark, plant a seed, or whatever the appropriate metaphor was. Their presence was one of the reasons he continued to live in Oxford after his first publishing successes. That and the fact that the hundred chief buildings in the Oxford area summed up, architecturally speaking, all the periods of British history he was most interested in. He would come back to his desk from a visit, or perhaps a walk somewhere in the university town, alive to the potential vitality of historical record — and even with a few specific clues or ideas to start him going again on the right track. Soon he would be turning the filled pages of his foolscap pad with rapidity and burning zeal.

"You should have been an historian," a new young don might say to him over tea, at the beginnings of personal familiarity, intending a compliment, of course, not perhaps realizing the extent of self-flattery and down-putting involved, in so addressing an internationally successful novelist. St. Cyr could have replied that he indeed started out as an historian. A doctoral student, in this very University. A part-time tutor as well. But he soon left that comparatively pedestrian career behind. He discovered a flare that couldn't be contained in the mundane exercises of historical scholarship and teaching.

"You're more English than the English," was the comment that usually preceded or followed hard on the other, whenever it transpired that St. Cyr was not a native Englishman, but a colonial, a foreigner really, for all his quarter-century in Oxford, his acquired Oxonian accent, manners and clothes, and his dozen-odd books about Britain's past. And yet, truly, he had never before in his life been more comfortably at home.

Faint sounds of morning activity around him in the tall, narrow house penetrated his consciousness as he sat staring at the blank half of the page in front of him. His charwoman had arrived, his Scout, as he called her to himself, a left-over term from his undergraduate days in College. The four Merton College students who occupied the top-floor of his house were, of course, not yet stirring. It would be an hour before Mrs. Fleece worked her way up to their rooms, and goaded them into their Saturday morning business or pleasure, with her clattering mops and pails and brushes. Downstairs, in the basement flat, although he couldn't hear them, he knew that Sarah Ponsby and her silent sister Jenny were tidying up after breakfast and getting ready for their weekly shopping expedition to the Market.

Though he had left it before dawn as usual, the warmth of Sarah's bed still clung to his pajamas. He imagined her giving his pillow an extra plumping as she made the bed in her room tucked away by the back stairs. It was familiar, pleasant, comfortable, the routine, the house, the way of life. The four lively young undergraduates stopping in once or twice a week for tea or sherry in term time, over the years. Not always the same young men, of course, they came and went, but his agreement with Merton College stipulated the number four, and out of that sampling there were bound to be several every year that were congenial enough. In any case, they were better to him than his own sons would have been in manners and respect, he felt sure, had he married and produced any. And Sarah, a little plumper than when she first came, with her thin nervous sister Jenny, to take a secretarial job with the Clarendon Press and to live below, over twenty years ago now, was still more amenable and consistently gratifying than any wife could possibly be. Or so it seemed, from what he could garner of such experience from his circle of acquaintances and from Oxford gossip. These were his home, his family. Giving him the support, comfort, pleasurable distractions and stimulus that any human being needs, never involving him deeply when he should be engaged in his vocation, but allowing him the mental and emotional freedom to pursue his work single-mindedly according to its demands, however outrageous by normal domestic standards.

Why, then, this fit of despondency that had overtaken him so inconveniently? Why this descent into gloom? Why this eruption of pointless remorse? It was as if worship of the youthful beauty of his Duchess Blanche had been transmuted, while he tried to capture it all in words, into the morbid despair of her husband and lover, the Man in Black, at her untimely death in 1369. But, after six hundred years, not even a speck of dust likely remained of Blanche's famed radiant flesh. Miss Sarah Ponsby was more real than a century's longevity in that dim past, let alone the scant two decades Blanche was allowed. And he, Edwin St. Cyr, was alive and triumphing in his consciousness over the moldering archives of John of Gaunt, for all of that great nobleman's sometime power and grandeur.

Abruptly St. Cyr got to his feet and went to the door. Mrs. Fleece was in the hallway, dusting the pictures, peering carefully at every frame as if to demonstrate that she was seeing it for the first time.

"Good morning, Mrs. Fleece, has Miss Ponsby left yet?" He asked quickly, into her kerchiefted, button-eyed, perpetually surprised-looking face with its wrinkled toothless mouth. He was in no mood to provoke or give pause for her garrulity this morning.

"Why, I think that's Miss Sarah now, sir."

Mrs. Fleece pointed her feather duster at the main stairs. He heard the door open and immediately called down.

"Sarah, love, anything in the post this morning?"

Sarah Ponsby came to the foot of the stairs, foreshortened, dumpy in her bulky sweater and slacks, and empty shopping net in her hand. She looked a little startled, as well she might be, since, in all the years he had accepted her services as his unofficial corresponding secretary, he had rarely evinced any interest in whatever letters she thought fit not to bring to his attention at once, or ever for that matter.

"Nothing special that I could see, Edwin."

She avoided greater familiarity than first names, even in front of her totally uncritical sister, who was waiting for her, uneasily no doubt, just outside the open entrance door. Certainly she never gave Mrs. Fleece anything to gossip about.

"Nothing from Canada?" he persisted, despite his reluctance to expose his unusual interest any further.

"Ah," she said, staring up at him with the beginnings of an understanding. She remembered the only letter from Canada recently, a week or so ago. An odd letter by any standards, though his correspondence from readers was often unconventional. From a literary admirer, of course, but this time an old acquaintance, as Edwin later confirmed, who had just come upon the extensive fiction that the author had created over a period of two decades. She — the correspondent was a woman — had been exploring it, working her way through it volume by volume. She felt compelled to write from out of his probably long-forgotten past, taking courage from the fact that his pen-name was obviously not intended to obliterate all traces of the plainer Ed Cyr she had known, to offer him her congratulations, her gratitude, and her good wishes. Was it perhaps this letter, conceivably the beginning of a nostalgic epistolary exchange of some scope and significance that inspired Edwin's uncharacteristic interest in the mails from Canada? — to Sarah a remote colony, a large, vague domain holding out to her only a faint threat of eventually arousing in St. Cyr some latent home-going instinct of which to date he had happily shown no signs. Sarah put the letter in the pile for him to read, but answered on St. Cyr's behalf in the formula they had long ago agreed upon: the distinguished author was presently abroad, but would hope to reply to the kind and generous letter in due course — which sometimes he did but more often did not. Conceivably this formula might provoke a further message, but it seemed rather unlikely so soon.

"Ah," Sarah repeated. "Nothing at all from Canada."

She turned her face downwards, away from his gaze, standing with one hand still on the banister. She was waiting — as unofficial secretary, as woman perhaps — for some gesture of reassurance from him. She required so little, demanded nothing.

"Well, fetch a bottle of the good stuff, on my account, won't you love?"

She beamed up at him. On her soft face the pleasurable prospect showing of an evening before the fireplace, if the temperature dipped overnight again, in any case an after-supper noggin of whiskey and lemon, one round perhaps shared with Sarah's unresponsive sister before she took her therapeutic embroidery to her room, a second, a third, a fourth even, while Sarah knitted and rocked, until at last, judging the moment right, she put the needles and wool away and went to turn down the covers in her bedroom. He would go up the main stairs to his own official bedroom, possibly even stumbling a little, prepare for the night, and come down the back stairs to join her, all of course just for form's sake. God knows, anyone with half an eye in the neighborhood, let alone in the house, who was interested must know how they lived after all these years. However, the English will turn a blind eye to any morality, St. Cyr understood, as long as departures from the conventional were never deliberately displayed.

He looked around to see Mrs. Fleece disappearing up the stairs to the third floor, no doubt relishing the moment of awakening the grumbling students with her bright industry, leaving St. Cyr an opportunity to wag an index finger teasingly and smile down at Sarah, sending her happily after her sister, while he stepped firmly and quickly back into the sanctuary of his "writing room," as Mrs. Fleece reverently called it.

Once seated he didn't immediately take up his pen. Let Blanche wait a little longer, he thought discourteously, already she has waited six hundred years. He reached for the big book of medieval baronial history which contained, as a bookmark, the week-old airmail envelope from Canada.

When he looked at it now, it seemed familiar enough. The handwriting on the envelope stirred indefinite waves of recognition. Should he not have immediately identified those small, tight curves and carefully dotted "i's" and crossed "t's"? Still, he suspected the validity of this reflection, having the first time read half-way through the closely-written lines on both sides of the four blue sheets and then leaped down to the name Roberta Moncrieff (nee Dell) at the end before he finally woke up and faced the Bobbie Dell of twenty-five years ago whom, understandably, his correspondent the Mrs. Moncrieff of today, was sure he wouldn't remember at all. But of course, my dear, dear Bobbie, of course I remember you. He sighed deeply, suppressing a wave of the same uncharacteristic personal sadness that overwhelmed him an hour ago, in the midst of the mundane exercise of shaving a countenance that fully showed the passage of all the intervening time, and surely would be almost unrecognizable to Roberta Dell now.

That was how it began. It was largely a delayed reaction, starting like a serious illness with a few twinges a week ago, hardly noticed, certainly not focused on, but getting steadily worse. He smoothed out the creases of the pages and began to read the troubling letter through again. It was all there, if he was interested and cared to read between the lines as well as the words themselves: Roberta's life in the twenty-five years since they parted, since he abandoned her, to use the cliché of romance. He would have to work at it with his mind and imagination to bring it truly alive for himself, and why should he? Why should he tamper with his dimly but sweetly remembered twenty-five-year-old Bobbie, young, fresh, graceful, not frail or ethereal in the slightest, but healthy and athletic and full of fun? Throwing back her silky blonde hair, laughing with delight at his ineptness on the tennis courts at Stanley Park, or his tumbles on the snowy slopes of Grouse Mountain, through two summers and two winters in Vancouver, just before he took flight for Europe in pursuit of scholarship. Mrs. Moncrieff's descriptions were simple and matter-of-fact. They expected nothing of him, made no direct claim on his feelings. Why should he transform his own faint images into those of a substantial middle-aged small-town housewife, living with her older retired husband on the outskirts of Nanaimo, Vancouver Island, three grown-up children and a long history of psychological ailing behind her? The reason was, perhaps, that between the lines she did seem to be asking him one question. Asking him as a man of the world, as a source of wisdom, experienced beyond her adopted small-town comprehension, not as an old boy-friend or whatever the current North American phrase might be, but asking him in a way all the harder to ignore for not really assuming he would answer.

In the two years they were together, he had answered many of Bobbie's questions, he the somber, responsible elder of the couple by five or six years, she the playful, teasing, reliant one. The truth is he answered more questions than she could ever have thought of asking. He was that sort of young man. He wouldn't have such confidence now. He had long ago lost his certainties about life's directions and about moral judgments. He had developed many quirky prejudices, no doubt, but he had ceased to have any considered views whatsoever on modern experience. All those upsetting and disturbing things he used to say to her in his quiet way, making her think she should throw over her conventional, shallow family and community life, centered on the big house in Vancouver's Shaughnessy Heights, reject everything comfortable and familiar as he seemed about to do, venturing to England and farther places. All those iconoclastic gestures on his part were really so superficial. In the end it was she who made the radical break, however little she intended it that way. He travelled farther, but maintained his old habits of mind to keep him warm. She went mad. Or so he gathered from her words.

Madness is bad management, St. Cyr said angrily to the pages he was gripping tightly in his fingers. Bobbie, Bobbie, how did you let yourself get into such a state? How could you? Well, that was a question he couldn't attempt to answer. The mystery of mental balance. One can't even begin to understand unless one permits the closest, the most intimate and vulnerable of relations with other people. Sarah Ponsby's sister, two years younger than Sarah, was out of the same loins as herself, the same home, social class, schools. But how different they were. Sarah, calm, warm-natured, sensible, accepting whatever the world brought her. Her sister, hiding under a thin brittle shell a tangle of nerves stretched to the breaking-point, though in twenty years never quite breaking, huddled near the benign presence of her sister, never speaking, never giving an overt sign of her inner turmoil, unless one listened outside her door and heard her sob, or unless one chose — as St. Cyr learned not to — to look at her eyes when she thought she wasn't being observed.

This frizzy-haired, thin, pale, drying stick of a woman. Surely Roberta Dell isn't, wasn't, and could never be like that? And yet, her letter told in simple words of recently waking up as if after a twenty-year nightmare. Days, weeks, years of dreading the trivial daily encounters of house and town, the mundane responsibilities of home, family, domestic duties. Friends and ministers and doctors and, at last, psychiatrists, a long list of well-wishers demonstrating to her that nothing could be done for her, that she must help herself. A hideous disease that didn't even offer the comfort of being terminal. And now, returned to life as mysteriously as she was grievously exiled, aware of possibilities for pleasure and even joy she had long forgotten, she discovered she was married to a tired old man who had long ago given up any interest in regions beyond his rocking-chair and his vegetable garden. Now for the question, crying out from between the lines. How much did she owe that man, her husband, who remained with her throughout her ordeal, which surely was his also? Did she owe him loyalty after all those wasted years? Fidelity to a man whose sexual interests had completely atrophied (or so St. Cyr deduced)? Did she have any right, revived, rejuvenated, to try to rescue happiness for herself in the remaining time?

St. Cyr thought of her sitting in the kitchen of her drab little frame cottage on a five-acre lot outside of Nanaimo, watching the husband stooped over the tomato patch, his head grey or bald, wearing old trousers and his undershirt, no doubt. Nothing left of the romantic hero, the young bush pilot who flew into the small village in northern Manitoba where Roberta Dell had gone to work with the Indians, and eventually flew out again, almost literally with Bobbie on his arm. St. Cyr knew nothing about all that before, or about the dreary twenty-year aftermath. When he and Bobbie broke off their transatlantic correspondence, with its passionate yearnings that flared and faded and flared again, she was still talking bravely about a new life in the North, and he was confidently sketching his budding career at Oxford as a professional historian.

St. Cyr could have put the following twenty years for himself in a much shorter space than Roberta took. The only really noteworthy event was the day he delivered four hundred pages of typescript to his doctoral thesis supervisor, Sir. John Neale, six months before the deadline they had agreed upon for the job, and left them with the ambiguous note: "Sir: This is my completed project. It may not be quite what you expected — I know it isn't. But I'm convinced it's the best that I can do. Edwin Cyr."

St. Cyr was fully prepared for the worst reactions. Indignation, contempt, mockery, outright laughter. For, of course, it was not a D. Phil. thesis at all, not a three-year study of aspects of Papal influence on English life in the early sixteenth century. Instead, it was the first historical romance he had ever attempted, the one that was soon to launch his literary career, a fictional version of the biography of the sixteenth-century Prioress of St. Leonard's nunnery, at Bromley, Middlesex, whose abduction or elopement was a minor mystery of the period. The usual terse note from Sir John Neale summoned him to Magdalen College — "Dear Mr. Cyr, do please come by for tea at four on Wednesday next, if you are free, so that we can discuss the progress of your 'project'. Yrs., Etc., Neale."

He mounted the stairs to his supervisor's rooms with a sense of dismay at his own effrontery. Seated in the opposite corner from him in the big, deep-cushioned sofa in front of the fire, Sir. John was his usual calm, urbane and charming self. He obviously found the situation immensely piquant and amusing. His tolerance was no doubt all the more benign for the outrageously complete surprise of St. Cyr's change of direction, which he obviously relished. Until then St. Cyr had shown less of the alleged originality and brashness of North Americans than Neale had perhaps expected and even hoped to find.

"I suppose, my dear man," he said at one point when their conversation approached jocularity, looking with a hint of whimsical disapproval over his spectacles, "I suppose you will have to throw over your fellowship — Imperial Order of the Daughters of the Empire, I believe?"

Tea drifted on into sherry as they talked about the manuscript, about St. Cyr's future, about the relations between fiction and history. St. Cyr walked back down the stairs and into the front quad of the College with Neale's half-mocking absolution and blessing, to "go on in that line and be a splendid success," and more thrilled and exhilarated at this turning-point in his life than at any of the more tangible evidences of success that in time followed: the publisher's acceptance, excellent reviews on the whole, renewed writing, further publication, in due course a quite substantial income, invitations to address Oxford societies and speak or be interviewed on the BBC. And of course, an immense correspondence suggesting a kind of mass communication through his books that he could never have achieved as an historian. Though his scholarly friends refused to treat his work with entire seriousness, even they as often as not admitted it interested and entertained them, and their wives even more.

St. Cyr had already broken off his outdated relation with the girl back home by then, of course. The end came after he had been at Oxford for a year and a half. Roberta wrote to say that she was thinking of spending the summer in Europe. Mightn't she visit him in Oxford, and perhaps travel with him if he was going to spend some time on the Continent? Well, what was poignantly sentimental to contemplate from a distance of time and place became an alarming and oppressive burden in urgent prospect. St. Cyr was just at this moment becoming deeply involved with his first heroine, the beautiful, austere Prioress of St. Leonard's, safely separated from him by four hundred years of history, and he was just becoming involved more superficially with the not-so-beautiful or so austere but considerably more accessible, convenient and immediately pleasurable Sarah Ponsby. Roberta accepted his high-flown epistolary eloquence about new directions, turning points, sacred, unchangeable but unrenewable pasts and so forth first with saddened, reduced claims on his time and attention and then with tearful regrets turning to tender resignation. And finally with silence. Silence that lasted more than twenty years.

"I wanted to do that for so long," St. Cyr murmured passionately into Sarah Ponsby's ear the first time he kissed her, walking with her one dark June night along the tow-path near the college boathouses. Having just closed the chapter of his life that held Roberta Dell's shapely, enthusiastic body, he found his own words not too far from the truth. Lust was overflowing the reasonable bounds within which he normally managed to contain it.

"Darling," Sarah answered, leaning comfortably against him in the dark, "then why ever did you wait so long?"

For the next few years Sarah's practical and sensible nature made it seem inevitable that their lives should become increasingly meshed. Even when she brought her mentally-ill sister to live with her and (in due course) took over the basement flat of St. Cyr's leased house, it was one further step towards solidifying their unofficial union. It was as if Sarah were saying, "You see, you needn't marry me, what we have suits me quite well, thank you, as long as it does you."

Sarah helped in a thousand ways, and never interfered. No London socialite, no titled lady, no county matron, no sweet enamored undergraduate (in love, surely, with St. Cyr's fictional imagination, not with his portly manhood, which he knew was pleasant enough but hardly exciting), no other living woman at all had so far competed with the capacity to fulfill his needs that Sarah Ponsby deployed. And sober or drunk, jaded or virile, he found in her bedroom a warmth of receptiveness and responsiveness that allowed him vicariously all the female faces and shapes that fact or fancy could bring to his mind.

Moreover, there were a few occasions (no literary biographer or journalistic enquirer would ever be privy to them) once or twice a year perhaps, when a stranger need seemed to appear with a kind of inevitability related often to the maturing of his current literary work. A need that overtook him to enter into the role of a heroine more literally than he had done so in the effort to capture her life in words. In a certain sense he felt he must *become* that woman, not as was more often the case, merely woo and make love to the heroine, which Sarah's generous and unspecific womanhood readily allowed, even when she might not be particularly aware of it. On those special, rare occasions Sarah, in her calm, unsurprised, amenable way, participated completely. Participated in whatever dramatic casting of roles or reversals was wanted. Her matter-of-fact acceptance, so English, St. Cyr was at first inclined to think, made the outbreak of such tastes and desires seem no more ridiculous, no more perverse, and no more difficult to accommodate — to prepare for, with stage and wardrobe, to agree to without hesitation from the first hint, even to take the lead — than an invitation to a costume ball. Now, Sarah my dear, may *I* dance for *you*?

In the midst of these last meditations, St. Cyr woke at a tap on the door to discover, with a flutter of embarrassment, that he was in a state of some physical turmoil and disarray. He adjusted his black dressing-gown around himself, and only half-turned from his table to receive Mrs. Fleece's proffered tray of coffee and biscuits: elevenses. Sometimes on Saturday mornings he would go down to the kitchen and sit with Mrs. Fleece while she had her coffee. Not today.

"Thank you, Mrs. Fleece," he murmured, miming a part he often found useful, the famous author deep in his creative thoughts, barely able to notice with a fraction of his attention the trivial realities of the present moment. She left silently, piously, like a minor priest ministering to Archbishop or Pope.

St. Cyr took up Roberta's letter again, and this time read it through to the end resolutely. Not a word presuming undue intimacy, not a trace of assumption about what he might or might not remember of a personal nature. Was she real? This girl, this grown woman now, whom he had held in a variety of embraces of the most intense, absorbing, almost pedantic kind, some with the remarkable complexity likely only to youthful athleticism, experimental enthusiasm, and extreme limitations of convenient circumstances. What came back to him now, with a rush, was the memory of a shared train trip across North America, their last days together, a journey which symbolized, in a way, their whole relationship: beginning with mutual need, travelling in the same direction some distance away from home into new spheres, becoming more desperately intense as they got farther from the familiar, and their time together drew to an end. And then the splitting off in different directions, she to New York, in search of a career or vocation, he to Europe believing he knew exactly why. How he made love to her, night after night in the upper bunk to which he climbed to join her, when day seats were changed to sleeping accommodations, and the corridor emptied of passengers and porters. He had to admit, there was more fever and fury in those few nights than in a year of lovemaking with Sarah Ponsby. It was fierce, ferocious. More like rage than love, though just as mutual. What he wanted to do to her. What she wanted him to do. There were no words for it. It was utterly exhausting, but never satisfying.

"Our bodies knew it was goodbye forever," St. Cyr said aloud.

The truth of that strange forgotten episode was slowly emerging in his mind along with powerful memories of claustrophobic darkness behind the bunk's closed curtains, the deadening roar and vibration, the jolting, clacking rhythm of metal on metal, always the same but never exactly repeated. Their perspiring limbs would untangle, as a peek through the curtained windows showed light growing across the stretch of prairie or of treeland or lakeland the night train was relentlessly surging through, and they would end the nocturnal struggle for ease and gratification in their separate beds, peering up at the black low ceiling above each, as solitary and confined as if already in their coffins. A day of meals and talk and silences, brooding silences, walks along the corridors to the observation car, walks together — or apart, as if to rehearse the future. And then the night's madness all over again.

For St. Cyr there had been so many directions, so vast a change in the months and years that followed, that he never really thought of what that last brief period of frenzy meant. Now it came to him fully, as he clutched the letter in his hands. It dawned as it ought to have, characteristically for him, with the brilliance of a single eloquent sentence. He laughed to himself as it flowed through his mind to its final period. He pretended to write it down, invisibly, with his finger. He wrote it in air. The ultimate eloquence of historical romance, but twisted into a terrible meaning that had no place in the kind of book he loved to write. Splendid truth of statement combined with the most devastating self-mockery. Savage irony directed at his own character and his own career, as he relived those nights of lust and savagery, remembering in amazement. Remembering how she lay for him, and how he vandalized her, that burning, willing body, as if by skewering each of her tight hungry athletic entrances he could destroy himself and her together at the height of their need for each other.

"She died in my arms!" he cried aloud, exulting, laughing hysterically at the cruel accuracy of the summation. That was it! *She died in my arms.*

He re-read the flat phrases of her letter in which she sketched her twenty-years' exile from sanity. Those irrational suspicions of everyone around her, as if the whole world had betrayed her, and could never be trusted for a moment again. Those radical self-doubts. Her literally pounding heart that kept her awake in panic at night, her baseless dread, her fear of people discovering her fear. Twenty years of agony, relieved only by drug-induced depressions. St. Cyr had Sarah Ponsby's sister to help him comprehend, or the words might have meant nothing to him. From this she now wakes, eager to salvage whatever the remaining time might allow her. Turns to St. Cyr, rediscovered by accident through a book in a small town library. St. Cyr, whose personal fulfillment, personal glory, she so wrongly infers from the richness and worldly variety of his *oeuvres*. Not realizing that the works were all there was, the very substance of his life, not its glistening effluent.

"I'm sorry, my dear, I'm sorry," he whispered to the pages. Sorry to have led her away from home and family and abandoned her as the first premonitions of her illness were stirring in her. Sorry to have denied her years ago when she thought she wanted and needed him, God knows how mistakenly. Sorry to have seemed to survive, flourish even, after she had perished — "Died in my arms."

There was a light tap on his door, and Sarah Ponsby entered, still in her outdoor pullover. As he turned to her, he read his own distressed expression in her quick grey eyes, and saw that she recognized the letter in his hands.

"Dinner at one, love?" she asked quietly. "Jenny's tired from shopping, she'll eat in her room."

If her sister's frailty ever wore Sarah down, she never showed it. She took every turn of Jenny's mental instability with the same calm acceptance, like the weather. St. Cyr reached a hand impulsively towards her, a rare demonstration. At once she came closer, stood touching his cheek as he pressed his face briefly against her broad hip.

"I'll be down, love," he said. "I'm almost finished for today."

By the time she had closed the door quietly behind her, he was writing. My dear Roberta: I was deeply moved by your generous tribute to my books. I am now in the midst of my thirteenth novel — I shall send you a copy next year when it is supposed to be published. Unless I run into difficulties — one never knows with this writing business, never. In my new book you will find, I think, the fullest, the only proper reply I can give to your letter, so generous to me in its confidences. Although I make my living now by re-creating history in fictional form, I have never been able to understand what kind of reality the past possesses, how it relates to the present and the future, how indeed it differs, if at all, from dreams and imaginings. My new book is about a splendid English nobleman, John of Gaunt, who lived six hundred years ago, and about his first wife Blanche, sweet, beautiful, and greatly loved. She died young. *She died in his arms.* As he held her, he whispered to her: 'I shall join you soon. Without you, life means nothing to me.' In fact he lived on, in ever-growing worldly splendor and glory. But what few knew, and what I want to show, is this: he never escaped the sense of loss, grief, remorse. Not for a moment. Never. 'I'm sorry, Blanche, I'm sorry,' he was heard to say on his deathbed. Sorry to go on living, he must have meant. To have been flesh and blood, deserting her, while she grew more and more distant in the memory's darkening vault. His recollections of her, pulsing an ever-more-faint light towards his thriving earth, like the flickering of the farthest stars lost in a drift of cloudy midnight skies. Life beckoned to him, and the Man in Black had to walk away from the grave. Then there was no one to hear his apologies, and to forgive him. Not after that. There never is, my dear Bobbie. There never is. For the selves of history are dead, the sinners as well as the sinned against …. You see, Roberta, my book is at its most difficult stage. There is much to be done, and it may be a long while.

St. Cyr paused for a moment, at a loss as to how to finish a letter that, despite himself, had swelled into magniloquence, when all he had wanted was to be simple and honest. Was there any truth in what he said about John and Blanche? Who knows? For now the historian was silenced. All the novelist could say was, it makes a good story.

He began to write quickly — two more sentences that sprang fully formed together into his mind — before putting down his pen for the morning. The first sentence, to complete his personal letter to Roberta Moncrieff. The second sentence, imitating the style of Geoffrey Chaucer's closings, across the bottom of the page of his half-finished novel manuscript, under a double-scored heavy line which, with a sudden surge of strength, he ruled across the sheet from margin to margin. After all, he thought, as he made the strokes, longing to enjoy the finality implied by the gesture: the moment of decision is overdue. He simply had to make up his mind whether to go on with his book, at the risk of diving deeper and deeper into an ocean of feeling, or to give up on this one and stop, put a finish to it, and cut his losses. The discipline of his art and craft, indeed of his life, brooked no interference. It depended on his historical characters continuing to arouse and then to liberate all his creative energies. And so he again plunged his pen into the full stops after each of his last two sentences, first one, then the other, and went down to dinner, leaving the pages side by side on the table, the ink still drying.

> May the skies rain blessings upon you, my dear Roberta, whom, oh yes, I do remember, remember well, and may the years ahead bring you all the freedom and happiness you have missed and ever been hopeful for, yours in friendship, Ed.

Here endeth Edwin St. Cyr's Book of the Duchess and her Man in Black.

Bayley And I

Bayley sent me a wedding invitation. It was in the mail this morning. I haven't seen him for years, in fact not since we were in school together out there in Vancouver. That was in the war years, when kids had to grow up by themselves as best they could, and they didn't always know how to go about it. I remember Bayley well. We used to spend most of our spare time in his room on the second floor of his mother's big old house near Tatlough Park. Bayley was our mainstay, the consistent one, the one we felt we could always rely on, during those last two or three years in high school.

Bayley's room was his great pride. It was small, but every inch was put to use. Against one wall he had a two-tiered set of bunks made of metal. A couch stretched along another wall. Hanging above it in a glass case were some of Bayley's specimens. He collected just about everything: insects, gun-shells (his father was a Major in the Canadian army, prison-of-war in Singapore, I think it was), matchboxes, bottle-tops, and of course Petty girls, but mainly butterflies. And he used to change his displays every week or two like a museum, though nobody else ever showed much interest. His drawers and closets were like storage vaults and he seemed to be able to produce any number of displays from them. Sometimes if you came in early, just after supper, you would see him at work, sitting at his desk in his wicker chair, carefully sticking pins in new butterflies. I never really noticed how he did it. It was funny how seriously he took them — after all, Bayley was hardly what you would call the studious type — as if he saw something in them that none of the rest of us could see. He would hardly look up at you then, peering at his new additions until he had them set just as he wanted them.

It used to be quite a pleasure to come into Bayley's room in the middle of the evening. There was a tailor-made greeting for each of us. Standing in the doorway you would have your head banged by a lazy foot hanging down from the top bunk, a hand reaching out from the lower would pull you into the room, and Bayley himself, stretched out on the couch, would kick a stool across to you and yell, "Well if it isn't Kerr-dog, you old dog! Where've you been, Kerr old boy?" or, for example, for me Gordon Noble: "On your knees, everybody, the noble Noble has arrived! Bow down, you varlets, bow down! (Anybody who did, of course got kicked from behind.) Close the door behind you and be seated, my lord." No matter who was there, the crowd then always seemed complete.

When the door was shut the Native Princess danced into sight (she was tacked on the inside of the door, and anywhere in the room you could sit or lie and watch her). She was almost life-size on glossy paper, and was supposed to be a South Sea Islander, I suppose, judging by the dark skin and the long loop of flowers hanging round her neck and stretching down her naked body to the sands at her feet. The Petty girls on the walls, with their long legs and over-size breasts, were in a way quite sexless by comparison, because they were so fantastic. Their style of drawing cooled instead of fanning the flames (cooling was really what we all needed). But she was different, her breasts and thighs lit up by the firelight, the rest mysteriously in shadows or hidden by the flowers. She had hung in Bayley's room so many days and months and even years that no one ever said anything about her any more. Though she belonged to Bayley we all shared her, and no one could forget she was there. Nights when everyone was lying about too lazy to think of anything to do she seemed nearly alive, standing there watching us all with a little smile on her lips, as though waiting for us with some kind of secret promise. I guess for many of us she was as close as we had come so far to what Woman was or what we wanted her to be. Lie and look at her too long though, in certain moods, and you could get very restless.

Bayley's strong point of course was that he didn't seem to know what restlessness, boredom, and so on, were. With his endless collections around him, his friend or two or three come in to see him, his Native Princess on the door, Bayley always seemed sort of content. If there were any volcanoes in his life, you never heard them erupting. And once you tasted Bayley's brand of contentment, you kept coming back for more.

It was Kerr-dog, if I remember rightly, who usually supplied Bayley with his girls the times when Bayley gave a party. He did well sometimes too, bringing along quite lively and attractive girls. But even so Bayley treated them always in the same way, friendly and polite to their faces, proud and facetious or just plain dirty behind their back. Maybe his South Sea Islander gave him unrealistic standards. Anyway he never got to know any of them on his own, and always had to call on Kerr-dog to help him out for the next time.

"Well good evening my dears," he would say to a couple of Kerr-dog's women arrived for a party, "come in and take off your things." And they would smile at one another over his standard joke and his mock-politeness. But they would soon drift away into other rooms, in their thick over-socks, and start to dance on the polished floors cheek to cheek with somebody more interesting to them. And yet from a girl's point of view Bayley ought to have been a good-looking fellow himself. He seemed just to miss it somehow. He had regular features, but he used to make his big eyes bulge out on purpose when he was trying to be funny. And though he was tall and broad across the shoulders, when he laughed he used to throw back his head and cackle in a high-pitched voice, making his Adam's apple stick out and shuttle up and down. So Bayley would usually stand joking with the stags, or go around filling glasses.

"Drink it up, Waller, you old walrus. You're as sober as an owl," he would whisper in a hoarse voice. Waller was the quiet little fellow who had to wear glasses about an inch thick. "Have another beer, Zeke?

Lots more in the bath-tub. How about you, Kerr-dog? A little more of the mountain-dew special?" and so and so on, throughout the night.

When the last dancers couldn't stay awake any longer in each other's arms, the records were stacked away, shoes dragged on, glasses and bottles heaped together, and yawning waves and shouts passed back and forth on the doorstep and up the street, regardless of the neighbors. Bayley and a few unlucky (or maybe lucky) stags would be left behind to go to Bayley's room — which was closed during the party — and burn themselves out with stories of the night's doings, while finishing off the refreshments. After they took their girls home some of the others would be sure to drop in again too. Bayley's voice by then was always loudest, full of glee or sarcasm: "Where did the noble Noble pick up that nag? Cracky, he must be hard up. I wouldn't be seen on the same street-car with her." And he would throw back his head, screw up his bulging eyes and cackle like a mad hen. "As for that little dog with Hank — did you see her? She was just waiting to be asked. That's the only reason I could figure him spending two minutes with her. What a sack!" He would lay back glass in hand on his couch, opposite the Native Princess, and join the jokes of the others with high-pitched laughs and wild glances from his big eyes. Or sometimes he would just sit shrugged up into his corner, watching.

I brought Joyce with me once to Bayley's place. She was from our high school and I'd seen her around the school lots of times but had never tried taking her out anywhere before. After all she was only in Grade Ten. Her family liked her to be in early, so I thought I'd better tell Bayley in advance to cut down on the kidding. On my way by after supper on Saturday I stepped in to say yes I would be bringing a girl to his party that night but we would be leaving early. He didn't know her by name.

"What's the trouble, Noble," he said, "Won't Mommy trust you out with her little treasure after dark?" Bayley gave his usual cackle, but didn't look up from the little spotted butterfly he was trying to mount.

"Don't see why not," I said, "I didn't let on I was bringing her to your place, Bayley …. Anyway, she never lets Joyce stay out late. She's only fifteen." I knew I was in for a ribbing, but I blurted it out anyway.

It would have been worse to try and leave early without saying anything ahead of time.

Bayley almost choked. "Fifteen? You lousy cradle-robber, Noble. Well, she'll grow up fast enough around here. Bring her along, my boy, we'll see that she has all the lollipops her heart desires."

He pushed a pin a little further into the mounting board and then held up the butterfly with its spread wings for me to see. I suppose it was one of his rare ones, he looked so pleased with it, standing up to admire it and pushing the cardboard under my nose.

"Yeah, nice," I said. "Well, I have to shove off now. Joyce wants me there early to meet her mother."

"Holy cow! Meet her mother! Mommy has to give you the once over? God help you if she sees into that dirty mind of yours."

For some reason this time his laugh really got to me. I was suddenly fed up with everything. "Here's your damned bug," I said. I flicked the cardboard out of my hand and sent it sailing right across the room, while I headed for the door.

Bayley was still standing there, speechless, flabbergasted, his eyes bulging out at me, as I left. Out on the street a few big flakes of snow had started to fall, very unusual for Vancouver. They melted as fast as they landed.

Bayley had nothing much to say to me when Joyce and I got there a couple of hours later, but to her there was a lot of 'Joycey this' and 'Joycey that'. We danced together most of the night, hardly stopping. Bayley kept offering her drinks, but she just leaned on me and smiled and shook her head. Being called 'little girl' didn't seem to bother her at all. She hardly paid any attention to what Bayley's words and looks meant, but I could see him more than once over her shoulder while I was dancing with her, go over to one of the others and stand nudging and whispering and cackling in his usual way.

I'd only had one drink myself and Joyce was as fresh and bright as ever when the time came for us to leave. For some reason, early as it was, our going started other people going too, while we were putting on our overcoats and rubbers. At the door Bayley was trying to talk some of them into staying, but to me he just said, looking from me to

Joyce and back again, "Well, noble Noble, come back and see us after you get your little Cinderella safely home. We'll be here till morning." I started Joyce down the stairs before he could get any more cracks in, as he was trying to. He was well under way by then.

Outside it had stopped snowing, but now it was cold, one of those clear quiet nights, an odd sort of moonlight. The snow had really changed things. The street seemed to have disappeared. Instead there was just a wide stretch of white like a park with dark trees dotted along the sides. No cars anywhere, not one in sight. Joyce and I started off down the middle, kicking through a new path ankle-deep, and pretty soon a line of people from the party laughing and singing were trailing far away behind us. She had mittens on her hands and I had bare hands but I held one of hers anyway. I tried to forget I was mad at Bayley. We didn't say anything, just walked softly along listening to the muffled voices away behind, watching the whiteness and the sky a million miles up and our breath drifting towards it. It made you dizzy to put your head back and stare. Once we turned a corner well ahead of the others, and all of a sudden she ran to the side to see a little pine-tree like a Christmas tree covered with snow. It was very quiet. We were all alone and I held her hand and it was then that I kissed her for the first time.

When I left her at her house I took my time walking. Really I felt like going home to bed, but I knew Bayley and some of the others would be up in his room if the party was over. On the way by I could hear them but not what they were saying, so I went inside and up the stairs, pushed open the door and walked in.

"Well, I'll be damned, here he is, the noble Noble, the arch-baby-snatcher himself. Back already. That was quick, quick, quick, my boy. Fastest draw in the West."

I kept my mouth shut and just climbed into the top bunk where Zeke was sitting with his legs dangling down. He was a prairie boy of course, a year or two out from the farm, and looked it too. One or two others were there. Bayley was pouring a glass of beer for me, still talking and winking at them. "Have a drink, Noble. God knows, it must be thirsty work breaking the young ones in."

Zeke in his good-natured heavy way made a joke and tried to change the subject, and Waller behind his owlish glasses chipped in a little too, but Bayley had to keep on. "The way that little princess looked up at your noble face, Noble. You'd swear it was Prince Arthur himself, right out of the funny papers. Hey tell us, what did she think of your trusty sword? Did it bring the blushes to her pretty cheeks, you rascal?"

He walked over, reached up, and pinched my cheek, grinning in his insane way right into my face. I didn't move. Finally still looking him in the eye I said, but quietly:

"Listen, Bayley, I meant to say …. My kid brother's been wanting to meet you. He's only twelve, but he's got a nice lot of birds-eggs."

I was leaning down and smiling at him. Bayley brought up his glass of beer and sloshed it all onto my face. I emptied my glass on his head before he could move. He stood there quite still, goggled-eyed, beer dripping down from his hair and cheeks, looking amazed. And then without warning he started to cry. It was the last thing anybody expected. So we all left.

Well, we forgot about it in a few weeks and later on I used to go back once in a while. But meantime Bayley had changed things around. The Native Princess he moved to the inside of the closet door, so I hardly ever saw her. Not that I cared. He hid some of his collections too, or maybe they just didn't happen to be out very often when I was there. Anyway, I don't remember ever seeing another butterfly in Bayley's room.

That was so long ago. Ever since the card arrived this morning inviting 'Mr. and Mrs. Gordon Noble' to his wedding, I've been thinking about Bayley and wondering. As soon as I came home from work this evening I said to Joyce, "Why do you suppose Bayley bothered to send us an invitation to his wedding, anyway? I haven't seen him for years and years. Not really since we were high-school kids."

Joyce always has the answers. "Well maybe," she said, "maybe he just wants you to know he's a grown-up now."

I had to think that one over for a while. I was mixing us a drink before dinner. Finally I said, "O.K. then I'm going to write to him.

About the old days when we used to be friends. Say thank you for remembering us, and give him our good wishes. Then he'll know I've grown up too." And now I've done it, and I'm glad.

Dans le restaurant

("De quel droit payes-tu des experiences comme moi?" T.S. Eliot)

I have always found expensive restaurants intimidating. It's not so much the money, though God knows my mind panics when I run my eyes down the price list, trying mentally to finger the bills in my wallet at the same time, and to decide whether the numbers stand for a whole meal or only bits and pieces of one. What really bothers me is the effort to translate the foreign names into images I can see or taste, and the fear that I might order some ridiculous mixture of courses that would bring a smirk to the lips of the waiter. Or worse still, something I don't know how to eat. Of course when the time comes for the bill, I have the dilemma of getting a signal to the waiter, or just patiently hanging on, as if I have all night ahead, or my thoughts are so absorbing I can't remember where I am, until the card appears on a plate at my elbow. Then of course the agony of having to glance casually at it, gather in all the pertinent facts, feel confident I haven't been robbed, make a fierce, rapid calculation of the tip — what, ten percent? Fifteen? Is it twenty nowadays? Pretend I'm an easy spender. Assert a high standard of service. Or pass as a hardened realist, meting out exact measure, whatever that should be.

No, expensive restaurants always intimidate me. That's why I have long been grateful, whatever other feelings I may have, for the simplicity and comparative peace of — McDonald's.

This isn't a commercial, just an honest confession. The fact is the commercials are a lie. The place I go to, anyway, up in the north end of the city, is nothing like the TV version. Those fresh, energetic, clean, bright, laughing young boys and girls behind the counter, greeting you with their shining teeth and cheerful eyes. Their friendly alpine helloes. The song on their lips. Well, where I go I have to shuffle up one of the three or four lines — why do I always pick the slowest, the one with the Italian mother and her three kids, or the brawny young tough in the sweat suit who turns out to be ordering for the whole baseball team — I shuffle along until I get to a depressed, acne-ridden schoolboy who hardly looks at me, his face flushed with the strain of pushing buttons for Big Macs and Quarter Pounders and Fries (Large or Small) and all the rest of the possible items, to the number of no more, surely, than twenty-five. And even then the arithmetic is all done for him, and the machine pops up the total and subtracts from the folding money I give him and tells how much change to hand me back. Maybe the fact that he finds it so intimidating keeps me from feeling that way. The same with the others on staff, the teenage oriental girl who remembers to blurt out the company slogan, "Thanks for coming to McDonald's come again" to every second customer from her impassive face, as if she has no idea what the words mean. The frizzy blonde who has just invented hips and breasts and who takes my order while she's talking to friends at the side of the line-up. The unhappy fat girl who's always in a sweat, and wiping her brow — does anyone check to see if they ever wash their hands? The gangling tall pony-tailed boy, all neck and wrists, who ought to be behind the counter instead of walking around cleaning up — he's so full of energy, always on the go, but maybe they found him a bit quick with the till. I wouldn't expect him to miss anything a person accidentally left behind, or ever return it.

Anyway, I eventually do get my order, which is always a Quarter Pounder, a Large Fries, a Vanilla Milkshake, and a Hot Apple Pie. To Stay. I pick my seat very carefully. Unlike the chairs and tables on TV, these are likely to have squashed fries or ketchup or the odd slop of ice-cream or milk decorating them. And of course, the people that do that kind of spilling are all around. But there's usually a corner table or back-to-the-wall chair that's out of the line of fire. You might have to look across the aisle at a brat in a high-chair pawing his meat patty out of its bun, or a toddler pouring her orange juice down her daddy's pant-leg. You might have to see a double picture, once in the flesh and once in the mirror, of a long-haired foursome of ambiguous sex filling a booth with their silent pointless yearnings. But as long as I have a little elbow room, as long as nobody actually crowds me or, a rare affront, touches me, I've learned to tolerate the scene.

I put down my tray and lay out my newspaper beside it to ensure a little more space. And then I carefully push the small, stiff flap of the cardboard burger package out of the slit and open the lid flat out. I pour the open carton of fries into the lid, and there before me is my main course, meat and potatoes and a little bun and relish and tomato sauce to round out the diet. I eat with my left hand, first a few fries, then a bite of the burger, and then the fries again, until I get down to the very last. It's always a dilemma to know whether to end with a mouthful of burger or of fries. I don't want to leave it to chance. Somewhere before the last I make a decision. And to tell the truth, I invariably have a slight feeling that I've made the wrong choice. However, there's always the next time.

Meanwhile, of course, I turn the pages of the newspaper with my right hand. And from time to time I raise my eyes just high enough to be able to get some sense of the comings and goings around me. Or the stayings. Because there are a few who seem to stay at least as long at a stretch as I do.

I suppose that's how I first noticed the person who has become the most familiar one in the whole changing crowd. The one I seem to have established a peculiar grudging sort of relation with. You see, when I finally leave, pick up my tray and take it to the wastebasket to empty — typical of McDonald's that when I dump my scraps in, struggling as usual to get the paper mat to slip off with the rest of the debris, the flapping lid says "Thank you" for being stuffed with garbage — anyway, when I get up I just leave my newspaper where it lies on the table, or at least I used to. I've finished it. It's got so skimpy nowadays. Even so, I can't quite see myself putting it in the garbage, such a waste having cost me too much three-quarters of an hour ago. I did that once, and had the odd feeling that eyes were staring in hostility or disbelief into my back as I went out. So now I just leave the paper where it lies. And of course, in a routine that's developed in the last weeks or months, or God knows perhaps its years now, that man — that old man — is soon at the place where I was, as if it had never been empty, following the same track I did through the ocean of printed space spilling out over the table.

That old man, the one I'm talking about, he doesn't appear in the McDonald's commercials either. Nor his smell. It was the smell I noticed first. If McDonald's commercials were to smell at all, it would be the smell of youth, innocence, possibly a little whiff of harmless sex. This old man stinks. I don't know whether it's his armpits, his feet, and his dirty underwear — invisible though it is, it has to be dirty, because the once-white open-necked shirt is so dirty, the thin grey hair. Of course, some of the stink is probably from his mouth, which seems to be toothless, though he manages to mumble his burger and fries, his pie and his milkshake. Eyes don't smell, or I might blame them, because his faded brown eyes with their brown-specked whites look dirty, and certainly they are the strongest feature the old man possesses. If you try to look past him, you get snagged on the eyes, which you discover are staring at you out of the sallow, creased face slumped between the slouched shoulders, somewhere over by the mirrored wall.

I must surely have been at least four tables away when I first noticed him — his smell, that is. I know because I carefully set myself down at a spot with empty tables all around. I raised my eyes a little from my newspaper, thinking at first that the aroma was from the washroom — I forgot to mention the washroom, it doesn't appear on TV either. But it's there in McDonald's, its sickly sweet stench a slight undertone to the general atmosphere wherever you are in the room, even around the corner and out of sight. Where was I? Oh yes, the old man's smell. It wasn't a variation on the washroom perfume. It was coming from the opposite direction. I half-turned, and despite myself, I was snagged on a pair of old man's eyes. I looked down again quickly, and tried to immerse myself in my meal and my reading. I was hooked, though, under the surface of my consciousness. A thin line played me, played me, ignore it as I tried, until at last I had to leave. I got up, picked the tray off the table, let a hand rest on the newspaper and paused a split second, still not looking around, still staring down at my tray. Then, almost despite myself, I gave the paper a little push, just a couple of inches, in the direction of where I sensed the old man was sitting, and walked over to the garbage receptacle. I'm sure I didn't at any time look back that day. And yet I felt for certain that if I had I would have seen him, my newspaper in front of him or he moved over behind my newspaper, those smelly eyes moving slowly along the track of my reading.

That was the beginning. As if I knew it was going to go on, and as if I were trying to break the pattern before it became confirmed, the next time I was there — and of course he had to be there too, not far away — I actually tried speaking to him. The one and only time. To speak at him, I suppose I should say. When I was finished my Quarter Pounder and my Large Fries and my Apple Pie (not as Hot by then as it should have been) and had dredged up as much of the sludge of my Vanilla Milkshake as I could, and when I had turned the last page of my newspaper and laid it out on its back on the table again, I got up in the usual way, tray in hand. I could feel the tension between his eyes and mine, even though I was carefully avoiding a direct gaze. I could feel the tension between his slouching, clumsily dressed, dirty old skeleton and my own familiar body, my finger-tips resting on and pushing the newspaper an inch or two towards him. So as I started to walk away I said, in a voice low enough for only his ears to hear, though God knows maybe he's deaf, "Have you seen today's paper?" I hurried on. I didn't wait to find out if he'd heard me. If he was going to respond in any way. To me. To my permission, my authorization. I dumped my cardboards into the garbage container. I scraped off the paper mat. I put my empty tray on top. I nodded to the flap which was flapping its "Thank you" for my garbage. I walked out quickly. But as I was letting the glass door shut behind me I couldn't resist half-looking. A quick glance. And there I'm sure he was — whether at his table with my paper, or he at the table where my paper was I couldn't tell, his sunken face submerging into the print.

Now I mustn't give the impression that any single person at McDonald's could ever seem particularly important to me — that would be misleading. One of the reasons I don't find the place intimidating is that there's an ever-changing crowd. Not a closed-in community, just strangers, people pouring in and out in an uneven stream. If you find yourself always watching people, if you don't yet consider humanity too revolting to be observed, you couldn't have a better vantage point. It's amazing the variety of human beings who come through the doors. I'm pretty certain that lots of people who, unlike myself, don't view expensive restaurants as especially intimidating, come here sometimes too. As well as people who wouldn't dream of going to an expensive restaurant, who wouldn't be let in the doors, who couldn't even afford to pay the tip on an average meal, let alone be able to figure out what the tip should be. Personally I don't really look at people unless they force themselves on my attention. But it's hard not to notice some things. You can't get far enough from the others eating here. And when people talk in this place, their voices carry. In expensive restaurants, there is privacy, everybody seems to be whispering. Here, nobody cares. It doesn't matter if others hear you. It's as if no one listens anyway. Those two lean, dark-skinned, tough-looking kids, no more than fourteen or fifteen at most, rolling cigarettes and talking out some scheme they had. Stopping only now and then to look at themselves in the mirror, run their hands through their thick dark hair. It was going to be easy, easy money. In the back way. Up the stairs. Just an old watchman and he slept most of the night. One of them worked there and he knew his way around. He knew what was worth taking, what would be easy to get rid of. They laughed out loud from time to time, as if they were already big spenders. Hard to imagine them behind school desks ever. Easy to see them behind bars.

I met their eyes in the mirror a couple of times, but they weren't showing off for me. They were hardly aware of anyone around them. They were acting it out before a larger audience already, a bigger world than McDonald's could offer. I was staring at my newspaper but really trying to remember a friend and myself at their age, in another city far away. He had a plan. It was wartime. Butter was rationed. He worked all day for the shipper, and he handled those pounds of butter as if they were gold bricks. He knew the way over the wall when the gates were shut. He knew how to jimmy the doors where the trucks were loaded. He could do it by himself, but there was more than twice to be gained if I could help. I tried to think of myself as a thief. It was strange. It was exciting. It was frightening, but my friend and I couldn't talk about that. I didn't say no. I didn't say yes. The time drifted by. He didn't discuss it with me again. But one night when I met him on the street outside his house he handed me a brown wrapped package. He smiled under the street-light. Later at the back door of my house I weighed it in my hand. I opened the brown paper, and the wax paper inside. It lay heavy on my open hand like a brick of gold, shining dully in the moonlight. I folded the paper over it again and dropped it in the neighbor's garbage can. My friend went his way, and I mine. And I suppose I always envied his clarity and certainty a little. These two in McDonald's had their roles to play as well. In fact they were already lost in their parts.

It's hard to know how or where such creatures are spawned. Could any of these infants and toddlers, these noisy restless preschoolers, quarreling and egging each other on and nagging their parents, could any of these grow up into such purposefulness, such hardness? The ones being led to their places by their drooping pregnant mothers, the ones being exhorted by their overbearing fathers, "Come on now, honey, give me a kiss, give your daddy a kiss," as if love could be confirmed by enforced and reinforced demonstrations. I'm not the only one who shrinks from these domestic maelstroms. That calm, detached, elegant middle-aged gentleman in his cool blue summer suit and glinting spectacles, carefully knotted grey and blue tie, manicured fingers, tanned shaven cheeks. A banker, surely, an advertising executive, a vice-president at the least. He is here, among the Big Macs and Quarter Pounders, but not here, as well. And then in a minute he is on his way out, pausing only long enough to purchase a high-curled ice-cream cone, which he licks with a confident flick of his tongue as he pushes through the glass doors and is gone. I feel a moment of irritation that he, a man who could obviously summon a Head Waiter with a snap of his fingers, send back a bottle of wine or soup too cool with just the right amount of insistence — that this man should invade my eating place, sail right through the center of the McDonald's world as if he were an admiral of the fleet or the master of an ocean yacht. The man lost none of his own dignity or stature by being here even if a trickle of ice-cream ran down his hand, but neither did he lend any to his surroundings. He simply came and went untouched.

Not that I envied the man his worldliness. If I have a weakness, it's not for that sort of temptation. I noticed, too, no sign of the old eyes that waited for my newspaper looking at that blue-suited gentleman. Obviously neither of them could have existed for the other.

No doubt McDonald's would rejoice in the great equalizing power of the hamburger, that should bring so many diverse people together, or if not together at least to the same cash registers. Certainly those cash registers rang a continuing tune. The youngish middle-aged foreign man in his fine tennis shirt and shorts standing behind me took out a large roll of bills as we got closer to the counter. And he didn't look up at the display overhead to calculate how much his order was going to cost. Instead, he kept calling over to his family gathering, already at a table and waiting, and he kept stepping in their direction to hear their calls and answers, as they added more and more that they wanted. Eventually I had to lift my eyes from the front page of my paper to see. Three expensive little children to go with their expensive father, but no mother in sight. Instead, an expensive girl-woman babysitter. She was settling them in their places, tidying and teasing and cheering them up as they waited, laughing at them and with them as they asked for more, new to the job, surely, judging by the atmosphere of fresh fun and chaos they were all giving off. And the father, on the way to his club no doubt, taking them there to spare their expensive mother a few hours' peace, or perhaps she had her club to go to as well. He talked in an urbane adult way to his offspring, let himself be amused by their antics despite wanting to get dinner over with and go on his way, and he was obviously as charmed by his new young helper as — as I found myself being.

Because she was remarkable, any objective observer would have to agree. I placed myself at least a table closer than I ordinarily would have with a pack of children nearby. I opened my box, spilled my fries in the lid, laid my right hand on my newspaper, and attempted to carry on as usual. But my eyes were lifted as if by magnetism. From my place in the line-up I had followed her employer's gaze as she went back and forth from the children to him. I had observed her slender girlish shape, her long golden legs, her close-fitting brief white shorts, the graceful arms bared to the shoulder, her young breasts delicately defined even to the hint of their peaks in the soft white material of her sleeveless top. I felt an old and terrible pang as she stepped away and a rush of hunger as she turned and came back. But it was her face, her eyes that drew me when I was seated. She was laughing at the children, at the jokes of their father, she was laughing with them, as young and inexperienced as they, it seemed. And every now and then, as if she and I were previously acquainted spectators or in some sense colleagues or co-conspirators even, she would turn her face towards me, her neighbor, light me with her laughing eyes. Had no one told her what poisons fester in the hearts of men? Had no one told her that eye contact with strangers, especially males, in a city like this was to be avoided at all costs, or if engaged by accident, to be ended abruptly with suspicion, hostility, frigidity? I could feel a smile tugging at the corners of my mouth. I wanted her to look again. I would smile for her. And yet I wanted her not to look, so that I could watch her at my will. See, she's looking again. I can hardly go on reading my paper. But soon, very soon, they'll be finished. They'll gradually close their ranks, tidy themselves, get organized, and then they'll be gone, the whole happy family. Will the father really go on to his club? Or will he perhaps decide that after all he should spend the evening with his children? Will he discover an urge to exercise his urbane, foreign charm on this young creature? I feel a rush of envy, a rush of irrational anger. I want to get up and follow them. I want to speak to her. I want to warn her. *I want her for myself.* The absurdity of it. As they go through the door I find myself breathing heavily, being pulled after them. I watch her long legs stepping with easy springing stride down the concrete steps.

I turn my head down to my newspaper. It's not that she has walked out of my life. I have directed my attention elsewhere.

In a moment I look up again, at the doors, as if hoping in a ridiculous way that she will have rushed back, perhaps to exchange a quick word. Of course there's no one there. Not even, and I look around quickly to be sure, not even the old man. Thank God for that. He's nowhere in sight. Not a whiff of him. That would have been awful. To have him in the same room as that beautiful young creature. I slip deeper into the sea of print.

But the feelings persist. Yes, many years ago I too knew such a girl-woman. I even touched her. I was a school-boy, ignorant and loutish, and full of clumsy desire. She was long-legged, long-haired, fleet of foot — a runner, in fact, an athlete, not an Amazon but perhaps a Diana, though then I knew nothing of such matters. She was too young for me in the strict code of the schoolboy, but I walked the streets one night with her and at her door turned to exact a senior's reward. I don't know what I expected. Perhaps a prim refusal. Perhaps flight, a rush up the stairs to the safety of home. Perhaps, in some grimy depths of my feelings, I hoped for a token of an obscene fleshly encounter, a gesture towards wickedness, any hint of a counterpart to the lust that knew no name or direction, yet, even for me. Instead, she turned to face me with a radiant look. She lifted her eyes to mine, she placed her hands on my shoulders, she smiled into my heart with an outrush of warmth, of generosity, perhaps it should even be called love, though it could hardly have known me as object. And she gently put her lips up to mine. She held them there for a moment (I didn't dare move), drew back to look into my marveling eyes again for another second, then spun around and left me standing to watch as she slipped effortlessly up the steps and through the door without a backward look.

I'm almost through my newspaper now. There's a heaviness on my shoulders that makes them slouch over the table. The pulse at my throat flutters, but seems almost to be stifling. I run my hand to my

Dans le restaurant

collar and discover that it's unbuttoned, that I have no tie, that my skin is wrinkled and slack to my fingers. And now comes the smell. Unmistakable. I lift my gaze from the newspaper and survey the tables. Where is he? Why can't I see him? I pick at the remaining fries. I try to decide whether to end with them, or with the last bite of the Quarter Pounder. The Apple Pie is cold in its package. The Milk Shake will hardly come up through the straw. I suck my lips in. I close my gums on the tasteless food.

The smell is so strong it dominates the atmosphere. It comes from close by. It's here. I droop my chin on my chest …. I can smell my feet. I can smell my crotch. I can smell my armpits. I can smell my breath. My breath. My chest is full of pain, full of yearning. I raise my eyes to look into the mirror. There he is. The disgusting old man. There. He is staring back at me from the mirror with his smelly eyes. He is crying. He has slumped back against his chair. Now he is shutting his eyes. Now he has disappeared.

Paddy the Horseman

Paddy says it's cold in the hay loft. It's so cold the pigeons don't stir from their perches on the top beams as he comes up the stairs. His breath billows like white smoke into the shadows of the high roof. There's dead silence except for Paddy's footsteps and the hollow sounds of horses snorting or raking in the stable below the mow.

Paddy's told them there'll be no riding today, but they don't believe him. They're making short work of their morning feed. Enjoy your peace, my friends, is Paddy's advice. They'll all be here to ride tomorrow, it's Christmas day — the Colonel and the whole family, even the black-sheep daughter Sarah-Anne.

Right now, Paddy is going to enjoy his peace too. Three or four days to himself is all he ever gets in a year. He opens the granary door. The scamper of mice in the gloomy bins inside reminds him he should have let Meg out of the dog-run as the Colonel asked. The bitch loves to come up here with him to mouse. Paddy stuffs his leather mitts into his parka pocket and reaches his arm over the shoulder-high boards that hold the bags in the second bin. Wrist-deep in the stack he feels the cold neck of the bottle and pulls it out. He sits on a bale as he uncaps it and quickly puts it to his mouth. Cold in the mouth, but hot, lovely and hot down the throat. He coughs and spits. Tonight at feeding time, if there's anything left in it, the bottle can go back into its hiding-place.

From below comes the first nicker. Pete, of course, the big chestnut. Finished his hay, and ready to lead the boys out to the west paddock.

The rest of the bunch would be starting up soon. Before you knew it, they'd be tearing the place apart. Devil of a hurry to get out into the foot of December snow, and an east wind to cut the hair off a rhinoceros. There's no accounting for tastes, Paddy suggests to his bottle as he holds it up in the dim light. More than half of it still there, to be tucked away safely and zippered into his jacket.

Out on the mow floor again he bends to slide the loft cover off. Pete nickers louder, knowing Paddy is now standing almost on top of his head. A puff of hot air comes up through the chute from the manure and straw of the stable floor, and from the dozen well-fed animals drinking and staling and turning restlessly around in their stalls.

"Heads up," Paddy calls through the hole, automatically. Though he knows every human being but him is off the farm for the day.

A dozen bales of hay to be tumbled down onto the aisle floor one after the other, fast. Paddy can work fast when he has the right fuel in him. He reaches down and rolls the chute cover back in place with a crash against its metal guards. The blood rushes to his head, so he has to put a hand on the wall of mowed bales at the side to steady himself. On the way down the stairs he carefully lowers the trap door in place after him to keep out the draft. Johnny Pearce the stable manager will be looking to see how well he's done everything, all by himself. Expecting the worst, so much so that he almost didn't go down to the City to spend the day with his lovely wife and new-born baby, bless their sweet souls and thank God he did.

"Won't be long, my friends," Paddy says to the rows of long faces that turn to him as he walks down the aisle to the jumble of hay bales. He stacks half of them at the east end and half at the west end, ready for the evening feed and tomorrow's morning feed as well, if Paddy divides it right. He's sure of the twelve, because he counted off his fingers and toes and added two thumbs as he put the bales down the chute.

By this time it's late and Pete is getting worried. He's stopped nickering. He's sure it's a riding day, and he'll have to stand-in till somebody comes to hack or hunt him. The others in his gang of geldings take their lead from him. Jason, the big black Percheron type, Pete's right-hand man. Then the little scamp of an Arab colt with the funny name Paddy long ago gave up trying. The old grey hunter Dougall who hasn't taken a sound step for ten years and still cries to go out as loud as anybody. The homely buckskin cowpony, Mort, busy cleaning up the last shreds of his hay but keeping one eye on Paddy. And the two big half-brother twins who never put a foot wrong. They all have got quiet and watchful. Sir Peter's the boss, alright. The heavy bones of his Belgian breeding aren't to be argued with. But Paddy's the boss of Sir Peter and all the rest, make no mistake.

"When I'm ready, you devils," he yells, threatening, "not before," as Pete rakes at his door.

Paddy leans against the feed-bin and pulls out his bottle for another warm-me-up before taking off the blankets and turning the horses out for the day. It's not a big job, because the Colonel himself has built the paddocks and lanes in a way that takes all the work out of turning out and bringing in the horses. But everything goes so much slower when there's only one man, and especially when there are things Paddy himself never does except when Johnny Pearce the stable manager is away.

Usually Paddy doesn't have to think what he's doing. It's all habit, from milking the four cows at six-thirty every morning to eating the breakfast old Mrs. Pearce, Johnny's mother, puts on the farm kitchen table, to mucking-out the horses and putting down the hay. The rest of the day it's fence work and odd jobs, but Johnny or the Colonel himself tell him what to do. Except today, of course.

"Mind you keep your wits about you, Paddy. Don't want any trouble with those horses at Christmas time," were Johnny's last words as he got into the farm pick-up with his old mother for the hour's drive south to the City. And she said, "Dinner's in the oven, Patrick, be sure to turn it off when you take your plate out."

A nice old lady, even if she is death on the drink, and treats him, a grown man older than her son, as if he was a baby. Paddy in the ten years he's lived with the Pearce's on the Colonel's farm hasn't dared to take more than a sip on Christmas Day and New Year's Eve — in the house that is. During haying season, the Colonel sends out his housekeeper from the big house on the hill to the fields with bottles of cold beer, but you sweat that out so fast it hardly counts.

Paddy has his jacket unzipped, his mitts in his pockets. The stable is nice and warm compared with the hay-mow. The tack-room of course is even warmer. He watches the horses watching him as he opens the tack-room door off the west aisle. Half-a-dozen nickers at the sound of the door opening but he ignores them. Walks in leaving the door ajar. Baseboard electric heaters, not the cold stone fire-place, keeping it comfortable in there now. Trophies, pictures of the family and friends and their horses on the paneled walls. Paddy slumps down on the deep sofa and lights a cigarette. The bottle he puts between his feet on the carpet. Windows on one side are dark with the darkness of the unlit arena next door to the stable. Windows on the other side are bright with sunlight reflected from the snow of the paddocks and fields, stretching away to the west. Paddy lifts his bottle in salute to the big picture of the Colonel over the mantel, before he puts it to his lips.

Even in the picture the old man looks like the boss: dressed for the Hunt, top hat and pink jacket, mounted on Sir Peter. The Colonel never says much. He's kind of gloomy. But when he says he wants something done everybody hears him. At least, his two younger brothers do when they're around, their families, and people like Johnny Pearce and Paddy who work for him. The Colonel's daughter, Sarah-Anne, never pays much attention to him though. Married twice despite the old man's No, and just now getting rid of the second. She'll be here tomorrow, even so, Paddy's heard. Unless she's already got her tail up and is running after number three. Johnny Pearce says it must be her shenanigans that make the Colonel so sour most of the time. Great big farm, house on the hill with rooms enough to breed rabbits, fancy house in the City too, more money than he knows how to spend, no need to work another day of his life — and only this silly twit of a woman to pass it all on to.

Paddy swigs a mouthful thinking nice thoughts about Sarah-Anne, who comes to stay for a month at a time, rides hard every day in her tight-fitting riding pants and swinging blonde hair, jokes like a man with Johnny and Paddy, and then disappears for half a year, maybe more. Paddy leans back on the sofa. Puts his feet up. He can hear Meg barking, probably at a squirrel near the dog-run. He can hear the thumping and calling of the horses, keen to get out. But he's warm and sleepy. He lights another cigarette. Life is good to him. No family troubles. Steady job, the best he's had since he came as a lad from Ireland. Good warm room upstairs in the farmhouse. Comfortable mattress. Three meals a day. He scratches his belly, which is getting itchy with the heat. What more could a fellow ask? He yawns and lights another cigarette, takes another swig, dozes again.

He knows inside his head that he's had a fair amount to drink, because he feels so good and because he can't tell whether he's dreaming or not. Afterwards, even, he can't quite sort things out.

Pete and his gang are pretty annoyed with Paddy for being so late, that's for sure. Mort, the buckskin, has the heaviest winter coat, and as the stable warms up he's getting itchy. He's rolled a couple of times so his blanket is under him, and he's covered in straw ends, but it hasn't helped much. He has to get out and roll in the snow. He starts to knock against the door. Just a little reminder. Oldsters are supposed to take things easy, but the aged grey hunter Dougall is fit to be tied. He's crowing away to anybody who'll listen, in between fits of mumbling at his hay with his worn-out teeth. The Arab colt isn't really all that bothered. The young seem to be able to find things tolerable if there's something to keep them busy. So he's butting the door catch of his stall with his nose. He's found out long ago that if he can hit it twice just right — ta dum — it will bounce open. He'll do it too, though it may take a few hours of steady trying. The twin three-year-olds aren't doing much, they're so easy going. They're just leaning against the partition between their stalls, making it squeak back and forth. Someday it will just fall down. So much for the west end. But the east end isn't so simple.

There you've got the couple of old ponies Sarah-Anne outgrew, happy enough knee-deep in hay at first, but now eating their way through their straw bedding. And then there's half a dozen of the Colonel's breeding and show-stock, developing colic and bad habits and God knows what. There's a pair of thoroughbred geldings, three and four, he keeps hoping Sarah-Anne will come home and break. Getting to be quite a handful just to bring in and out. There's the mean natured liver chestnut Irish hunter the Colonel has never ridden since the horse kicked and broke the younger brother's leg when the two were out hacking five or six years ago. Then, of course, there are the two fine brood mares, thoroughbreds, the nice old grey dam Snowdrift that's produced a foal a year since Paddy's been with the Colonel. And the hot-blooded bay mare Johnny and Paddy call Sarah-Annie, because she's always looking for it, but hasn't taken for good yet, for all the trying. The Colonel paid twenty-five thousand for her, Johnny says, and she's the one they have to watch.

Right now she's weaving. Back and forth, back and forth, a bundle of nerves. Makes you dizzy to watch. No use saying anything to her, she's got herself hypnotized. The older mare, Snowy, just yawns at her across the aisle. She doesn't care. Turn me out, ride me, tease me, breed me, I'll take whatever comes along, even Sarah-Annie bugging me out in the paddock. Eat what the Lord has given me, drink my water, and lie down all the afternoon on a good bed of straw. Listen to my neighbors snuffling and munching and complaining all around.

Now what's all this? It's Peter, yelling at the top of his lungs. Everybody looks. Paddy's got up. Coming out of his own stall, or wherever he's been hiding, and is going into Peter's. Peter's telling him it's about time. Now everybody's up and yelling at once.

"Peter, don't let him forget us," Snowy calls down the aisle, but they're all making so much noise she thinks he probably can't hear.

Paddy hears. Paddy hears everything. Paddy smells everything. His ears twitch and his nostrils open.

"I'll be back to slap your fat bum in a jiffy," Paddy neighs as he goes around the stalls of the gang for the west paddock, taking off their blankets. Then the doors are all opened, and off they go, Pete first of course, Jason second, Mort crowding close behind, then the twins and pushing not to be last, Dougall and the little Arab colt nipping at his mottled withers.

"Keep off," Dougall croaks, testy old devil.

"Get along, the lot of you," Paddy trumpets, prancing along himself behind to shut the gate when they're out through the barnyard and into the west field.

"Paddy lover," Sarah-Annie croons, seeing him frisk out the door.

"Soon my dear," Paddy tells her by a twitch of his ear and a swing of his shoulders, "I'll be back for you."

It's cold out there. Paddy wastes no time in the east wind fastening the gate. He gallops back into the warm stable. Out go the ponies to the north paddock, the miserable liver chestnut by himself in the arena yard, and the three and four year olds race off through the east gate into the east paddock and disappear to its far end. It's lovely there, sheltered by the evergreen plantation. They roll and roll. Paddy itches to get his hide against that white scouring pad too. But there are still the brood mares to go into the wee south field next to the big west field.

"Snowy my girl," Paddy nuzzles her warm neck as he takes off her blanket. She walks sedately out the stable door, turns south to the open gate of her paddock, swinging her fat hips.

"Thank you, Paddy love, you're most kind to be sure."

Paddy knows better than to love up Sarah-Annie. You never know about her. She might kiss you or she might kick you. He steps out to hang up her blanket, opens the door wide and out she comes on her toes, tail in the air.

"Sarah-Annie, you're a lovely sight, sweetheart," Paddy says as she passes him. He's still shaking his head admiringly when he sees she's turned west, not south, west towards the gate of the west field, instead of following Snowy to the wee south field where she belongs.

"You witch! Have you lost your way?" Paddy yells, trotting along behind her. "Don't you make a fool of me now."

And then he sees the extent of his troubles. The west paddock gate is swinging in the wind, instead of being shut tight. Sarah-Annie is already brushing her way through. She's after the boys, and nothing's to stop her. Paddy's alarmed neigh reaches the gang before they know what's happened. They're in a group to the far west, under the now-bare once-loaded apple-trees, nosing in the snow hopefully.

"Good God," says Sir Peter deep in his throat, "look who's coming." They all raise their heads so high they're like giraffes in a fright, even Dougall, the dirty old man, and the little Arab, a randy kid. Pete is already making his move towards her, to meet her, galloping so high his feet hardly touch the ground. Jason comes half a step behind. Then, ears back, teeth bared, not missing a stride, Pete sends Jason and the others scattering off his track. There he is, Pete, right there, as they join together again and come crowding up behind as fast as they can run, Pete, nose to nose with Sarah-Annie herself. Nostrils meet, flaring. They both stand rigid.

"Get back!" Paddy whinnies, half the field away, husky voiced from puffing along in Sarah-Annie's tracks through the snow. Nobody pays him the slightest attention, least of all Sir Peter and Sarah-Annie — every muscle coiled, turning around now, so that there's Pete, his nose to her quivering flanks, her tail high, her eye rolling white.

"Look out, you damn fool!" Paddy squeals, but it's no use, it's too late anyway, she's wheeled, she's let fly, there's a flurry of legs, and Pete's bloody lucky he's missed by an inch a pair of hooves like cannons in his knees or face. Now they're off, all of them, the mare ahead, galloping and twisting and kicking and breaking wind and the laggards stretched behind like a swarm of bees, even old Dougall on three legs lumbering and lurching, calling Wait for me, Wait for me, Wait for me, with every labored breath.

Paddy groans, drops into a walk. What can he do now? No use chasing that circus another step. They'll go till they're tired now or have lamed or maimed each other. He turns his back on them and ambles wearily towards the stable for a bucket of oats which later they might be interested in. Inside, he stops for a swig or two from his bottle. Not much point in hurrying. Twenty-five thousand, Paddy thinks, twenty-five thousand, and she'll surely break a leg. Just my luck.

As he goes out again with the bucket, not all that soon afterwards, Paddy peers to the west, watching them still running through the drifts. Then he grins and slips into a trot to the west gate.

"Luck of the Irish," he wheezes.

On a great sweep around the field, snow churning behind them, the mare half-a-length in front of the pack, she has slipped through the open gate into the barnyard, and Pete's gang, old habits working, misses the opening and goes on galloping past it, on their own side of the fence. Sarah-Annie didn't intend this. She sees she's got only Snowy and Paddy out there with her, not her idea of fun, but it's too late. Before she can turn and chase into the west field again, Paddy has slammed the gate shut. Ha! He's got her back! He feels so good he kicks up his heels and sprays out the oats from his bucket in two wide sweeps, one for the geldings on their side of the fence and one for the mares. Anyway, now if they'll come to the fence he can see what the damage is.

They're all blowing and snorting, too hot to care much about the grain, brown-yellow against the whiteness of the snow. Other things on their minds. They meet again across the fence, Sarah-Annie still performing, squealing and wheeling, the geldings pushing near as they dare behind Pete to sniff her over the rails. Paddy looks at their legs for blood. Not a trace, not a single trace. It's a miracle!

"So if there's lumps and bumps tomorrow, who's to say where they came from?" he asks the whole party. Paddy watches them for a few minutes more. "All that trouble, Sarah-Annie," Paddy says. "There's nothing that lot of geldings could do for you anyhow, my love. I'm the only one around here who's just the way the Lord made him."

He goes back into the warmth of the stable, leaving the mares to find their own track into the south field, when they're ready. They'll come to no harm in the barnyard.

Paddy's tired as he clomps down the aisle. He puts the bucket back in the feed-bin, and lights up a cigarette, striking the match on the No Smoking sign stapled to the beam above. Johnny and the Colonel are death on smoking in the stable, so he's very, very careful. The aisle needs sweeping, but the stalls look good, he's mucked them out well, for all that the horses have stood-in an extra few hours today.

Paddy needs to relieve himself as he smells the straw, and he can hardly wait to unzip when he steps into Pete's stall and hears the rustle of the stalks under his feet.

Paddy the Horseman 111

Horses are the same, it affects them that way. No wonder they all stale together when they come in at the end of the day. That feels better. He walks out and down to Sarah-Annie's stall, sniffing his way along the aisle. A deep bed, fit for the queen herself. He pushes a foot into the fresh bedding in the darkest corner. Ah, he groans, as he has the urge to lie down, right there. He uncaps the bottle, and takes a swig. Not too much left now, a little dribbling down his chin, but oh, the rest is where's it's doing the most good. He sinks deeper, groaning and sighing and breaking wind. No, it's not too bad a life, not too, too bad....

Paddy doesn't remember much after that. His lungs and throat feel as if all the cigarettes he's ever smoked have been rolled up into one big one, and he's smoked it till the butt burned his fingers and mouth. That's about all.

Actually, Johnny Pearce is the one who has the biggest shock. It was dark, Christmas Eve, when he got home. He was just coming along the Aurora Sideroad to the spot where you can see the lights of the big house on the hill, his old mother in the pick-up beside him, when he realized something was terribly wrong. He started ahead, grunting to wake up his mother who was dozing. It was the kind of thing you sometimes imagine happening just like that, but you don't really believe it ever will. As he rounds the curve he sees clearly — the barn is burning to the ground.

Across the fields and through the trees came the glow and flicker of flames, as if the fire in a huge fire-place was dying out. All around, on the side-road, up the entrance lane, cars were parked, those of the voluntary firemen empty, some with people in them or beside them, sight-seeing, a few of the neighbors watching helplessly. And further up were the fire-trucks, and three police cars. The firemen were playing their hoses onto the smoking, flickering ruins of what used to be the Colonel's pride and joy, his barn and stable. In the fields beyond were the dark shapes of horses, standing in groups and now as Johnny picked his way in slow gear past the cars and up the lane, he could see that some of them were running, galloping in great circles round and round, stopping and then circling again. He couldn't count them, but all the paddocks seemed to have movement. His mother had screamed in horror at the first glimpse and he had sworn a string of curses. Now they drove on slowly in horrified silence.

Their own house fifty yards away from the stable was untouched. The arena adjoining the ruins was still standing too, its roof and near side hissing from the firemen's hoses. Their pumps were going strongly, supplying their tanks, lucky to be able to suck enough water from the frozen pond behind the house in weather just below freezing. A police car blocked the lane where it divided for the driveway up the hill to the big house. Johnny knew the Colonel wouldn't be there yet, thank God. He was having a dinner for his family in the City, and Sarah-Anne and he were coming north after that.

"The horses must be alright by the look of it." Johnny said to his mother as he parked at the side of the driveway.

"But where's poor Patrick?" the old lady gasped out, saying what they both were thinking at the same moment.

Johnny left her sitting in the truck as he walked over to the group of uniformed men around the fire chief's car. The Colonel's housekeeper and her husband, the grounds man, come back from their shopping trip in the City, were sitting in one of the police cars. Paddy was nowhere in sight. Johnny looked at the piles of foundation stones and crumbling walls covered in collapsed smoldering beams. The skeleton of the barn was still recognizable. Every now and then a rafter would fall in a cascade of flame and sparks and billowing smoke. But there was nothing much left to burn. God help any creature caught in that.

"Your man's in the hospital," the chief explained as soon as he recognized Johnny Pearce. "We picked him out of a snow-drift this afternoon when we got the alarm. Some nasty burns, but he should be alright. The smoke knocked him right out. When we brought him around with the inhalator we had to keep him from running back into the barn. Just like that pair of crazy horses," the chief went on, pointing towards the south paddock, closest to the buildings.

Sarah-Annie was standing there, looking as if she was about to jump the fence from a standstill to get to the remains of the barn, her neck and shoulders in a white lather you could see even in the dim starlight and the blaze of car lights and fire-glow. Snowdrift was standing still behind her, huddled close. Then they wheeled suddenly together, and bolted off again into the dark, lost, homeless, and terrified.

When Johnny was sure the arena would be safe, he and the grounds man set about rigging up some loose-boxes so they could get the horses inside for the night, before they ran themselves to death. By then the Colonel and his daughter got back too, and faced the horror. It was three in the morning before everything that could be done was done and they could get to bed. The emergency work would go on for days, and then there would be the re-building to think about.

Now it was Christmas Day to wake up to. The Colonel and his daughter took Johnny with them at ten in the morning to visit Paddy in the Newmarket hospital. During the short drive Johnny heard the Colonel's latest report on what had happened. The fire chief thought it was either a short-circuit in the electric heaters in the tack-room — "Damned aluminum wiring," the Colonel said, "I was going to have it all taken out" — or rats exposing the wires in the east end of the stable, that started the fire. Must have broken out just at nightfall, and all the horses in their stalls. It spread surprisingly fast, as though it started in several places at once. But that's the way a barn fire often goes. There wasn't enough of the place left for them to be sure. They were lucky to save the livestock. Lucky the hired man was on the spot so soon, doing his night check.

The fire chief gave Paddy the credit. It looked as though he just got the last of the horses out before the roof fell in. Could have caught him. He was probably driving the last two out again — they were in the barnyard — after they tried to run back into the burning building, when he passed out from the heat, smoke, pain. That's the picture as the officers figured it out. Of course, Paddy was in no condition to confirm it yet.

The Colonel spoke to Paddy's still body as if he were talking to a soldier wounded at the Front.

"How are you, my good man? The doctors tell me you're going to be all right, perfectly all right. We're very proud of you, young chap."

Paddy's eyes stayed open for a few minutes, perhaps even widened a little, and then he seemed to fall asleep. At least, he didn't move or say anything. The Colonel and Sarah-Anne looked at each other across the bed. Johnny stood at the foot of the bed, wondering if he should say anything. He was so used to speaking for Paddy. Sarah-Anne reached down and touched Paddy's uncovered fingers.

"Does it hurt very much, Paddy?"

There was no answer. As hospital visitors often do in such situations, those at the bedside started to talk about their own business as though the patient didn't exist. The Colonel folded his arms and cleared his throat, addressing the air over Sarah-Anne's head.

"It would be awfully good, Sarah-Anne … I mean to say … awfully good if you could stay at the house for a bit. I mean to say," he went on, finding no relief from her for his awkwardness, and turning to include Johnny, "we'll have to build again right away, won't we now? It would be awfully good if …. You could do it just the way you'd like, of course. Whatever would suit you."

Sarah-Anne grinned across at him.

"You know the way I feel about my freedom, Daddy. I'm not a good soldier."

The Colonel kept his solemn look, saying gruffly:

"Carte blanche? Put up a cottage of your own too, if you prefer?"

Her grin turned to a throaty laugh. The sound made Paddy's eye-lids flutter.

"My own place, Daddy? We could give it a try . . . . Well, what do you say? Shall we go back and look at the ruins?"

Paddy raised his eye-lids a fraction as they walked towards the door. Perhaps Sarah-Anne noticed. She came back for a moment to stand by the bed.

"They tell me you're a hero, Paddy."

There was complete silence.

"Get well soon," she said. "You know, there'll always be a place in my new stable waiting for you."

Paddy lies in a daze after they leave. Is he dreaming? His skin is mostly numb, but now he is beginning to feel itchy. He needs …. It would be good if somebody would come and take off his blanket and let him rub himself against the bed-posts or something. Well, there's nothing to be done about it.

He slides deeper into his warm, still bed, around which seem to hover vague smells and sounds. Like the sound of clean, cold water being poured into the water buckets. The sound of straw when it's forked into a stall and you lie down flat and stretch your neck over it and get it into your ears. The smell of hay, when a bale is freshly opened. And then, strangely for this time of the year, the smell of spring pasture. The swish of tall grass as hooves gallop across it. And then the crunch and snap of wind-fall apples under the trees.

Paddy doesn't have to think about yesterday or tomorrow. Paddy's at rest right now. Paddy's in clover.

An Oxford Anecdote

Hello again myself. I'm enjoying these recording sessions more than I ever thought I would. They come naturally to me. A professional politician is always making speeches or telling stories, whether in the House, on the hustings, on TV, radio, or even somewhere trying to be alone for a holiday. If he's not talking to the Public or the Press or the Opposition, he's talking to himself in the mirror. Now, for example, I could say to myself, for God's sake turn the machine off, shut up — but the flow would go on in my head regardless. It really doesn't matter whether I get around to writing the memoirs of my personal and political life in later years. These times for reminiscing, like right now, are the closest I can get to any sort of private meditation, given the life I lead. I wish I could sit down alone and spin the reels more often.

A woman reporter once said to me, "You're the handsomest politician in Ottawa — doesn't it infuriate your wife to have us all chasing after you?" "Not a bit, I said, with a modest blush. "She tells me it's O.K. with her — as long as I keep running."

So a man in my position doesn't get as much privacy as he and his family would like. It's a choice you make. Just one of the penalties you pay for holding high public office in the 1970s, the kind of constant exposure you get in the mass media today. You always have to think twice about what you're going to say. Which is a bit hard for someone like me who enjoys the sound of his own voice, as my wife frequently tells me. Well, the old Chief claimed that a good politician has natural good manners: he never puts his foot in his mouth in public. Before I joined the Cabinet there wasn't nearly as much pressure of course. Those first few years on the back bench, they were great, they were all too short. My wife and I always think of them nostalgically. Of course we can afford to now. But there's no way around it. Nowadays, Mary, our in-laws, the twins even, the whole family, we have to be political animals all the way through. My friends say it suits us. At least there's never a dull moment. My idea of a good time is certainly not to sit around contemplating my navel, or anyone else's for that matter, ma'am.

I've been a candidate four times in twelve years, and so far I've never lost a race, thanks to a great team. In fact, I suppose my performance is a darn sight better in politics than it was in track-and-field, when I was a student. I once told a reporter that when I got into politics it was easy, I just went from fast running to fast talking. I guess the only track records of mine that still stand are two intramural ones. The two-twenty I ran for the University of British Columbia Faculty of Law team in 1947 and the one-hundred I laid down for the Queen's College, Oxford, in 1949. My national collegiate times have all been wiped out years ago. My record as the youngest man to be brought into the Federal Cabinet in this century stays right there on the books.

Anyway, I was trying to say something about how my various experiences of English life influenced me, especially my student years at Oxford, a century or two ago.

I took Mary down to Oxford from London last year after the Commonwealth Conference broke up. I'd hoped to be able to show her some of my old haunts and have a bit of a holiday before returning to Ottawa. The boys were still in school of course. Mary was enjoying London, but with private discussions every morning and formal afternoon and evening sessions and press briefings and so on, she and I were like ships that pass in the night. Not as close, I remember kidding her, not as close as Mackenzie King and his mother used to be. Anyway, I accidentally let it slip to a reporter that we were going to spend a few days at my old Alma Mater, and before we knew it we had two magazine writers and two photographers sharing our compartment down to Oxford. Not quite what we had in mind, but that's politics.

It was kind of fun, even so. We had a couple of fairish days, weather-wise, just a little drizzle on Sunday morning, most of which anyway we spent in bed at the Randolph, reading the Sunday Times and the Observer and the News of the World. I told Mary, the two of us lying in the big double bed, VIP suite, breakfast leavings and papers scattered all over the place, and her looking just great in her new night-dress from Harrods', I said, Twenty years ago when I was a miserable undergraduate in my cold lonely bed in Queen's College half a mile from here, with only my Rhodes Scholarship to keep me warm, I would have given my right arm for a morning like this. Why just the thought of it would have raised the temperature so high, palm-trees would have sprouted in the Front Quad.

The sun came out in the afternoon and we wandered over to the old College to have a look around. Some great pictures, which I've kept copies of, of Mary and me in the dining-hall and the chapel and the Buttery and then standing by the fireplace in my old rooms. They were smaller and dingier than I remembered, but the young chap living there then — by coincidence, he was a law student too — seemed as content with them as I was in my days. He was very friendly, and didn't object to being inspected by a Canadian cabinet minister, his wife, and the Press. Of course he was more sophisticated, in the English public school tweed-jacket and corduroys way, than the brash colonial I was in my days there. I could never have kept my cool as he did. He probably dined off that story for weeks. You've got to hand it to the English public school system: they know how to put polish on a man.

Sunday evening we had dinner at the College with my former tutor, B.K.S. Sandford and a dozen guests. Poor Mary, I don't think she enjoyed it very much, though she put on a jolly good show all the same. She didn't know most of the names B.K.S. and I kept mentioning. The other guests talked more generally about the Oxford scene and that sort of thing, amusingly enough, but such matters wear thin after a while, unless you have the place in your blood, as a college man always does. Personally I lap it up. I find myself thinking and sounding more and more frightfully English when I'm in a group like that. Did I say that among the other guests, besides the Provost and the Senior Tutor and their wives, were an old friend, Douglas Petrie, who was Honorary Secretary of the Track and Field Club when I was up, now a philosophy don at Worcester College, and his wife, Vera, a tutor in Russian at St. Hilda's interestingly enough? Decent of Sandford to pick them specially to join us. Fascinating people in their way. Vera is a perfectly charming woman, a dark Slavic beauty in her thirties, quite a surprise to me, since I remembered old Petrie as the tallest, shyest and most awkward chap on the Oxford team. Brilliant lad, though, and a certain kind of beautiful women do seem to find brain irresistible.

Anyhow, it was a donnish sort of occasion. Sherry in the Fellows Garden, then a seven-course dinner with four wines served in Sandford's rooms by his scout and several others. Just delicious, down to the last detail. Sandford's round bespectacled face has hardly changed, except perhaps that his thin hair is even farther back from his brow. Certainly the rooms are the same as they were those Thursday mornings twenty years ago when I used to read my weekly essay to him, both of us buried from sight, almost, in the two big tatty old armchairs by the window. Sandford's wife may have left some marks on the place, but they weren't evident to me — she of course had been in hospital off and on for the past several years. It was the same old bachelor don's suite I was familiar with from college days.

In fact nothing at Oxford ever seems to change. B.K.S. still sits in his chair hearing the dronings of undergraduates reading for the B.A. or the B.C.L. and looking over his thick glasses in that characteristic stiff-lipped way. And Petrie, as lean and fit at forty as he was at twenty, still trains with the team three times a week at the Iffley grounds. Easier, of course, for a long distance man to keep up an active interest in running. He could still pace the team lads for a few laps. But I don't suppose he would care to risk the famous kick finish that won him the ten-thousand against Cambridge in 1950.

"If you're going to be here tomorrow," he said to me as the dinner party was breaking up, "come down to the grounds and work out with us. We usually put in an hour or two on Mondays. At least join us for tea afterwards — as usual, at the Iffley Hotel. You look as if you've been keeping fit, have you?"

Mary laughed at that, and started telling Douglas what a physical fitness nut I am. She didn't realize that what has made me famous by Ottawa standards is just the normal amount of exercise for an Oxford hearty: a few games of squash a week, a little jogging or skiing in the season, a couple of swims, and of course the daily calisthenics. I wasn't too worried about being able to keep up with Douglas Petrie, anyway. Though as I think I've said, I'm not much for bringing up the rear at any time. So I said, yes, if we decide to stay over for a day or two more, I might just do that.

Dear old Oxford. It was nice to walk through the heavy gates of the College, wave goodnight to the porter who let us out, turn west along the almost deserted High street back to the Randolph, and know that in some ways this funny sleeping little town has hardly changed in five hundred years. Maybe not everyone would have the same reaction. I'm not sure Mary really got the spirit of the place. Otherwise she wouldn't have mentioned so often how enclosed life must be in Oxford. But it gives me a feeling I never understood: until I realized that it's the very one I used to get when I was a choir-boy in St. Patrick's Cathedral out in Vancouver, oh, thirty-five years ago. I was quite a religious boy, a credit to my Roman Catholic mother. In fact at one point it was a toss-up whether I should go into the Law or into the Church. The call of the active life got to me, and I've never looked back since.

My campaign biography always lists me as Anglican, which is Mary's church, and I'm no more a Roman Catholic now than she is. But I've actually never been confirmed in the Anglican Church. So I'm really neither Catholic nor Anglican. Mary is practical about these things. Off the record, she once said she'd be as religious as the Liberal Party wants her to be, and those are really my sentiments to a T. But there's nothing like a few young years in the Faith to give you that sense of ancient buildings that point to the heavens and things that have been and will be forever. Well, it's hard to put it in words. But Oxford at night gives me that kind of feeling.

Mary was due in London by noon Monday to go round the galleries with her old friend from school days, the wife of the First Secretary at Canada House. So, we agreed that I would spend the day in Oxford, and come up to the City to join her on the last fast train to Paddington, the 11.53. We have the Press pictures from my afternoon at the Iffley track, me in borrowed togs, a towel around my neck, stepping out strongly with the old leg action, Petrie with his fine effortless stride a pace behind me, at the turn over on the university tennis courts side. It was a great workout. Made me quite nostalgic. The members of the Club were all so friendly. I said good bye to the Press chaps after tea at the Iffley Hotel. In fact, I gave them the slip, telling them that I would probably see them on the 6.40 to Paddington. I had other plans, plans I hadn't even told to Mary.

Mary is the ideal wife for a man in high public office. I once said to a reporter that as long as my wife keeps voting for me I'll keep winning elections. Bounce, energy, good spirits, great public presence, pleasant to talk to, and of course, very easy on the eyes. She likes the challenge of political life. She likes to keep busy. She likes the sense of getting things done. England was her holiday, and I didn't want to depress her by taking her to Aylesbury Hospital with me.

B.K.S. Sandford talked to me about his wife in Aylesbury Hospital when I first telephoned him. Or rather he answered my questions about her. Elisabeth Cary — I don't ever think of her as Elisabeth Sandford — Elisabeth Cary was an undergraduate when I was up at Oxford. Just a lovely person. I met her first at the Newman Club. She probably went to the Club because she was a Catholic, but I went there to meet girls like her. It turned out that we were both reading law with B.K.S. Sandford. It was great for me. I took her punting on the Cherwell, played tennis and had tea with her, even dinner in my rooms (scrambled egg on toast, I think it was). We had lots of jokes about old B.K.S. Of course he wasn't old at all, really, except in manner, probably still in his early thirties, but already set in the habits of a life-time, a measured, grave, almost stately sort of man. Fads, fashions, the whole 'now' thing meant nothing to a man like that, you could be sure. Not that he wasn't capable of sharp and sardonic comments on the flow of current events.

When I think of it, Elisabeth must have got special amusement out of seeing the two of us — me, bouncy, full of beans, always on the go, a public career ahead already, and B.K.S. dignified, reserved, restrained, an intellectual's intellectual. I suppose I was half in love with Elisabeth. Certainly I would have made love to her, and damn the consequences, if she'd given me the slightest encouragement. But something in her calm face and serene, sort of open-eyed, gaze made me take her, and myself as well, more seriously, I suppose, than I really wanted to. We became good friends whose paths obviously were leading into different worlds. We said goodbye without ever putting anything into words.

Years later I heard that she had married old B.K.S., and I felt a twinge thinking of her sweet fresh face and body and that stiff, withdrawn, even armored, donnish nature she had given herself up to. I couldn't see much that drew those two together, at least on the face of it. Still, by then I was married myself, and hadn't given her a serious thought for years. She would have been a lost soul in Ottawa in any case, even more so than me in an Oxford college.

B.K.S.'s reaction was unfathomable when I hinted on the phone that I would like to see Elisabeth, and followed it up talking to him on Monday morning after Mary went back to London. But he definitely didn't put me off. Indeed, he seemed to be encouraging me. Anyway, no one has a better command of the old British ice if someone needs chilling. So, I felt confident in accepting his suggestion that I drive over to Aylesbury with him after dinner, and go on to London from there by train when visiting hours were over.

I braced myself for the worst. B.K.S. was admitting nothing about her condition. Lots of talk about benign tumors and remedial treatments of various sorts. But I knew that nobody goes to Aylesbury unless he's considered by at least some doctors to be a terminal case. And she'd been there for two years, with occasional brief holidays arranged by B.K.S., at Oxford or in the country nearby. Some pleasant quiet pub on a river where she could rest from the treatments and get some fresh air away from the dreariness of the sick and dying.

The pallor was as I expected. But she wasn't emaciated or anything like that. The three of us talked in quite an animated way, if B.K.S.'s conversation could ever be called animated. I think Elisabeth was pleased to see me, as far as her quiet unsurprised manner showed. There might even have been a little more color in her cheek for a while. I had this sense of them together, their eyes watching me — B.K.S. was in a straight chair by her pillow, I was perched on the arm of the easy chair towards the foot of the bed — watching me as if they were in some other country or on the other side of a glass window. Watching, polite, kind, but from an uninvolved distance, where I couldn't be invited and didn't belong.

As a present for Elisabeth, I'd brought along a witty, satirical book about contemporary British society, *From Caesar to Harold Wilson*, by Donald Bamfield. Everybody was reading it. It was reviewed very favorably by both the Observer and the Sunday Times. Sounded like great fun and very sharp. Just the thing for hospital reading, I thought. I was chatting away about it and everything else that came into my head, holding up my end. B.K.S. made wry comments with that tight-lipped grin of his. He had brought me in to her with some sly references to what a famous and distinguished Canadian politician I'd become. Elisabeth was sitting up against the pillows. I got a little smile out of her from some of my best Ottawa stories, but I could see she was tiring quickly. Her eyes kept drifting away from me down the white sheet and up to something beyond and behind me, on the wall or ceiling towards which her bed pointed. I half-glanced around at one point to see what drew her dark eyes, but there seemed to be nothing but a big old-fashioned wardrobe reaching almost to the ceiling. Anyway, from my angle, I couldn't find anything that could be distracting her attention.

I could understand that with all my colonial bounce and energy I was a little overpowering for a sick person, so I made my move to leave before the visiting hours were over. They didn't really try to keep me, despite their politeness. I took Elisabeth's hand, standing beside the bed and looking down at her pale face. What do you say in that kind of situation? Well, they weren't admitting anything, so I talked about seeing them again on my next trip to England and so forth. There was nothing left but a little pressure on her soft damp hand, a smile, and a 'well, cheerio for now'.

B.K.S. followed me down the hall to the foyer. As I turned to say my goodbyes to him, there was perhaps just a little more stiffness than usual in his bearing. His look warned me against entering forbidden territory. I found myself looking at him hard in return but exchanging platitudes about how well things seemed to be going, and how confident everyone was about improvements and so on. The British aren't great hand shakers, as everyone knows, and I was almost afraid to offer mine. But as I once said to a reporter, a handshake to a politician is like a drink to an alcoholic — it may not do him much good, but he can't do without it. B.K.S.'s hand was firm and warm, his face expressionless behind his glasses. I respected that man. I liked him more than I had ever done before.

I was striding along through the gates on my way to the station when I remembered my umbrella. You don't travel around England without your umbrella. Dreadful anticlimax, I thought, to go back. Maybe I could get the orderly to fetch it for me. Nobody was in sight to help when I got back to the right corridor. The door seemed to be open and after a step or two down the hall I realized the bed was empty. They must have stepped out for a walk, perhaps with the wheelchair, before visiting hours ended. I stood in the doorway. The faint unnamable smell that I hadn't even admitted to myself was there rose to my nostrils as I looked at the empty white bed and the sparse furnishings. I retrieved my umbrella from just inside the door. There was a neat stack of new books in the bedside-stand, mine on top, and all looking unopened.

As I straightened up, my eyes followed the line of the bed pointing towards the big, high walnut wardrobe against the wall, reaching almost to the ceiling, dominating the room. On the top of the wardrobe, pushed back against the wall, in a direct line of vision from the pillows at the head of the bed, was the thing that must have drawn

Elisabeth's eyes when I was talking to her. It was barely visible from anywhere else in the room. I certainly hadn't been able to see it from where I was sitting. I could feel an uncomfortable pounding in my chest, it was so startling, so out of character, irrational, childish — pathetic. I was uneasy, sort of embarrassed to be there looking at it, as if my presence was sacrilegious. What it was, was a small wooden model of a great church, a great cathedral. Not an especially good model either. Just a cheap, crude toy, by the looks of it, maybe something her father or an older brother made for her when she was a child. Painted grey to simulate stone, and with fake lit windows, as though the place was packed with people, and Christmas or Easter Mass was being celebrated. A medieval cathedral, I'm not sure which one, or even if it was meant to be any one in particular. Lying back in the hospital bed and waiting, surrounded by the smell of her own decaying body, her eyes could rest on that, that great cathedral. In fact could hardly avoid resting there. I had to hurry out.

When I got to the Station, half a mile away, I was still so preoccupied, I guess, that I did the kind of thing I pride myself on never doing. One of those minor boobs of the unorganized and inefficient who don't know their way around. I got sort of disoriented for a moment. I ended up waiting on the Down platform instead of the Up platform. The toot of my train coming in through the fringes of Aylesbury had already sounded when I realized I was on the platform on the wrong side of the tracks. I wasn't going to spoil my plans by a silly mistake. And I had no intention of being beaten in a race by one of those absurd little playthings the English call trains. So I made a run for it and put everything I had into it, as if I were running for my life. Up the long flight of stairs, over the crossway, and down the other side. Under thirty seconds, which must be some kind of record.

Half a minute later I was in the first-class carriage, puffing away, the old heart thumping. Alone, for one of the rare times in the past twenty years, on my way to London, then Ottawa, on my way back to Mary, to my family, to my public life in politics. Alone, looking at the reflection of my best profile in the window, as we rattled along the tracks. Waiting, I suppose, for that other public face to say something. But for once there just didn't seem to be anything important to say.

Anyway, I'm sitting here now, watching the reel go round and round, surprised to find myself, as I was then, uncharacteristically speechless.

Frenchmaid and the New Sci-Fi Age

A human being is not just a machine that can be turned on and then off, with a push of a button when its work is over. We all know that, don't we? People are always talking about how important it is to be prepared well ahead of time. Prepared financially, of course, but even more so, psychologically, spiritually — not to mention physically. Professor Peter White had been listening to this sort of talk seriously ever since he himself turned 60 back in the last century. The year that Mulroney's Conservative Government conducted a poll on the question of removing the compulsory retirement age for public sector employees. The poll proved conclusively that no political gains could be made by such a change, and that was the end of it for the foreseeable future. Professor White had come to the same conclusion through his own more informal poll of those among his aging colleagues he cared to talk to on this delicate subject. Half of them believed in early retirement, half didn't want to retire ever, seeing their retirement as the end of a life-long affair, whether passionate or not.

Peter White's solution, during his last years in the English Department, was simply to plan for leaving at 65, on the conventional and statutory deadline. He would have been perfectly happy to accept that terminal date (it turned out, of course, that he had no choice). But by the time it came, he had realized already that all this business of preparing for retirement was utter nonsense. The world was too unpredictable. How absurd to imagine that RRSPs and annuities and government bonds, plans for travel, cruises and second honeymoons, retirement cottages and hobbies and projects for idle hands and minds — how absurd to imagine that all that elaborate machinery could have any relevance to the retirement of a man like himself, whose wife (by then a professor in Sociology) died of lung cancer when he was 63, whose daughter was killed in a car accident when he was 64, and whose last year of employment at the University saw his son being denied tenure by the History Department, getting a divorce from his alcoholic and promiscuous wife, and going off to teach social studies and physical education at a third-rate private school in British Columbia. It was like designing a bridge before you discover it's supposed to go over an ocean.

Well, of course he made adjustments, both financial and social. Instead of renting out the basement apartment to some suitable young couple who, they once thought, could offer a little additional income to supplement their pensions, and whose presence would become in time a friendly reassurance for an aging pair of professors in their retirement, he himself moved downstairs. Then he let the upstairs, not to a couple but, as chance would have it, to one of those legal threesomes which were becoming so fashionable in the modern era. An arrangement which would (he hoped) lend a little vitality to a big ravine house that now seemed somber indeed — while still being stable enough not to be a constant worry to a solitary widower.

And he continued to go down to the University four or five days a week, dropping in for morning coffee with his active colleagues, and working in a carrel in the Library on his outrageously novel scholarly project: A History of the Treatment of Sexuality in English Language Science Fiction.

Usually he ate lunch in a corner of the Great Hall of Hart House, but sometimes he forced himself to join the others in the College dining room. On those occasions he always catered to the expectations of his old friends by bringing along some suitably raunchy or bizarre discovery, a sample from his growing collection of scholarly oddities in the field of futuristic sex.

But whether it was an observable fact or only his paranoia, his presence seemed to be progressively less appreciated, and his best stories, even, more and more likely to provoke uncomfortable instead of amused responses.

Sensible as Professor White's retirement adjustments might appear, they had little to do with the prior ten years of discussions with wife, son and daughter, as well as with insurance agents and investment counselors and of course with confreres at various stages in their own approach to retirement. He found himself surviving not because of careful planning, but largely because of the biggest single factor in his post-retirement life — inertia: that is, the tendency of a body in motion to remain in motion, and in the same direction.

In view of Peter White's state of mind, it was more luck than good management that his three new tenants were immediately compatible — with him, as well as so obviously with each other. He liked them from the beginning. First Tom Selzer and Margo Denny came together to answer his For Rent video — he ran it only on the East York TeleNetwork, and for just one day (five years of zero housing growth in the City made it a landlord's market). Tom, who turned out to be a quiet, sensible young lawyer, did the serious talking, while his young woman friend did the interrupting, and set the mood.

Professor White hadn't completed his own packing. He explained that he was having trouble fitting his life-time's collection of books into the existing downstairs shelving.

"Please don't move another single one, if it's for our sakes," Margo Denny said. "Sheila and I" (the third member of this trio was a woman, a primary school teacher) "— even Tom, sometimes — all three of us love to read. We'll take good care of your books. We'll dust them, we'll put them back where they belong, we won't turn down the corners, and we won't ever, ever get stains on the covers!"

Margo was a dark brunette with long, free-flowing tresses perpetually in motion, which she kept throwing back from her face with both hands. She ended by dropping onto the arm of Tom's chair and seizing his hand and crying: "I love Professor White's house, Tom, I know Sheila will too. Now you have to make sure he'll take us. Tell him what good tenants we are. Here," she reached towards the cardboard file case

Tom was holding on his lap, "show him our references.... Show him our contract, why don't you? He'll want to know how legal we are."

Tom was a little embarrassed, but all three had to laugh with pleasure at her enthusiasm. Tom hesitated a moment, obviously having a better sense than Margo that Professor White might very well cherish his roots in another era, with its different values and ways of doing things — after all, not everybody embraced The Age of DiversiValues, as the journalists liked to call it. But then he slipped a folded document out of the file, opened it to reveal an official seal, and passed it over to Peter. Margo got up and toured the room again, talking steadily about the beauties of the house and its location and view, so much superior even to what the Video had suggested, as Peter glanced over the several sheets of legal jargon.

Whether there was anything special about the agreement, Professor White didn't particularly care to know. He could see that theirs was indeed a "Registered Relationship," that their liabilities and responsibilities to each other were spelled out, and that procedures for altering the arrangements were dictated contractually. That was the most these pieces of paper could ever guarantee, popular as they had become. They were clearer, certainly, but no more impervious to changes of heart than the old mid-century sanctified marriages and orally-pledged liaisons.

"Perhaps, your third party won't be quite as enthusiastic as you both are," Peter said, handing back the document to Tom Selzer. It seemed necessary to inject a note of realism before the mood became positively euphoric.

"Oh Professor White," Margo cried, as if she sensed a real problem, that might be bothering him under the surface, "if you can think of having Tom and me here, you will certainly want Sheila Cain. Tell him, Tom — Sheila is the nicest person you can imagine. Everybody loves her."

Tom caught the hand Margo was waving at him, and drew her down to the arm of his chair.

"Sheila is the quiet one," he said, with a smile at Margo's expense, and she accepted the message with a self-mocking pursing of her lips.

"Sheila likes to cook and knit. And she plays telebridge two nights a week in her school-teachers' league. Basically, she wants to take it easy and relax when she's home."

"It's true," Margo said, "if we let her, she'd spend all her time-off just pottering around the house, making things tidy and …."

"And leaving nothing for these clever machines to do," Professor White concluded for her. He was holding a handful of brochures Margo had given him earlier. Margo was a sales manager for Century Robots. One of her efforts to convince Peter White to accept them as tenants was to offer his house a whole range of state-of-the-art samples. She was always trying out new models, wherever she lived, to substantiate her sales pitch. GarbageMan he liked, WatchDog was eminently practical, especially for a house on a ravine lot and the crime rate where it was, but he thought he might just draw the line at FrenchMaid, with or without the optional cap-and-frilly-apron wardrobe.

"May I suggest," he went on, "that we talk about it after your friend has come and had a look around?" Once again he felt it was time to assert a little control. These charming young people — Tom was square-faced, reliable-looking, not overly so, though a handsome enough specimen — these people were beginning to sweep him along before he had a chance to judge them properly as prospective dwellers in the rooms of his house that were still haunted by twenty or more years of his traditional family life.

Later that day, just before the dinner hour (Peter was about to put an instant omelet into the Micro), the door-chime rang and Margo's long hair and laughing eyes showed up again on his hall screen. He pressed the door release, and looked with interest at the face of Sheila Cain in the doorway behind Margo. She was as blonde as Margo was dark, as soft and sweetly plump as Margo was slender and athletic.

"Professor White," she said, with a warm smile that parted her perfect teeth and showed the tip of her pink tongue, "Margo has been telling me such nice things about you and your house." Her handshake was surprisingly firm.

"I've been looking forward to meeting you," he heard himself answering, with a courtly bow over her hand, though in truth he hadn't given her a thought in the gloomy trance he had slipped into, all afternoon, at the prospect of actually going through with the rental. "Why don't I leave it to Ms. Denny to show you around?"

He stood at the living-room windows, looking over the trees of the ravine that shielded them from the nearby Don Valley Copter Pad. He could hear the faint hum of arrivals and departures, but he barely remembered how he and his wife first used to grind their teeth at the encroachments of the changing modern world on their peace. The two young women were moving quickly about the rooms and up and down the stairs, filling the air with their talk and laughter. All that youthful energy made him straighten his slumping shoulders and take a hand from his trouser pocket to feel whether his belly muscles were firm, as he turned to greet them.

"Well, do you have the picture now?" he said to Sheila.

"I certainly do!" she answered with a cry. Her face was flushed with pleasure. The two women stood hand in hand in front of him. Now they all were smiling.

"Well then ….." he said at last.

"Do you mean …?." Margo asked, her dark eyebrows raised in her excitement.

"If you wish."

He bowed his head to each in turn, waited a moment to enjoy their rising happy hopefulness, and then reached out a hand.

"Professor White! That's wonderful!" Margo cried. "Sheila loves it as much as Tom and I do. We're going to be so happy here!"

The two women seized his outstretched arm in all four of their hands, and the agreement was confirmed.

"Do call me Peter, won't you?" were his last words, spilling out after them without premeditation, as they walked down the steps to their separate cars, and waved goodbye.

Then he stood for a minute at the kitchen window and watched as Margo followed Sheila to her car door. Just before he turned away to brood on his own rashness — their references as yet unchecked, their deposits, their signing of the lease still to come, their manners and appearance their only real guarantee — he observed with a caught breath, when the blonde opened the door and sat behind the wheel of her car, how the brunette bent down, put a hand to the back of her fair head, and kissed her full on the lips.

****

"How are things working out at home, Peter?"

It was Arthur Kettle joining him by chance in the West Wing washroom, a shrunken, grey-bearded, near-contemporary of his, one of the few remaining Departmental colleagues Peter felt he could talk to about personal matters. After all, he reflected as they looked down into their respective urinals, although he and Arthur had never actually acknowledged it, they had slept with each other's wives three or four times, experimentally, earlier in the century when they were all in their twenties and thirties, and they had compared notes about their children from time to time over the years.

"No problems so far," Peter said, picking up the conversation, as Arthur had done, where they left off a couple of weeks before. "They're reasonably quiet, friendly — even had me to dinner a couple of times — and I haven't had to put out the garbage once since they moved in."

Peter and Arthur exchanged grins in the washroom mirror. "GarbageMan," Peter had decided, was a safe and simple subject of conversation. "WatchDog" also, certainly —programmed innocuously not only to patrol the grounds but also to turn the outside lights off and on. The third machine was a little trickier. Peter hoped he hadn't let slip anything in their earlier conversation to get Arthur too interested now. Arthur had always been a bit of a prig, a literary liberal only, and he certainly would not approve of Peter's involvement with "FrenchMaid."

"Ethel is after me about your GarbageMan," Arthur was saying as he dried his hands. "I told her … after she's been pushing me for the last thirty-five years to put out the garbage every week, why should she stop working now? It wouldn't seem right. I tried to explain to her that it's different for you — I mean, you're a Sci-Fi man. These gadgets are a professional interest for you."

Peter laughed.

"Not very professional, and not that interesting," he said, knowing how to cater to Arthur's prejudices, though in fact he had already found Margo Denny's machines pretty effective and useful. Sometimes even more than he could have imagined, now that he was getting the hang of operating them.

"What I want to know is," said Arthur as they walked up the stairs together, with no suggestion that he was changing the subject, "what do these young trios think they're going to do when the game begins to wear thin? Do they really believe these complicated relationships can have any enduring value? And what do they think is going to happen to their children?"

Then, when Peter hesitated, he went on:

"I suppose your three do have that sort of relation, don't they?"

"Oh yes!" Peter said, startled into a certainty of response he didn't intend, and that didn't seem decorous. "Well, I imagine so," he added lamely. And then, quickly, "Still, I wonder if there isn't a lot to be said for expanding the nuclear family. Look at you." (Arthur's wife had only been able to bear one child, despite their earnest efforts.) "Look at me." (Arthur was one of the few who focused on what it meant for Peter to lose wife and daughter.) "Wouldn't we all be better off with a doubling or tripling of our family pool? Our potential. Our bonds. Our … our support-system?" (A phrase his wife might have used, he realized as it came off his tongue.) "Maybe these young people are on the right track. After all, this is a new century."

That was enough to set Arthur Kettle going on one of his monologues about changes in social history as evidenced in the literature of the last two thousand years. But Peter's mind was off, even before they parted company at Arthur's office door, in a different direction: back to the present, back to an evening more than a week ago, to his three new tenants, and himself with them, as a result of their first invitation, sitting in the living room in which he and his traditional family foursome had made such a different spectacle night after night for so many years.

It was still an improbable and memorable evening in his mind, though really nothing very much happened. A delicious dinner: some sort of mysterious plankton protein concoction that reminded him of the old lobster dishes you used to be able to get in restaurants all around the City, before the species got so rare. Drinks in the living room, wheeled in by FrenchMaid, at Margo's finger-tip control, a show-off performance, though everybody seemed to take it for granted. Music and classical video, selected no doubt for Professor White's antiquated tastes. And the most relaxed after-dinner mood Peter had ever experienced. He could hardly believe midnight had arrived so soon, finding himself quite absorbed into their generation, stretched out casually on the sofa under the ravine window, his bare feet in FrenchMaid's massager unit, one much-lined palm resting upwards in Sheila Cain's lap — she was amusing them all by palm reading in heavily accented tones — and nearby Margo having her long hair combed as she sat on the floor at Tom's knees, with Tom absent-mindedly operating the scalp-soother comb on its long cord from the massager unit.

With an effort Peter eventually extricated himself from these pleasurable coils. He had the barest inkling of a feeling that he might have made a fool of himself or outstayed his welcome, as he stumbled downstairs to his own quarters, cheerful and friendly thankyou's echoing in his ears as if the gratitude were all on the other side.

Where and how the trio were distributing themselves after he left, he had no idea. All he knew (they had earlier given him a tour of their re-arrangements) was that in some sense, and for some occasions, Sheila Cain and Tom Selzer slept in the big north bedroom with the double bed, and Margo slept in the small south bedroom with the twin beds.

"I'm so restless at night. I have to have a bed to myself," Margo had explained to him, with disarming candor and cheerfulness.

It was only when he was sitting in his basement living room, looking straight out at the dark tree trunks lining the ravine that he realized he had not entirely severed his link with the apartment above. Margo's robot system, with its dual control-set and surveillance screens, which she had been patiently teaching the skeptical but willing professor to operate, was still alive and active.

He only intended to tune in to Watchdog on his rounds — actually what Peter wanted was to know whether his cat had returned and was waiting to come in at the basement door — but instead he got FrenchMaid. It — she — was upstairs, cleaning up after the dinner party. He hesitated a moment before switching over to the correct channel control. And by then it was too late. Curiosity, loneliness, sheer voyeurism, call it what you will. He wanted to watch.

At first it was a little frustrating. Glimpses of the trio moving about the apartment as the robot sucked in empty glasses, ashtrays, dinner debris, and trundled it into the kitchen. But then it (she?) — Peter still felt the gentle, almost human warmth of that foot massage — settled down at the end of the sofa to service Tom Selzer's feet freshly bared by Sheila, on one side, and Margo, on the other. The music and video had changed to something stranger and the women had slipped into silky gowns that were too revealing for any but the most intimate of audiences.

Peter watched in a state of sweet, guilty astonishment as the two women sleepily and slowly undressed the helpless man, his only movement being now and then to raise his head to kiss one and then the other. They lay their limbs against his naked body, and caressed it again and again, their arms and hands intertwining. How aroused the young man was, became more and more evident on the little screen, until the women's heads bent together over his body, the blonde and brunette locks interwoven, shielding their most intimate address from the calm gaze of FrenchMaid's camera. Eventually, after a long while all movement seemed to end, and the three young people lay stretched out side by side in evident peace.

But then, after a few moments, just as Peter was reaching forward to turn off the control, Margo's head lifted and she moved closer to Sheila across Tom's sleeping chest, and Sheila's head turned to meet her. In the center of the screen, their lips joined. Then slowly and carefully they helped each other rise, they each slipped off from the other the silken gowns that had half covered their bodies, and they spread them over Tom's naked shape. They stood side by side, hand in hand, looking down at Tom silently.

Frenchmaid and the New Sci-Fi Age

Peter's breathing was becoming almost painful at the twinned spectacle of these naked creatures. And it stopped completely, for a moment, as they turned and embraced. Together, they disappeared from view, leaving Peter to stare in disbelief at the stretched form of the young man, unstirring on the sofa.

After switching off the control, Peter White sat looking at the blank screen and trying to assess his turbulent reactions. But first, there was the question of his own body. How long had it been since he felt like this? It was not pleasant to calculate because, for several years before her death, sexual congress with his wife had presented embarrassing and unmentionable problems. He recalled not the general, broad, comfortable release from tensions often reported by older married couples as an achievement of marital intercourse, but a precise, localized, frustrating sensation — rather like a sort of rough tweaking, really — which was the direct result of his wife's fits of coughing at untimely moments, often beginning with almost unnoticed stirrings somewhere deep in the lungs and ending with uncontrollable diaphramic heavings and intimate convulsive closures that were detrimental and even dangerous to a male partner's physical intrusions.

In the last several years of her life, they tacitly agreed to express their feelings for one another, which intensified as the period drew to its end, in a more and more spiritual way. It seemed wisest to both of them simply to ignore the fact that they had bodies, whenever that was possible — to treat them merely as machines necessary for certain functions only.

Now Peter was beginning to let the unaccustomed flow of vitality in his body, in his skin and blood, carry him back in time beyond those difficult last years. Indeed, his invigorated feelings were taking him through a whole disused file of experiences he had shut up and locked away as being of no further relevance to his present elderly condition. He scanned his lifetime's sexual history with an increasingly easy and rapid sweep. It had not been such an arid project, after all, had it? Who knows, perhaps there could be some literal truth in those old romantic notions about living on your memories. There was no need for it to be buried and forgotten entirely just yet, was there?

And then he was here again in the present, reflecting on the trio in the room or rooms over his head, abundantly alive in whatever postures might now sustain them. He reached over and switched on the reading lamp behind the sofa. On the coffee table was Margo Denny's set of Century Robots brochures. He pulled out the only one he had failed to read carefully, fully, and began now to make amends.

He leafed quickly through to the section on "Personal Services," with its glossy illustrations. He applied his warm thumb to the inviting Thermal Release point on one page and then the next, and let the subtle perfumes loose into the atmosphere around his head. In a moment he was chuckling to himself at the inventiveness of the designers of FrenchMaid, and the richness of the functions she could provide for her purchasers. Or in his case, a borrower.

This creature held out a plentitude of reminders of what people can do for each other, or attempt to do, suggestions of how their affections might be lavished, in the sheer joy of material existence.

"How ingenious," he murmured, allowing his hand to slip between the buttons of his shirt, and touch his bare skin. "How wonderfully, beautifully ingenious."

A Jar In Tennessee

(I placed a jar in Tennessee,
And round it was, upon a hill.
It made the slovenly wilderness
Surround that hill …. W. Stevens)

His office desk presented its customary pleasant disarray of books and papers and correspondence. The only bare spot was the right-hand corner, across which, leaning back in his chair, he stretched a leg, carefully straightening the trousers under the calf to avoid creasing.

The appearance of chaos was of course deceptive. Basically his life was nothing if not orderly. He felt he could lay his hand on whatever he wanted. Most days one item would be central, though possibly not to a stranger's eye: a letter he was answering, a book he had to consult for his edition of modern poetry, a note pad on which he was listing points to be made in a lecture. Today there was the little knife.

It lay on top of some papers on the blotting-pad where his visitor, Woodman, had dropped it. Its brown wooden handle and shining blade, snouted like a barracuda, were almost lost in the clutter. But the scattered things on the desk and the seemingly confused flood of talk between him and Woodman spread outwards from this common kitchen implement. It could have seemed, perhaps, more ridiculously out of place than sinister, there among the books and letters, so far from its familiar domestic context. In any case, its blade was short:

considerable force would have been needed to make it a dangerous weapon. However, you would have to say that the kind of focus it provided for everything around it was likely to be temporary, unsatisfying, if not positively ugly and evil.

The interview had long ago passed the stage where he could stop Woodman for a moment and telephone his wife again. Helen was going to be upset no matter what he did now. Since it was Friday, and she had already called to make sure he would be home on time, of course she would worry. She hated the unexpected, breaks with settled habits, as much as he did, especially on Fridays, which they customarily spent quietly at home together.

He lowered his wrist below desk level and stole a glance at his watch while Woodman continued to glare out the window at the setting sun and rage on. A turning-point in the harangue had been reached, the crisis was passed, and yet he felt it was still useless, if not actually dangerous, to try to influence the tone too obviously. A volcano erupting. The violent spurts of fire and lava had to subside first. Then the rumblings fade away, and the fearful observer, feeling himself once again on firm ground, could approach closer as the smoke and ashes and steam began to dissipate.

Not a bad metaphor, he thought, looking at his visitor's thick-veined throat, full lips, strong jowls, swollen eye-lids. From somewhere within or under the heavy shoulders and deep chest that seemed too big for his wrinkled grey tweed jacket came the barely repressed power, the anger, the bitterness, the passion that kept that frothing flow of words pouring from the grimacing mouth. Rolling eyes filmed with tears. Lips specked with spittle. Each wave of blood surging up the throat shown by the open-necked shirt seemed about to burst through the contorted features into a molten chaos. The trick was to know when to challenge those wild eyes to come back to him, to widen in realization of the presence of another person, and then to focus, to steady, to stay fixed long enough to bring the man back from his private nightmare to communication with a human being. To restore some order out of this dreadful chaos.

Now the rush of talk slackened for a moment. There was the catching of breath, the biting of the lower lip. Now he must interrupt. Before the cycle began all over again. Before his wife called and asked what was keeping him. Before he would be forced to simply break off in the middle of a spasm, and leave the poor devil suspended in his anguish. Now was the time to risk the move.

"Woodman, Woodman. It makes me very sad to see you so sick and miserable."

The filmed eyes turned on him like the headlights of a runaway truck.

"Woodman, you've been doing so well until now."

A tremor ran downwards over the broad face from the dense cap of brown hair above the forehead to the square jaw, leaving a calm expanse, empty of expression. The eyes settled into a heavy-lidded stare.

"When you first talked to me, Woodman — what was it, a year ago? — you said you couldn't go on the way you were living. But you have gone on. You've managed. You've survived. You've held it all together in spite of everything."

Woodman's eyes slipped away from his gaze. The pupils shrank as they searched the waning sunlight again. But he knew that across those eyes was passing the pitiful, the self-pitying shadow that had lived through those endless dismal months, the laboring ghost who had dragged himself along the narrow path between an abyss of suicidal despair and a landslide of violence and brutality. Woodman could see only Woodman, nothing else out that window.

He felt Woodman's despondency eat like acid at his own bones. If only the man would accept ordinary reality for what it was, instead of making his insane demands on people and the world around him and then hating them when he couldn't be satisfied. He passed a weary hand back over his thinning hair. Why was he here, watching this man's death-struggles? He was a professor, a Ph.D., a doctor of philosophy, not a doctor of medicine, let alone a psychiatrist. Any frail emergency lines he could throw out were no use against that dark destructive current. Home, his waiting wife, some drinks and some comfortable domestic chat. Then a quiet dinner and an early night. If the damned Psychiatric Institute couldn't or wouldn't save Woodman, what could he do? And if the Institute let Woodman walk the streets with a knife in his pocket, was he supposed to do something more? Lock him up in the office? Take him home with him? The situation was totally hopeless. Woodman knew that better than anyone. Was right a year ago. He either ought to kill himself, as he put it then, or commit an act that would force society to incarcerate him in some sort of human environment. A prison. A hospital. An asylum. Somewhere where at least there could be no more of that dreadful isolation. And yet?

"Woodman, we never claimed, you and I, in all the times you've come to see me — as my student, and, I think I can say, as my friend — we never, either of us, claimed you could suddenly be happy. We said you could find ways to endure. You couldn't jump into a new life with friends and things you like doing and were good at and some meaning to it all. But you could take just one little step, just that inch in the right direction. Then maybe another would be possible. And another. Until you could look back some day and say, that's where I was. I'm not there any longer. I can go on."

Woodman's eyes were rimmed with water. He turned the broad face to follow the other's open-palmed appealing gesture of arm towards the object on his desk.

"But this, Woodman. This. To take such a leap. To think of taking such a leap. Backward. Miles, miles, light years backward."

The energy returned to Woodman's face. He rubbed moisture from his cheek with his big fist. His eyes widened and rolled upwards to the top of the window where the last rays of the sun slanted from across the campus. His voice thickened with conscious feeling.

"I don't want to do anything like that."

His arm warded off behind him the almost invisible knife enshrined by the cluttered desk. The passionate grieving voice rose higher.

"I don't want to hurt anyone. I don't want to hurt a living person on this earth."

Yes, Woodman seemed really to mean it. More knowledge and more experience with unstable minds than a doctor of philosophy possessed was needed to fathom Woodman's nature. But if he meant it now, wasn't he also sincere a half an hour ago, when he was saying very different things?

He risked another glance at his watch. Contemptible, no doubt, to be thinking of his own habits and creature comforts, while this man was being torn apart by his good and bad angels. But this was Friday. And ordinary life had its claims and rights as well, especially after a long hard week. At forty-five habit was part of what made life tolerable, for Helen as well as for him. Perhaps childless couples tended to rely on routine a little more than others, without the changeableness and unpredictability of off-spring to disrupt the pattern of their lives. In any case, Friday was ordinarily their special night. He always tried to be home in good time, in a good frame of mind. A few drinks, a quiet dinner, an early night. Neither of them liked to be disturbed. For the past few years it wasn't always the easiest thing in the world to nourish just the right sort of attention and interest, tenderness, warmth, whatever it should be called. The border-line between contentment and plain apathy was just as narrow as its opposite boundary, that between contentment and chaotic desires. Obviously happiness lay somewhere within those borders, if you could find it and hold on to it. Helen had the same difficulties, he was well aware. The curse of middle-age, no doubt, and a familiar story.

Woodman's thick-set body wasn't that of a young man either. He must be at least thirty. But his life had never settled and crystallized in a constructive way. He had never in all his years been satisfied with anything. From unhappy childhood to the wilderness of maladjusted adulthood, if you could believe everything he said, through several colleges and a hundred part-time jobs his devils had pursued him. The Institute had attempted more than once to help him, and might still be seriously trying, despite Woodman's versions of his relation to the doctors. But really, he was the spirit of destructiveness and chaos incarnate, or perhaps not yet incarnate but in potential, waiting to become so. What self-abuse and what secret crudities, barbarities and obscenities on others he had committed at one time or another, in his fantasies or in fact, probably his own distorted introspection couldn't even be certain. Somehow, to the threshold of middle age he had brought a mask at least not so marked that he could be identified as a monster or fled from in the streets and hallways of respectable society. In fact, for all his compulsions he must have shown few people the expressions he had exposed to him half an hour ago.

The stolid mask belied those earlier obscene dreadful mouthings. Looking at Woodman's thick thighs in the wrinkled brown trousers, he found it easy to revive the sense of those worst moments in the past hour. The way that now heavy, deadened body miraculously became light and frail and elusive, without moving from the chair beside his desk, as Woodman mimed the woman's response, and even while at the same time he was actually mocking that lightness and frailty and elusiveness. The look of surprise, the mouth opening in a coy O, first with growing comprehension, then with rising terror. The little laughable, pathetic flurry of helpless feminine hands, held forward to protect — to protect not that actual massive, no doubt hairy male chest, but rather a quite easily imaginable smooth, slender female torso, in fearful contortions, revealing, indeed offering, flaunting, while in the very act of defending, its liquid breasts and floating frantic nipples. O no, no, no, no, no, she cried.

"The bitch wanted it," Woodman had snarled. His thick lips were wet. "They'll never admit it, but they always want you to do it to them. They want it ….Whatever they pretend."

Woodman's eyes had flared around the office walls. The fingers of his right hand had groped in his pocket.

"They just need an excuse," he groaned. "They want to be able to say they're forced. When you give it to them."

He had pulled his hand out of his grey tweed pocket. The blade of the little kitchen knife gleamed in the afternoon sun. The handle was buried in his big right fist. His left hand convulsively fingered the blade held between his bulging thighs.

"Woodman, for God's sake," he'd cried.

Woodman's eyes had lifted, startled and focused on his face.

"That's what all my friends say," he'd muttered, the color draining from his face. Pathetic. Of course the man didn't have a friend in the world. His sweating lips twisted into a wry grin. "*I* don't claim to know anything about women. That's just what all my friends say."

"Woodman."

"Of course I don't believe everything they say."

He started to explain as much as he could to Woodman, the poor, dumb, lost, lecherous, violent, lonely soul. Women, he said, never, never, never want to be raped. That's just a male dream, an illusion. Surely, a woman, like a man, may have fleeting images cross her mind, fantasies, images of assault, and images of violation. And it's possible they point to unsolved mysteries hidden in the depths of human nature. Maybe they're, well, hints of the insatiable need to be at one with another body, even at the cost of destroying yourself and the other. I don't really know. What I do know is that aggression is just one small insignificant portion of the whole mature experience of sex. There's consideration, there's affection, there's loyalty, there's respect, there's tenderness. These are what make possible a good relation between two people. No woman wants the aggression alone. Put it out of your mind, Woodman, right out. That way lies chaos, madness.

Woodman threw the knife onto the table, where it clattered into the scraps and shreds of learning and scholarship: how incongruous, how grotesque it seemed. Lying there among the tools and results of intellectual life. There it remained untouched, unlooked at directly, all through the troubled ebb and flow of the next half hour. Until eventually they had worked through the orgiastic excesses into a phase of calmer talk.

This time he felt he could deliberately glance down at his watch so Woodman could see him doing it. Woodman flinched, his dull face waking with a sense of social awkwardness.

"I'm sorry, Woodman, but my wife's expecting me. We have plans for this evening. I'm awfully late. Leave that with me, won't you, please?"

He nodded down at the desk. Woodman was half-rising. He held up a hand to stop him, very much in control of the situation now. It would only take a minute to round things off. He turned on the full power of his personality, his experience, and perhaps if it wasn't too presumptuous to think so, his wisdom. Certainly a kind of confidence moved him, to pass on what he could about how a life should be conducted.

"Woodman, God knows there's nothing I can do to help you. In the end, you're the only one who can do anything. But I just want you to know that I would be terribly distressed to find that if, after all you've been through, after all the efforts you've made, the inches you've gained, you should suddenly blow it all up."

He rose from behind his desk and perched on the bare corner. His left hand reached down and toyed with the knife. Woodman's dull broad white face looked up at him hopelessly.

"You've got to realize, Woodman, that for most of us most of the time, life isn't ecstasy. It's endurance. Plain simple endurance. If that weren't enough to justify being alive, we all would have torn the world up and thrown it away long ago."

They walked to the door.

"You've got to level out these ups and down of yours. Build some sort of orderly pattern into your life so that all this irrational energy can be kept under control. You know what you have to do. We've talked about these things so often."

Woodman looked at him directly before going out, struggling to maintain his precarious equilibrium, swallowing his tears. "Thank you," he said, bobbing his heavy head. "Thank you. I really do appreciate everything … everything you've done for me."

As he drove north from the campus towards home, he put Woodman's dreary fate firmly out of his mind. The sight of the broad back, stocky legs, and large buttocks moving slowly down the hall like a sleep-walking rhino was completely blotted from his mind by the time Helen greeted him at the door of their spacious St. Clair Avenue apartment.

"How've you been, pigeon," he said, touching her thin, worried cheek after he had given a brief explanation and put his brief-case in his study. It would sit unopened tonight, delightful thought, books, notes, letters, annotations and all, and not require his loyal services until tomorrow morning.

"I'm just glad I didn't know you were seeing that awful man Woodman this afternoon," Helen said, leading the way into the immaculate kitchen. Her shoulders shivered in revulsion under her loose-fitting frock.

"Now Helen."

He put an affectionate arm around her waist. The drinks were waiting in the freezer compartment. He carried the cocktail shaker into the living room and she brought the glasses.

"I know you hate talking about it," she continued, "but I still say you shouldn't ever be alone with that man. You can never be sure he won't do something .... You said yourself he should be locked up."

He poured the martinis. Sometimes she looked so tense and fierce that her slim body, so attractive to him when he first saw her browsing in the Boston bookstore fifteen years ago, seemed as rigid as a skeleton. Soon, he hoped, the soothing symmetry of their comfortable, well-furnished rooms and their habitual ways would take effect.

"Helen, relax, relax. If I said that, I didn't mean it. Anyway, Woodman's already been locked up. The Institute didn't think it did him much good, except to make him more conscious of the terrible state he's in. He's still got the basic problem to solve: how to relate to other people. He just has never learned that it's possible to be really close to people through mutual respect, friendship, kindness, loyalty, and all the things that make normal people normal. Ordinary human relationships aren't sufficient for him, and therefore he's never sufficient for them. He can only see two ways of behaving: retreat into depression, total isolation, a horrible icy apathy, or else aggression, violence, attacking other people."

Helen put down her glass without tasting it. Her voice went up an octave.

"That's just what I mean!"

He put a hand on her knee as he raised himself to his feet to mix another drink. He was glad that at least he hadn't mentioned the incident of the knife to her. Already, though, he was afraid the evening was spoiled.

"You know, he's really no different from the ordinary person as far as his problems go, he's just an extreme case. I couldn't turn him away from my door. I had to talk to him, poor devil, considering the state of mental chaos he was in. Come on, pigeon, its Friday night. Let's forget Woodman's troubles. They're for the Institute to worry about. None of our business, really."

Later that night, much later, after he had tidied himself up and stretched back again in the bed, he found that the waves of alcohol were still passing dizzily over his head. He had drunk more than usual even for a Friday. The Woodman encounter had shaken his equilibrium more than he thought it could, perhaps. But it had been alright after all, he felt sure. More satisfactory than sometimes, despite all the worries. She was still in the bathroom with the light on and the door ajar. Her little habit, to stay there dozing a while, dreaming perhaps. Remembering? You could never know for sure what was in another person's mind. It wasn't even safe to take you own mind for granted. He thought he was satisfied. He had, in a sense, been satisfied. But he wanted more, something else. Under the smooth surfaces of habit some deep need moved, and the surfaces rippled and shook. Was she satisfied? Content? Happy? He didn't even know. He felt very alone lying there in the dark, very cold and isolated.

He raised himself on one elbow, suddenly restless, in a strange way curious, not really quite himself, as though invaded by a disturbing force. He swayed a little getting to his feet. He saw her through the half-open door, sitting with her nightie tucked up to her waist, leaning forward on her thin thighs, her long loose hair flowing down over her bent head, face hidden. Standing there in the shadowy bedroom, he was aware of that access of foreign energy all the more strongly, the blood throbbing up in his throat, almost choking him, almost erupting. He took a step forward as she heard him. Her head came up, vaguely, eyes searching the darkness beyond the doorway.

"Honey, I'm in here," she warned. They were always very discreet in their personal habits.

He ignored the warning. He walked into the bathroom and right up beside her, looking down at her startled, annoyed, nervous face. She abruptly laughed and started to get up from the toilet seat.

"I've always said we need two bathrooms."

The strange energy overflowed into action. Without answering, he caught the bottom of her nightie before it could fall to cover her thin body. With a single movement he pulled it off over her head. She stood in the light, her arms instinctively crossing over her tiny breasts. Her mouth opened in a little O. She seemed like a stranger, and he was a different person. Reaching for a wrist, he pulled her to the doorway. Her voice broke out, confused, alarmed.

"What are you doing? Don't be so rough."

Turning in the shadows, with the bathroom light full on her naked body, he let go her wrist and slipped his hands up over her bare shoulders and slender throat. He started to pull her down to the floor, sinking to his knees in front of her, wooing, worshipping, pleading, slumping out of control, it was hardly clear.

"Good God, what do you want? Are you sick? Are you drunk?" she cried, trying to break loose from his fingers. Her eyes were staring down at him in disbelief, and then in fear. He clung harder, dragging at her, sinking his nails into her bare flesh. Suddenly she twisted her naked torso away, and darted back into the bathroom.

"No no no no no, how could you? You're like an animal."

She slammed the door and turned the lock.

In the shadowy bedroom he stretched out where he lay on the rug. His body throbbed. To his own hands it seemed alien, strong and hard and massive, more powerful and more terrible than he had ever imagined it could be. Until gradually the power began to subside and fade away. What am I doing? She must think I'm …. It's a nightmare. I must talk to her. Helen. He couldn't move, Crossing an arm over his eyes he fell into a doze.

Woodman, Woodman, he muttered in his sleep. Self-control, peace, strive for that. Avoid intensities like the plague. Leave desire, ecstasy for others. For you, for you, the best hope lies in a well-ordered life. Write that down, Woodman, write that down, and remember it.

The Offering

She closed the door quickly and hurried back through the dark hall to the kitchen, holding the letter in her hand. "Victor dear," she said, "please stop, please stop teasing that bird. I'm sure the postman heard. You can hear it all the way out to the street."

She sat on the edge of the chair just inside the door.

"It's only a little game, Frances," Victor said quietly. "Is that a letter from your mother?"

Through rimless glasses his calm blue eyes watched her face closely. He was kneeling in the middle of the floor.

"Oh Vic, you know he hates it .... I could hear his screeching." She ran a hand through her brown hair and looked away.

"I was teaching him to jump through my arms. Why don't you look?"

Victor lifted up the side if his coat. Out from under his arm stepped the bantam rooster, shook its red comb fiercely, bridled its blue-black feathered wings, strutted indignantly on its orange toes. Linking his long fingers together Victor made a hoop of his arms and in a quick scything motion swept them under the rooster's strutting feet. With an angry screech and flutter the fowl tumbled through the hoop. Quickly again the arms swept around, and again the screech and the flustered scramble. Victor was smiling at the humiliated creature.

"Stop. You're ... you're cruel." She stood above him, her face white and thin-lipped, but she didn't touch him. He looked up at her quietly. Then he got up and took the letter from her stiff fingers.

"Here, Chaunticleer," he said quietly, almost tenderly, opening the basement door so that the rooster could run jerkily to his box and his corn cobs on the landing.

Frances went to the clothes basket, and began folding diapers, piling them on the kitchen table. Victor stood reading the letter, holding it in one hand, and the cheque which he had taken from it in the other.

"How much?" Frances asked.

"One hundred dollars," he murmured without raising his eyes from the letter. "She says she can't spare a cent more this time. One of her roomers has been sick and she's carrying his rent for a month. She says she hopes we can manage without sacrificing any necessities."

He put the cheque on the table and took a pen out of the cluttered drawer, adding. "Do you think she's being sarcastic?"

"How should I know?" Frances creased a diaper roughly. "You're the one who's always guessing other people's motives. What else does she say?"

She took the pen he offered her and signed the cheque.

"She says she hopes the baby is over the skin irritation. She hopes your art school is doing better and the children are enjoying their new pet. She hopes I'm better now and have given up my visits to the psychiatrist and have found a nice new teaching job. She's full of hopes. She says she hopes …."

"Alright, alright, I'll read it later," Frances said, throwing down the pen. "You don't always have to be so sarcastic. You know she's trying her hardest to understand."

"And I know how difficult that is." He was putting the cheque into his pocket, a little smile on his lips still.

She followed him to the door. "I didn't say that. Why must you put words in my mouth?"

He kept going, through into the long hallway with its cracked linoleum covering.

Her voice rose sharply to reach him. "Why must you always put words in my mouth?"

At the doorway he turned his blue eyes down on her for a moment before going out. "I never put words in your mouth that aren't already in your heart."

She couldn't stand with the door open to watch him walk along the street because, behind her, the rooster crowed. A man across the road carrying a briefcase looked up in surprise.

She was always shutting the door quickly these days, lest someone complain to the police about the new pet. The little children who came to paint and draw in the mornings would be broken-hearted if Chaunticleer were taken away now. In the kitchen she threw down another ear of corn at the basement door and sang chuk-chuk to the handsome rooster, before going back to the laundry basket.

Victor walked north to King Street. Their tall old house to which they had moved when his school asked him to resign a year ago stood in a backwater of the city between King and the Lake front. Its wide streets and large houses still had an air of dignity about them from happier days, but the people who mattered had long ago left them, moving northwards to newer, more thriving residential and business areas. Large, run-down houses like theirs could be rented for very little by those whose needs or resources were small. It was out of the way, but that no longer mattered since they had long ago stopped seeing what friends they had in the city.

The tall bespectacled woman-teller in the bank at Dufferin and King showed no sign of recognition, while Victor watched her carefully with his steady blue eyes as she counted out the nine tens and two fives. She never did, none of them did, though he had come in once or twice a month for a year, and they all should know him well enough. She avoided his eyes. Her fingers snapped the bills almost contemptuously. He went on his way without a word.

The streetcar and then the subway car were nearly empty. None of the passengers looked at him though he roamed his eyes over their faces and bodies continually until it was time to get off. At St. Clair a policeman turned on his heel and walked off down Yonge St. when Victor paused beside him at the traffic light. And then Dr. Dornreimer's secretary — the doctor shared her with two others — only glanced up from her typing when he came in the doorway of the big converted mansion. He sat down quietly in the paneled waiting room, and let his hand run over the sheaf of bills warmed in his inside pocket. He fixed his eyes on the secretary's head and thought of nothing as she hammered rhythmically at the typewriter without looking up.

Frances at the kitchen table was adding figures in her dog-eared black account book. She had used it during her one and only year's school-teaching, before she got pregnant and married, and now her disastrous finances seemed somehow more controllable when entered in the same neat columns. Six pre-school children playing at art four mornings a week. Two roomers, a German man and wife, both hard-working and on their way to better things. A monthly cheque from her widowed mother that had come ever since she had brought herself to tell her about Victor. Minus rent, household expenses, art supplies, prescriptions for herself and the baby. And minus fifteen dollars a week for Victor's psychiatrist. They should give up and go on welfare.

Taking a sheet of paper from the drawer she began to write quickly: Dear Mother, and you are a dear, dear mother, thank you so much for the hundred dollars, I know how hard it is for you. It comes just in time, and it very nearly with what we've taken in this month covers all our costs. We're only about twenty dollars short. Would you, could you possibly go to Uncle again and ask for just that much? I don't know otherwise how …. As she looked blankly at the page wondering how to continue, Chaunticleer crowed suddenly and loudly, and she shushed at him in his box, with a smile relaxing her lips. The baby stirred and whimpered. She got up to warm the milk.

Dr. Dornreimer was withdrawn and preoccupied. Victor could see that his mind was elsewhere, probably planning the weekly article on mental health he wrote for the *Star*. He watched the short fat body shifting about restlessly, and the mobile face contorting and grimacing in all the ways he knew so well. He heard his own voice fade and grow thin and weary. Dr. Dornreimer was just not interested in him this morning. He tried, though the hour was nearly over, to think of something to bring back the doctor's wandering attention, but the effort was tiring. The doctor was even repeating himself, like a reproving parent, now that he had lapsed into silence.

"No, no. It is not quite the same thing …. That money with which you pay your bills, money which you yourself have not earned, that won't do any more. You know that yourself."

Dr. Dornreimer's accent was faint, but his syntax was too elaborate to be that of a native. His tone became more dignified and foreign and aloof to Victor's ears.

"The health of the mind — what we choose to call sanity — this is what our ancestors would say is a blessing, a gift, a gift of the gods. Basically I'm sure they were right. To get back the health of the mind once it is gone, even a little, one must work for it, earn it. I can't give it to you. No one can. One must, as it were, make sacrifices. Make offerings. In German we have the one word for both. Das Opfer. Offering. Sacrifice. You see?"

His thick lips were touched with a wise smile and he was looking into the distance. It was one of his women's club speeches. He was always performing somewhere. Victor hated that tone.

"Of course," he concluded, "Das Opfer must be one's own, not someone else's. That is the essence."

Victor's voice was low, without expression. His anger was too deep to surface.

"I was told to come to you for help. I still need help. I can't earn money. I can't go back to teaching again until I'm well enough to make people look at me and accept me. It's nine months … nine months since I first came …."

Dr. Dornreimer leaned back, and for the first time, it seemed, turned his face directly towards him. From this angle it was not fat, but a square strong face. Victor stopped, unable to finish his sentence. The doctor waited a moment and then:

"Victor, you must no longer attempt to shift the responsibility for your progress — nine months, a year, it doesn't matter — onto my shoulders. It rests entirely with you, you know that. Well, well. Come back next week with that in the front of your head, and tell me … tell me exactly how it makes you feel."

He began to write at his desk. Probably recording his own fine phrases before he forgot them. It was a dismissal. But Victor would not leave without replying.

"You think you know me so well. You once admitted that my wife could be hurting my ... my self-respect by her lack of understanding. You hurt it more by ignoring me this way."

Dr. Dornreimer continued to smile at him. His tone was mild but final.

"My dear Victor, you know I am not ignoring you. Far from it. It is no use to argue with me. What is there to gain? It is really only arguing with yourself. I thought you had given up all that months ago. Do please go away now. I have no more time for your big pride this morning. We will talk again next week."

He did not look up. There was nothing for Victor to do but leave, with his frustration and anger unexpressed. He set out to walk home.

The ravine into which the east end of St. Clair plunges without a backward glance leads its winding course all the way through the city to the Lake. In June it was grown over with green leaves and deep grass, and the city leaning over it could scarcely see to the paths at its bottom. A man walking north looked aside up the treed slope as Victor passed him by. His dog was invisibly threshing about in the bushes. No one else passed as Victor walked slowly south, except a pre-occupied teen-aged boy peddling energetically northward on a rattling bicycle.

In the distance ahead appeared a little girl in a short skirt bouncing a ball against a viaduct pillar. He fixed his eyes on her as he came nearer. She might have been the absent-minded child he had strapped into tears at school for not paying attention. Her legs were skinny, and they flashed brownly under her green kilt. Her throat was bare, as thin as her legs. The ball escaped her and rolled to Victor's feet. He picked it up, bounced it once and made to throw it to her. She stood feigning surprise, her hands hanging by her sides, her slim legs close together, and her neck long and straight, like a bird too young to fly from the nest. Her look changed, seemed more than a child's, as she suddenly smiled and called to him.

"I can catch, sir."

He bounced the ball in front of her and quickly walked past as a group of laughing girls came down the path from the street to join her. He climbed out of the ravine and hurried along Bloor St. to the subway, homeward.

Chaunticleer's cry echoed and spread like a flare of colour along the dark hall as he quietly closed the door.

"Victor?"

Frances sounded anxious. The house was large and lonely in the daytime, and the district not the safest. But he was not in the mood to answer, and he stood thinking until she came to the kitchen door?

"Why didn't you answer me?"

"Did you call?"

He followed her back into the kitchen, where she was ironing. He went over to the baby's basket. The infant's eyes were closed. Its mouth was opened and its round featureless face lolled above the weak neck. The infant did nothing but feed, sleep, and cry and Victor wondered if he could even distinguish it from any other baby in the city. Certainly the child was too young to know its father. He touched its cheek.

"Don't fuss her, Victor. She's just gone off."

Victor took his cigarette maker from the cupboard, sat down at the table and began to roll cigarettes. He watched Frances at her work.

"Are you afraid someday I might decide to get rid of her?"

Frances flushed but did not look up or answer.

"Things would be a lot happier for you if I did, wouldn't they? You would be rid of us both at one stroke."

"Don't joke about things like that," said Frances, leaning hard on the iron.

"I'm not joking," Victor continued in a quiet reasonable tone. "I remember what you said a year ago when I was fired and the baby was still in your womb. You said you wished we were both dead. What's happened since then to make you change your mind?"

Frances put down the iron carefully, and turned to him.

"Don't you start talking in that tone of voice again. You didn't have to marry me. I'd have had my baby and taken care of her and brought her up properly whether you married me or not. You married me because you couldn't bear to be alone, to leave me alone, to be … left out of things."

She began to iron again energetically.

"I think that's the real reason you slept with me in the first place, Victor. But you're too proud to admit it. You're still too proud to admit you needed anything but my body. You want to be loved but you don't want to love anybody. That would mean you would have to be responsible for others and you don't want that, do you? You can't bear that."

Victor went on quietly cutting up the cigarettes he had rolled in the machine into proper lengths with the old razor blade, carefully so as not to cut his fingers. When she left to take the pile of finished laundry upstairs he walked over to the basement door and with his foot tipped the rooster's box open and tumbled the bird into the room. He knelt in the middle of the kitchen floor and again began to force it to scramble through the hoop of his arms, smiling as it tossed its bright comb and pecked and struck at his sleeves with its sinewy spurs which had been trimmed, and protested deep in its pulsing throat and breast.

Upstairs Frances was spreading clean sheets on their big old double bed when the screams, the terrible screams echoed across the landing. She burst through the doorway drowning the thin throaty unidentifiable cries with her own voice.

"Victor, for God's sake Victor, what's the matter?"

She plunged down the stairs blindly and stumbled through the kitchen door. Victor stood looking down. The bird hung twitching by its neck from his big hands. One blue-black wing was faintly flapping, a scattering of feathers lay on the floor beneath. As the big hands twisted again she heard a crackling sound. In its basket the baby was whimpering, and now its voice rose in a frightened wail. Before she could pick the baby up, Victor had rushed down into the darkness of the basement.

Several times in the hours that followed Frances stood at the basement door listening with held breath. But she felt so sickened and hopeless that it seemed she no longer cared. After the baby's night feeding, she crossed the moon-whitened landing bare-footed and entered their bedroom, leaving the door ajar. She stood at the window for a moment looking down into the back garden, a narrow oblong between its high rickety wooden fences. Victor was still there, where she caught sight of him hours before. She could see him plainly, standing motionless with both hands resting on the long-handled shovel in front of him. She turned and crept wearily between the fresh sheets. She drew the covers up over her eyes. The mantel clock chimed three times, and she heard the floors creaking downstairs. At last he came, and eased himself down to sit on the bed beside her. He drew the sheet from her face.

"Keep away," she said.

She pushed his hands off.

"I think it's over now."

His voice was just above a whisper.

"How could you," she said. Her voice trembled with despair. "You aren't even sorry."

"Not now," he whispered after a moment. "I was. But now I'm glad."

She threw herself over, her back to him, and lay limp and still.

"Listen," he whispered again, reaching to put a hand on her shoulder in the dark. "I know it was horrible. I know it was horrible."

His voice rose. The bird had had life. It wanted to live. It had struggled, beating its wings, thrusting its neck like a little arm, fighting wildly even after he broke it in his hands. Frances moaned and pulled the sheet over her head as the torrent of words grew more and more incoherent. Then abruptly he was silent. At last he spoke again, putting his lips close to her ear.

"For God's sake, Frances, I'm not insane. I know what I've done. I had a life in my hands. I killed it. It could have been anything, anyone. It could have been me. But I .... It's different now. I feel so different. Everything's different now, don't you see?"

She waited, resisting him silently, not believing him, listening to his breathing as he sat without moving. But she knew there was no choice. She was the strong one. If she abandoned him he was finished.

The Offering

She would have to believe him, if that's what he believed and hoped. Perhaps it was true. She wanted it to be, so much so that it almost had to be. She had always been waiting for something terrible to happen, and it never did. And now he was right. It felt new and strange. It had to be different.

At last she turned towards him in the dark, accepted him, drew him into the bed beside her. His cold fingers stroked her hair and warmed themselves against her cheeks. In a little while they stopped moving. Without warning, sleep had engulfed him. She lay awake as the moonlight slowly crept across the covers, and her tears veined his hands.

Old Friends Of Farmer Smith's

Usually when Dan Douglas makes these trips to Vancouver, which he does three times a year, buying for the Kelowna Rotary Club sports programs, he stays at the Bay Shore Towers. It's handy to the downtown firms he deals with. He has no personal connections in the city any more. In fact it makes him feel lonely, as if he were still a miserable adolescent not really in the game, just trying to watch and learn how to live with (and without) other people. Even though he's away from home no more than three or four days, he telephones his wife every night during what he and she like to call the cocktail hour, a name which they know is a bit grand for Kelowna. You could say the calls are just a comfortable habit, but that wouldn't bother Josephine and Dan. They know each other's minds pretty well after twenty years.

He figures she'll especially like to hear from him this time, because she has her widowed mother visiting from Victoria for a week. Her mother is a nice old girl who never stops talking. Not that Dan blames her. Her husband was Mr. Justice Henry Sales of the British Columbia Supreme Court, a man with more tall stories than a whole convention of politicians put together. Dan remembers when he was taking Josephine out how awkward the parents made him feel, being always a little on the shy side anyway, and Josephine his first real girlfriend. The father's elaborate stories, his wife's silence. Sitting in the living room of their Point Grey house while Josephine finished doing her hair upstairs in her little bedroom at the back, which Dan had such nice erotic reveries about but, as a matter of fact, never got into.

Dan usually calls person to person, from his hotel room, to make sure it's Josephine he gets on the line, not one of the kids.

"Hello dear, am I disturbing you?" he says in his high-pitched, slightly whining, not-bad imitation of her mother, "Are you just settling down with someone — oh goodness, I mean, something — nice?"

One of the banes of their lives is that whenever Mama Sales calls long distance from Victoria, where she lives now, it's the minute Josephine and he are starting their first of two drinks before dinner. That shoots the whole cocktail hour for another day.

"Hello, Daniel, how are you?" She answers, her cheerful public tone telling him right away that she's got her mother there in the room with her. He goes on for a little while in Mama's line (questions about everybody's health down to the last bowel movement) and then switches to another favorite patter in his 'I'm a Rotarian out on the town' style, both knowing that's the last thing she has to worry about. But the phone bill is mounting. So he has to hang up now. The bright lights and the music and the flesh-pots of Vancouver are calling him.

"Don't forget to take your Vitamin C, Daniel dear," she answers. Which with her mother there is as close as she can come to kidding about whether at his age and stage he's up to a night on the town. Ordinarily she clowns around on the phone like a high school kid.

"Kisses to the babes, and of course to Mama," he says. And then, knowing the things that flash through her mind — street accidents, heart-attacks, muggings, bridges falling, avalanches (she's the scary type) — and being a little superstitious himself, before he puts down the receiver he whispers in deadly earnest, "I love you." That's really all he's phoned her for anyway. As he always tells her, upwards of twenty years of their life is a pretty big investment in each other. Gilt-edged securities, of course.

He takes the elevator up to the bar on the twenty-second floor of the Towers. It's a nice quiet spot before dinner, with a great view of the bay and mountains, when and if it ever stops raining. He usually picks a stool at the end of the bar, so he can talk to the bartender when things aren't too busy, and watch the action from the side-lines.

Tonight there are only half a dozen in the room. His favorite corner is occupied, so he settles into a seat on the other side. As he starts to give Ed his order, he realizes the fellow sitting across from him, in his spot, is someone he knows. He's obviously been at the bar a lot longer than Dan has. He raises both hands high in the air as if he was a cheer-leader, but silently, and then brings his ashtray around while the bartender transfers his drink to Dan's side.

O Danny boy, he croons softly as he approaches. The old high school joke. All Dan's former high school friends in Vancouver seem to react like juke-boxes every time they see him, especially the ones like Jack Mason, who played on the Lord Byng High School football team with him. Maybe it's because when you've known someone in school, and then don't see much of them afterwards, they tend to stick in your mind forever as you first knew them, no matter how different they become. They're still your old buddies. They've never grown up for you, probably because to your adolescent mind it was all just a game, they were never real people to you anyway. For that matter Jack Mason was still BlackJack, the star quarterback of Grade 11 and 12 to him, with just a touch underneath maybe of the earlier Grade 8 and 9 kid they used to call Jack Rabbit, because he won all the races, and because of certain advanced sexual characteristics of his.

As he sits down Dan reminds himself not to say anything to him about his own reasons for being in Vancouver, not to mix business and nostalgia. Jack played pro-football with Vancouver and with Edmonton for a few years after high school, never quite good enough to get to the top. And then a couple of marriages and some wandering from job to job before he went into Spelling's Sporting Goods. Things seem never to have developed the way they should have for a man who was born to show the way and be a big success in whatever he chose to do. Now he gives you a sense of just drifting through life. Anyway, Kelowna Rotary does a great job of sponsoring local sports mainly because — if the man has to say so himself — Dan buys for all the teams, and he shops around and doesn't get taken over by wheeler-dealers like Jack Mason. Although he's only a high-school principal, and not a businessman, he's had enough experience to know that the first thing BlackJack would do would be to offer him a kickback, old friends sticking together and all that, if he would put the Kelowna Rotary accounts into BlackJack's hands. That's the way business is done, whether it's in Vancouver or in a hick-town like Kelowna.

"I'm buying," Mason says, as soon as Dan finishes his first drink. "Let Spelling's do it, is our motto. On the account, old chap." Two is Dan's limit anyway, so he does let him.

Mason's thick wavy hair is as jet black as it was twenty-five years ago. Dan even for a moment wonders, does he or doesn't he? His face is certainly showing signs of wear and tear. Nevertheless. Big square jaw, marvelous bright even-toothed grin that lights up everything and everyone in half a mile, bushy dark eyebrows, intense eyes. Now of course he's all fuelled up with too much drink, but basically as always damned handsome. These modern safaris type clothes suit his trim shape, too, and he looks as if he could still get stripped for a football game with half an hour's notice. Maybe Dan is just influenced by the contrast of the two of them in the mirror behind the bar, himself with his balding head, glasses, and baggy 1950s tweed suit Josephine keeps telling him he should leave in a garbage can in Vancouver on his next trip and come back 1970s style.

"Well Danny Boy, you're looking One Hundred Percent." Mason says. He still has that enthusiastic energy and blindness to the facts that drove their high school football team into the finals two consecutive years.

"Funny thing," he goes on, "I was just talking about you today. I was out in Kerrisdale seeing our old pal Farmer Smith.

"How is the old Farmer?" Dan asks. An image flashes across his mind, bearing little relation probably to the Harold R. Smith, Master of Arts (Phys. Ed.) who he knew was now the head of the Kerrisdale Community Centre. Mentally a door opens (Dan's grade 10 classroom perhaps) and a tall gangling red-faced boy is led in. (Thank God, Dan thinks, we've got enough sense not to introduce new kids into classrooms that way anymore.) He's all wrists and ankles. His blond hair is standing straight up and his big ears are sticking straight out. One look and you knew right away — fresh from the Prairies. He had to be nick-named Farmer. What he really thought God knows, but no amount of kidding seemed to bother him on the outside. From that first day his long horse-face had a cockeyed grin on it whatever you said to him. And so it was Farmer Smith from then on, in the halls, at recess, at dances, on the football field. Probably it worked for Smith just the way it did for himself. Danny Boy became part of the group, but Daniel Douglas still felt like an outsider.

"The Farmer brought up your name," Jack is saying. "He doesn't seem to know where you're living or what you're doing nowadays. I had to tell him we've all sort of lost touch."

"Well, I guess I haven't seen Farmer since …." For the moment Dan can't even remember when. Certainly not since Dan got married and took a job in the Interior and left all the old Vancouver gang behind him. Actually, sometime before that, in fact.

Jack orders another drink for himself. Dan refuses, still nursing his second. Jack wheels on his stool to face him.

"Listen, you wouldn't recognize Farmer now. Not a trace of hayseed anywhere. I'm surprised you two haven't kept in touch. He always looked up to you, didn't he? He was so dumb and you were so smart. Yeah, he really respected you."

"You were the one he looked up to," Dan says, laughing. Because BlackJack Mason was the big man in his high school days, no question about that. The born leader. The natural athlete. The head lover boy. The man most likely to succeed. There's one in every school. He was everything Farmer Smith and Dan Douglas could never be and would have given their last dollar to become, though Dan at least would never have admitted it at the time.

Ed puts another double whisky in front of Jack, and Jack knocks a third of it back before answering. He can sure put it away. His forehead looks hot enough to light a cigarette against.

"You were always my booster," he says. "I counted on you to back me when things got tough. You were a real team man. I can still remember the way you always used to say, 'Great call, great call,' and lead the guys out of the huddle keen enough to make it work, whatever dumb play I might have picked."

Dan laughs again. If they don't watch out, this is going to turn into one of those comfortable mutual back-slapping sessions. He's never heard Jack so friendly.

"That's because I was just a dumb lineman."

"Jesus, Danny," Mason says, putting a heavy hand on his shoulder and peering into his face, "don't hand me that bull. Farmer Smith was a dumb lineman. You were a smart lineman. The best left guard in the league. The smartest guy on the team."

Dan snorts at that. Jack shakes his shoulder, insisting.

"Course it's true. The Boss told me that himself."

That does surprise Dan. The Boss was their coach, better than the average type you get volunteering for these jobs, Dan realized now, doing a psychology Ph.D. part-time at the University of British Columbia. A real little sergeant-major he was.

"He said that if I'd been blessed with half of Dan Douglas's brains I'd be the best quarterback he'd ever coached.

"He was just trying to shake you up," Dan says. Which could have been true. The Boss used all kinds of tricks like that on them to get them to behave the way he wanted. He manipulated them all. They were more useful than a bunch of white rats to him.

"No sir, he meant it."

Jack is quiet for a moment, looking into the bottom of his glass. Then he turns his big smile onto Dan, with just that little touch of sheepishness that makes him seem such a nice guy when he wants to be. No girl could ever resist that look.

"I'm going to tell you exactly when the Boss said that to me. I bet you have no idea."

Dan shrugs his shoulders and grins back. He's actually very curious to know. He could have used a little ego-boosting of that kind when he was in school.

"The Oval, January 1st, 1946. High School Final, Kitsilano High versus Lord Byng," he says slowly, with a touch of momentousness, knowing it will all come flooding back to Dan as it does for him. They're both eighteen again. The big stadium, the crowds, the bands, the nerves and nausea in the dressing-room, the mob pouring out onto the field, that last agonizing two minutes of play when Lord Byng pulled it out by a single point.

"Remember?" he says, watching Dan's face. "Us down on our own twenty-five, our ball, with two minutes to go?"

Remember! It was the most exciting moment in Dan's whole high school life. Of course BlackJack Mason was the hero of the day, everybody agreed.

"You really got us going again when you had to, Jack. Otherwise we would have been finished. There's been nothing like it at old Lord Byng before or since, I'll bet."

"Yeah," he says, taking a sip from his glass, watching Dan still in that intense friendly way. "I got us going. Four damn good calls, Right 4, Right 3 the reverse, Right 400 the pass, and the Quarterback Sneak. Sixty yards on four plays. But then where were we? Still twenty-five yards out, right on the sidelines instead of between the goal-posts where I should have run the ball for a field goal try. And time only for one more play."

Dan begins to feel a little awkward. Mason is creeping up on what he thought was his own sly little private memory. Maybe it's been there in Mason's mind as clearly as in his own. The crowd was going crazy. They got wilder with every play in the big march up the field. And then after Right 400 clicked — that's the pass to the left end off the same basic play as Right 4 — and after the Quarterback Sneak slipped Black Jack through the middle for twenty more yards (big hole courtesy of the best left guard in the league) they couldn't control themselves any longer. They came piling down from the stands and those in front got pushed out onto the field itself. The game had to be held up. God, the suspense, having to wait at that crucial moment. The players were just as crazy as the crowd. You couldn't hear yourself think for the roaring. What could poor old BlackJack do at that stage? Dan's heart was thumping again twenty-five years later just thinking about it, with Jack sitting next to him at the bar.

"Well, you did the right thing, anyway, Jack, the way it worked out. You called the right play."

Mason sitting there and watching with that grin on his face and those intense eyes made Dan have to say something. He didn't mean to sound so phony. Mason's reaction is a snort of rueful laughter. He shakes his head, looking into his glass again.

"Do you think I've forgotten?" he says. "It was you. You're the one who did the right thing. It was your call." He taps a finger on the bar counter. "You said it. Until then my mind was just a great big blank."

The Boss's unbreakable law was that his quarterback called the plays. You could be benched for a whole game if he found out you were trying to tell his quarterback what to do. Silence in the huddles except to answer the quarterback's questions. But there's no rule against thinking, even for a dumb left guard. Dan always liked to figure out what he would call in a given situation. It kept up his interest in the game. Even now when he's on the sidelines at a game he still likes to double-think his school quarterback. But of course nowadays the coach sends in most of the plays from the bench anyway, which takes half the fun out of it. This time, with the long delay because of the crowd on the field, they were all just bent over in the huddle in a kind of daze, waiting. BlackJack was standing straight up and looking at the other team over their backs, pretty much alone in the middle of the storm. After all, the last real move was up to him.

Five years of the Boss's discipline suddenly went out the window. Dan stood up, blurted out "Quick Kick" into his blank face, and ducked down again with the boys. BlackJack didn't move. He didn't say a thing. But half a minute later when the whistle came to start the game again, he put down his head, called his play — of course it was Quick Kick — let out his famous lion's roar to send them at the opposition, took the ball out of the single wingback formation, faded back, and booted it into the end zone. Luckily their safety was more stunned than his own team was. He should really have returned the punt, the only move he could make. When he woke up he was lying under Farmer Smith, Dan and half the Lord Byng line, three yards inside his own end zone. Lord Byng had just got themselves a championship by one point.

The gang came out on the field, chaired BlackJack Mason and carried him to the stands for the trophy presentation. Why, they were celebrating for weeks afterwards. But neither of them, BlackJack or Dan, in the twenty-five years since has ever mentioned what passed between them on the field, in that last huddle.

"Jesus, Jack," Dan says, suddenly sorry to think that what was a nice little satisfying memory to him was one Mason must have carried around like a sliver for all these years. "I just blurted it out. I never even knew you heard me, or if I was just thinking out loud what you were thinking."

"Oh, I heard you," he says quietly. "I was drifting along in a fog. My next call would have been another pass or the Sneak again or something just as stupid. The game would have been down the drain. You threw me a life-line. It worked, and I got all the credit. Except that afterwards I told the Boss what really happened. And he wasn't all that surprised. He said he thought it was too good an idea to come out of my thick head."

The ridiculousness of it comes over Dan as he looks at Mason's face, which is starting to turn lugubrious and self-pitying. When the mighty fall. Anyway, what the hell, if it was always that clear to Mason, why did he never say anything to him, not even a private thank you? Well, it's comfortable not to have to envy him anymore, the way everybody used to. Dan laughs and slaps him on the back, trying to end the subject lightly the way it should be treated.

"Come on, Jack, it was a great game and we all had the time of our lives. What does it matter now who called the damn play? Listen, I've got to make some phone calls tonight. Have you eaten yet?"

That's a mistake. Mason is set to drink the night away. Food is the last thing on his mind. But he talks Dan into staying for one more drink with the promise that then they both are to go downstairs to the dining room. Dan pities him. He's turning into a lush in front of his eyes. Fifteen minutes later he has his black book out and is trying to persuade Dan to double-date a couple of girls he can guarantee. Dan fends him off with jokes, but finally has to tell him the truth.

"I'm a happily married man, Jack."

Dan can see that that gets his goat, but to hell with him. Mason's big smile turns a bit sneery. Then, as he's thinking over what nasty comment to make on Dan's fidelity, some memory starts to light up his face.

"Oh sure," he says, "I forgot all about that. Yeah. You were married before me, weren't you? When you first went into the Interior to teach school. You sent me an announcement."

He grins into the bottom of his glass, stirring the ice-cubes with a swizzle-stick, enjoying himself for some reason that escapes Dan.

"Women," Jack says, as if changing the subject, "they've always been bad news to me. Other guys seem to manage. Even the old Farmer is married now. Jeez, I remember the first girl Farmer ever got without my help."

He looks at Dan out of the corner of his eye. His grin is sort of unpleasant now. It's all gone sour. Mason starts to tell him about Farmer Smith's first girl, that is, the first one he got all by himself. I've forgotten her name, he says. Lived over in Point Grey. Daughter of a judge or something. How Farmer managed to meet her, he doesn't know. By the time he graduated from high school Farmer was getting quite civilized, but there were still lots of hayseeds in his hair. BlackJack, who had all the girls he wanted, used to set up double dates with Smith, but in a joking way so that it seemed very amusing for girls to go along and meet this big red-wristed yokel who was always happy to be a straight man for BlackJack's jokes. He would have done the same for Dan too, but the whole business of girls was too much for Dan even to try, until he left high school.

"You won't believe this — I didn't find out about it till it was too late — the Farmer and I actually shared that girl." Jack leans his elbow on the bar and watches Dan sideways out of his alcoholic cloud. "It's true. We both had her."

Dan looks back at him and realizes he could hate that face, maybe always could have. Mason goes on. Farmer Smith had got a job as a life-guard at Bowen Island the summer before going to the University of British Columbia to take Physical Education. Somehow he met a girl there, a girl who apparently didn't consider him to be just a joke.

Well, he was a big strapping fellow, muscles on muscles, Jack concedes, and in a bathing suit and tan a girl might even find him good-looking. This girl was spending every weekend during the summer on Bowen Island to be with Farmer Smith. Then BlackJack, who was working out with the Vancouver Lions at that time, met her on the college campus, and started dating her during the week.

"Christ," Jack laughs, "I never used to ask a girl who else she might be seeing. I wasn't interested as long as she was treating me right. This girl, Jo — yeah, that was her name, now that I think of it — Jo never mentioned the Farmer, and whatever else she might have told him, she obviously didn't give the Farmer my name either. I knew there was some competition because of the weekend thing. My big ambition was to get her to stay in Vancouver instead of leaving for Bowen Island every Friday night."

You would have to know Farmer Smith and BlackJack Mason in those days to realize what a mismatch it was. Of course it was only a matter of time before Jack won. Dan feels a shock wave of bitterness, and another, and another, as he looks across at Mason, with his dark head bowed over his drink.

"So you stole Farmer's first girl," Dan says, not showing anything he might feel, but having to hear the rest of the story, even though he'd rather be a hundred miles away. BlackJack wouldn't understand. But for Dan there was only one girl, the first and the last, the one his life was built around.

BlackJack angles his head so he can see Dan out of the corner of his eye again. His little sneer comes back.

"No way, Danny. I didn't even know he was in the picture. She just preferred me, damn it."

BlackJack asked the girl to go out with him Saturday night, as he'd been doing for weeks, expecting her still to say no. But she didn't. She said OK, and in fact invited him to come to her place for dinner.

"Her Dad, the judge or whatever," Jack says, "was away back East with her mother on a holiday, and the house was empty."

BlackJack's eyes get brighter as he remembers. Dan wishes he could get up and leave, but he sits there listening, even letting Mason wave to Ed for another round before he continues the story. A few drinks before dinner, a nice quiet meal for two, everything moving along so well, with BlackJack calling the plays. She was green, but enthusiastic, which was the way BlackJack used to like them.

"After dinner, we're half way up the stairs, on the way to her bedroom. Leaving a piece of clothing on every step. Damn it all," Jack snorts, slapping a hand on the bar so loudly Ed looks up from the drink he's mixing, "at the crucial moment the doorbell starts to ring. Forget it, I say, holding onto her. But Jesus, it went on and on. I think she must have known right away who it was. She got more and more miserable. Finally she crept down the stairs, one at a time, putting things back on as she went. I just pulled on my pants and sweater. Hell, it wasn't my problem. Anyway, I was drunk as a skunk."

The girl opened the door. Jack couldn't see who it was, but the conversation went on so long in low tones that he came down the stairs to have a peek. There he was, Farmer Smith, standing under the veranda light, with his big hands by his sides, his mouth moving more than Jack had ever seen it do before. The two were finishing their talk. Farmer was turning to go. The girl was just about to close the door. But he looked over her head and recognized BlackJack in the shadows of the hall.

"You should have seen the poor bastard's face," Jack says, covering his own with both hands and making a kind of awed giggle under them.

The girl saw the look between the men. She turned past Jack and ran up the stairs. So there they were, the two friends a dozen feet apart.

"My first thought was, jeez, the big clunk could probably break me in half if he ever got mad. But I decided to play it cool, let him make the first move."

Farmer stood with his jaw going up and down for a minute.

"Well then," Jack says, with the amazement still in his voice, "what do you think he did? What would you expect him to do?"

"I don't have any idea," Dan says numbly into the bottom of his glass, wishing he'd never come into the bar, never met BlackJack, never heard of Farmer Smith again.

"Nothing. That's what he did. Nothing. He said 'sorry Jack, I didn't know you were here or I wouldn't have walked in on you. I just came by to see why Jo wasn't on the Island last night.' Well, what could I say to that? He really made me feel like I'd kicked a stray dog or .... I started to apologize and explain too. But he wouldn't have any part of it. Wouldn't even let me finish. He cut right across what I was saying with something I'll never forget. Where the big clunk picked it up from I don't know. I guess it was an idea of his own. He said — you're going to love this, Danny — he said, 'I hope you don't think I'd let a girl come between friends.'"

Mason slapped his hand on the bar again, laughing almost out of control, apparently.

"Can you beat that? The old tongue-tied Farmer? 'I hope you don't think I'd let a girl come between friends'"

Jack turns on his stool and looks straight at Dan. He's determined, it seems, to get a rise out of him.

"Can you imagine Farmer Smith saying something like that? The girl upstairs crying her heart out over him, for all I know?"

Dan gets up slowly, a little dizzy from so much to drink, resisting his impulse to slap Mason across his sweaty face. After all, what's the point? It wouldn't help, nothing is going to help.

"Well," Dan says at last, getting a grip on himself as he stands looking down at Mason, "it just goes to prove what great friends we were, doesn't it? BlackJack, Danny Boy, and the Farmer .... We stuck together like three pieces of shit."

There's not the slightest change in Mason's expression. Dan can see he's wasting his time. Mason's too far gone to get back at with words. Dan turns to go, but the words come anyway, growing louder than he intends, while he puts a hand on the bar to steady himself against the whirling room.

"Jesus, Jack, what I can't figure out is .... Did we have to go through all that crap to grow up? I mean, was it really worth it just to get where we are now?"

Mason's eyes go a little glassy as the tone of voice penetrates and he struggles to make sense of what he hears. Dan grabs his limp hand from the bar top and shakes it quickly.

"Well, I have to go now, Jack. Let's be sure to get together next time I'm in the City. Great to remember the good old days."

Mason doesn't try to keep Dan. He's too drunk even to look surprised. Dan walks carefully through the tables that are beginning to fill up now. At the door out, as he fumbles to make sure he's got his lighter and cigarettes with him, he glances back to see BlackJack still sitting by himself at the end of the bar, hunched over his drink, finishing the day as he probably has got into the habit of doing.

The first bitterness fades a little. But he thinks, *I know now why she never let me call her Jo.* And his mind begins to wander back over all the things in his own life he hasn't yet been able to tell her about, and has tried to put behind him, grievances, shames, disappointments, humiliations, as well as some long-buried happy things. He doesn't want to be angry with the world, with Josephine, with himself. It's not good to be alone. Christ, who is Jo, anyway? Not the Josephine he loves and who loves him.

As he waits for the elevator, he wonders whether he can think of an excuse to telephone, even though he's called once already, and the cocktail hour is over.

The Jumbo Special

That very morning he had said to Clara, *Thank God, I think things are settling down at 36 Ashley Road.* Partly of course he said it to reassure Clara, who was as uneasy on Saturday mornings as he was. But it was also what he really thought, despite recurrent dreams and waking doubts to the contrary.

Clara never for a moment suggested that she begrudged Peter or his wife and children these Saturday visits. Just the reverse. It was she who for the past few difficult months had been understanding and sympathetic, offering to go down to her studio and leave the apartment to him all day so that he could bring the children there for lunch. She made it sound so natural, too.

"You've got to have somewhere domestic to take them, Peter. Restaurants and parks are alright for a change but sooner or later …. And as far as I'm concerned, I'm so far behind in my work — thanks to you, my darling — a few Saturdays at my desk are just what the doctor ordered."

Peter was behind in his work too. But his partners with the help of the junior accountants were quietly filling in for him as if he was ill or temporarily seconded to the United Appeal or whatever. There was nothing urgent to worry about. Whereas Clara had to come up with detailed interiors for half-a-dozen newlyweds setting up their first homes, for a bevy of bored or neurotic matrons who wanted to do everything over and catch up with the times, and for a handful of small commercial jobs, all before the end of the summer. As well, new business was coming into her studio, Future Design, every week. The tall elegant Clara dispensed, at appropriate rates, the same tact and flair that made her own apartment in the downtown converted warehouse a showpiece in a unique sophisticated modern manner. She had been in the interior design game for almost fifteen years, the last five, since her husband's death, on her own. So it was no wonder she was in demand. However, she was marvelously efficient. She would manage to catch up and please everyone.

At first Peter thought he couldn't impose his unruly brood of three boys all under ten on Clara's stylish furnishings. But she was quite persuasive.

"Goodness, Peter, do you think I design rooms that are just to be looked at? Here, see?" She cried, kicking the curved stem of a tall, graceful lamp, raising an equally graceful, long pant-suited leg like a ballet dancer to do it. Miraculously the lamp swayed over and settled itself again on its base, as if rooted like a palm tree. She lifted both arms in a languid gesture of triumph.

"My materials are indestructible. I design not only for the present, not only for the future, but for eternity."

They both laughed a little hysterically, surrounded as they were by the debris of a good dinner for two at home and the mixed time currents of a flourishing affair and a disintegrating marriage. A second and third cognac in the big glasses often tided them over the moments of unease.

But still, Peter had never brought the children to the apartment. When he had run through all the likely excuses, Clara made it easy for him not to have to produce more reasons. He seemed to want to keep a sort of firewall between the two parts of his life. All the more surprising that weeks after the first natural opportunities had passed, Peter abruptly introduced the possibility with those optimistic words.

"Yes, at last, thank God, I think things are settling down at 36 Ashley Road. I wondered about bringing the lads here for a bite of lunch."

Clara was delighted. Even more so when he continued:

"I think it's time they met you, too. If you're willing."

"Willing? You know I've been dying to meet them. Just as soon as you felt the right time had come."

Lunch was no problem. She knew already what all three boys liked and didn't like, from Peter's wry descriptions of those Saturday meals, usually hot dogs or hamburgers or as a special treat Kentucky Fried Chicken. And her fridge and cupboards were full of things that could please them in a jiffy. She had often said how wonderful it would be to make up for her lost years and catch a full-blown family in one net.

"I'll tell them you're my best friend — which is the truth," Peter said as he was about to go, "and I won't say anything about my living here. There's no need to make it any more complicated than it has to be for now."

At the door after kissing her goodbye he turned her around so she leaned back against him, and together they looked through the sunken living-room and the open door into the bedroom. It was semi-circular. A huge circular bed occupied the main space of the room. Around it were curved chests of drawers against the walls. Above the bed hung a chandelier consisting of a circular mirror as large as the bed, surrounded by a dozen lights which could be aimed at different parts of the room.

"That room," Peter said, pushing Clara towards the bedroom with a loving pat on her buttocks, "is a conversation piece even for a gang of dumb, unobservant, pre-puberty boys. Maybe you'd better lock that door while they're here."

As he drove northwards in the direction of 36 Ashley Road through the downtown traffic his good spirits faded. When he was with Clara it seemed right that their hours should be full of wit and laughter and good food and wine and rich silences. What was wrong with happiness, if you were lucky enough to find it? After the long evenings came the wildness or tenderness of loving, every meal and every mating conducted as if it were the first, or the last. Nothing habitual, nothing taken for granted, nothing predictable. Even the sadness, for there was the sadness of an old almost forgotten past, hers, which they relived, talked through, and the sadness of a newly ruined past, his, pasts which were not theirs and which both separated and brought them together.

Especially his past, which united them only since its ruination was what they two had brought about because of their discovered need for each other, a need to be satisfied whatever hurt and harm they might cause anyone else. Even sadness was sweet when they were together.

The only really bad time for him was very early in the mornings, or very late at night — anyway, about three or four a.m. He wondered, in the daytime looking back dimly at the half-sleeping, half-waking nightmares that often filled those hours with groans and sweat and stifled writhing, he wondered why he didn't wake up Clara beside him and bring alive the happiness that they shared. Pour it like a cool spring shower over the hot coals that seemed to be eating into his body. But that solution came clearly out of his day-time thoughts, was inconceivable at night, and the whole problem with these nightmare hours was that they belonged to a totally different order of time and reality. Nothing in the one sphere had any relevance to the other. He could sweat and cry in the one, while a few hours before or after he was laughing or singing or sharing new highs of ecstasy in the other.

He didn't believe the phases of night-misery were real except when he was actually enduring them. If he did in fact groan aloud at some contorted image of his wife or his children, some facial expression of disbelief or grief or some gesture of pain, gaping rents in the smooth familiar surfaces of an intimate fifteen-year-old relationship through which bottomless depths of irreversible loss and wrong could be glimpsed, Clara was too sleepy or too tactful to draw such discords to his attention at night or in the morning. Probably everyone had times when remorse or guilt or humiliation or shame or despair wracked them with an almost physical pain. Blame it on our Puritan heritage or if you prefer on cross-currents in the subconscious, overdeveloped superegos, dietary considerations, the influence of the stars or the weather. Once, wryly, he contemplated the effects of that circular bed. Perhaps he was the kind of man who had to have a square bed and a head-board or wall at his back. In any case he was sure that time would help everyone, including his wife and children, to adjust to the new situation.

The boys were playing in the living-room when he arrived. The outside door was ajar, so he was once again relieved of the bothersome impossible choice of whether to knock on the door or just open it and walk in, as if he still lived there. A little push made his arrival known and the three children ran to meet him and pull him into the hallway. His wife was nowhere in sight.

"Mommy would like you to have us back by four o'clock. We're going to Craig and Sally's for dinner," young Peter said at once. He gave the message solemnly as befits the eldest and most responsible of them, and the one who at almost ten had no doubt been told often enough that he must now be the man in the house. Craig and Sally, with their happy ordered lives, their two older children, were the most kind and reliable of friends.

"Where we going, Dad?"

Mark, the seven-year-old, always seemed most anxious to get the day's activities under way. He looked as much like his fair-haired mother as young Peter looked like his dark-haired father. Frail, worried, hardly bigger than his five-year-old younger brother, he was happy only when things went smoothly and quickly. He got upset with too much excitement. But Ricky, the youngest, was dragging his father with both husky little hands into the living room to show off his cardboard-box castle. Though Peter Senior was as impatient to be off as Mark, sometimes it was quicker in the long run to yield a little at first.

The living room was in a state of disarray that could be understood only archaeologically. In the top layers were the games, books, and assorted clothes of the three boys' last few hours. Below that were signs of adult habitation, a few empty glasses, ashtrays, plates here and there suggesting little parties or snatched meals or buffets over the past days, coffee cups with butts in the saucers, newspapers mainly unopened, some pens and scraps of stationary, letters, bills, telephone books, a set of potted plants dying on the windowsill, a vase of long-dead cut flowers on the mantel with a card he would like to have glanced at to see who they were from.

"Come on, lads, let's go," he said more grimly than he intended, feeling a growing depression. He didn't want to think of what conditions, physical or spiritual, the rest of the house might reveal. "Go up and tell your mother we're on our way, Pete."

He ushered the other two into the car, ignoring their "where we going's" for the moment. The grass and the hedge were immaculately groomed, in keeping with the neat green expanses of the neighborhood, courtesy, Peter knew, of the gardening contract they had signed and paid for before the crisis. Young Peter came running to the car and to the place in front reserved for him. He would sit without saying anything, leaving the uproar to the two in the back seat. Occasionally Peter Senior turned around to break up a quarrel before it came to blows.

As they neared Clara's apartment, he began to trim his crew to the mood he hoped to achieve and maintain over lunch.

"Simmer down, you guys, O.K., now, what are the rules?"

"Do what Daddy says." Ricky was the first to speak the basic rule, though he was usually the last to obey it.

"Don't keep asking for things," said Mark, directing the moral to Ricky, more than to himself, which was fair enough, however untactful.

Young Peter had the vocabulary and mature mind to get into the spirit of the catechism. "No weeping or wailing. No groaning or gasping or ...."

Peter Senior helped him. "Groveling or grubbing or grabbing."

And the boy's turn. "No sobbing or shrieking or sighing or ...."

With the father to finish rehearsal off. "And definitely no snarling or snapping or slobbering."

Peter had explained that he was taking them to lunch at the home of his best friend, a lady called Clara. They were not very curious, except that Ricky wanted to know what games there would be. Peter Senior thought of that white shag rug in the living room, which Clara claimed was stain-proof and of the wine and cognac glasses displayed on top of the huge wooden cross-beam that marked off the dining area. Could his boys climb up on that beam? He would have to keep an eye out. From them he expected the noise and activity level of a monkey-house.

"Now don't tell me, let me guess," Clara said in the hallway. "This young man is Peter Junior, I'll bet." She put a hand on the boy's downturned head. She pursed her lips and thought hard as she studied the next face. "And this must be Mark." Mark looked unsmilingly up at her. Then with both hands thrust under his chin, and a tone of delight: "Last but not least, Richard, the shy one."

Ricky had pulled unceremoniously away to press his face against his father's leg. Pulling at his hand, ignoring Clara, he muttered, "Where's the games?"

It was strange. The quietness of the boys through lunch and afterwards, ranging from impassive withdrawal for the eldest, to obvious sullenness for Mark, and to deep restless boredom and resentment for Ricky. Clara was trying very hard. The artificiality, the forced high spirits, the touches of flirting, the direct appeals for responses. This was a Clara Peter had never seen and wouldn't have expected. He could feel himself getting stiffer and more embarrassed, becoming the heavy father, treating the boys as if their table manners and talk had to meet the standards of the high Victorian Age. In fact, that's of course what Clara suggested to his mind: a childless Victorian lady, maybe a would-be governess between positions, trying to win the master through her tenderness for his children. He looked across the debris of peanut-butter cookies and jello covering the ceramic-mosaic table top, and wondered how he and this charming sophisticated woman, perfect companion and lover, could have found themselves cast in these dreary deadening roles.

Early in the afternoon, Ricky and Mark capped the disaster of the visit, the younger by setting up a refrain, Daddy when are we going home? And the older by quietly throwing up on the Danish sofa.

"For God's sake, Mark, why didn't you say something?" Peter cried in exasperation as he mopped up what he could with his handkerchief.

"I didn't know," was the only answer before the silent tears started and would not be stopped.

"O.K., O.K., simmer down, it's alright."

"Of course it is, Mark," Clara called as she got a bucket and sponge from the kitchen. "I'll have this cleaned up before you can wash your face. Let's have a race."

As if yielding up at last to failure, Peter lay out on the carpet and watched while Clara removed the mess. A few minutes later he reached back through the doorway to pat her cheek ruefully, sending the boys on a few steps ahead to the car.

"Thanks for all that, Clar," he said.

"See you soon, darling."

They were both too disappointed and flat to make more, or less, of the occasion.

The car arrived in front of 36 Ashley at four p.m. sharp. Peter would have liked to have let the boys go in by themselves, but he felt he should make sure his wife was there.

"Tell your mother we're back," he said to young Peter. He stayed in the hallway with the other two swinging on his arms while he waited for word from upstairs.

"Mommy wants to talk to you before you go," the eldest boy said from the top of the stairs.

"Is she coming down?"

"She wants you to come up."

He looked in from the doorway of the bedroom. The pillows were crammed against the quilted headboard with its two dark patches. Newspapers and magazines and books were scattered over the rumpled blankets. On the bedside table and on the floor were the plates and cups of several meals. Three or four dark brown bottles of prescription pills lay in the half-open drawer of the table. The lamp was on, although sunlight poured in from the west window onto the scattering of clothing at the open closet door. He said nothing, but waited for her to speak. His coming triggered her words, but her rapid blue eyes darted past him and around him. He stared at the sunlit window as she talked, so that their looks were never joined.

She had to discuss the children with him. They were getting beyond her. Richard was waking in the night crying. Mark had started wetting his bed again. Young Peter had simply refused to do several things she had asked, and he had once been very insolent with her. He was too big for her to spank him. They needed a man, a father. He had no idea how difficult it was. What did he intend to do about them?

Peter broke in with rising exasperation. "I've told you, time and time again, if you don't want them or can't manage, I'll take them to live with me."

"With you! Do you think I would let you have them? What kind of a home could you give them? You and your …."

The words poured out in ever widening circles. It was going to end as always. "Pull yourself together." "Don't you dare speak to me in that way." And the flow of anger, bitterness, pain, flooding off into hot tears, if not blows as well. He longed to be somewhere else, anywhere. He tried to stop the rush towards that inevitable tearful catastrophe.

"Listen, I thought you were going to take the children and go out to dinner. It would do you good to see Craig and Sally."

The effect was abrupt, complete, and the reverse of what he had hoped.

"I can't go, I can't take them."

The words came in an anguished wail.

"For Christ sake, why not?"

"I told Sally I would …. I told her I would bring the dinner. I was going to buy the jumbo special, at the chicken place. Enough for everybody. That was my reason. I got the day wrong. The jumbo special is tomorrow."

He writhed in silent humiliation. To need a reason. An excuse. To take the children and have dinner with their oldest friends. The jumbo special. To have to try and make it casual, frivolous, not a desperate need. Keep the balance of a relationship by doing them a little fun favor, by bringing the jumbo special, enough for everybody. Not to be a receiver of Craig and Sally's charity, not their burden. Not subject to people's pity, impatience, boredom. The turning away of others from grief, loneliness, dreariness, disorder, calamity. Abandoned. Alone. The sweat began to ooze from all over his body. His neck and face throbbed as if he were on fire. The uncontrolled wailing and weeping. Come back, the children need you, I need you, come back, come back. His heart pounded. This was their private unacknowledged sharing, this tearing anguish. The night-misery in broad daylight. There was no waking up. It was real.

"You don't have to buy the goddam jumbo special," he raged. He didn't want to think about it anymore. He didn't want to understand. His wallet had some tens and twenties. "I give you all the money you need. You couldn't be out of money."

He threw the bills on the bed.

"I can't go now," she sobbed, pulling the sheet over her head, "I can't go now. Go away."

He turned and walked out the door. The sobbing was a muffled sound in his imagination when he got downstairs. The boys were silently reading and playing in the living room. They were miraculously calm and independent. He stood in the doorway for a moment watching them. They ignored him. Their visit with him was over. He didn't exist for them until next Saturday. Well, maybe it was kind of a reassuring thing.

"See you next week, lads."

"Bye Dad."

As he drove back to Clara, his blood cooled. And now, getting the matter in a clearer perspective, he reflected that there had been worse occasions. *Perhaps at last,, things were beginning to settle down at 36 Ashley Road.*

Prospects of Employment

I haven't felt particularly nervous during my weekend as Colonel Scott-Smythe's guest, though from his point of view I'm a young man being looked over to see if I'm suitable for a job. The truth is, I have a perfectly all right job in Ottawa. I'd like to move to the Toronto area for lots of reasons. But I can wait. What the Colonel has to offer isn't necessarily the best opportunity. There will certainly be others. However, I shall have to do some serious thinking. It's so easy to make the wrong decision and waste years of what could be the most important stage of your life, or at least of your professional life.

As usual, there are at least two sides to the question. People whom I respect have told me the Colonel is an impossible man to work for, demanding, overbearing, treating all employees like personal servants expected to be on call day and night. Technically of course I wouldn't be working for him, but for the Canadian Association of Horse Exhibitors. However, as founder, original financial supporter, and board chairman, the Colonel is the man you have to get along with if you intend to take the job of Executive Secretary of the CAHE. Although he is still on a few company boards, and is a fundraiser for the Conservative Party national organization during election years, and is the most active seventy-year-old sportsman I know of, the Colonel spends more time trying to influence the CAHE in one way or another than on all the rest of his businesses and hobbies put together.

That's why he's taking such a personal interest in me, a mere junior accountant in a small Ottawa firm, which he could buy up lock stock and barrel just with, say, the amount he has spent developing his herd of prize cattle this past couple of years. It's me as writer, magazine editor, and horseman, not me as accountant he's really interested in.

I think it all dates back to my great success at the Royal Winter Fair last year when I beat the Colonel's entry in the Lieutenant-Governor's Cup with my seven-eight's Thoroughbred Hanoverian cross. Always the officer and gentleman, the Colonel was a good loser considering the fact that entries from his King stable have won the Cup more times in the last twenty or thirty years than they have lost, and he did have a nice big chestnut gelding by Sultan Mahmud that he thought was too good to be passed over. Naturally I took advantage of my position as owner and editor of the *Ontario Pony and Horse Journal* to put in full page pictures of my horse being pinned first, and the Colonel's horse waiting for the second ribbon in the background.

A month after the Royal the Colonel was in Ottawa on CAHE business and he condescended to come out to my little converted cattle barn and look over my horses. I may have postponed making some good money but raised my own value in his eyes by turning aside a couple of strong hints he dropped about buying up the competition if you couldn't beat them. My father, a retired master from Ridley Boys School who spends all his time gardening and reading history books, said I was a fool not to make enough to pay for the mortgage. He's interested in my writing, not my horses. My mother agreed with him mainly because she would like me to have a fuller social life, meet the right girl, get married, have a proper house instead of an apartment over a barn, produce children and perpetuate the family. Well, I really had nothing I was prepared to sell at the time. I certainly wasn't going to stop exhibiting just when my stable was coming along so well.

One of my reasons for wanting to come to the Toronto area, in fact, is that it offers much more scope to a horseman. For example, Colonel Scott-Smythe lives within thirty miles of the City, but he's in the heart of the horse country. I couldn't hope to settle that near, real estate values being what they are, but even a little farther out …. It was baiting the hook for the Colonel to let me stay at his country estate and see the neighborhood on horseback. Of course being his house guest for a couple of days I would be able to show him whether I was sound in ideas and cooperative in attitude and in other ways an Executive Secretary to his taste.

The only thing he didn't calculate too well was that his horse should have jumped him off over a coop a week before I arrived and cost him a broken collar-bone. But he's one of those men nothing slows up. Tough old bird that he is, he didn't postpone my visit or forewarn me. Instead he met me and his chauffeur as I was driven up to the door of his mansion. Arm in sling under his smoking jacket, white hair, standing straight and tall.

"Glad to see you, good man, how was your flight? These Friday night flights from Ottawa are sometimes rather crowded. No, no it's nothing at all, just a hair-line fracture. Expect to be riding again in two weeks at the outside. Don't you worry, my stable manager, Flynn, will show you the country. Knows it as well as I do myself. He'll take you out first thing tomorrow. I must be in the City until noon. We'll talk over lunch."

Well, it's very difficult to get a word in with Colonel Scott-Smythe until he puts his questions to you, gets you to make your response at what he considers to be the appropriate moment. I find all this rather restful. Everything is in his hands. And frankly I enjoyed that session in his trophy room which lasted almost all Saturday afternoon. He's a fascinating old devil, reeking with power and money, always expecting to get the most out of people and life, fancying himself as the country gentleman, but genuinely charming when he wants to be. By the end of our talk it was fairly clear that he would like me to have the job. Now it's up to me. I have to be careful not to get swept along without really making my own decision.

That's why I all the more gladly accepted the invitation to ride out again this morning, and why I suggested to Flynn — Flynn was, to say the least, unenthusiastic about coming in the first place — that he could leave me to find my own way back while he took a short-cut home to his Sunday lunch. I have a chance to do some thinking by myself. When the Colonel comes back to see me at tea-time, bids me goodbye at the door, and watches me being driven off to the airport by his chauffeur, he'll want to know whether I'm leaving as his man or not. I've been totaling up the pluses and the minuses.

A big plus is the size of the salary, for what is really a half or three-quarter time job. I would have lots of time for my magazine and my writing, as well as for building up an accountancy clientele. Another is the range of contacts. The Colonel himself can do a lot to send useful professional opportunities my way, and then there must be a good percentage of the wealthy and propertied people in Southern Ontario interested in the activities of the CAHE, with part of my job being to cultivate and expand that membership. Also on the plus side is being involved much more fully in the various aspects of exhibiting horses, something I've always found enjoyable and am beginning to find profitable. What better way to spend leisure time.

However, and it's a big however, Colonel Scott-Smythe for all his charm is a strong-minded and difficult man, showing signs of senility. Committing myself to three years with the CAHE, as he wants me to do, might be the worst possible waste of time. The secondary prospects might never come to anything. I might return to Ottawa the older and the poorer. And have missed whatever other chances might have come my way. I don't think I would want to go back to being an over-worked accountant earning not much more than wages, and a week-end horseman and odd-job man tied to a small barn and a big mortgage. Realizing that not everyone can live like Colonel Scott-Smythe, with his six-hundred acre cattle and horse farm, his forty-room mansion, his polo arena, his sixteen-horse model stable, his swimming pool, tennis courts, artificial lake, his chauffeur-driven cars, his six field hunters, his archery range, his .... Well, there's no end to the list of that old man's possessions. It makes your tongue hang out.

Just as there's no end to the lanes and trails that spread out from his mansion into the woods and farmlands around it. I have been ambling along for half-an-hour in what I know is a westerly direction, back towards the stable. I have passed through a fifty-acre field of yellowing wheat, a huge hayfield with its second growth of alfalfa well up, a pasture with a dozen prize Holstein cattle day-dreaming in the corner, a long wooded valley in which I saw a deer and some birds I think must be pheasant, and then a rolling field over which I sent a flock of sheep scattering though I slowed up to a walk. But since talking to the Colonel's next-door neighbor, Ladislaw Boro, and saying goodbye to Flynn, I haven't sighted another human being. All this within an hour's drive of the City.

I suppose being neighbors Flynn has heard Ladislaw Boro's conversation too often to be the slightest bit interested. Or perhaps the Irish and the Hungarians have a natural antipathy. I found Ladislaw amusing and interesting, and a nice diversion from my own brooding and Flynn's rather morose comments on the weather, the crops and the state of the world generally. Irishmen, contrary to popular opinion, are not all cheerful. In fact I was glad of an excuse to suggest that Flynn leave me. I must have stood talking to Ladislaw for half an hour after Flynn introduced us across the fence-line and took his horse off at a lazy jog to leave us together.

By the time I turned my horse southward along the Colonel's side of the fence-line and waved goodbye to Ladislaw Boro, I felt as if I had had the privilege of being the theatre audience for a one-man play. It turns out that Ladislaw has the only small farm in the neighborhood. Most of it is sand and rock, rather, I must admit, like my place outside Ottawa. His hayfield slopes up from the cedar rail fence so that as he stood on his almost empty hay-wagon watching Flynn and me canter along the path towards him he was looking down at us. We halted forty feet away on our side of the fence to say hello. He took off his old felt hat and bobbed an odd little military bow at us that made me think at once that he must be a European. A rather comical and unexpected sight in the middle of Southern Ontario farmland. Until his hat came off, he looked like a youngish man, his body wiry and muscular and tanned in the brown cotton patched trousers and shirt he was wearing. But his hair was iron grey. He smiled cheerfully when Flynn introduced us. The day suddenly seemed more pleasant. I took the chance to tell Flynn to go back the way we came, leaving me to have a chat and come home in my own time.

I was mounted on a big black mare, Colonel Scott-Smythe's favorite hack, a little fresh from lack of work but with beautiful manners.

"That is the kind of horse we had in my country," the Hungarian called across the fence, taking a few steps closer to the edge of the hay-wagon on which he was standing to make a better appraisal. "Yes, that is like Hungarian horse."

He put his hat back on his head and strode three paces to the middle of the wagon, hands on hips, voice rising to cover the forty feet between us as if I were at the back of the theater.

"I was sitting on horse, just like that, when the Russians captured me."

There was a moment of silence in the early morning sun as we contemplated this very strange memory, strange I mean, in this quiet Ontario countryside thousands of miles from where you could even imagine such a thing happening. I was brooding on it for the first time, probably he was taking the memory out and opening it like a favorite pocket knife. The big mare swished her tail at the flies and stirred her feet in the long grass, not realizing she was part of a composite human picture, a sort of double exposure, I suppose you could say.

"Now I am too old to ride, of course," he said, breaking the spell. He bent down and idly shifted a bale of hay, as though demonstrating a stooping or a weakness in his back.

"No, never," I called, "never too old."

I was really protesting more or less spontaneously for myself as much as for him. I wasn't really focusing on him. He shook his head in a stubborn sort of way.

"Too stiff. Too sore. Last time I rode was, oh, ten, fifteen years past. When I used to work for Colonel. Before I bought my own farm."

He began to pace back and forth on the wagon, stopping for a special gesture, a raising of both arms, a look into the bottom of his hat, an expressive movement in the air with his tanned fingers. Talking all the time. Loud and soft, fast and slow, happy and sad. A wonderful stream of words, a life's experience being orchestrated for breath and vocal chords and tongue. All I did was smile and laugh occasionally, nod, agree, show I understood the sounds. That was the only encouragement he needed. A man who loved to talk, who had a deep well of half-articulated memories and thoughts that perhaps he rarely got around to dipping into any more. That's the impression he gave me.

When I first came to this country, he was saying, I worked on the Colonel's farm. Yesterday I was officer, today I was farm laborer. But I was alive. Cowman, fieldman, all kinds of work, what does it matter. This country is beautiful. He waved an imperial arm to take in the whole neighborhood. Very good farming, also very good riding and very good foxhunting for the ladies and gentlemen. One day I was clearing brush. I stop to watch the Hunt go by, oh, very pretty, sixty or seventy riders. They jump a chicken-coop, little coop about so big. He put a hand down to show how insignificant the jump was. They all go over except for one nice lady. What is she to do? Poor lady. Her horse wouldn't like to jump today, thank you, though the nice lady ask him very politely. She has no crop, she has no spurs. She would like so much to jump. After a while I cut her a piece of branch and I present to her: Madam, may I offer you this to help you?

Ladislaw mimed the soft lady-like taps she gave her horse's side and demonstrated all over the wagon floor how the horse would not change his mind. Now the lady is so far behind the others, all alone, very unhappy. At last I come to her (Ladislaw mimes his little military bow) and I say, Madam, perhaps you would wish me to take horse across?

Desperate and clutching at straws, the lady decides to dismount. Ladislaw in his overalls makes a few small adjustments to the tack and vaults into the saddle. A gathering of the reins, a little forward urging, and a few small circles to collect the horse, all reenacted on the wagon floor for my benefit. Then a calm determined approach to the fence and over they go. At once, a circle and back again, and yet again. Ladislaw's strong hands look very delicate as he lets out the imaginary reins, pats the imaginary horse, and the neat exercise completed beams down from his stage on the remembered lady and on me, his weather-brown face lit up with delight at the little challenge and triumph.

And now, an ironical grin settles on his lips. Before he realizes what she is doing the lady, whom he has helped back into the saddle, reaches into her sandwich case. Madam, he says quickly, trying to prevent the embarrassment, it is nothing, please. In Hungary, where I was captain in the Hungarian Hussars, we hunt twice a week over difficult, difficult country. Much more difficult than this. But always for each lady there are two officers. Ladislaw goes on to tell me what he couldn't tell the lady. Yes, yes, if you were lucky it would be a young lady, a pretty lady, if not, that's too bad, in any case, you must never, never leave the lady behind. To leave the lady behind? Ladislaw's face expressed bewilderment and disbelief at the kind of manners which had allowed such a thing to happen. But the lady he had just helped, the happy Canadian lady, reached into her sandwich case and pulled out a bill to tip him with. Misunderstanding his embarrassment, she thrust the money into his overall pocket, burying it there in the midst of the nails and binder twine and hayseed. Then she rode off leaving him to shake his head wryly in his humiliation. If I could have found that lady, he says, I would have bought her something with money, some little gift, some flowers perhaps. But I never saw her again.

A week or two later Colonel Scott-Smythe showed that he had heard about the matter. He knew now that he had an experienced European horseman on his farm staff. One morning, and he did it sometimes later on too, he invited Ladislaw to take time off from his work and ride across the property, Colonel Scott-Smythe in front, as always, with two neighboring landowners, and Ladislaw with the Colonel's stable manager and groom following.

Oh, I was big man that day, says Ladislaw, with an ironic grin, blowing himself up a little to show physically the effect on his vanity of being part of such a distinguished group. Very big man.

After this, his cheerfulness and self-mockery and irony seemed to flag a little. My Hungarian friends said to me, when I bought my own farm, they said that I would now have horses of my own too, and be able to ride again all I want as I did in Hungary. But, he shrugged his shoulders in resignation, it is never that easy. When you have done your chores, milked your cows, can you look up and say, here is my horse, now I ride? No. No. It is finished. All that is in the past. Never mind. I have had my riding. I have had my youth. He paces the wagon thinking. He straightens a bale of hay, bending his back slowly over and up again.

I was sitting on my horse, just like you, when the Russians captured me. Three years gone from my life ....

He stands looking at me, as if trying to decipher some dim, mysterious image of himself as he might have been, horse, uniformed rider, lifted out and held from the flow of time forever thirty or forty years ago. He seems to be looking right through me. Then his eyes focus on me gathering my reins, and knowing that I have to go sometime he grins, raises his hat in that curious mixture of the military and polite civilian that had caught my eye before. It was his curtain call. I return the farewell with a salute from my hunting crop, and head my horse homeward.

As I say, that must have been half-an-hour ago. Since then I've been ambling along through pasture and woodland, generally in the right direction, I'm sure, but probably not the shortest route. I have this feeling that before I get back to the stable I should make a choice that could be very important, but I also wonder how much it really matters. I guess this is the kind of acquiescent mood you can get into out in the country — I have had something like it creep over me when I've been working in my own barn outside of Ottawa — and it's fatal to any chance of decisions that make the most of your opportunities.

There's a nice looking chicken-coop in the fence ahead, and beyond that I think I see the Colonel's tennis courts. I'll slip into a canter here, and we'll see how well the Colonel's mare can jump. A little excitement will wake us both up and get the blood flowing again, before I have to commit myself for the future.

The Mare

From the stable door, Patience can see that the mare is sweating in her stall again. More likely, she hasn't ever stopped sweating since Clyde brought her in. She's always in a white lather for hours after Clyde works her. He's too big for her and he asks too much, trying to make her into exactly what he wants. After all, the horse is still very green.

Clyde is in the stall rubbing her with a sack. His scowl hardly lightens as Patience comes down the aisle, followed by John MacNeil — who is there with her not as a friend or anything else now, but as the veterinarian. Patience wishes she'd stayed in the house. Let her husband and John deal with the horse, instead of coming out to be there as soon as she saw the car pull up at the stable and John get out with his black vet's bag, and look down towards the house. The stable is her husband Clyde's job. Her job is to teach kindergarten, babysitting really, over in the sub-division in the mornings and look after the accounts and the house in the afternoons. Has been for the three years since they got married and began renting the run-down house and barn and set themselves up in the horse business. Horses are just a hobby for her now. They're his work, his responsibility. She could keep right out of the practical side, especially since from the beginning Clyde has stuck to it so much better than anyone predicted.

Usually she does, in fact, but with the mare it's really difficult. The mare was hers as a filly, her high school graduation present from her father. His reward to her for agreeing to finish school before thinking of getting married. Joking to herself she thinks of the horse as her dowry, since not long afterwards her disappointed father said: Well, go away then. Don't come back if you're still going to hang around that conniving womanizing no-good Clyde Barnes. And you might as well take the filly with you. What use have I got for her on a dairy farm if you're not going to be here? And Patience did what he said, risking everything.

When they reach the end of the stable aisle, John MacNeil puts down his black bag on the cement floor and leans his elbow on the open door of the stall, assessing the state of the mare as Clyde continues to rub her down.

"Would you be wanting me to jog her for you, Doctor?" Clyde calls over his shoulder in his imitation of an old Irish horseman well into his cups.

A sour sort of joke. It doesn't need a veterinarian examination to locate which limb is the problem. Patience can see at a glance. In fact, the mare is standing on three legs now, holding the near-hind clear off the ground. The one with the white-stocking. Apart from that, and her white star, she's dark bay. She is obviously in pain. Her eye rolls to watch what's going on behind her. She doesn't believe we're here to help her. Patience is sure it's Clyde's fault the horse won't trust people any more. She used to be so sweet and easy to handle. However, there's no point in being sentimental about horses when you're in the business. You'll only get your feelings hurt, one way or another.

"It looks as if she's jogged enough already for today." John says.

Patience looks away to avoid having to meet John's wry grin under her husband's angry eyes. John MacNeil knows very well what a touchy subject the mare is. Even having a vet in to see the horse is touchy enough. Clyde would never have called him in if it weren't that there's a rich buyer up from the States, and he wanted the horse ready to show the man by the weekend.

Clyde bundles the damp sack in both hands and throws it past John onto the floor of the aisle.

"She's had a lot harder work than I gave her this morning, and been none the worse for it," he says. "She's fit."

He smacks the hard muscles of her haunch for emphasis. The mare's rump quivers under his big hand. Silent suffering. She hates him, Patience thinks, he's so rough. If she weren't so scared of him, she'd let loose, sore leg and all. I should never, never have let that man touch her.

"Let's have her out on the floor," John says.

Small, fair-haired, compact, sometimes he looks so young and worried. But he's the vet now. She's glad he slips right into that tone. Quiet but firm. Otherwise before you know it Clyde will be telling him what's wrong with the mare and what's to be done. Her husband is all heaviness and darkness, stubbornness and anger, beside the small, mild, thoughtful John. Two men could hardly be more different. And yet right now, concentrating on the job as they are, standing close together, they seem more alike, farther from herself than from each other. Men, alien, absorbed in their work, unconsciously or maybe consciously excluding her.

The mare lurches herself around in the stall, head held as high as Clyde's strong hold on her halter will allow, as he turns her. She lowers her nose almost to the floor before daring to clomp awkwardly off the straw bed through the doorway and onto the cement of the aisle. Patience snaps a chain shank onto her halter. The two men move to look at the mare's back legs, while Patience watches, her head close to the mare's, humming softly under her breath.

The other horses in the stable are all standing quietly, subdued, even though it's getting near feeding time. Funny how they can always tell when there's a vet in the stable. But it's not the smell, as some people say. She feels sure of that. Except perhaps at worming time. She looks back at John Macneil who is running his hand over the mare's haunch and stifle and then carefully working down towards the hoof. Soap, car upholstery, rye whisky, cigarette smoke, wool, linen, the sharp male smell. Never anything like medicine. She suddenly becomes conscious of Clyde's eyes, under his dark bushy eyebrows, watching her across the mare's back from where he stands opposite John, as if he can read her mind.

"Is it the hock?" she asks, speaking to Clyde's angry face.

John's voice comes up muffled from where he's stooping to feel the fetlock joint.

"Could be."

John isn't ready to commit himself. He always takes his time. Now he lifts the hoof and tries to draw the leg back. The mare tenses her muscles, tucking it higher under her as if she's coiling to let fly. Clyde's deep voice growls a warning. The tone Patience hates most.

"Don't you dare, you bitch."

It was his roughness, more than his ambition — greed, her father called it — or his playing around, that made her father hate Clyde. Or maybe it was just jealousy, the way a widower father is so often supposed to feel about his daughter. Never come back, he said at first. But lately when their paths occasionally cross, it's Come back any time you want if it doesn't work out with you and Clyde Barnes. Sometimes the big old dairy farm, one sideroad north and two concessions west, an easy ride over graveled roads, seems very near and inviting. But she doubts whether even now her father can accept her as a grown-up person with a life and a will of her own. Maybe it's because things aren't clear enough to herself yet.

John continues to pull the mare's leg back gently.

"Sore," he says, as though excusing the horse.

John doesn't have to be rough, Patience thinks. He gets the job done his own way. Clyde, Stephens the blacksmith, old Sandy MacNeil (the race-horse trainer, John's father) — many of the professional horsemen around the country seem to get so rough, Clyde worst of all. An occupational hazard. Always in a hurry. Never willing to take the time to coax a horse, to be understanding, to go half way. John's different. She enjoys watching him handle a horse. Strange that he doesn't like his job, and keeps saying he wants to get out of it. John has let the leg down and now proceeds to make the mare put her weight on it by lifting up her off-hind.

"There," he says to Clyde, holding the off-hind hoof in his left hand and running the fingers of his right hand over the other leg at the back just above the hock. Clyde pulls her black tail out of the way to see. "I think it's the tendon sheath. Could be just a small tear, but very painful all the same."

He puts down the sound leg and stands back from the horse. Her bay coat is dark with patches of wet sweat at the neck and loins. But she's an animal nobody would be ashamed to own. You didn't have to see her papers to know she's well-bred, worth the fancy price her father paid trying to bribe Patience to stay at home. Small head, good sloping shoulder, short back, tail well set on, clean hocks, lots of bone, open dished feet, a touch of a splint on the near fore but hardly noticeable. A fine top line, and, as Clyde's advertisement in the Horse Chronicle said, a brilliant mover. From her angle, Patience can see the welts from Clyde's stick on both sides. This is the worst ever. He must have really got after her. If Patience does decide to leave him, it will be more because of the way he treats the horses than because of his other women or his treatment of her. But where will she go? Crawl back to her father, apologizing for her mistakes? He'd sooner or later try to bully her and boss her as much in his own way as Clyde does. Besides, she doesn't really regret what she did, and in any case there's no way to undo what's done. Of course there's John but ….

"Were you jumping her?" John asks Clyde as he turns to fish in his medicine bag.

"A little cavaletti work, I'm just starting her over fences," Clyde says. "I told you, she seemed fine," he goes on in an aggrieved and defensive tone, more to Patience than to John, "I didn't notice a thing until I put her back in the stall."

"Sometimes the way," John mutters through lips closed on the cap of a needle he has taken out of his bag.

He fills a syringe from a bottle of Bute. His fingers are quick and sure. The mare is hardly aware of the three sharp knocks on her neck, the third of which sinks the needle into the spot he has swabbed with alcohol. She flares her nostrils as the fluid surges into her neck muscle but Patience, watching her eye carefully for warning signs, sees that there will be no trouble. Patience rubs her velvety nose comfortingly.

"I'm giving her ten c.c.'s now to control the swelling," John says as he fills another syringe, "and I'll tranquillize her to settle her down.

DMSO may be the answer for quick results but …. I don't like to suggest it this soon. Tonight we'll have a better idea where we are. I'll come by about nine."

"OK John, you're the doctor."

Clyde takes the shank from Patience when John is finished, unsnaps it and stands holding the mare by the halter. He seems reluctant to leave it at that, frustrated to think he can make no more progress. John is kneeling by his bag.

"OK," Clyde says again, leading the horse back into the stall, "thanks for coming so soon. We'll see what it looks like tonight."

Even though she knows she can see John again in the stable at nine if she wants to, she can't let him just go away now. Not this afternoon. It would be so bleak.

"Do you want to come over to the house for a coffee before you go?"

Her voice sounds stilted to her own ears. School-marmish in her effort to be normal. She hates playing a role.

"Sure, great," John says, with a glance at his watch. He seems more natural and casual. He snaps his bag shut, and stands up wearily to follow her. The busy vet on his rounds. "You coming, Clyde?"

"Almost feeding time," Clyde says. And then, waving them both away but trying to be more gracious, "I may be in before you go."

She's happy walking down the aisle ahead of John, aware of his eyes on her body, suddenly feeling her sensuous self again, young and attractive and graceful, desirable to at least one not too familiar man, different from the kindly mommy figure she is at the school every morning doing her job. Now the afternoon isn't a total loss. The wanting is almost as good as the having. Cynically you could say it was better. They can sit over coffee and talk and brood for an hour or more. And plan. Plan for another afternoon when she can meet him and they can talk and then be completely together and there'll be no emergencies to stop them doing whatever they want. The dreariness of her life is bearable then.

They sit as they usually do for their occasional times like this, at the old wooden kitchen table where you can see the rutted lane from the barn. John takes her hand in both of his over the table and leans his fair head on it. A few months ago he would have started at once trying to persuade her again to leave Clyde, but they have talked all that out. He has an image of her set up in some apartment in Aurora or Newmarket, some place where he can go and make love or cry or have a meal whenever he needs to. What he should have is a nice town or city girl who will always be available and who will wait patiently for him until he's ready to marry. Certainly she can see no possibility of herself living with John in the present circumstances.

She runs her other hand over his hair and neck. When they're together it seems that he's always the unhappier of the two, the more troubled and lonely. She has to play the comforter, which she loves to do. Is that because it's true, or because she's a woman? Is he really the unhappier, with his domineering old father and his sickly mother, so demanding and depressing lying there all day with her Parkinson's disease or whatever it is? It sometimes seems to Patience that perhaps unhappiness is a way of life for John. He'll always find something hopelessly wrong to keep him like that, never far from despair. She turns her hand palm-upwards to feel his almost boyish cheeks. Neither speaks for a few minutes, and then they sit back and begin to talk quickly about everything and nothing.

"What do you think about the mare?" She asks. "He'll be so mad if she has to be let down for any length of time. After all the work he's been putting into her."

"I treated Jamie Carlson's three-day event horse for a tendon tear, last year, something like this. Dead lame one day and two weeks later he was in the ribbons at Caledon. I wouldn't have believed it."

"Don't you tell that story to Clyde. It's the kind of thing he loves to hear. He's in such a hurry, and he always thinks he knows exactly what he's doing. He'd risk killing the horse to get what he wants."

It's a troubled pleasure to talk to John about Clyde this way, as she often does. There's no one else she can talk to, really. She sums it all up in a sentence.

"You know Clyde. He's convinced there's nothing he can't do by brute force."

John looks at her with his pale agitated face.

"And is he right?" He asks.

She understands exactly what he means but she pretends she doesn't. It hurts too much.

"He's got that little mare so nervous," she goes on, "he can hardly go into the stable without sending her up the wall. He rides her for two hours at a time, brings her back in a white lather. Some horses you just can't treat that way. She's not stubborn, she's wild and scared. If horses could talk …. She needs some tact and understanding. I can't bear to see her standing in the stall, still in a sweat, at ten o'clock at night."

Like last night. She vowed not to say a word about the mare to Clyde. But walking back to the house from the stable Clyde caught up with her and she blurted out her anger. He was ruining the mare. He would break her down grinding away at her like that day after day. It was criminal. She knew the horse better than he did, having raised her from a filly and started her schooling at her father's farm.

"When I schooled her I never had to touch her with the stick," she cried, as he stamped angrily into the house ahead of her.

He turned in the doorway. It was she who always had the words. She was the educated one, the talker. He had left school at fourteen. But sometimes he could say things he really meant.

"You call that schooling a horse? She never did a damn thing for you unless she wanted to. If you don't like my riding her, say so now, once and for all, and take her to hell out of here, the both of you."

Yes, she thought, in the long silence that followed, in the hours of his glowering, yes, some day she would saddle up the mare and ride off into the sunset and leave them all behind her. He didn't say another word on the subject. In fact his dark, tanned face barely changed its fierce look until he switched out the light and turned to her in bed. It was a hot night for so early in the month of June. She lay on her edge of the bed under the single sheet, naked as they both had always slept. He said nothing, but he reached a hand to her thigh. Big, calloused, the fingers spread round her leg. He never changed. The directness, the urgency of his need for a woman — that had thrilled her so much when she first knew him. Sometimes she still reacted, still wanted to be wanted that way. But as often as not if she let herself go he might be after some other woman and she would be left soon to nurse her anger and jealousy. Other times she just couldn't care less.

She lay still. She was thinking of the day to come, the afternoon with John. It was hard for her to cast her mind any further ahead than that. She willed him to take his hand away and go to sleep.

"It's so hot," she whispered to the shadowed ceiling.

The fingers eased their hard grip. The palm grew wet, warm flesh on warm flesh. She could hear his heavy breathing. His sprawling limbs lifted and fell restlessly, heavily, but his hand still lay hot and damp on her thigh. He stretched beside her, stirring and sweating like a big animal.

"When?" he said.

It was almost a groan. He had tried everything since the first months of their marriage when he discovered that wives weren't always available. Insisting. Demanding. Waiting. Taking. And now, it was asking.

"When?" he said again.

"I'm hot. I'm tired. Maybe tomorrow. Tomorrow."

He drew his hand away and slowly turned his broad back to her. She fell asleep still aware of his tensed, heavy, sweating muscles and harsh breathing, mute and helpless for all his strength and his wanting. They hardly spoke again until noon the next day. Coming in to lunch from the school, she found all her beautiful plans spoiled. The mare was lame. Clyde wanted her to telephone John MacNeil, who had always been their vet, keep telephoning till she got him, since Clyde hadn't been able to contact him and now had to go out to the horses. Of course John returned her call as soon as she left her name with his answering service. He was expecting her, but not to be asked to do his job as a veterinarian.

She looks across the kitchen table at John, late into an afternoon that should have been so different. Six afternoons in six months is all they've been able to manage. More would have meant bringing it all into the open, something she doesn't feel ready for, and probably John doesn't either, despite what he says. Whatever Clyde may guess, he'll never talk about anything as vague as a suspicion or feeling. Besides, to talk is to invite discussion of his own behavior.

At times life is miserable for all three of them in their different ways. John because of her, but not just that. She's John's escape, as he is hers. He and his father worked so many years to get him through veterinary college, and then he discovered he hated the job. Loves horses still, but hates the people he deals with and what they do to their horses. The horse world in which he's no longer just a boy, and which he can't accept as an adult, where people will do anything to win or make money. Wonders what the point of all that effort is. Now at the table John's fair complexion is darkened with the thought of what he wants her to tell him right out about last night, and can't ask. They talk on about Clyde and the mare, painful as that subject is to her, because it's less painful than the other unspoken subject.

"Maybe he does know what he's doing with her," John says, wanting her to deny it, no doubt, but trying to sound fair. "He's made a lot of good horses."

It was true, she thinks. Remembering the shows and the buying and selling in the three years of their marriage, and the years she knew and admired him before that, when she was living at home and riding her father's horses at all the shows. Of course she was crazy about him then, despite her father's disapproval, his insistence that she continue in school. Her first lover. Though even then she knew her father was right in one respect. Clyde would reach out for any girl or woman who came near. But how can she be sorry about all that now, whatever the future may bring?

Clyde started out on his own, with nothing, in a tough business. Patience had to give up serious riding and work in town, they needed the money. But his stable is becoming known and he's making money at last.

"The mare is different from any other horse he's had to deal with," she says. "Sooner or later there's a temperament you can't force. He thinks he can dominate them all, and that's not the way it is. She'll beat him, even if she has to break a leg to do it. It makes me want to cry."

John gets up and puts his cup in the sink. As if he can't let her see his face. He looks out the window as he speaks, watching the lane from the stable. She understands the waves of jealousy that roll over him in this house, in Clyde's house, making him clench his fists and sending the flush up the back of his neck.

"Does he still get his own way with you?"

She looks into her cup. What can she say to that? He's such a child. He can't accept the fact that they're living in a grown-up world.

"Does he?" John turns his back to the window and looks down at her. For the third time, in a bitter voice: "Did he last night?"

Quickly she gets up and steps into his arms. Her eyes watch the lane over his shoulder as they hold each other close. "John, don't ask things like that. What's the use? As long as I'm married to him…."

"Christ, Christ." He buries his fair head in her hair, and stands holding her tight for a long while. Then without looking at her he rushes out the door, runs to his car, and spins the wheels up the driveway and away.

She's alone again. But she's getting used to that, whether it's with her kids scattered around her at the school in the mornings or sharing board and bed with Clyde, or having these scenes with John, it makes no difference. She leans her cheek onto the hand that John's gentle fingers had held. For a moment it had been fierce and sad. Now she doesn't mind. It's as if, frustrated by the way things turned out, he had to have his climax another way. It wouldn't be the first time he had it by himself.

She could have said to him, 'Not last night,' but it wouldn't have changed their situation. Such things are nice, but they can't last. There's no future for them, they both know that by now, though he won't admit it. A life with him would be as hopeless as with Clyde, though the opposite. Seeing the two men together beside her mare has made her more clear and firm about it. She lets him go now with hardly more than a sigh, hoping he will come back but not really needing him.

That night she makes an excuse to stay in the house, and hopes Clyde won't bring John back for a coffee or a drink. That will be too awkward. It's late, after ten, before Clyde returns, alone. She's in the bedroom reading, her hair nearly dry after her shower, wearing only an old cotton shirt of Clyde's because of the heat. She puts down the book when he stands in his jeans at the bedroom door, toweling his tanned neck and arms, looking at her body stretched out on the bed.

"How is she?"

"Dead lame," he says. "Does that please you?"

"Don't be stupid. I'm sorry. For her and for you."

She picks up her book and starts to read again. He drops the towel on the floor and comes to stand beside the bed. She doesn't look up, though she can almost feel the heat of his body hovering over her, until he pulls the book out of her hand.

"Today is tomorrow," he says.

She laughs. But he isn't joking. He doesn't even realize how silly it sounds. Last night she said 'tomorrow'. And the night before. And the night before that. It can't be like that any longer. Either she's married to him or she isn't. His bare neck and chest are dripping with water or sweat. He hates talking about things openly. She looks at his face calmly.

"All right then," she says. "Come to bed."

The lights are out. For a long while he lies over her laboring and sweating. He grows more and more violent forcing himself against her stillness until a last convulsion stills him too. He lies on her, sodden and heavy, a seal of sweat holding their bodies together. It's no good for either of them. He has taken, but she has given nothing, and so in the end even he realizes there's nothing he can take. She waits until his breathing quiets, and then she disentangles herself. Soon, without words, they sleep.

In the morning he has left for the barn before she's fully awake. Her body feels alien to her. I can't go on, she thinks, being his woman whenever he has to have me.

Coming home from school at noon, she sits in the car for a few minutes to watch the mare in the small paddock closest to the barn. She might have known Clyde wouldn't let her stand-in, even for the day. He'll try to keep her going. She's moving quietly along the split cedar rails, nibbling the long uncut grass on the verge of the lane, pausing now and then to raise her head and look across the fields where the other horses are turned out. At the walk, at least, she uses all four legs. It isn't impossible. She might come out of it very soon.

She's alone, like me, Patience thinks, as the mare raises her head to gaze off in the distance. Only worse, because for her it has to be that way, whatever she thinks or does. Not really tamed, not really wild, not able to live by herself or take care of herself. A creature waiting to be made into something by people and things that happen to her. Not caring what her life is until somebody someday tries to make her into something she doesn't want. Mute, but there's no point in talking anyway, nothing to be said. I don't want you to give in, little mare, but I guess you've got no other choice as long as you're here. I can't bear to see it, though I know Clyde and all the other professionals would call me sentimental. She slips the car into gear. As she continues on her way along the curving lane to the house, Clyde, with lunge line and lunging whip in hand, comes out of the stable to catch the mare. Tears rush into Patience's eyes so that she can hardly see to drive.

Well, nothing's settled yet, she thinks, sitting for a few minutes by the house before getting out of the car, then drying her cheeks with the backs of her hands. Whether its people or horses you can never be sure how these things will turn out. She begins to hum softly to herself as she walks up the steps of the house. Without knowing when it happened, she has the feeling her mind is made up.

She'll be clear and calm and realistic. Tomorrow she'll saddle up her mare — her dowry — and ride at the walk, or walk beside her if she has to, one side road north and two concessions west to her father's farm. She'll get her father's pick-up truck and come back for her clothes and books. Leave the rest, there isn't that much. Her father wants her to come back and she can be of some help to him there, enough to justify her staying for a while. She doesn't really care anymore what her father thinks about it all. Now, that is, that she understands better how people always think whatever they need to and whatever they want to think. But she can live with him as long as he treats her properly, leaves her personal life alone, and until she can decide where she'll go from there. In this mood it seems she can make her life into anything it should be.

But tomorrow is not today: she concludes her planning with a rush of her old confidence and energy. Today, she thinks, heading for the bathroom to shower, Clyde Barnes is still my chosen husband. It couldn't go on forever, it won't go on. It's really finished already. But even now sometimes, though never for long any more, it's just the way it used to be — both of us feeling the same thing, daytime or in the night, not having to talk about it, not caring then about anything else in the whole world. I'll live out today to the end. Tomorrow …. Tomorrow he'll be free to do whatever he wants. And I really will saddle up the mare and ride off into the sunset.

Naked, showered, drying her hair with a big towel, she stands by the kitchen telephone. She hesitates a moment longer, looking through the window down the lane towards the stable. Then she quickly dials.

"Dad? Can you put up a couple of stray females for a month or two? …. Me …. Me and my mare."

She can tell right away by his laugh that at least she's started off on a new note. A nice beginning.

"Not tonight," she answers into the phone, looking down, testing the youth, the firmness, the shapeliness of her naked body with her eyes. "Tomorrow. Expect us before the sun goes down."

As she hangs up she hears Clyde's footsteps on the graveled lane. She hums to herself, as she begins in her mind to prepare an evening they both will remember as good.

A Very Special Tuesday

It was quite possible for him to look at his own face in the mirror. Or to look at his body in the mirror. Even his naked body. Full length. He was not, after all, a hopeless neurotic. But wasn't it … unnatural? That he found it hard to look at his face in the mirror, and at the same time — full length, naked — his body? This face, so familiar, these eyes. And then to run down the white figure that held it up, the neck with its loosening skin, the shoulders hunching a little (he knew he did that, and from time to time he tried to push them back and stand more upright), the chest a little more concave than ever, hairless, resting on the swelling that he could still suck in if he thought of it. Below that …? Eyes rushed up again to the face. The utter nakedness. It was embarrassing to have this impassive public mask crowning this private … obscenity. Hairy, limp, dangling. Hide the face or cover the body. Don't just show them openly together, as if they belonged to each other in some civilized order of things. Slip on the underwear, stoop precariously, pull one sock up and then the other. Ridiculous sight now, but at least the relationship was clear, the whole picture was on the way to being made acceptable.

"Admiring your muscles, my dear?"

Sal patting his behind, her tanned bare skin flashing past the mirror as she returned open-robed from their bathroom, going to her closet to find her clothes.

"Don't tell me, I'm getting fat and shapeless."

His answer more to himself than to her, as he pretended to be using the mirror to help him button up his shirt and do his tie. Over his shoulder she was not at all fat and shapeless. Knew it. Breasts perhaps a little slack? He wasn't sure. He hadn't a very real sense of standards. The sex symbols in magazines and movies are all of course posed. Mightn't they look like her in private hitching up their panties, bending over to put a leg into their slacks? Other men always praised his wife dressed, in any case. Especially in her tennis dresses, or even rising, dripping, tugging up her straps, from the club swimming pool. Not bad for forty-two, his wife would say to him afterwards, enjoying her triumphs realistically and calmly. Not bad, but then I do try,

This last for his benefit, of course, with a wry glance at his blurring outlines. You married me for my mind, not my beauty, his only reply — a weak joke to escape the reality that he was …. Not getting old, that he could understand, she could tolerate (he was half a dozen years ahead of her), but that he was getting old and didn't seem to give a damn any more. However, she was not the type to worry about it unduly. She was going to manage her own life in her own way, without help or hindrance from him, and even if he did choose to let himself go to seed and fade away.

"Daddy." From down the hall.

He began to hurry. Yes, he'd forgotten it was Tuesday, even since the breakfast table.

"Daddy? Have you forgotten it's Tuesday?"

"Of course he's forgotten it's Tuesday." His wife, already dressed, fetched his jacket from the cupboard and held it for him as he tucked in his shirt, straightened his tie. She smoothed it over his shoulders in a maternal way. Inspected his face, as he did too, in the mirror, catching her eyes, hand covering mouth to stifle his professional-sounding smoker's cough. Double breasted suit, knife-edge crease, polished shoes, a not undistinguished perhaps even craggy face and fashionable graying hair just close enough over the ears. Nothing incongruous, nothing embarrassing. Not a hint of what the decent clothing hid.

He turned away from the mirror, reasonably satisfied. "Start the car, love, I'm coming."

"Snap." That from his daughter Sue, passing by the doorway and glancing in to catch a glimpse of his wife's turtle-neck sweater — green. The girl with her blond hair six inches longer than her mother's, locks never for a moment still around her changeful face and slim shoulders. Her green sweater, the same colour but, unlike his wife's, showing only the smallest of swellings.

"Move," his wife said, pushing him after the girl and down the hall. "I'll get the big monster from the music room." An instrument that size should have wheels.

No time for dawdling over coffee, cigarettes and the newspaper after breakfast Tuesday mornings. His daughter's 'cello lesson at eight downtown, his wife's tennis foursome at the club at eight-thirty, leaving him to do the chauffeuring. Surely not too much to ask, my dear, one day a week? In any case, it gave the girl another chance to practice her driving, and in fact he ended up at the office hardly later than usual, having served the family cause.

Except that, of course, his mind wasn't really given over to his wife or his daughter on Tuesday mornings. This day was (usually, with luck and good management) his own, his little weekly self-indulgence. For several years now his special day. The one that made all the others in the week worthwhile, the dreary round of briefs, reports, consultations, business lunches with friends or colleagues on the other side, a routine ordinarily changeless and unrelieved even by the spurious excitement of court appearances. Not, as he long ago insisted to his partner, that he had any hankering for that side of the law, let's not spoil a perfect relationship. In fact no one could be more understanding than his partner — than his two partners, for that matter, the legal as well as the matrimonial one. Sal gave him every encouragement, whatever private reservations she might have, about his Tuesday ritual. It was one of the few things about his life she really admired, perhaps mainly because she couldn't understand it unless it was something she should admire. And John Rowland made sure that he himself or one of the senior juniors was always on hand, for even the most unexpected crises at Sargent and Rowland's, on Tuesday mornings, so he would be undisturbed for as long as he wanted.

"How am I doing?" Sue murmured as she eased the Olds back out of the double garage and the driveway. She was sitting up as high as she could, holding the wheel tightly with both hands on the top half. Flicking her hair from shoulder to shoulder as she peered back and forth to keep her bearings in the unfamiliar reverse gear.

"Great," he said. He was busy easing off the buckle on the seat belt. The passenger side was always too tight for him. "You might let off the hand brake," he added.

"Sorry, dad."

How casual the young were. So sure of themselves. Ruthlessly independent without even thinking about it. How little they worried about the possibility of doing damage to things — or to people for that matter. She grinned at herself in the rear-view mirror.

"Will I ever learn?"

"You will. Before you get your license."

The fact was, she was already as good as lots of drivers he knew. Better than any other seventeen-year-old, not that he really knew any others. A foreign breed. She was good at everything, of course, music, sports, school-work, acting. John Rowland used to twit him for talking about Sue all the time, nicely though, and without a trace of jealously, despite the fact that his own daughter Elly was only a couple of years or so older and, frankly, not nearly so talented. John Rowland and he had quit comparing notes in detail years ago. It was too embarrassing.

What would Sue Sargent be doing when she was Elly Rowland's age? He found it very hard to imagine. The future seemed a blank. Certainly not like Elly quit school and tramp around the world and work fitfully part-time in her father's office or at other odd jobs. Nice to have Elly around once in a while, everybody agreed, even the secretarial staff at Sargent and Rowland's. But Sue was destined for …. Nothing he could picture seemed to justify that youthful energy and ability. All that he could think of was that sooner or later the bird would fly away somewhere out of his life.

"Got time to come in, Dad?"

They had pulled into an empty space in the Conservatory parking lot, an adequate job of parking. Usually he would help her out with the big black case (his wife had dumped it in the back seat to hurry them on their way) and then ease over into the driver's seat, leaving her to go into the old brick building and meet her teacher by herself. He looked into her bright blue eyes which had caught him in a moment of watchful thoughtfulness, tempting her to ask him for a variation of the routine. He was aware of her young body eager to be off and moving, yet offering to share its morning exuberance with him, maybe drawn to him like air to a vacuum. He hesitated, one hand on the rear door to close it, the other joined with hers on the grip of the big case. He held on and took the weight of the instrument.

"Why not?"

"Great, Dad, you can hear me zap through my new Bach," she laughed, skipping off ahead of him to the back entrance, which was busily opening and shutting for a stream of children and young people, all shapes and sizes, instruments not necessarily matching.

"Just ten minutes," he called after her, as he stepped along as briskly as he could to catch up with her dash through the corridor and up the stairs, struggling and sweating a little to keep the case from banging his knees. His breath shortened quickly as usual.

"Good morning, Mr. Sargent. Hi, Sue."

Donaldi, dark-skinned, tall, lean and energetic in his rumpled corduroy jacket and brown turtleneck, came up behind them as they hesitated at the closed door of Room 231. He fished a key ring from his pocket and swung the door of the little room wide for them. Four wooden chairs and two music stands.

"May I stay a minute?"

"Good," Donaldi's smile and nod generously including father and daughter, his teeth bright and even. A confident thirty-year-old, knowing exactly what he wanted from his pupils, from life probably. "Sue needs an audience."

They've forgotten me, he said to himself only a few minutes later. Sue was sweeping her long elegant wrist across the strings, delicate pale features embowered in strands of her fine fair hair, slim body swaying, eyes half closed, lips parted. Absorbed, trying so hard, a form of ecstasy. Donaldi walked around behind her, hovered over her, stood above and behind, leaned down, tapped her bowed head at the part with a long finger. Largo, largo, please, please, and now again, from the beginning. Fragments, eloquent phrases. Clearly he would never hear the whole thing, all the parts put together, at least not here and today.

Neither looked, as he eased up from his chair and stepped out into the hall, closing the door behind him carefully. He stood for a moment peering back through the small glass rectangle set in the door. Donaldi, a hand on her shoulder, saying something to her with passion, his other hand appealing to her, her flushed face looking up at him and laughing. Body more slender and fragile than ever, it seemed, behind the rich, solid, dark curves of the instrument. These two, strangers to him in their energy, their dedication, their youthfulness, their sense of direction. He turned away wearily and found his route through the muffled cacophony of musical echoes breaking into the corridor from all sides. Fifteen minutes later, the deep tremolos of the 'cello still vibrated in his mind as he entered the underground parking lot of the Centre, perspiration cooled by the fall air through the half-opened window during the drive, and pulled into his reserved space. In the elevator he leaned against the padded wall to catch his breath.

Good morning, good morning. Martha, Roger. How are you, Mrs. Raines? Good day. It is, it is. Problems, John? Good, good. Until tea then? Very good.

The door of his inner sanctum on the sixteenth floor now closed, now safely shut. The phone off-call, the secretarial barriers erected. Tuesday morning was about to begin. His heart beat slowed.

"Tales from a Prairie Youth." The neat pile of typescript was sitting in the middle of his desk where Mrs. Raines had put it as usual last thing before leaving Monday night. The end part of chapter five, this was. First he would reread it, making corrections and changes in careful inked marks in the margins and between the lines, using his treasured old-fashioned pen. Then, putting the pile to one side for re-typing, he would push on with chapter six, writing slowly and meticulously on the lined pages of another of the many black foolscap binders stored in his bottom drawer.

It was all very neat and orderly and systematic. Quite different from his first sporadic attempts to write out of office hours at home or at the cottage, when he was younger and nursed more romantic ideas. How else could he work, after twenty years of the discipline of preparing insurance case briefs? And why shouldn't he build on a hard-won efficiency, just as he could now take advantage of the leisure a successful career earned him. John Rowland had his yacht and his golf, he had his occasional social tennis and his writing. Actually, just as John's yacht was a prized and rather useful embellishment of their firm's prestige, allowing in the season the best of entertainment for out-of-town visitors, so his writing was something of an asset at times. He hated to think of how many complimentary copies of his first book, *Tales from a Prairie Childhood,* John Rowland had proudly handed out to colleagues and clients.

It could have been a humiliating disaster, an embarrassment at least. The laughter of the members of his profession. He had kept his writing a secret from all but a few that first time, until it was at the printers'. However, it turned out that there was nothing to be ashamed of. Nothing to change his life, either. Perhaps what surprised him most was that in the end there was so little really to show for all those secret months of labor. He was, frankly, let down when the publishers, and the reviewers (the modest handful who could be expected to notice a book of this kind), had done their bit. To top it off, now he felt just as uneasy as ever about sitting down to try to follow it with a second work. More so. It got harder instead of easier.

He sat almost motionless at his desk, working his way quickly through the typed sheets. This was less agonizing than having to look at the blank pages of the foolscap folder. He could even pretend he was revising the work of someone else, just as he did a dozen times a week when he looked over the briefs prepared for negotiation or litigation by the firm's juniors.

In a while, inevitably, he faced a blank sheet on the desk in front of him. Procrastinating still longer, he reached to open the pages of *Tales from a Prairie Childhood,* a copy of which he brazenly kept always somewhere on his desk within sight. As he had got into the struggles of the new book 'Youth' he had gradually realized why it was that he had found it possible to write the first book so ... if not easily, at least steadily and, relatively speaking, confidently. It was because that book really dealt with his parents and their generation, not with his own life in any way that touched him closely. And it had a sort of implicit argument, too, an argument which he later recognized he had pursued all through the memoirs of his early life in the small Saskatchewan town of North Bend. The novels and stories by others he had read dealing with small prairie towns had almost all depicted a narrow-minded, repressive establishment group at the center of town life, rebelled against by younger and freer spirits. That's not how he remembered it. His father was the town banker, his uncle the chief barrister and solicitor, his grandfather had owned the biggest store. It was partly to show the color and richness of their lives, yes, the establishment, from the inside and sympathetically, that he had written his book. That was his start in life, and a good one too, not something he mocked or rejected. It was the warmth and variety and subtlety of those days and the people in that town that made the book, as many of his friends said, so highly readable.

The problem was that now he had to leave 'Childhood' behind and get into 'Youth', get into the experiences and the thoughts that had led the way to his becoming Edward Sargent, solicitor, husband, father, comfortably well-off citizen of Toronto, amateur author, an establishment figure himself, no doubt, many would say. It was a broad highway that petered out beneath his feet into construction work, detour signs, gravel and sand piles, excavations, trees and bushes.

This was getting to be embarrassing. Instead of the eight or ten reasonably legible pages he expected to have ready for typing by lunchtime or at least by teatime, he found himself lucky to produce more than two or three each Tuesday without driving himself relentlessly. Mrs. Raines would be wondering what he was doing closeted by himself all those hours. Could she possibly understand that he, famous for his ability to dictate an entire brief without stopping from the merest sketch of a case in his rough notes, might find himself at a loss for words? Might sit, in effect hemming and hawing for minutes, hours at a stretch, might rip a sheet from the folder and dispatch it in an angry ball into the wastepaper basket? It was enough to make you believe in inspiration, or the Muse.

He eased back from his desk and gazed out the window at the geometric glass patterns formed by the tall sweep of the matching tower opposite. For months, years even, everything he looked at had staleness, a tiredness at its heart, as if he had seen it all once and didn't want to see it again. He was embarking on a phase of the memoirs that should have been exciting, fun anyway, 'Youth' was encountering sex for the first time that he could remember. If he could just find some way to suggest delicately what was going on. The tomboy cousin from Regina, he remembered her so well, who caused — and tried rather unsuccessfully to teach him a way to deal with — his first erection, in the high airy attic of the old house on Main Street, North Bend. And the sweet understanding of his mother, who, he realized later, had seen enough to know and had simply turned her back and let them be. A faith in the young, in sex, in life that as a parent now he could more fully appreciate but in fact could hardly fathom.

An image of Donaldi hovering over Sue and her 'cello suddenly flashed through his mind. Completely irrelevant. He shook it off. The young today could take care of themselves. They were so much more sophisticated, not having to pick up the clues on street corners or in the back seats of cars. Sal talked to the girl in terms that startled him, almost embarrassed him. A typical situation last year: the two of them, laughing and joking together the first time Sue went to Donaldi as a music teacher, and her mother had met the man.

"God, he's beautiful," Sal called out from the hallway in answer to his 'how did it go'. Hugging the huge 'cello case to her body in a passionate embrace.

"Daddy," Sue said, trying to pull the case away, "tell her she can't have him, he's mine. I'm the one who has to do the stupid practicing."

"Just keep your pants on, little one, he's much too old for you."

"And he's much too…."

"Don't you dare say that, you little brat, you're speaking to a woman in the prime of her life."

"If I may interrupt this little family quarrel," he had said, his mock disapproval hiding not a little of the real thing, "what are you two talking about?"

Donaldi, they both sighed. The new 'cello teacher. Charming. Gorgeous. All Sue's for the next year, worse luck.

"Well then," he had said finally, as close as he could get to the spirit of the occasion — picking up one of Sal's broken-stringed tennis racquets from where she had leaned it in the corner of the hall and handing it to his wife, "maybe you'd be better off sticking to your own best instrument."

However, they were too cheerful to let him get away with even a hint of sourness. They took hold of him from both sides and began to hug and kiss and tease jealous Father Bear into a better mood. And they succeeded. Nevertheless, how could his daughter know, so early, anything about the power of sex, the extraordinary power, and the complications of it, and the way it could fade and drain away and leave a core of drabness in the oldest and most familiar relationships.

There. He had thought it — there was a kind of pattern. He turned back to the page in front of him. Was that what he was working up to in his laborious chronicle? Is that where the lines that started in childhood and youth were leading irresistibly? Beginning in ineffable innocent gropings towards the heights of first ecstasy and ending in the flat clarity, the level prairie of adult anti-climax? He capped his pen and threw it onto the desk.

There was a soft knock on the paneled door. He looked down at his watch. Ten o'clock already. He leaned his elbows on his desk and allowed himself the indulgence of the heels of his palms deep in his eyes for a moment, while he waited for his secretary to come forward with his morning coffee.

"Good morning, Mr. Sargent."

He glanced up in surprise. Not Mrs. Raines, the homeliest as well as the pleasantest and most competent of secretaries, product of some twelve years of dedication to Sargent and Rowland's business. For a moment he didn't recognize the slender pretty young woman in white blouse and long black skirt and a mass of tightly curled black hair.

"Elly."

He didn't know whether to go on feeling startled and annoyed at a break in routine, or to lapse into a sudden sense of pleasure at the change, which Elly Rowland's quick awkward movements with cup and sugar and cream made it hard to resist.

"Father asked if I would fill in. Mrs. Raines had to go to Oakville, something unexpected. I hope I'm doing it right."

She finished stirring and put the cup and saucer directly in front of him, laughing despite herself, and glancing expectantly into his as yet uncommitted face as she blurted out the rest of her thoughts.

"I really didn't think secretaries did this kind of thing anymore."

"Would it appease your revolutionary ardor — if I made a cup for you?" he said, deciding to enjoy himself after all, and starting to get to his feet.

"Don't you dare," she answered, turning back to the open door. "Father would fire me."

"Well, then, at least bring in a cup for yourself and join me."

"Sure," she said. And was gone, leaving the door ajar.

In a minute she was back, gently pushing the door shut with one foot as she balanced an over-full cup and saucer in both hands. He cleared a place for her on the desk.

"Shit, I'm sorry!" Stooping to put the cup down, she half-tipped it and sent a brown stream across the desk top. Quickly she began mopping what she could with napkins, plucking papers and books out of the way.

"Don't worry."

Their busy hands were colliding and competing until he sat back and watched her finish. She had his handkerchief to wipe the edges of *Tales from a Prairie Childhood.*

"Isn't that awful. I never was much of a waitress."

"You made your point."

"But your beautiful book."

He studied her across the desk. The flush still darkening her cheeks. She knew about the book. Had she read it? He didn't know whether to ask. She seemed content to look candidly back at him in silence with her very large, very dark brown eyes.

"I liked it," she said at last, as if she could read his mind, laying the book down on the desk in front of her. "But it was so sad."

"Sad?" He grinned across at her in disbelief. Everyone said, how funny it was, how charming, how warm.

"Yes, sad. All the good things, all the fun things are in the past, are gone. There's just this lonely voice, sort of nothing-voice, talking about them. Remembering them. They're gone for good, all of them, everything."

Her face darkened as she spoke, as if the vision she had remembered or conjured up was actually going to depress her. Then she shook her mass of black hair and smiled instead. "I don't pretend to be a critic .... It's nice to be able to tell my friends I know a real author."

He couldn't decide how much of her quickly restored good humor and amusement was directed at him. In any case, he didn't find his reaction too unhappy. He rather enjoyed her attention, whether she was laughing at him or not, as she went on. "I guess I shouldn't ask you what you're writing about now. Father said nobody is supposed to know."

He grinned broadly again, and lifted his arms in the air to both sides of the room, grandly. "YOUTH," he said resonantly.

Then he dropped his arms in despondency, with the same touch of self-mocking display. "But it's a subject I find I don't know much about any more. Foreign territory, foreign language."

And then quite seriously. "It's not going all that well at the moment. Anyway, you'll see for yourself. I'll get you to type this for me, please. Or you could leave it for Mrs. Raines."

He handed her the black folder from last Tuesday.

As she took it her lips parted as if she were going to speak. But she kept her silence long enough for him to say impulsively, as the thought popped into his mind, looking at her transparent skin and clear eyes, "How old are you, anyway?"

"How old are *you?*" She folded her arms over the manuscript and gazed back, a half-smile challenging him. It was a deadlock.

A Very Special Tuesday

They had finished their coffees. She was picking up the cups with one hand, holding his writing in the other, and turning to go. He held her up for a moment.

"Come in again. Come in at lunchtime, won't you?"

She was standing at the door, waiting, no surprise on her face, not snapping the fragile link. He plunged on, feeling gauche as a schoolboy.

"If you're free, that is. I'll take you out for a bite. Small return for your help."

His turn for amusement, he ended with a slight ambiguous gesture and a faint nod to his desk top.

She smiled at his little joke, or possibly at his invitation, throwing her answer over her shoulder. "Sure, Mr. Sargent."

Again he had the not unpleasant inkling that he was the one who was providing most of the entertainment between them. After the door shut, he picked up the book and for the next hour or so leafed through its pages, still moist at the edges, without so much as uncapping his pen.

At twelve-thirty he buzzed the receptionist. Left two messages. One for everyone: 'Out to lunch for a couple of hours.' One for John Rowland: 'Gone to dine with a beautiful lady — thanks to you.' That should give John something to think about for a minute, or maybe longer. He didn't know how much Elly told her father about her movements. Certainly Sue thought nothing of skipping around the city without a word to her parents.

Elly came to the door as he finished his call to the receptionist. She was carrying a bulky wool cardigan and a small leather bag. He stood up and buttoned his suit jacket. "Let's go through here," he said, proceeding her to the door that led directly into the hall.

"Your escape hatch," she said. "How convenient."

In the elevator she kept her silence, but leaned against the wall and watched him. "Where are we going?" she asked as they got out on the floor where his car was parked.

He hadn't really thought. He was just drifting along in an uncharacteristically aimless way, now that he was outside the territory governed by his appointments book, like a boy playing hooky. "I don't know. Where would you like to eat?"

She stood by him for a moment as he opened the car door for her.

"Know what I'd really like? A cream bagel and a smoke," she said, looking to the sky and touching her lips with her tongue.

"What?"

In a few minutes by way of an answer, she had navigated him to a delicatessen off Jarvis Street, and they were supplied as she wished with the first part of her order. Then she directed him along the Lake Front road, past the railway yards and the warehouses, until they could see the breakwater and open lake ahead. "Over there, pull onto the side road by the gap in the breakwater. It's nice there."

It had begun to rain, a chill windy rain that spread sheets down the windshield once they parked in the by-road and the wipers stopped, and at times rattled violently on the roof over their heads. It was snug in the car, however, even more so to look over the soaked grass, and out into the lake, where grey waves were sweeping up and splashing high against the breakwater. The eye trying to penetrate through the gap in the breakwater was soon lost in the grey swirl of water and air and rain.

Elly leaned back into her corner of the car and ate her bagel with gusto. When she was finished, she wiped her hands and mouth on a napkin and then took her leather bag onto her lap. "Smoke?" she asked, pulling the makings from the bag.

He looked at her for a moment before he realized what she meant. She had her half-grin on her lips, her watchful brown eyes wide to wait for his reaction. "Why not?" he said.

She finished rolling one, pinched the end and handed it to him. As he waited for her to do the second, he wondered if he should admit he didn't smoke — except of course his usual pack and a half a day. The lake by-road was almost abandoned on a day like this. An occasional car cruising by, though the highway a hundred yards away was streaming with traffic. All perfectly normal. Still, a parked car could attract attention. It would be rather embarrassing to have to explain how he came to be picked up on a possession charge in the company of his partner's daughter less than half his age.

"We're so ... solemn," she said, accepting a light from him. "This will do us good."

"Do you think so?" He inhaled deeply, as she leaned back against the door and watched him closely through the curling smoke.

"I was right," she said. "You're a virgin."

The smoke came from his lungs in a prolonged eruption between a laugh and a coughing fit. He covered his mouth with the back of his hand. "That's the sweetest thing that's been said to me in years," he panted, still struggling for his breath.

Then, despite himself, despite a deep resistance to all this kind of thing that he realized he had never really put to the test, it began to come, it began to inch over him. Calm. Peace. Willingness to accept this moment, however nonsensical.

"You are a very wicked young creature," he said, blowing smoke towards the rear window of the car as he half-turned in the seat to look at her with a new lazy directness. "Corrupting a man old enough to be your father."

"So, do you like it?"

As she asked, she leaned her head back against the side window and shifted her skirted legs up to rest on the dashboard by the steering-wheel. She had kicked off her shoes. His left arm, draped over the steering-wheel, almost by accident allowed his fingers to rest lightly on the soles of her feet. He was in no hurry to answer.

"Yes," he said at last. "I like it."

His hand closed gently over her toes. She turned her head away slowly to look out over her shoulder at the wind-tossed lake. He studied her slender ankles and calves, the smooth firm skin, following their shape where the long skirt was riding up over her knees. *This is crazy.*

"This is crazy," he said, not sure if he was repeating himself. "I haven't sat in a car. By a lake. With a girl. For twenty years."

She turned her large brown eyes towards him slowly again, inhaling deeply. "Do you like it?"

His breath shortened, his heart pounded noisily. "I like it," he mouthed, his face turned up towards the rising smoke.

She leaned forward to put her cigarette butt in the ashtray. Then, reaching down with both hands, she slowly drew her skirt up to her thighs.

"Enough," she said, after what seemed a long while, bending to cover his hand that still held her toes with hers, and then squeezing it for a moment longer. "Too much."

She still studied his face and eyes without moving, then abruptly sat up moving away, and swept her skirt over her knees.

"You had the advantage over me," she said, surveying his rumpled business suit, her arm tentatively reaching towards his waist, then for a moment fingers slipping between the buttons of his shirt to touch his skin with their tips.

He put his hand in turn over hers, breathing deeply, keeping hers captive against him. "I told you. This is crazy," he said once more.

"Who cares?" she answered with a shake of her head, running both hands through her mop of black hair, laughing at the expression on his face. The new nakedness, perhaps. He hardly knew where to look. He could only listen.

"Well, I didn't realize you were such a … such a crazy old man."

Despite himself, despite the flush that he could feel spreading across his face, he joined in her laughter. He hadn't quite decided how much of a fool he was making of himself, or she was making of him, but he didn't mind in the slightest.

She picked up her handbag and proceeded carefully to roll another cigarette. He lit it for her and then accepted it back again, turn for turn, as they sat in silence watching the rain gradually ease until they could see the breakwater's concrete form clearly in the restless grey water. When she finished the cigarette with a last breath, she butted it out and, in a business like way with no further words, did up her seatbelt. He did the same, and started the car.

"It really doesn't make any difference now, does it now?" she asked.

"What?" he said, easing the car towards the entry to the highway. "What doesn't make any difference to what?"

"What you said. That you're old enough to be my father."

He raised his right arm off the steering wheel and pulled her shoulder under it against his chest as he drove along. Huddled together, he thought, like survivors on an ice-flow or river raft. He didn't care a hoot who might see.

"Drop me here at the subway, please. I don't have to go back to Daddy's job this afternoon. I'm heading North with some friends."

He had only a moment to decide whether he was more sorry than relieved.

He pulled up at the curb by the subway station, where they sat smiling silently at each other. In fact, she was almost laughing again. She squeezed his hand and suddenly put her open lips to his cheek. In a moment she was outside on the busy pavement, about to shut the door.

"Maybe I can come in and see you next month when I get back from my trip to France …. Anyway, I'll read your book when it comes out." She turned to go, waving. "Thank you for lunch. So nice. All of this. Goodbye."

He watched her as she darted through the glass doors and the turnstiles and disappeared into the underground.

On his way back to the office, despite himself, he kept shaking his head in disbelief, and chuckling again and again. He could hardly wait to sit down at his desk to squeeze a little more out of what was left of his special Tuesday.

But he was suddenly so tired he could barely steer the car into the Centre parking garage. On the way up in the elevator it seemed the ride was interminable. He leaned against the wall breathing heavily. With a new pain in his chest, he realized. Everything around him seemed to be ascending away from him forever.

Now his whole body felt numb. But he didn't really mind. He was strangely content. What was happening was happening. He didn't mind, whatever it was. He coughed deeply three or four times, more deeply than he ever had before, bowing his head, looking down at his creased trousers and polished shoes.

Breath came more easily when he slid flat onto the floor and stretched his legs in front of him. Then the doors were opening. He lay without struggling. Voices. Faces over him. He couldn't hear what they were saying. Strangers and friends, Mrs. Raines' graying head above him, John Rowland pushing from behind, his mouth open, calling to him. It was embarrassing. It was sad. It was strange. It was crazy. And then suddenly it seemed to be over. The page was completely blank. Now he had to shut his eyes. Whenever he woke up, he would try again to make sense of the whole amazing adventure that he thought 'Youth' must be.

The Last Ride Together

It was just sitting there in the loose straw, very still, with its bright little button eyes staring out at a world it couldn't understand, its wings bedraggled instead of neatly closed or spread wide in the air. Its beak kept opening, but the young girl couldn't hear a sound. When she bent to look more closely, it fluttered a few feet farther into the corner of the shadowy barn loft. Then it was too sick or too exhausted to go any more. She went down on her knees and scooped it up gently in both hands. It was fragile and light, resting without a struggle in the soft loose cage of her fingers. She held it close to her body for a long time.

"Look, Mother," she said later, walking slowly along the aisle to stand inside the stable office door.

Mrs. Clive was at her desk tallying up the accounts of her boarders and her pupils. She was surrounded by chits which she was trying to put into appropriate totals. It was a job she didn't very much enjoy, though she did it conscientiously the last weekend of every month.

"What is it, Alice? You can see I'm busy."

"It's hurt, Mother. It can't fly."

Mrs. Clive put down her pencil, ran both hands through her curly black hair, and stood up with a quick, exasperated movement. Alice stepped back a little from her mother's glare, protectively holding her hands closer to her breast.

"You seem to attract troubles, Alice. What have you found this time?"

Her daughter was almost as tall as she. She had the same alert dark eyes, the same tangle of black hair, showing now to the nape of her neck as she bent over the injured bird.

"I think it's the leg. See, it's sort of bent. Is Dr. Kelty going to be here today?"

"Oh, Alice," her mother said, sitting down in disgust after a glance at the bird, "get that poor creature out of here."

"I thought the vet might be able to fix it."

Alice crouched down in the doorway. She was absorbed in watching the tiny feathered stirrings in her hands. "I would take care of it till it could fly again."

Mrs. Clive had picked up her pencil. She pointed it now impatiently at her daughter.

"Listen to me. Take that bird out to John, right this minute, and tell him to deal with it. You have to learn that there are some things you simply can't do anything about. All you're doing is prolonging its misery. You're too old to play silly games like that."

Standing silent in the doorway, tears rising in the corners of her eyes, looking down at the bird, Alice seemed more like nine or ten than the teenager she was. But her body was beginning to mature. Even now it was a form more like her mother's than like the slender stem she had stayed until her thirteenth birthday a few months ago. She turned without speaking or looking up.

John the stableman was busy elsewhere in the barn, or was supposed to be. He had some quick way with wounded animals that had to be put down, with mice, barn-pigeons, rats, newborn kittens, which Alice had never been able to bring herself to watch. He accepted it as part of his chores. Along with mucking-out the school-horses, mending fences, raking the arena and the yard, filling the feed-bins, watering, putting down the hay, sweeping up, cutting firewood, and the thousand jobs required of the one full-time man in the riding-stable of thirty horses and ponies. Mr. Clive had long been dead and buried, leaving Joan Clive with the whole business to occupy her thoughts. Having so much to do, even more than Mrs. Clive's sharp eye, was what kept John mostly sober most of the time.

"John, Mother says I should ask you to deal with it."

She held her hands out towards him, a reluctant offering, ignoring the middle-aged man and woman in riding clothes who were standing in the open south doorway with him. They were all three watching the horses grazing in the paddock nearest the stable and talking quietly.

"What have you got there, darling?"

John bent his weather-raw face over her hands. She could smell the rich atmosphere of whiskey and manure that always surrounded the wiry old age pensioner. He lifted his shapeless felt hat from his head for a moment with one hand and scratched his bald pate with the other. Then he slipped both hands into his bib overalls and smiled benignly.

"You've got yourself a little birdie, darling. That's nice."

He turned to go on talking to the adults. But she insisted.

"It's hurt. It can't fly."

"Oh, it'll be alright, don't you worry."

John bent over her hands again. His blood-shot eyes were trying to focus. A more concentrated look was beginning to settle on his unshaven jaws when Mrs. Clive's strong impatient voice reached them from the office doorway. Very little ever went on in the stable that her quick dark eyes didn't see.

"John, take that bird out and deal with it, please. It's almost ten o'clock."

John took his hands from his bib-front and without a protest Alice tumbled the bird into them. He shuffled off down the aisle towards the north door, leaving Alice and the middle-aged couple together.

They began talking to her, both at once, before she could escape. Mr. Smith and Mrs. Edwards had come in for lessons every Sunday morning, rain or shine, since Alice could remember. He was short and fat, she was taller and thinner. For Christmas and birthdays they brought her little presents. But they were very boring, both the people and the presents. When her mother was busy, she sometimes made Alice take them out for trail rides through the conservation park instead of herself giving them a lesson in the arena or the paddock.

Now Alice felt claustrophobic with them attentive to her, Mrs. Edwards' large short-sighted eyes, so pale the pupils and the whites almost merged, Mr. Smith's small hazel eyes buried in pouches of loose skin under bushy, sandy eyebrows. Separately the pair looked ridiculous enough in their ill-fitting riding boots and rumpled hacking jackets. Together, posting unevenly around the arena one behind the other or clinging to their martingales on a gallop along the trails, they were twice as silly. And still more so whispering and giggling in the horse stalls or aisles like the girls in Alice's class as they helped each other tack up their horses. But they were always very sweet to Alice, as her mother occasionally reminded her.

"I'm sorry about your little bird," Mrs. Edwards said. "But I guess it's for the best. You wouldn't want it to suffer."

"I was going to look after it," Alice pouted, finding a sympathetic audience at last.

"Try one of these, my dear. They're very special."

Mr. Smith's Scottish burr was always more pronounced when he spoke to Alice. He was the kind of man who just loved children, having none of his own, and his chronically ill wife neither able to bear them nor care for them. He produced a roll of peppermints and let her take two. Mrs. Edwards huddled close to receive hers, as if all three were in a corner of their school playground.

"I think we're going to ride out this morning. Won't that be fun?"

Mrs. Edwards's voice struck that girlish artificial note that infuriated Alice.

"Mother didn't tell me," she said coldly. "I'll have to find out who she wants me to ride."

And she left the pair standing by themselves as she walked down the aisle to the office. She marched in and looked down at her mother seated behind the desk.

"Do I have to go out with Smith and Edwards this morning?"

Her mother's face flushed with anger at first, and then before she spoke her glare softened. She looked at Alice's face, thoughtfully tapping the pencil against her teeth for a moment before answering with unusual mildness.

"I'd like you to, Alice. Take them the long way round by Scadding's. And don't hurry back. You can ride Jason."

That caught Alice by surprise. Jason was her mother's own horse, reserved for very special occasions, usually to be ridden only under supervision. But Alice couldn't allow herself to show too much pleasure.

"Oh alright. But I hope they won't chatter and giggle all the way."

"You behave yourself and don't get smart-alecky."

Her mother picked up a pile of chits and started to add them up again. Then she held Alice in the doorway with a final word.

"Be nice to them, Alice. This will probably be the last time you'll have to take them."

Alice went off to tack up her horse without entirely understanding the words. Smith and Edwards had been fixtures around the stable for years and years and years.

The trees in the conservation park were almost all bare. They trotted through a layer of yellow and brown leaves so thick and drifted the paths had disappeared. Mrs. Clive always allowed Alice to take Smith and Edwards over some of the series of little jumps, fallen logs and brush piles and poles wired between tree-trunks that were scattered through the woods.

"Do you want to jump?" Alice called over her shoulder when she neared the first of them at the trot.

"We're right behind you," Mr. Smith answered. She caught a glimpse of his bushy eyebrows and little moustaches, his strained red face, his dumpy body bouncing precariously on the back of the big slow chestnut school-horse. And farther back, the vague excited face of Mrs. Edwards bent over the neck of the calm old bay ex-hunter. Alice lifted the willing Jason into a brisk canter and skimmed the long serpentine of little jumps, six or eight strides apart, doing the whole line of them without stopping. She halted and turned at the edge of the woods in time to see the others trailing behind her. Mr. Smith lost a stirrup over the last jump, but hung on by the reins. Mrs. Edwards followed blindly, face jutting forward, without ever shifting her stiff perched position over the horse's neck. Alice felt conscience-smitten at having set such a fast pace and given them more than they bargained for. They drew up beside her and began laughing at once like a pair of school-children just off the roller-coaster.

"That was so exciting!" Mrs. Edwards sang out. Perspiration dotted her upper lip. Her pale vague eyes were running.

"Are you alright, my dear?" Mr. Smith panted, putting a hand on Mrs. Edwards' knee.

"Oh yes," she cried, "I enjoyed that so much. That's made my ride."

Jason was up on his toes, his blood aroused a little from the gallop. Alice had her hands full for a few minutes, but she settled him so that her little troop finished the ride, around Scadding's cornfield and back along the edge of the conservation park to the stable, without having to go out on the concession roads, in a safe, sedate trot and walk. Jason's long effortless walk put Alice well ahead out of hearing for the last ten minutes. She was lost in her private thoughts and glad not to have to listen to the laughter and chatter and whispering.

Back at the stable she and John took the three horses to be washed and returned to their stalls until they were needed again, while Mr. Smith and Mrs. Edwards went into the office to talk to Mrs. Clive. They were there for quite a while. Riders for the eleven-thirty group lessons had begun to arrive before they came out.

While they were in with her mother, John congratulated Alice in his comical way on bringing back her pair of riders and horses all in one piece.

"It's always so boring," Alice said.

"Cheer up, my darling, you won't ever have to be doing it again."

Alice looked under Jason's neck, which she was rubbing with a towel, to show her puzzled expression to John.

"That's just what Mother said, I think. How come?"

John was on his way to the tack room but he paused, pushing his old felt hat back from his bald head.

"Did you forget? Mrs. Edwards goes into Hospital for her eye operation next week."

"Ah," Alice said. She vaguely remembered the talk about it now. The thought of Mrs. Edwards' pale watery eyes being operated on, cut into with a knife, sent a shudder down her spine.

"How long will she be gone?"

John put his hat back on his head, and answered quietly and quickly. Mrs. Edwards and Mr. Smith and Alice's mother were just emerging from the stable office.

"Never be back again, so it seems, darling. That's what I've been telling you. Her husband's a weak-hearted old codger, never liked her riding and now won't let her ride again after the operation."

Never? John was gone before Alice could talk about it anymore. She led Jason past the group in the aisle and put him away in his stall. Then she followed John into the tack-room where he was sitting in the corner starting to drink his morning tea. She took her cup and stood at the window overlooking the parking lot. On the far side, under the bare-limbed maple tree, Mr. Smith was leaning down to speak through the car window to Mrs. Edwards who was in the driver's seat of her Toyota. Alice could see Mrs. Edwards' pale vague face turned upward, listening.

"What about Mr. Smith?" Alice asked John over her shoulder without turning her eyes from the window. "Who's he going to ride with now?"

John chuckled into his tea-cup.

"Now that's a darn good question, Alice. I bet you he's wondering that very same thing himself. It's not easy, a man of his age, to find a friend. He was lucky to meet Mrs. Edwards."

"Did he meet her here then?" Alice asked. She couldn't remember that far back. For her they always seemed to be together. She was watching Mrs. Edwards start the car, and Mr. Smith bend closer and closer to her face.

John laughed louder. "Meet her here? Why, he met her here and here's the only place he meets her, the poor devil." He was about to go on, but he caught a glimpse through the open door of Mrs. Clive's form approaching, riding boots and crop, and he ended abruptly.

"His wife and her hubby don't approve of all this riding business, my girl, they just don't approve."

"Alice," Mrs. Clive called through the open tack-room door. "Come and give me a hand with the cavaletti."

"Yes, Mother."

But Alice, before turning away from the window, saw clearly with widening eyes that Mr. Smith's face drew nearer and nearer and then for a moment actually seemed to touch Mrs. Edwards' face through the open window of the car. The Toyota pulled slowly away and the dumpy figure of Mr. Smith stood at the door of his Buick watching it leave.

"Mother," Alice whispered, as they went down the stable aisle together towards the arena door. "Mother. He kissed her. Smith kissed Edwards."

Mrs. Clive slowed her stride. She looked down at her daughter's wide eyes and smiled.

"Not to worry, Alice. They've been good friends for a long time. Now they've had to say goodbye."

Alice half-grinned in return, imitating her mother's expression, uncomprehending, and whispered again, mostly to herself, "But they're so old."

Her mother sent a peal of laughter echoing down the aisle, making John at the other end of the stable look up in surprise. She didn't laugh often. It was a pleasant sound. Mrs. Clive slipped an arm around Alice's shoulder protectively.

"And you're so young, little one. Someday you'll find out for yourself. Nobody's ever too old for kissing."

She tugged the girl's down-turned head against herself for a moment before releasing her as they entered the riding arena side by side.

"Alright, let's go." Mrs. Clive called in her sergeant-major's voice: "Everybody circles to the right and, Trot!"

Winter Wheat

The old man lay still under the heavy quilt. The light from the east window was strong enough to show the worn hardwood floor, but not the ticking clock on the bedside table. All night he had stirred and turned and settled and stirred again, until in the early hours his wife beside him had sat up patiently and offered to get him something more to make him sleep.

"What's the good of it?" He had growled. "There's no medicine to help me. You know that as well as I do." And he had buried his white head in the pillow, holding his stiffened back away from her rounded form and soft hands.

In the long wait till dawn, each lay silent, listening to the sounds of the big, old, half-empty brick farmhouse, drifting in a dark sea of restless, homeless thoughts.

A faint low of a cow to calf sounded from the distant pasture to the west. The water pump started its rhythmic pounding in the basement. He refused to pretend sleep any longer. Pulling away from her hand on his shoulder, he stood up in the cold shadowy room. She moaned through pursed lips as she clambered out from under the quilt and sat with her bare feet on the sheepskin that made a patch of floor on her side of the bed tolerable. She switched on the bedside lamp. His thin wiry body was stooping and stretching as he struggled into his thick clothing.

She sighed heavily.

"Dear, dear, dear, it's only five o'clock. I do wish you could rest. You'll wear yourself out and the day still to come."

He turned on her angrily.

"For God's sake woman, do you think I'm enjoying the game of it? I won't lie around for no purpose. There's things I must do."

His crooked hands wrestled with the buttons on his cuffs. She stepped off the sheepskin and went to button them for him.

"You're not to go out in this raw weather, certainly not until the sun takes the frost off the ground."

"Get on with it," he muttered, shaking the wrist she held in her two hands, and over which she bowed her short-cropped grey-tinged head. "Never mind, never mind." He pulled the second wrist from her grasp and strode to the door.

"At least let me make some breakfast. It's much too dark to go outdoors, you won't even see to put your feet. Such a miserable morning."

She followed him down the hall, her dressing gown trailing as she drew it over her shoulders. He was already at the side door, freeing the bolts.

"Where have you put my crop," he barked over his shoulder. "The cattle will be in the wheat field, I know it for a fact. Three mornings in a row that fool son of yours has forgotten to shut the middle gate. Where's my damned crop?" He ended with a shout.

Her eyes darting in every direction, her lined face flushed, she hurried round the living-room searching the mantelpiece and the hardwood chairs and tables. At the door to the hall again, she looked back along it to see the black hunting-crop hanging from its hook by the side-door, a yard from her husband's hand. His white head came up slowly as he rose from lifting the bottom bolt. His cheeks were scarlet, his eyes closed, his lips twisted in a grimace. He leaned an elbow against the door. She rushed forward to take his arm.

"Come. Come into the kitchen, dear. Please. Come and sit down. There's no need for you to go out anymore. This has got to stop."

His thin body was rigid. Letting her take him down the hall step by step, he opened his eyes, unclenched his teeth.

"It's no use." His voice came from the back of his throat, as if he were choking. "It's no use anymore."

"You have to be patient, take more time, take each day," she said, seating him in his chair by the Franklin stove, where he eased back, filled his lungs, stretched his chest and groaned.

"Patience, patience be damned to hell. Shut up and make the breakfast if you're going to. I've got things that won't wait. I have to go out."

Three hours later, the weak sunshine of late October was glancing across the old man's white head as he dozed in the deep chair by the Franklin stove. His breakfast tea-mug rested in one clenched fist between his legs. His wife, dressed in grey slacks and a heavy grey cardigan, was quietly tidying up the kitchen, with occasional anxious glances over her shoulder at his sleeping shape.

At eight o'clock there was a sudden roar in the distance as the Diesels were started on the construction site half a mile to the south. The old man raised his head, his pale blue eyes opening wide, his arms and legs drawing together as though to protect himself from a blow in the center of his body. His wife dropped the tea-towel in the sink and hurried over to him.

"You left me for a while, dear, you were off in another world. Don't get up. There's no need."

The old man put his hands on the arms of the chair and struggled to his feet.

"I wasn't asleep," he said, "I just closed my eyes for a minute. Get out of the way, you silly woman. I've got to go up to the wheat field and drive the cattle back."

His wife followed him into the hall, her face flushing and paling and flushing again.

"I want to know why you won't let Paul go. You don't have to. It's his responsibility now. I'm sure he'll go back there, he'll see to it as soon as he's finished in the barn."

The old man had already got his sheepskin coat on and was opening the side-door, hunting-crop in his right hand.

"Yes, and the damage will be done by then," he said as he walked out into the chill morning. "The boy is useless. If you want something done properly, you have to do it yourself."

"He's not a boy," she called after him. "Paul is a grown man."

But he didn't look back as he marched like a soldier on parade along the graveled lane to the barn.

At the dog-run he paused to open the hatch and call out his little white terrier. The small body bounced about him on its short legs, senseless with energy, the stubby tail seeming to pull the dog up and down and around as though shaken by an invisible hand. The small sharp teeth showed as he yapped continuously, the staring eyes gleamed.

"Up," the old man ordered, stooping and cradling one arm as he reached the barn door. The dog leaped onto the arm, and settle into the crook against the man's chest.

"What's the matter, Dad, getting tired of the soft life?"

The voice came from above, as he shut the barn door behind him.

"Not a bad morning, for the time of year," the old man said gruffly straight ahead, without stopping to look up at the speaker. He pushed his way along the barn aisle past the pile of hay-bales his stepson was dropping down from the loft trapdoor. He could hear the voice of Sammy, the hired man, echoing from up in the loft behind his stepson. He didn't have to hear the exact words to know the kind of thing he had overheard lots of times. Wouldn't catch me getting out of bed on a frosty morning if I didn't have to. Thinks the barn will fall down if he doesn't keep an eye on it day and night. He'll tan your bottom if you forgot to water the horses last night. Has he got that miserable little rat of a dog with him? Why doesn't he go away to Florida, spend some of that quarter of a million he got for the south fifty?

"Oh, shut up, Sammy. Get back to your wheelbarrow and mind your big mouth."

Paul's laughing voice came down along the aisle before he let the loft trap fall shut.

The old man put his terrier on the floor at the feed-bin, lifted the lid, and fished inside for some dried food. While the terrier gobbled from his bowl on the cement floor, he watched Paul and Sammy stack the hay-bales they had put down and then take their forks out to the cattle-shed.

As they left, the barn door at the end of the aisle opened and a girl's voice called.

"Daddy? Are you there?"

The old man looked up to see the girl's slim silhouette against the morning light from the open door.

"Daddy," she called again, taking a step down the aisle and peering into the relative gloom of the barn.

The old man cleared his throat.

"Your father's at the cattle-shed, Peg."

The girl stooped and put her lunch-pail on the floor beside the door. She walked quickly towards him. Her green ski-jacket was open. She wore high white rubber boots over her green corduroy slacks.

"Granddad, I'm late for the school-bus. Could you please tell Daddy … well tell him that Mommy would like him to call her at the house. She has to go shopping in the city this morning."

The old man opened his coat and fished in his vest pocket as the girl approached.

"And Granddad," she continued, coming to a standstill in front of him now, and imitating a grownup lady's disapproving hands-on-hips manner, "Granddad, that bad little doggie of yours has been after the ducks again."

He leaned back against the feed-bin, his grim face beginning to crease into a smile.

"Now it's not funny, Granddad. He would have killed one if Mommy hadn't come out with the broom. And then he snapped and snarled at her."

She shook her pigtails energetically and glared down at the little terrier who was licking his bowl energetically across the floor.

"He's a mean little dog, that's what he is," she finished, stamping a rubber boot for emphasis.

The old man held up a twisted taffy in red wax paper for her to see.

"And now you're so mad at the two of us, Peg, I'll bet you won't get down on your knees and say pretty please for a taffy."

Her frown changed instantly to a smile and her brown eyes shone.

"I thought you didn't have any more."

"This is the very last one, I just found it in my vest pocket this minute."

He held it high in the air.

"Please," she said, stepping forward and reaching for it.

"Pretty please," he said, raising it higher.

"Please."

She stood up on tip toes and gave a little leap. He brought his arm down and put both hands behind his back, leaning on the feed-bin.

"Oh, Granddad," she cried, flushing with pleasure. Suddenly she threw both arms around his neck and flung herself against him. She reached up with her warm wet lips and kissed the white stubble on his cheek. Her hard little buds pressed on his chest. He slipped his arms around her in a bear hug lifting her off her feet.

"Pretty please," she whispered into his neck.

"There," he said, letting her go free and popping the taffy into her upraised hands.

She turned and raced down the aisle.

"Thank you, thank you, Granddad. But he's still a mean, nasty little dog and I hate him," the call trailing off behind her shape as she disappeared into the sunlight.

He stood looking down the aisle, his hand stroking his vest where the little unformed breasts had pushed at him, until at his feet the terrier's whimpering rose to an impatient whine. Then he took his crop off the feed-bin and walked out into the barnyard.

He headed west through the gate into the center lane. The footing was dry, though the long grasses and rushes on each side were still silvered with frost. To the southeast, far away, the unfinished frames of the new housing development rose beyond the row of trees on the edge of the field. He now habitually looked the other ways, to the north and to the west. Southeast, land he had worried and watched over for years was stripped and bulldozed out of all identity that meant anything to him, even the hills and hollows. It had fetched more money than the crops and cattle of three generations of his family, but he had not had time yet to focus on the figures his wife and stepson kept pointing to in his bankbook.

The terrier yapped in pursuit of some invisible or imaginary creature in the tall grass. The old man yelled twice without effect.

"Come here, you little scamp," he bellowed for the third time, emphasizing his call with a swishing crack from his hunting-crop. The movement of his arm and shoulder seemed to carry further than he intended. He stumbled forward and eased down on one knee with a groan. After barely a moment he rose pushing his crop against the hard ground and staggered forward weakly until he could sink onto the trunk of a large fallen elm tree. He sat still, drawing shallow breaths and peering west beyond the next fence-line, where the ground dipped sharply and then climbed again to the wheat field, from here still out of sight.

Two big swaybacked patchy grey geldings nosed in the brown weeds in the middle of the field to the north across the split-rail fence. Once they had galloped the countryside with the hunt in the fall and summer and pulled the cutter in winter. But now they only picked their half-blind way out from the barn in the morning and back again at nightfall once a day. As he watched, the heavier of the two geldings wheeled ponderously on his haunches and, ears sourly flattened against his head, showed his worn teeth to send off the unbroken chestnut two-year old that came frolicking up too close behind him.

The old man shut his eyes for a moment and drew a few deeper breaths. The terrier circled the log snuffing noisily and then jumped up and tried to climb on his lap. The old man absently drew him close to still the thin-skinned shivering that began from his little paws to his wet nose as soon as he stopped running about. Chill air enveloped them both. There was no heat in the wash of morning light.

The old man ignored the sound of the tractor approaching from the east, until it surprised him by stopping in the field to the south of the lane, across the split-rail fence. He got up at once when he realized his wife had ridden out with Sammy who was now going on, pulling the manure spreader.

"What are you following me around for, woman?"

As she awkwardly climbed the fence he turned his back to her and began stalking off westwards on his way again up the lane. She followed a pace behind.

"Mr. Stanley phoned, dear. He and his wife would like us to drive over for tea today."

The old man shook his white head impatiently and walked on more quickly.

"I can't go. I'm too busy. Go by yourself, I haven't time for that sort of nonsense."

She tried to catch up, reaching to pull on his sleeve.

"But you said you liked Mr. Stanley. You said you thought his sermon was … you said you thought his sermon was more interesting than anything you'd heard since you were a boy. You told me yourself you'd be glad to meet him personally."

He pulled away from her to crack his whip and call the terrier off a new scent. Then he stood to face her in the scrub-lined lane.

"I just finished saying, I haven't got time for that sort of thing. Churches, sermons, you know I'm not interested. Never have been. I only went to church because you nagged and nagged. I only went to shut you up. Now leave me be. I've got work to do."

He shook her restraining hand loose and walked on. She stood calling after him.

"You should be resting. You shouldn't be out here by yourself."

He refused to look back or slow up.

"You're not supposed to be alone." She raised her voice almost to a wail. "It's too cold. Please don't go any farther. Come back."

She waited with eyes filling with tears, facing the chill wind. Then she turned and walked away steadily towards the barn and the houses. The old man was disappearing into the dip when she stopped at the gate into the barnyard, for a moment, to look again. An occasional flake of snow sifted down from the blue-grey sky.

Paul was sweeping the barn aisle. He glanced at her set face and went on with the job.

"He's going all the way up to the wheat field," she said, "what should I do?"

He swept energetically.

"Nothing. There's nothing you can do, Mother. He's too damned stubborn to listen to anyone at the best of times."

She followed his progress up the aisle, talking continually. How happy they had been about the real estate sale that left them the largest part of the farm and no financial worries any more. How pleased his step-father had seemed when Paul graduated from agricultural college and came back to take over the place. How they looked forward to easing up and being able to travel. But now he was so restless, so angry always, so ill. He hardly slept a wink at night. For a week he had vomited blood. He wouldn't listen to the doctors. She couldn't make him keep still and stay in.

"Look, Mother," Paul said at last, taking away the second broom she had begun wielding uselessly, and speaking into her vague, preoccupied face, "he's been doing things his way for over sixty years. You always said you could never make him do anything he didn't want to do. Why don't you just leave him alone? He'll figure it out, I guess."

Her moist eyes focused on him.

"But he shouldn't be back there all by himself. He shouldn't ever be alone …."

"You go on to the house. Make yourself some coffee and forget about him for a while. I'm going to check the fences before noon. If he's not here by then, I'll take the pickup back there and give him a lift home."

They had gone into the barnyard now, and Sammy's tractor was just coming into sight along the curving path through the fields to the southwest. Paul stepped across the rutted barnyard and opened the gate for him.

"I'll talk to you later, Mother, I've got too much to do right now."

She turned to stare at him for a moment, anger sweeping over her face. Then as she walked on past him to the house she patted his arm.

"I know you're trying, Paul," She said. "Young feet and old boots don't fit any better than old feet and new boots."

The old man, picking his way down the center lane through waist-high brown weeds, brome grass and timothy, had reached the field of cattle. He opened the hunting-gate into the well-grazed pasture. The far fence-line was dotted with the white shapes of the prize herd of Charolais. Only an occasional large head rose to gaze at him, jaws chewing without stop, large dark eyes unblinking, mournful. As he and his dog crossed the field, a big-uddered cow lowered her horns and snorted threateningly at the little terrier who dared to yap at her calf. The whole west fence-line, bordering the wheat field, was now visible. It was quite unbroken. The old man walked up to the hunting-gate and leaned on it to look over and beyond, still farther to the west.

The wide expanse there was dished and tilted so that it took the rising sun. The fields around were bare and brown, or tattered with weeds and scrub the cattle wouldn't eat until the autumn forage worsened. But the wheat field itself drew the gaze. There was nothing to match it. It was an unvaried sheet of rich green, a lush carpet inviting the eye irresistibly, but so unmarked as to forbid entry. It held all the soothing, nourishing life the dead, drab autumn countryside lacked. It looked as though it could swallow up all impurities and burn on with the same impassive, constant greenness forever. It was a crop well set to face the winter. Next year there would be a fine harvest of grain.

The old man ran his glance along the cedar rail fence line that ran around the four sides of the field. He had sunk every post and set every rail in place, solidly, five high, over thirty years ago. Some of the rails were bowed, a few broken ones hadn't been replaced, and here and there a post that had never been braced by a steel bar sagged to the west. Plugged and patched as it was, the cattle still respected it. There were years of use left in it yet.

Behind him in the pasture the dingy white cattle grazed silently, ignoring his presence. The little terrier was snarling viciously down a groundhog hole at the edge of the center lane. The old man groaned aloud and turned to go east, back to the barn. Then over his shoulder for a last time he let his eyes scan the whole green carpet of winter wheat tilted upwards to its western boundary. There, as if he were seeing it for the first time, on the upper edge of the sloping field, and spreading on over the whole top of the hill, stood the towering maple-bush. Planted a hundred or more years ago, it had never been given a reason to stop growing and it rose now high in the air like a fortress or cathedral. The giant trees had shed their colors, all except the faded yellows and browns.

It was so unexpected, but there is always the unexpected, the unpredicted. He hadn't been up that far in years, not to stand under the trees, but he remembered the way the fallen leaves within carpeted the spaces beneath the soaring trunks. He lifted the hoop off the gate-post, swung the creaking gate west, and walked through to the green wheat field that led up to the edge of the bush.

Gentle as the slope was, the border of the wheat field was furrowed, and he had to pause several times to catch his breath. The maple-bush seemed to grow richer in color as he neared it, as though he were seeing it in early October or late September, seeing it when its greens were just turning and it was blooming with reds and yellows, a glory to eyes for miles on all sides.

In the lea of the bush, the chill wind died. Now he had reached the point where the rich green of the wheat field stretched eastward, behind and below him, and he was on the fringe of the woods. He went through the last gate and closed it carefully behind him. He was there. A hundred corridors opened in all directions between the tall slender grey trunks as far as his look could travel. Their branches were high, high above, masking the pale sky. He walked forward through the crisp leaves sifting over the ground, otherwise bare except for a little scrub here and there, all that could grow so far below the sky-high network of branches that never let the sunshine reach the ground.

The air was cold and silent, the light a strange, blurred, shimmering, pale yellow. He stumbled over hidden roots and fallen branches, first in one direction, then in another. There had been nothing to do in the maple-bush for years, not since he was a young man, not since the death of his first wife, whose face now floated across his mind, or was it that of his granddaughter, he couldn't be sure. The sap still ran in spring in the veins of the trees, but no one had worked the maple-bush for a generation.

He leaned his white head back and looked up towards the tops of the trees. They were lost high above him in the grayish haze. Then to his silent amazement, the tall motionless tree trunks began to turn slowly round and round and round in an endless procession. Somehow he now felt the deep carpet of leaves under his back. And the icy breath of the ground surprised him seeping up over his body. Still, it seemed safe to close his eyes for a moment with those silent grey pillars above guarding him on all sides.

After a while the little white terrier came scrambling through the crackling paths, his nose tracking the old man's meandering footsteps back and forth. He yapped excitedly when the trace led to the shape stretched out half-buried among the leaves. He nosed at the feet, at the arms, at the chest. Then he sat peering at the white face, his mouth open, panting from his run. Whimpering a little, he lay down a few steps away, his face on his paws, his beady eyes staring. In a few minutes his tense body started to shiver uncontrollably. Abruptly he got up and began to run eastwards as fast as his little legs could carry him. The maple-bush was silent now, except for an occasional leaf or twig falling, and the distant drone of engines.

The Birthday Present

Hilda Dale is standing in the display window of the shop called 'Pants 'N Things,' which she has operated, under one name or another, for fourteen years. It was the only place of its kind in Richmond Hill until the new shopping mall opened recently in the north end. She can see, and can be seen by, George and Harriet de Vries and their teenage daughter, Debbie, who are sitting in their parked Buick Electra having an argument.

"But Mother," Debbie is saying, "If you don't like this place, I don't mind, really I don't, let's go somewhere else."

"Yes, of course," George de Vries insists, slapping the steering wheel with his gloved hand for emphasis, "there are a dozen other places we can go to, all of us together."

Harriet de Vries, sitting in the front seat, her fur collar turned up around her neck, is smiling frostily and refusing to change her mind.

"Absolutely not. Debbie wants to go to 'Pants 'N Things'. It was her very first choice. I personally do *not* wish to go here. But now that we're here, I insist that you take her in, George."

Debbie is used to finding her parents exasperatingly irrational. She knows she won't get an answer now, but she tries for a last time.

"Mother, at least you could tell us *why* you won't come in. It's ridiculous for you to just sit here twiddling your thumbs while we're inside. Besides, I may need your advice."

Harriet de Vries laughs out loud at that.

"My dear, tell me, when is the last time you took my advice about clothes? Don't bother to think," she goes on, as Debbie starts to say something. "Just take your father in there without any further discussion and do whatever you two decide is right."

George de Vries has evidently concluded the argument is lost. He gets angrily out of his side of the car. Debbie shrugs her shoulders, reaches to her mother and kisses her warmly on the cheek. On the sidewalk, before shutting the car door, she leans down and says,

"Tell you what, Mother, I'll stand up there when I've picked out what I want," pointing to the display window where Hilda Dale is pinning a pair of purple slacks, legs spread wide, against a wooden backdrop. "You can go thumbs up or thumbs down. OK?"

"Just buy something nice, darling," Harriet de Vries says coolly, blowing her a kiss, "take your time — and, Happy Birthday."

She switches on the radio and snuggles into the seat, looking straight ahead, ignoring them both, as if she very much prefers to be alone.

George opens the shop door to let Debbie in ahead of him. The little shop seems to be deserted, except for the racks and shelves of modish teenage and young women's clothing it's crammed with. George unbuttons his top-coat and stands against a wall as Debbie plunges into the search with pleased cries.

"Can I help you, sir?"

Hilda Dale has stepped back into the shop from the display window. She's trim and athletic-looking in her brown slacks and brown turtleneck sweater. Her expression is no more or less friendly than that of any middle-aged saleswoman addressing any middle-aged customer. George de Vries and she are prevented from a direct exchange by his daughter who calls from the other side of the shop.

"It's me. I'm the one who's buying," she laughs. "It's my birthday present."

Hilda Dale turns to her, smiling. She makes a little, studied, graceful gesture of delight.

"How very nice. May I ask which one? Your fifteenth?"

The Birthday Present

"Fourteenth. Don't give her ideas," George says, looking at his daughter too. "She's still just a baby, though she may not know it."

Debbie has taken a jump-suit off the rack in front of her, and is holding it against her full-breasted body with one hand, and snugging it into her slender waist with the other. She cocks her blonde head to one side.

"Father, if you're quite finished .... He likes to pretend he's too young to have a grown daughter," Debbie adds for Hilda Dale's benefit.

"Perhaps that *is* a bit old for you," Hilda says, walking closer. She smoothes the collar under Debbie's chin, and glides a hand over her shoulder. "Lovely though, isn't it?" She goes on, turning out of the way to stand side by side with Debbie so George can see. Hilda is more slender than his daughter. "It's her size, too. Would you like to slip it on, dear?"

Debbie lays it on top of the rack.

"Possibly," she says. Her tone makes it clear that she intends to do her own choosing.

Hilda turns and goes away to tidy the items on a rack closer to where George de Vries is standing.

"She'll be a while," George says apologetically, holding his gloves in one hand and slapping them into his other palm. His fondness for the girl is obvious, most of all perhaps in the fact that she seems to lighten his usual solemn public manner.

"That's quite alright. You should enjoy yourselves," Hilda Dale says. Then, with Debbie at the other end of the shop, she adds quietly, not looking up from her work, "She's a lovely girl. You're very lucky."

Clearly it isn't just an ordinary compliment. Hilda Dale recognizes George de Vries as surely as he recognizes her. As Harriet recognized Hilda Dale first, standing there in the display window ten minutes ago. The window of the shop both the de Vries knew existed years ago, under the name of Hilda Dale's Fashions.

Hilda's not saying anything openly, so George doesn't. In fact, what is there to say? George's anger at being forced into this position fades. He stands looking quite calmly at this trim, competent lady in her forties, with her heavy earrings, her long painted fingernails, her mascara-eyes, and the rich musk that surrounds her in an invisible but almost tangible cloud. Hilda's sideways glance at him is just as candid and appraising.

Fifteen years ago her hair was more the color of Debbie's now, golden, honey-colored. Harriet de Vries knew it was dyed blonde right away, but George had never even thought about it. Too naïve and too unobservant of the ways of women. Now there's no question. Hilda Dale isn't trying to make it look natural. It's a deliberate decoration, an artificial platinum color to fit a certain elegance of style. Chosen to go with the clear, bright blue eyes, startling under the plucked, arched eye-brows, which Hilda directs at George now as she says, smiling in a way that's almost mischievous, even mocking:

"How are you, George? It's lovely to see you after all this time."

Not unpleasant shock-waves can be seen to go through George de Vries, but he stands like the rock of Gibraltar. He has his own style, too. Fifteen years ago it wasn't quite as formed, of course, but there was already the reserve, the carefulness, the conservatism that was to develop into the dignity, the stateliness of the most successful senior partner of the most successful senior law firm in the City. Even at Osgoode when he was still a student he had found it difficult to unbend. Rehearsing for the Supreme Court already, his fellow law students would say, but not in an unfriendly tone. They seemed to know that he really wanted to joke and relax like everyone else, but didn't have the knack. Now he's standing rather pompously out of place in his dark coat and business suit, evidently unable to produce the right response. Somehow, his manner and presence which never fail to impress the court, clients and opposing lawyers only seem to amuse Hilda Dale, as indeed they often do his wife. He's saved by his daughter's voice.

"Is it supposed to go this way? Or this way?" Debbie calls, laughing at herself as she whirls a poncho around her shoulders in front of the mirrors at the other end of the shop.

"It doesn't matter," Hilda Dale answers, going to join her, "that's the beauty of these things, dear, you just suit yourself. Whichever way you like best."

The Birthday Present

George appears to be debating with himself whether he can beat a retreat. But then he'll have to sit in the car and talk to his wife. At least, he feels confident now, Hilda Dale won't deliberately embarrass him. It's unexpected, rather flattering in a way that she remembered so quickly. It's different for him — she was something of an occasion — but he was surely just one of many, a long list of men.

He checks the thought, remembering how well that way of putting it to himself fits his wife's ruthless version of the matter. To Harriet, Hilda Dale was a tart, a whore really — no doubt would always be one to her mind. George, watching the heavily-made-up fashion-conscious middle-aged woman move around his daughter's natural, youthful good looks, doesn't know quite what to think, any more now than he knew fifteen years ago, when he met her.

Then — Harriet and he had been married for five years — he hadn't known what to think about anything. Harriet was in the same boat. She had graduated from Trinity College in Art and Archaeology, taken a year to tour Europe, and come back to marry George, whom she'd met at University. His law career was launched by then. They both were thought to have married handsomely, with the approval of all the parents, in-laws and friends. The future seemed to open up with predestined ease and certainty. But he and Harriet, under their busy, smooth, elegant surfaces, were miserable. She was perpetually nervous and ailing, he was bored and depressed, all the more because he knew he was boring. They seemed to have found out all they ever wanted to know about each other.

When are you going to start a family? A friend asked who got a rare glimpse of their problems, after all, that's really what people get married for. Another said: Take a separate holiday, two people shouldn't be living in one another's pockets three hundred and sixty-five days a year.

Both ideas no doubt had merit. But no one in their group took separate holidays. It would look odd. They both felt they loved each other too much to do that kind of thing. Which is also why Harriet only laughed when one of her free-thinking college girl-friends suggested An Affair as the best cure for a lifeless marriage.

They were, and wanted to be, in all respects a traditional married couple. As for children, they had begun to try, but it wasn't quite so simple. They weren't like animals that just go on coupling till they produce. They both tacitly agreed that the sex side of their marriage wasn't the most important, and they both felt, perhaps, that the other rather held back a little. There were so many minor difficulties and awkwardness's and adjustments, even after five years. In any case nothing yet had happened in that line.

When Harriet's mother asked her to spend a few weeks helping her set up a retirement home in Florida, and Harriet and George agreed over a wine-full sentimental dinner for two that she should go, neither of them realized it was to be a turning point in their marriage.

Harriet found George waiting for her at the airport as she expected after nineteen days and nights apart in the month of February. Harriet, naturally fair, tanned quickly, and the stay in Florida was long enough to turn her a rich golden brown. It pleased her in a relaxed way to see the familiar dignified figure of her husband on the other side of the glass doors.

"You're so beautiful," George said, looking at her as if for the first time, after kissing her on both cheeks.

"Wait till you see the rest of it," Harriet murmured, kissing him again, responding to a quality in his attitude which wasn't at all what she had thought of first when she was getting her feelings in order for him as the plane landed.

Their dinner for two at the homecoming was never completed. Half-way through, fortified with a couple of martinis and a few glasses of the airport restaurant's best wine, George started to deliver his news. After a few moments of frozen silence at the first hints of what he had to tell, Harriet said quietly:

"I want to go home."

"Harriet ...."

"Right now."

Got to her feet and walked out, leaving him to mollify the waiters with a sheaf of bills, to pick up the coats and bags from the check-girl, and to run to the elevators after her.

At home there followed days and nights of tears and hysteria, waves swelling and receding and reaching new heights. George, I don't believe it, tell me it isn't true. You couldn't do such a thing. How could you? Why? Who was it? Don't tell me. Don't give me any sordid details. I don't want you to say another word. What did I do wrong? Was it anybody I know? Where? How often? Was it ….? Was it in this house? In our … in our bed? Oh, God.

George had rehearsed the revelation and possible reactions many times in the last few days. The reality was beyond the powers of his imagination, though rather to his surprise Harriet did not fall ill. The anger and grief he was, at last, beginning to endure without wincing. The intervals of icy calm grew more devastating. Evidently it was dawning on him that he had done something irrevocable, that there might be a price to pay.

"That's all I want to hear about it now, George. The details aren't really that important. But I want you to answer one question."

It was three in the morning, three days after she had returned. She'd spent a half-hour in the bathroom washing her face and tidying herself up, one of many such visits in the last few days. Now she seemed as determined and awake as he was exhausted and barely conscious. They lay side by side, fully clothed, on the bed.

"I want to know, George, why you decided to tell me? Why didn't you just keep this sordid little affair to yourself?"

He seemed to rise to the opportunity. His love for her, his remorse, his deep desire to be open with her, his refusal to live a lie. As he reached his most eloquent heights, she suddenly laughed sardonically.

"George de Vries, you … you …. Don't you dare give me that shit."

Harriet never swore. It was like a slap across his face.

"The truth is very simple. I see that now," she went on, "you think you can have your cake and eat it too. You think you can just dump all your guilt into my lap. You've done something dirty and disgusting, you've confessed like a good boy, and now you're pure as a lamb again. Well, I won't have it, George, I won't have it."

She burst abruptly into tears again, face down, sobbing into her pillow. After a long while, she felt him venture to touch her hair with his fingers, her long naturally blonde hair. She didn't pull away, as she'd done before, so he stroked her neck. Her tears eased a little.

He lowered himself beside her, not too close, but close enough to rub her back. If things that he might say ran through his mind, he discarded them all. At last, pulling himself closer, he drew one leg against her and tightened his arm across her back.

"I'm so very sorry, my darling," he moaned into her ear. "Please forgive me."

"Shut up," she said fiercely, turning her face away from him on the pillow. "What else can I do? Leave you? Because of that woman?" Then, after a long silence, just as fiercely: "Love me."

It was a command. With a strangely detached but passionate, even greedy deliberation, he undressed her prone form, revealing the white stripes left by her bikini which emphasized the darkness of her tan, as if she were a woman he had never seen naked or touched before. He took off his own clothes. He lay over her back and rode her newly violent body until they both collapsed into exhausted sleep. They had never been like that together before. It was strange, maybe even perverse, certainly more than a little frightening for both of them.

All that was before Harriet had even heard about the money, as she did a day or two later.

"You gave that woman five thousand dollars?"

Harriet's capacity for outraged disbelief was stretched to the limits.

"I told you, not gave, loaned."

Again the sardonic laugh. This new note from Harriet in her attitude towards George was becoming a permanent part of their communication with each other, as if his weaknesses were never entirely out of her mind. As if she had seen through him once and for all. The money George loaned to Hilda Dale, to add to her own savings and help her open a small clothing store, was the subject of thinly veiled sarcasm and oblique jibes off and on for the three years George's bank account received the repayment cheques — which he stubbornly reported to his wife every time.

The money part was the immediate reason for Harriet's going to see Hilda Dale — or more exactly, going to look at her without being seen — in the Eaton's women's fashion department where George had first met her.

"This I have to see for myself," Harriet cried in bitter mock-enthusiasm. "A five thousand dollar whore!"

There was nothing he could do about it. George had to describe Hilda Dale and say where she was likely to be found, so that Harriet could go down to the store and identify her, gaze on her, secretly heap hatred and contempt on her, no doubt.

"Don't worry, George, I have no intention of speaking to her," she said, giving the impression that contamination of the worst sort would result. And when she had done it, finally, and returned, Harriet summed it all up from her point of view.

"That woman's obviously a tart. You can see that at a glance. A dyed and painted prostitute. Hardly in the five thousand dollar range. Well, you've had your fun and she's got her money. You and I are going to have to live with this forever. But now please, please, let's not talk about it ever again."

She rushed off into the bedroom for what might well have been her last cry because of Hilda Dale. In the space of a week her tentative, pliant nature seemed to have changed into flexible steel.

Now as George watches Hilda help his daughter at the mirrors see herself in a pair of slacks she's trying on, he realizes just how unfaithful he has been to Harriet. Not that he has deceived her ever again, with Hilda or any other woman. Fear alone would have been enough to keep him from that. But to him Hilda Dale was never — could never be — the contemptible creature Harriet said she was. For Harriet to know and understand that would, presumably, have made the woman all the more hateful.

Of course all that Hilda Dale knew about Harriet was what George had told her. There was never any triumphing over the cheated wife, he was sure. More a kind of detached interest, as if Hilda knew all too well what it was like on the other side. The interest began when George first went to Eaton's to buy a present for his wife's return. He might have gone to a more exclusive shop, but those places made him all the more stiff and pompous and he found it hard to discover, let alone assert, his real wishes. Hilda Dale seemed to have the key to his self-protective façade.

"Can I help you, sir?" A slender blonde woman about Harriet's age. More conspicuous made-up, more obviously wanting to appear attractive to men, but that itself was rather reassuring.

"Yes, well, I wanted to find something in the, ah, dressing-gown line … something …."

"Well, let's go and see what there is," the woman said, and in a moment was holding samples against herself, one after the other in rapid succession, with a charming sense of the fun it was, perhaps even a little mischievousness at modeling on behalf of a wife who, by now she had discovered, had only in fact just left the country.

George had never picked up a woman in his life. He didn't know how. It never occurred to him it could be so easy. There was a visible rise of energy and daring in his rather stodgy manner. He had been bored and depressed. Now before he knew it, almost, he was taking Hilda Dale to lunch, exchanging private histories, views on marriage, hopes for the future, and inevitably arranging for dinner a day later. Not a dinner at some remote safe restaurant, either, followed by a night in an anonymous motel room, which he supposed you would do with somebody you picked up. Something more personal and more rash and risky. Even more uncharacteristic of George de Vries. She would come to his house. Cook him a steak. He drew the curtain and hoped there would be no awkward visits or phone calls. Once she was in the door, it all seemed so easy again. She wanted to see the house after dinner. They walked upstairs with full glasses of wine.

"So this is where you do your work at home," she cried with pleasure, as he opened the door to his study, with its imposing rows of books and its big mahogany desk and his lounging gown hanging over the chair. Hilda picked up the gown and tossed it across the arm with which she held her wine glass. With the other she mimed the action of taking off a jacket. It was at once comical, a caricature of his dignified bearing, and seductive.

"The distinguished barrister has work to do this evening," she intoned in a parody of the George de Vries brand of formality. "The distinguished barrister dons his smoking jacket."

Adroitly Hilda slid the gown over her shoulders, freeing her long blonde hair with a flourish, her slender body half-shrouded and half-shown in the folds.

"The distinguished barrister takes his place at his desk," she chanted, easing herself onto the chair, and striking a studious pose over a large law book. "The distinguished barrister must not be disturbed until dawn."

Then with a laugh she flung the gown onto the floor and skipped into the next room. Which turned out to be the bedroom, and the tour ended there for now.

"Darling," she said much later, looking up with wide startled blue eyes, from the pillows and her nest of hair, as he lay over her naked body, "I almost didn't make it."

Then she pulled him down and kissed his mouth in a display of gratitude. This was a language he had never heard, could hardly even understand. He lay in a warm daze. Somehow she flattered him and challenged him at the same time, with her expectations, with her evident pleasure and satisfaction, with her easy, candid ways. Even her nakedness was different, so natural and yet so conscious of its provocation. George de Vries had never before felt so happy, and also so pleased with himself, in bed. Of course, he was the one who was truly grateful. And so far he hadn't even begun to have a guilty conscience.

Two days before Harriet was due to return, George and Hilda knew that the moral holiday was over. For a while George had vaguely thought that he might try to continue the connection with Hilda Dale as a business relationship. It was she who had been more anxious than he that his proposal of a loan be put on a sound legal basis. And after all, he had a fair number of small and large investments on the go, though nothing quite as bizarre and hard to explain as a five thousand dollar loan at seven and a half per cent for three years to a women's fashion store proprietor. He was sitting across from Hilda at dinner in her little Willowdale house — earned, as she put it wryly, by seven years' hard labor in the service of her long divorced husband, an experience she wouldn't discuss except to say, with steely finality, she would never marry again, never let a man have the power to do that to her again. George discovered that Hilda knew the end of their affair had come before he tried to put it in words.

"Go home, get the house ready for your wife, darling," she said, tapping his hand with her coffee spoon, "and don't worry about me. I've had a lovely couple of weeks. You've been very generous, too. Now I can get started on my own, which I never could have done without your help. So you see, you've changed my life. I'll manage very well and yes …" cutting him off as he tried to interrupt, "you'll manage too. In a little while it will be just a nice memory."

That was the last communication he had with her, except for the bank transfers that came promptly, automatically, into his credit every quarter for three years, perhaps a little to his guilty and secret surprise. Although both the de Vries knew she had located somewhere in Richmond Hill, from the cheques coming out of the Hilda Dale Fashions account in that town, George had long ago suppressed his awareness of her existence and assumed Harriet had done so too, even when they bought an estate north of Toronto and drove through the town frequently on their way to and from the country.

And even when Debbie brought them to the shop to buy her fourteenth birthday present, the thought evidently didn't occur to either of them. It was only when they were parked out in front and were about to get out of the car that Harriet suddenly balked. Then George caught sight of what Harriet had seen — Hilda Dale, fifteen years older but still recognizable, with a hint or two to help — standing in the display window of 'Pants 'N Things'.

Dismay ran through his bones, dim vibrations of that old dread that caught up with him when long ago he realized he risked losing Harriet. Now, not in the least wanting it or intending it, he is put in this ridiculously compromising position. But he can hardly be angry with Hilda Dale. She has been, is now, a paragon of discretion. She waits until Debbie is back in the changing room to speak to George again.

"What do you think of it?" she asks in a low voice across several racks of clothing. She makes a light, gay, sweeping gesture around the place rather grandly with her arms that is strangely familiar to him.

He folds his arms, smiles in return, and surveys the neat little shop with fresh eyes.

"I'm really not much of a judge, Hilda. But I do like it."

"I'm glad," she says, her face lighting up. "You see, you've got your baby and this shop is my baby. In fact, I think they're just about the same age, too, aren't they?" She adds with a laugh, as she sees Debbie come out of the changing room in a pair of bib-fronted slacks with an embroidered jacket to match.

"Don't despair, Dad, I'm sure this is it, what do you think? Shall I show it to Mom?"

"I wouldn't," George says quickly. "If you like it, great. I think it's beautiful. I'll go and tell your mother we're nearly finished."

He pulls a cheque-book and pen from his pocket, rapidly signs a blank cheque, and holds it out for Hilda Dale to take. "Thank you so much for your help," he says, looking again into Hilda Dale's disconcerting clear blue eyes.

"Why thank you, sir," she answers, with a bright smile and a hint of playfulness in the gracious movement of her hands, "I'm so glad to be able to help you celebrate."

When George opens the car door, Harriet's face is hidden in the collar of her fur coat.

"Debbie'll be along in a minute," he says gruffly, turning the key and starting the car. Then he speaks his bottled-up anger to her muffled face. "Why did you make me go in there? Why dig up the past?"

At last Harriet moves around to look at him, and she can't avoid letting him see she's crying. She hasn't cried in front of him for years. His face shows his sense of dread reviving instantly. "The past?" she whispers in an anguished tone. "Can't you ever understand? There is no past. It's as alive to me now, right this minute, as it ever was. That woman ...."

Torn between anger and awakened remorse, he lashes out desperately:

"Don't call her 'that woman'. She's … she's a very nice person. The truth is, I liked her then and I liked her just now too."

Harriet's face distorts in pain.

"You stupid man, do you think I don't know all that?" She plunges her sobbing face into her hands.

Five minutes later, her eyes are dry and she is allowing George to kiss her gently on the lips when Debbie opens the passenger side door abruptly and tosses her parcel into the back seat.

"Aren't you two a bit old for that kind of thing?" she asks jauntily as she pushes in behind her mother and shuts the door. "Hey," she calls out exuberantly to the roof of the car, letting her blond hair fall over the back of the seat, "that was fun, thanks so much — what are we going to do to cap this on my birthday, Mom?"

"Personally I think that should be quite enough for one day, my dear, unless your father has something else in mind," Harriet de Vries says drily, her face averted from her daughter's cheerful glance. She doesn't wish to be questioned about her feelings, which she can hardly understand herself, and which in any case would probably be a foreign language to Debbie and her generation.

Putting a firm gloved hand on George's thigh, she directs her eyes at his familiar, dignified profile as he drives carefully out into the traffic, and heads homewards.

A Shaggy Dog Story

("A humorous anecdote about a shaggy dog,
a story with a surprise ending
Involving ludicrously unreal or irrational behavior")

One of my best friends happens to be — as many people of my generation still put it — homosexual. Lots don't know, even some who think they know him quite well. He teaches at the University, as I do, but for the sake of his privacy I'd better not mention his department. Though perhaps it doesn't really matter now, considering the way his situation has developed. And after all, this *is* the 1960s, when many think we're entering a new era of acceptance.

I will describe him, however. Nobody pays attention to the descriptive parts of stories anyway. And even if they do, it's almost impossible to get an identification of a person through words alone, no matter how accurate or eloquent, or how memorable the person being described.

My friend doesn't fit any of the crude caricatures. He's a tall, angular man in his mid-thirties with a weathered face and quick, alert eyes that look at you squarely and that you aren't likely to forget easily. Many a woman, single or married, young or old, has experienced a missed heart-beat at the first sight of him striding down the street or standing in the corner of a crowded cocktail party. That serious, rather sorrowful expression on his face in repose, alternating with sudden vivid smiles as if lit by a strobe light. At one time he was quite used to well-meaning acquaintances, and particularly the wives, trying to pair him up with deserving women. Even now, although he's basically a non-social rather shy man, he will accept being the decorative eligible bachelor at theatre-parties and dinners and so on. Not because, I know for a fact, he has any latent hankerings for heterosexual or playboy life, but because he has a dread of being cut off entirely from what even now he still takes to be the more normal range of human experience.

I respect his motives, if not his judgment. Personally I think he puts up with a lot of boring involvements for that rather questionable reason. We have lunch together in term time once or twice a week, and I often make the point to him, at least indirectly, without much effect. I have the feeling, though, that after his rustic weekend with the Sloans, he was more inclined to see things my way. In truth, it's obvious he was. Even by the following Thursday, the only day when we could get together to compare notes, he hadn't quite recovered from that weekend fiasco.

I knew well ahead of time that my friend — John, we'll call him in this story — John was going out to the Sloans' farm for a weekend visit. We talked about it over another of our lunches, a few days beforehand. Having been there myself a few times years ago, I thought I knew what to expect, so I did express a bit of mild astonishment, over our glass of wine and omelet aux fines herbes, that he'd got himself trapped into accepting that invitation. However, he claimed to be looking forward to it. So I said, lifting my glass in a toast across the table, "Good luck, dear boy. Tell me all about it next week."

It rather amused me to think of my friend John savoring the delights of nature and the country life with that dull, square family, the Sloans, and their set. John is even more city-bound than I am. I was sure he'd get a headache without his usual atmosphere of car exhausts and tobacco smoke. Fresh air would make his nose run, as it does mine. He would go into culture shock as I do anywhere that's more than five minutes by cab from a bar and a theatre. As for conversation, well the mind boggled at the prospect of such rustic delights after sunset. I remember the Sloans at home all too well. In vivid detail.

There were potential hazards of the worst kind, but I didn't feel I could go into them at that time, even if in fact he was about to face them.

So it didn't surprise me all that much to see John looking a little haggard when we settled down at the Café Dauphin on College Street the next Thursday, as pre-arranged, to a lobster salad and a post-mortem.

Of course, I was forewarned to expect the worst, after the enigmatic phone call I'd got from him on Sunday morning — long distance and collect — when he was supposed to be still enjoying the delightful weekend in question.

"You could use something a little stronger," I suggested, inspecting his wind-burned nose and tired eyes over my glass of Bordeaux.

I know that face so well. I longed to find a way to cheer it up. But then, all of a sudden, his expression was lit by one of his quick carefree grins that make him seem for moments ten or fifteen years younger than he is, just like a boy's. Clearly his powers of recovery hadn't been permanently impaired. Far from it. He was eager to unburden himself to a friend who would appreciate his ordeal.

"My dear man," he said, fixing me with his candid eyes, "let's face it, you're quite right — life in the country is not all that it's cracked up to be."

He then proceeded to grace the lunch hour as only he can do, recounting the tale of his weekend with the Sloans in full color down to the last bizarre detail. As he talked, he aroused so many memories of my own experience. But it was obvious that, however unsuccessfully, he'd worked far harder than I would have done to seem normal and make it work.

The Sloan place is a century farm a few miles west of Newmarket, which is a little nothing-place thirty miles north of Toronto. The estate has been in the Sloan family for five generations, but the present Edgar Sloan, like his father before him, uses it really as a holiday home only. The actual farming operations, planting things in the ground, keeping animals, or whatever (I've no idea, really) don't amount to much, I gather. The hired man and his wife do most of it, except for some amateur help from the Sloans, and of course from their unfortunate guests when they're around.

The drive north is about an hour and half, depending on the weather conditions, and it's probably pleasant enough if you enjoy that kind of thing, rural roads, forests, hills, farm-houses, barns and so on. Personally, when I've seen one old homestead looming romantically on the horizon I've seen them all. The Sloans and their twelve-year-old daughter might have driven John out with them from the City on Friday afternoon, but he had a cocktail party to go to first. So they agreed to pick him up at the Newmarket GO Station at 9 o'clock. John, of course, doesn't own a car. In the City he prefers to walk or take a cab, as I do myself.

Once you leave the lights and noise of the Newmarket station and head west along Highway 9, you're in a different world. Edgar Sloan, beside you in the front seat of his Volvo, is a comfortable, solid man who has been doing comfortable solid administrative work for the University for twenty years, and he smokes a pipe and doesn't say much. "Nice to have aboard, John. Hope you'll like the old homestead." That sort of thing. You can't not like the man for his simplicity. And John, well, you must understand that he is courtesy itself. "Thank you, Ed, I'm sure I will. But you realize, don't you, I'm strictly a city-boy, born and bred. I wouldn't know a cow from a camel." "Never mind, John, by Monday we'll have made a farmer out of you."

As I remember that jaunt, the farther you get from the bus depot, the darker and more depressing it seems, out there in the country. Soon you're off the four lane highway with its dwindling street-lights, and you go north onto a gravel road with nothing but occasional rural mail-boxes here and there in the growing darkness, and then an even rougher, bumpier, narrower road that goes on forever into nowhere and finally you turn up a one-car winding driveway towards a faintly lit sprawling two-story redbrick farmhouse in a clump of tall black trees. Silence, when the car pulls up in front of the indeterminate dark shape of the house, except for a dog barking somewhere and you hope he's chained up though he sounds safely far away.

Darkness, and all those queer, horrible smells in the autumn night. Sweet civilization, where are you? It sends a shudder down my spine to think of being that distant from it.

But then, of course, the door of the house springs open, and Mrs. Sloan, Joan Sloan, a plump friendly figure in her late forties or early fifties, a womanly woman, stands in the light of the hallway and the porch, calling out her greetings, a little more heartily and less decorously than you might have heard her doing at the entrance to her Dunvegan Street stone house in the City.

In a few minutes she has John sitting in front of the fireplace with a glass of scotch, while her husband takes his bag up the wooden staircase off the main entrance and along the upstairs hall to the guest bedroom. The young Sloan girl, Lucy, is supposed to be already in bed and sound asleep, ten o'clock being late by farm-time, you have to realize.

"It makes a nice change from the City, doesn't it?" Mrs. Sloan says, answering John's first compliments about the house.

He would have no difficulty saying good things about the cozy living room with its stone fireplace, its hardwood floors covered in a shag rug, its old hunting prints hanging on the walls, and its deep comfortable chairs and sofa. Just the kind of taste you would expect from the Sloans, in fact.

"We try to keep everything here simple and natural, as it's been for the last hundred years," Joan Sloan likes to say.

With her plump cheeks, her hair done in a bun, her long wool skirt, Mrs. Sloan is herself a picture of those plain virtues, exuding decency and good-natured warmth. She pushes the scotch, the coffee, the biscuits and cheese, whatever will please the guest, and quaffs generously to set a good example. Sloan comes back in to puff at his pipe in his favorite chair, filling the role of the country squire to perfection as the conversation turns naturally to crops and weather.

John is feeling comfortably groggy after his conviviality earlier in the evening, the bus and car ride, and now further hearty drinks and chat in front of a warm fire. He is keeping his eyes open with difficulty, although Mrs. Sloan seems to be getting livelier, when the clock in the corner chimes the notes for eleven. Just then he hears a throaty yowling at his feet, and is startled to his senses as his hostess cries out.

"Oh dear! Tabby's woken up."

Suddenly, hard upon the animal sounds, a grey shape thrusts itself half upwards from the rug onto John's lap, and drags the other half up with its claws. John finds himself looking down into a snarling be-whispered feline face with fierce green eyes.

"Sorry about that, John," Sloan says genially, blowing a billow of smoke to the ceiling. "She's not fit for human company right now. Just throw her onto the floor."

Gingerly John lifts the long, now limp, clinging, furry shape, hands under the front legs, and lets if slip onto the rug. It falls floppily between his feet and stretches straight out, its head twisting around to look back up at John, and from its pearly-toothed mouth comes an ear-ringing moan of anguish. The sound and the spectacle horrify him.

"Good God," he groans, "I've broken its back."

He hears Sloan chuckle for some reason, but he leans forward nervously to lay a hand on the dipped section of the animal's spine. At his touch it scrabbles its haunches upwards against his hand, its hind legs pushing it forward a foot or two, lifting its back and tail higher and yowling on, looking around with its fierce eyes half-closed.

Sloan calmly lays his pipe down and walks over.

"Not too many people nowadays have cats around the house if they're not spayed," he says, more proudly than apologetically, stooping to pick Tabby up.

He returns to his chair, stuffs the cat's now will-less rag-doll body under one elbow, its head buried in his armpit, its rump quivering upwards on his lap, and begins to smoke again contentedly.

"Poor little thing," Mrs. Sloan says, cooing across the room. Then, smiling at John: "She'll be all right again in a few days — as long as we don't let her get out to the toms."

The moans of the cat could still be heard, muffled by Sloan's heavy cardigan, until they gradually dwindle into silence.

Half an hour later, lights out, buried deep in the four-poster guest room bed on the second floor, John is trying to resign himself to the absence of the comforting hum of streets and traffic and normal people going about their business. Tabby's strange tormented yowling has ceased to echo along the downstairs hallway and up the staircase. The faint musical sounds from what he took to be a player in Lucy Sloan's bedroom next door have faded into silence. They'd intrigued and reassured him for the first fifteen minutes of restlessness, as if they were the signal from some neighboring prison cell, though the music itself blended all too well with the agonizing of the cat. By an effort of will John is about to go to sleep, so he can wake up early and begin to enjoy his weekend of normal country living.

Next morning, after tossing much of the night, John wakes from a belated deep sleep to hear Mrs. Sloan's cheerful call from outside the door at the agreed-upon hour, seven-thirty.

"Are you decent, John?"

Looking freshly-scrubbed and bright, in well-filled slacks and sweater, she presents his prostrate form shrinking under the covers with a cup of tea and leaves him to prepare for the first day ahead. He sniffs it, takes a sip, and in disgust puts the cup on the bedside table.

An hour later John is walking beside Sloan into the brisk October morning, a touch of rime on the ground, in a pair of Sloan's gumboots, intending to head out towards the back fifty and the cattle-pond. He's unusually weighted-down with pickings from a three-course breakfast, instead of his customary black coffee and dry toast and a cigarette. How could he refuse bacon and eggs, the pig having been slaughtered right here on the farm this fall, and the eggs having come out of the laying apparatus of hens that can be seen at this very moment scratching in the weeds in the poultry yard?

Smith is explaining the intricacies of cattle-breeding to John as they go through the gates of the barnyard. A chunky, well-developed adolescent female is in with the chickens, and she waves over the fence at them.

"Lucy, meet John," her father calls out to her.

She looks like the type who would be up and breakfasted long before any guests. She waves again, and they continue on their way.

"She loves the farm," Sloan says with obvious satisfaction. "I think it's such a good atmosphere for a child to grow up in."

"I'm sure you're right," John murmurs, trying to avoid an obstacle course on the path by the gate. Large, brown, oozing omelets, which he takes to be signs of the recent presence of real cows. Sloan seems to be able to miss miring his feet without once looking down, but instead walking on, pointing off across the fields with his walking stick, and talking continually about the pleasures of farm life, his ruddy face aglow.

They go up a small incline through knee-high browning grass. At the top they pause before descending the long slope on the other side that leads to the cattle-pond. Around it are shapes of cattle drinking or grazing. The pond is an uninviting shallow, muddy-brown oval. The weedy field is full of a certain faded yellow flower that sends a little tingle up John's nostrils. It's either goldenrod or ragweed, take your pick. If John was as allergic to ragweed as I am, he wouldn't have had any trouble identifying which it was. But he tells me he has only occasional sympathetic bouts, not the real thing. Or perhaps he hasn't had the opportunity of enough exposure to find out for sure. Personally, I never stray far from the comfortable reach of an air-conditioning unit from the month of August until October's frost.

The brown and white shapes of the cattle get bigger as John and his host go down the hill and approach them. John still hasn't quite understood Sloan's explanation of what it is they're there to do. Something about picking out the heifers that are in season and having them bred if they're old enough and ready, whatever a heifer is, and re-breeding some older cows. The two men stop a hundred feet away to watch the cattle again, John a few safe steps behind Sloan.

"Are they at all ...." John starts to ask, trying to sound casual, "are they at all...unpredictable?"

Sloan turns to him with a smile. A sturdy, broad-beamed, manly sort of man, looking more comfortable here than in his Administration office chair, despite the hair graying at the temples.

"Unpredictable? No, not really. They're a pretty placid lot. Oh, one might take a run at you if you got between her and the herd. Here, have my stick. Just give a good yell and they'll keep their distance."

He turns back to continue his inspection of the herd. John watches with fascination as below them, right in front of their eyes, one big, stout-horned animal suddenly lifts its huge front end up and mounts, yes, actually mounts a smaller creature barely able to support its weight. Quite an enthralling spectacle, for John. Together the animals surge forward with the beast on top making those impetuous urging movements of the back and legs and haunches and pelvis that John feels even a layman could interpret without too much difficulty. The blind forces of nature doing their majestic work.

"What about the bull," John says, trying to sound merely speculative, disinterested, and not at all intimidated at this display of violent passion now only fifty feet away. "Is he hard to control?"

Sloan takes his eyes off the herd for a moment to give John an enquiring baffled look, and then, seeing the direction in which John is pointing his stick, realizes what he means.

"Ah! No, no John, that's not a bull. We don't have a bull on the farm. Hardly anybody does any more. Too dangerous, too much trouble. No, the inseminator does all the breeding for us. Artificial insemination is the only way to go. Just pick your bull out of the catalogue. Wonderful quality, variety. We telephone by nine in the morning and they guarantee to be here before five."

Sloan points to the animal which was catching John's attention, and which has now pushed or squirted the small cow out from under its huge frame in its enthusiasm.

"That's old Mabel, the one with the crooked horn, our Number Three, the one on top. She's a reliable old girl. You see, as I was explaining to you, the one on top is always what we're looking for. She's the one that's ready to be bred."

"But she's a cow? A female? The one on top?"

"Yes indeed."

"And the one underneath is a female too?"

"Right on." Sloan bobs his head encouragingly.

"Amazing." John allows himself to murmur.

He's still digesting this intriguing feature of bovine behavior in the rustic world as he follows Sloan's instructions. He stands in the correct position so that, when Sloan begins to move the herd in the direction of the barn with loud cries of "Cow-up! Cow-up!", his presence, as much as his bravely threatening posture and his rather timid and self-conscious echoing, "cow-up, cow-up", can help to keep them going where they should.

Mabel, along with one other equally massive brown and white animal, takes advantage of the uniformly aligned heads and rumps of the dozen or so cows to attempt one back-side after another, thereby unintentionally aiding their progress back to the barn.

Ten minutes later they arrive. Once in the barnyard, Joan Sloan and her daughter emerge to help the men separate the two cows still trying their curious mounting exercises which apparently embarrass no one but John. He soon stands well back, because he has long ago lost any hope of being genuinely useful in the swirl of horns, legs, and voices. Somehow the two cows end up locked in the cow shed, mooing their protests, and the others are let out, to find their own way back to the pond.

Now it's time for morning coffee. Mrs. Sloan and John lead the way, with Lucy and her father a few steps behind.

"Do I get to call him Uncle John?" Lucy says to her father in a voice John is meant to overhear.

John turns around and grins at her, as Mrs. Sloan explains.

"She's a very spoiled young lady, twelve going on twenty-five. Don't let her bully you. She calls all our men guests 'uncle'."

Lucy steps up behind her mother and gives her a little push, running past as she's finishing her sentence, which causes the mother to raise her voice.

"Don't let her, John."

"Race to the house!" Lucy cries over her shoulder as she dashes ahead.

Just as suddenly, Edgar Sloan, solid, square-built, middle-aged man though he is, bursts into a stocky wide-gaited run in her wake. Mrs. Sloan smiles benignly at their disappearing backs.

"There's something in the air out here that gets to people."

John, who hasn't had a cigarette for over two hours, and who feels a little strained from the pull of his borrowed rubber boots over such terrain and distance, coughs slightly as he agrees.

"Yes, I can see that. I think it's getting to me too."

Over their coffee mugs, sitting around the big farm-kitchen table, Lucy and her father discuss whether John will go on the morning ride with them. They keep half a dozen horses, and they usually go for a hack on Saturday mornings.

"I'm sorry, I've never been on a horse," John admits as quickly as he can get a word in.

"That's alright," Lucy tells her father, "we can put him on old Jamie."

"Frankly," John decides to confess, "I'm terrified of horses."

"Oh, he wouldn't be terrified of Jamie," Lucy insists, still addressing her father.

"True," Sloan smiles at John. "Jamie is at least twenty-five years old by my reckoning. Nobody's ever been afraid of him." And then to Lucy: "Still, if John doesn't want to try it, there's no law that says he has to."

"Oh all right," Lucy says, shaking her pony tail and making a disgusted face at John. "I'll go and tack up."

"Just be firm with her, John," Mrs. Sloan says, as Lucy disappears out the door. "If she's like that at twelve, can you picture her at sixteen?"

Mrs. Sloan doesn't make it sound as though it's a condition or prospect too reprehensible in her eyes. Then she tells her husband:

"You two go and ride, dear. John and I will have a little drive around the neighborhood while you're gone. We'll see if we can pick up Toby along the way. You know where he'll be."

For John, these last words are somewhat enigmatic. It's the first he's heard of Toby. But he's happy to have escaped the horse-back ride.

John finds it quite relaxing to sit beside Mrs. Sloan's plump friendly body in the front seat of the Volvo. She does all the talking and the pointing out of places of interest. They follow one concession road after another, seeking vistas of fall colors. Some people seem to have a passion for nature in the hectic phases of its dying.

"We'll just slip in here for a moment and see if we can pick up Toby." Mrs. Sloan eventually says, uttering the mysterious name for the second time in John's hearing.

They pass a stately white house set well back from the road on a winding drive, with a cluster of white outbuildings behind it. And for a second time, John struggles to remember.

"Have I met Toby?"

"Oh no," Mrs. Sloan answers, "of course not, he was out all night again last night."

She heads the Volvo behind the big house and towards the buildings at the rear.

"Ah," she exclaims, "there he is, the little scamp."

John follows the pointing of her finger, and sees, in a clump of bushes running along the outside edge of the wire-meshed dog-run, a small, shaggy-haired, brown and white, spaniel-like creature slinking out of sight as they watch, tail and ears low to the ground. Mrs. Sloan pulls to a halt by the dog-run fence, opens the car door, and calls in a firm voice of surprising magnitude.

"Toby! Come! Come here NOW. TOBY!"

After a long pause, during which Mrs. Sloan glares confidently and authoritatively into the shrubbery where John can see no signs of life, from the far end of the cedar hedge, the brown and white mongrel emerges, looking even more sorrowful, guilty and low to the ground. It peers at them dejectedly, hunching down on the grass.

"Come here!" Mrs. Sloan insists from beside the car, with ruthless severity, and then: "Get in!"

Toby pulls himself along towards her, clinging to the surface of the earth like a snake, and finally drags his torso up onto the back seat of the car. She slams the door after him. She waves at an old man in bib-coveralls who has come outside from the cottage by the dog-run to watch the performance. The mesh fence of the dog-run is by now lined with yapping black dogs, all the same, and all twice the size of Toby. The din is alarming to John, though no one else seems to be worried.

"Thanks again, Mr. Carruthers," Mrs. Sloan calls through the car's open window as she shifts into gear, and gets a wave in return.

John and Mrs. Sloan drive home to the tune of Toby's faint moans and squeaks from the back seat, as she explains that Toby has had another cold and frustrating night ogling the neighbors' prize Labrador bitch in heat.

"You mean," John says in amazement, once he has the picture clear, "the dog just hangs around all night hoping?"

Mrs. Sloan glances over her shoulder at the depressed quivering shape of Toby, huddled in the corner of the back seat.

"Poor little guy," she says, "he can pick up the scent anywhere within a mile or two around us. If he catches a whiff, he'll trace it down and stay mooning about for four or five days and nights if we don't keep him in. Anyway, he'll be over it soon, once the bitch's time is past. Don't laugh at him, though. He's very sensitive."

John looks back into Toby's doleful pleading brown eyes. He shrugs his shoulders in answer to the inarticulate appeal there. He doesn't feel the slightest impulse to laugh.

Fifteen minutes later the car moves slowly past the Sloan barn, alongside which there is a station wagon John hasn't seen before. Edgar Sloan and a stranger in a blue smock and rubber boots are standing at the open back door of the car.

"The inseminator's come already," Mrs. Sloan says.

She waves at the two men as she and John drive on to the house.

John notes that the inseminator is pulling a clear plastic glove or sleeve up over one hand and arm. It makes him think of an over-sized condom, but he realizes just how contrary that association is. His imagination struggles to substantiate the likely state of mind of the two large animals waiting for the bull in the cow-shed. He silently wishes them the best of all possible worlds.

After lunch Edgar Sloan invites John to help him repair a corner of the horse paddock fence that has been weakened by horses playing over it. Edgar puts his hammers, saws, staples, fencing pliers and a roll of fencing wire into the wheelbarrow and leads John away to the spot under some trees in the north-east corner of the north-west paddock. Standing there is Sloan's big grey riding horse, a wet patch still showing on its back where the saddle sat a few hours ago, Across the fence is Lucy Sloan's little brown riding horse, also with a washed saddle mark.

"They're at it again, the rascals," Sloan says, sucking the flame of a match into the bowl of his pipe.

"Ah," John says, nodding knowingly, and looking to see if he could tell for himself, since he's becoming so experienced in these rustic affairs that seem to crop up every day.

As he focuses, he realizes that the big grey has its tail in the air and looks as if it would like to push the weakened fence down, like an aggressive male. But he stops himself from commenting just in time. He likes the feeling of becoming country-wise. The little brown horse, he now sees, is just as pushy, and besides, as he watches their noses touch over the fence and then graze down over each other's necks, he suddenly identifies with a shock of recognition the long cylindrical tube that is snaking downwards from the little brown horse's underside. It's a rather hideous scaled and discolored organ that even in its as yet relatively flaccid condition is taking on big proportions. John's amazement drives him to words.

"So the little one's the stallion?"

Sloan coughs on his pipe smoke.

"Not a stallion, John, just a gelding," he explains, pointing vaguely with his pipe stem at the brown horse, or perhaps locating as accurately as he can at that distance the site of the horse's missing parts.

As he speaks the little gelding and the big grey squeal in high-pitched voices and whirl around to race each other down their respective sides of the fence to its far end. There they take up the same strained, infatuated postures again.

"She's a devil, that big girl. She gets all the geldings going whenever she's in season," Sloan says. "But she'll be over it in a day or two more …. Well, shall we see what we can do about this fence?"

In the evening, while the senior Sloans prepare themselves and the food for the Saturday dinner-party at which John, of course, is to be the chief ornament on display for the neighboring gentry, Lucy leads the guest of honor off to the games room for the traditional pre-dinner contest.

"Don't let her bully you!" Mrs. Sloan reminds John, and then, varying the now-familiar theme: "Don't let her wear you out — she's a terrible tom-boy."

Lucy doesn't bother to look back, as John follows her be-jeaned, precociously developed shape along the hall. Once inside the games room, she shuts the door in a business-like way and goes directly to the table. There are two bats and a ping-pong ball waiting.

"This is my favorite," she says, grabbing the one which does not have its handle half-chipped off and its facing loose at the edges. "You get to choose ends."

John can see no difference between one end of the table and the other, but he chooses anyway, to stay in the spirit of the match.

"The first game is for two dollars," Lucy says, fishing in her tight jeans pocket for a bill, and putting it on the mantle of the stone fireplace.

"Put up your money, Uncle John."

"I'm not very good," John says, wryly, apologetically, reluctantly taking a bill from his wallet and placing it beside hers.

"We'll see," Lucy says, "Men always say that. If you get less than half my points, I'll give you a handicap next game."

A few minutes later it's obvious that it will be a miss-match. John is hypnotized by the girl's determined, efficient movements on the far side of the table, as well as by her scoring methods, as she toys with him, taking points at will.

"Enough," he says, fanning himself with his bat to cool down, after a second visit to his wallet and a second lost game, even with a five-point handicap to help him along.

"Oh come on, Uncle John," she pleads, "you're getting better and better, really you are."

"I don't have any more money," John lies.

"I can take a cheque," she says instantly.

John puts his hands on his hips, takes a deep breath, and looks down at her flushed, ingratiating smile, marveling at the lost innocence of youth.

"You little monster," he murmurs with a wry grin.

In a flash her expression changes. She laughs in his face, darts behind him and whacks him on the bottom with her bat. He chases her around the table, until she rushes to the door — but slows down enough to be sure he catches her there. She has suddenly become less robust, more feminine, helpless. She huddles against the door, hides her face in her hands. Unforgiving, he spins her around by the shoulder and smacks her bottom with his bat, perhaps a little harder than he intended. She flings open the door and runs noisily down the hall.

"Mother!" she calls in her most aggrieved tones, as she passes the kitchen door, "Uncle John hit me with his bat!"

Following at a more moderate pace, wincing a little at what the consequences might be, John meets Mrs. Sloan in the kitchen doorway, where she is now leaning out to call up the stairs after her daughter's disappearing form.

"Whatever he did to you, I'm sure you asked for it!"

At the dinner table Lucy stuck her tongue out at John for a split-second as she sat down opposite him, but apart from that the party went along much as he expected. Colonel Fox, a retired investment broker, and his wife, from the big farm north of the Sloans, and Charles and Janice Clutchey, who keep the antique shop in Tottenham, a fifteen minute drive away, were the other guests. A typical gathering, I imagine. Joan Sloan has gone through half the staff of the University extracting and supplying interest for neighborly country entertaining in the past few years. Some, like myself, probably don't come back often or ever. Others get to be regulars. John no doubt fits my category.

Not that Mrs. Sloan isn't a splendid hostess, a good cook if you enjoy those hearty roast beef and Yorkshire pudding sorts of occasions, an energetic — I was going to say conversationalist, but gossip might be a more accurate term. And Edgar Sloan, bless him, has a substantial and surprisingly varied and impressive cellar which he's not at all stingy about drawing on. By the time the guests leave, everyone can expect to be well-dined and pleasantly wined. Mrs. Sloan herself can be especially so.

When everyone else at the John feast has gone, and Lucy for all her protesting has been sent up to bed, Sloan refills his wife's liqueur glass, puts the bottle on the coffee table in front of John and says:

"Great dinner, as always, my dear. Must just step out and check the barn before turning in. You two stay and finish your drinks. Ta ta."

And he goes out through the back door, leaving John to his wife's hospitable care. She gets up and comes over to join John on the sofa, tripping a little on the rug's edge and almost slipping down against him.

"Dear me!" she says, one hand to her ample bosom, "I think all that wine and talk has gone to my head."

John gives her his hand to ease her down beside him. She holds it a little longer as she settles onto the cushions. John reaches forward for the security of his liqueur glass on the coffee table. Mrs. Sloan turns his captured hand palm upwards in her warm lap and begins to read his lines, tracing them with her finger. Her voice goes on eloquently if a little incoherently a long while.

John hears the sound of the back door opening again, and footsteps in the hall, but they continue up the stairs. Now he has the feeling that there is no outside intervention for this situation. Mrs. Sloan turns from her reading about the future revealed in his palm to the active present, grasping it with her two arms reaching around one of his.

"Why is it that such a handsome man as you has never married?" she murmurs, raising her eyes to look admiringly at John's still aloof profile.

John can see now just how slippery a slope he is on. He himself is not entirely sober. But he feels drawn to a desperate sincerity by the question asked of him often enough, though not usually in such dangerous circumstances.

"Me? Married? Who would want to be married to me?"

"Oh John!" she burst out, as if taking the hint, "most any girl in the world would want you. You're such a beautiful man!"

She slips under the arm she is hugging and presses closer. John spills a drop of liqueur down his chin.

"Well!" he splutters, searching for the right kind of banter, "most of the beautiful women in the world are already taken .... Like you Joan, you've already got a husband — and I think I hear him coming in right now."

At that she suddenly spins around and collapses, laying the back of her head in his lap, laughing.

"You're so, so sweet! Don't be silly. Eddie has gone to bed long ago. He knows I'm tipsy. He's very good to me. He doesn't mind it when I'm tipsy. I like being tipsy once in a while. Don't you like being tipsy?"

John looks down into her flushed laughing face so close to his. She's quite a handsome woman, he can see. Not too much make-up, stuff on an older woman that can really put a man off. Soft glowing skin, warm moist lips a little open, tongue teasing between her teeth. He realizes some men could find her really attractive. He realizes it's up to him. He will act now, resolutely, decisively.

"Excuse me, really sorry," he says abruptly, disentangling an arm, setting his glass on the table, and struggling out from under her head, "I think I'm going to be sick."

A little melodramatic perhaps, but wonderfully simple and effective. He quickly steps out of the room without a backward glance and strides up the stairs two at a time.

He hears several times a faint call of John John John as on his tiptoes he reaches the safety of the bathroom down the hall. Inside, he leans on the door to listen. There is no further sound. In a few minutes he has readied himself for bed. After another pause, ear to the door, he opens it quietly and negotiates the hazardous space to his bedroom as quickly as he dares to move in the half-light still glowing from downstairs.

Inside the guest room he contemplates placing a chair against the door, but decides that would be too ridiculous. In bed, he lies a long while with the covers over his ears before he drifts into a restless alcohol-fed doze.

Sunday mornings at the Sloans, he has been told, are for sleeping in. But John is awake early, before the sun is up. He hears the sound of music in the next room, movements outside his door, even what seems to be an accidental knock or two on the wall. His morning head and throat call out for help. He takes a couple of hang-over pills from his bedside table, dons his dressing gown and slippers, peeks out of the door, and heads for the bathroom.

As he picks his way in silent steps along the still dark hallway, he sees the light from the next room to his, its door half ajar so he could hardly ignore it. Transfixed, he pauses in mid-step.

Kneeling on the bed inside, a body, bare back, arms and legs, posing as if for Playboy in front of a tall oval mirror in a pine-frame stand, the naked figure of Lucy Sloan. Young, but undeniably female.

As John is about to hurry on, the girl suddenly looks away from the mirror and directly into his startled face outside her door. Abruptly, in a pantomime of surprise, she jumps off the bed and out of his angle of vision. As he hurries down the hall he hears a muffled door-slam. John can only wince as he dives into the bathroom.

After a wash and shave, he faces the return trip to his room. The hall is empty, brighter now as the morning light begins to filter in. Nearing the girl's door he realizes that it is ajar again, though inside the lamp is now out. He is about to hurry past, averting his gaze, when he hears a faint cry from inside, a low call of pain. He goes on a step, confused, uncertain, and there is another moan. Is the girl hurt? Is she suffering some sort of seizure? He can hardly just ignore it, can he? Gingerly he approaches the door. He can see nothing within. He knocks softly. The moans become more urgent. He edges the door open. He gathers up his courage and enters a few feet.

"Lucy, are you alright?" he whispers.

Moans answer him. He takes a step or two more towards the bed. It couldn't be just a nightmare, could it? She seemed too wide awake fifteen minutes ago. Now he can begin to see in the grey light. On top of the bed is a sheepskin rug spread out. And half under it, her naked back to him shining in the gloom, is the moaning figure of Lucy Sloan.

Agitated now, John raises his voice: "Lucy, is there something wrong?"

Suddenly the shape whirls around from under the rug, revealing white breast and flanks in the shadows and then covering and hiding in a flurry of grabbing and pulling. Lucy's voice flashes out accusingly.

"Go away! Go away! You, you ....sex-fiend!"

John gasps in amazement, turns and leaps quickly out of the room. He is striding into his own room when he hears a sound at the other end of the hall. The hall lights suddenly flip full on. Mrs. Sloan, in her dressing-gown, takes in the two bed-room doors open and John's retreating form at a glance.

"Really, John," she says, shaking her head, "the child is only twelve."

Abruptly, she turns out the lights and disappears.

John sits on the edge of his bed, chain-smoking and assessing the situation. Finally he makes up his mind. It's eight o'clock. He gets dressed, creeps quietly downstairs, telephones collect — who but me, his best friend in the City. In two brisk urgent sentences arranges for me to ring the Smiths by eleven, ask for him, and summon him back to the City immediately for an emergency. Leaves the nature of it to my own invention. He knows he can count on me. I ask no questions. I'm not that surprised. I'm only too glad to help.

By eleven Mrs. Sloan seeming to be her usual self is cheerfully making brunch in the kitchen. John and a perfectly normal friendly Edgar Sloan are returning from a morning visit to the stable, Lucy has fetched and showed off the eggs and unsuccessfully challenged Uncle John to a friendly game of table tennis. They are all about to sit at the breakfast table. My telephone call comes right on cue. The Sloan family seem distressed to have John's visit cut short.

"He can't go yet," Lucy pleads, "he has to have one more game with me."

"Now dear," her mother says, "John has to go, and we mustn't make it harder for him. He'll come back and see us another time, I'm sure, won't you John?"

Of course. Of course.

Safely back in the City again by mid-day, John takes a cab from the bus station to his apartment. He cooks asparagus tips on toast for a late lunch, stations himself in front of the TV set and fiddles with the remote until he locates the most popular Sunday afternoon movie, two and half stars, a family situation comedy which takes place in southern California. He then resolutely avoids until bedtime any intellectual or emotional reflex that might not be shared by many millions of his fellow North Americans.

By Thursday, John could begin to enjoy the lighter aspects of his weekend with the Sloans. It's taking on legendary qualities for him. He wants to give me more and more of the finer details. I help him along the way by comparing my own earlier experiences which are not without similarities. We really enjoyed our special aftermath lunch together.

After that, I pretty much forgot about the whole business. It must have been at least six months later when I got John's invitation to dinner at his place on Friday night — for a very important occasion. He said there would be others there, but he declined to specify. Naturally I was very curious.

In the meantime, there had been a substantial change in my own "life style", if I can call it that. You have to realize that I've been around the block (or clock) a few times, trying a little of this and a little of that, not really having things work out in any very satisfactory or permanent way. Well, finally I decided to take the big step. My dearest woman friend, Arlene, didn't expect romantic maneuvers from me. God knows, we've seen each other off and on, for better or for worse, much too long for that sort of nonsense, since she joined my University department ten years ago.

Quite simply, she's the most understanding person I know, next to John, though of course I've known him a lot longer. Anyway, she thought it might work. I thought it might work. We both had got to that certain stage in our lives. It was now or never. We had our little ceremony down at City Hall, got drunk afterwards along with most of our closest friends, except for John who was seeing his ailing mother in Vancouver. Then we took a trip to Europe over Christmas, and had just returned to settle in and try to make a go of it at my place.

Sad to say, Arlene has never liked John as much as I do. She's still a little unsure of him, I think. And of course with the big change in my domestic routine he and I didn't see quite as much of each other. Anyway, she's good about keeping surfaces intact, and we accepted John's invitation to his special occasion. I was dying to see him again so we could bring ourselves up to date.

As Arlene and I took off our coats in John's hallway, I realized it must be a truly special occasion. The apartment was completely redecorated, beautifully done with more taste than I and John put together could have summoned up. And there in the living room, in front of the fireplace, sitting on the sofa together as if for protection — Mr. and Mrs. Edgar Sloan.

Well, we exchanged our greetings in a suitably friendly way, though our surprise was mutual. I'm not sure the Sloans didn't look a little more relaxed when my wife came in behind me to be introduced. John asked us all what we were drinking. Went into the kitchen. There were voices I could faintly hear as Arlene and I chatted with the Sloans. It was becoming clear that we two married couples were the only dinner guests. All a bit mystifying.

All four of us turned our heads when the kitchen door opened again. John held it, and his companion entered with a tray of hors d'oeuvres.

It was quite a moment. John made the introductions to Arlene and me, while the Sloans looked on with what might have been a certain uneasy interest to see our variation of their own first meeting minutes before we arrived.

"Here we are," John said warmly, "this is David Bradley. I had to drag him away from the kitchen, he loves to cook and he's got something really nice going for us. David has come here from Montreal to join an architecture firm in the City. He's sharing the apartment with me. See what he's done for the old place already." And then, looking at me, "Tremendous improvement, don't you think?"

I gazed at John's changed cheerful, ingenuous smile and at the shorter trim, tanned, dark-haired and yes, God help me, wonderfully good-looking young man in a well-tailored blue suit with an apron still around his waist standing calmly beside him. I was so happy for John I had to turn away before I answered. My eyes took in the Sloans, my wife Arlene (lost in her own thoughts), and the elegant, tasteful, freshly arranged rooms.

"Yes, indeed, John," I said at last, glad to answer his waiting smile with a sincerely warm acknowledgement. "A truly wonderful improvement."

I won't bore you with a recapitulation of the evening. David turned out to be a responsive, witty, intelligent, charming talker, just a lovely person in every way, and a remarkably fine chef to boot! The Sloans and Arlene responded warmly to the food and wine and conversation. David had the Sloans sporting the beauties of their home in the country, and the precociousness of their daughter who was already showing academic brilliance and athletic prowess at the City's best girl's private school. Who knows, maybe it was preliminary to inviting David, or him and John together, for a weekend visit.

The hours flew by. David was the magic-maker. He made the Sloans forget their obvious uneasiness about John's completely unexpected invitation. He made Arlene forget she was still quite different from anyone else in the room, though it was filled with such unusual company, never asking her what country she came from (she *is* third generation Canadian, after all). And he made me totally forget my first dismay at the prospects of a revolution in John's life, and my relation with him.

In any case, I felt better and better about John. In all the time I've known him, I'd never seen him so relaxed and happy, so naturally himself. This must have seemed to him something close to what was missing for him all along — a full share of what he considered to be normal life.

"Arlene, love," I said in the taxi as we headed home, after we exhausted talking about David and John and the Sloans and what we each made of it all, "I wonder if you and I shouldn't consider, well, someday getting a home in the country, and maybe starting a family."

Arlene laughed out loud at that.

"My darling husband of three months! How adventurous you're becoming! You're always telling me how set you are in your ways. Don't you think we should try one thing at a time? Maybe after a while, just staying married to Your Favorite Little Black Girl won't suit you as well as you think it does."

"Nonsense, my sweet!" I answered. "So many of my best friends are married now. And I'm getting to like the idea more and more every day."

With that, I gave the dear girl a most uxorious kiss on her left cheek, and we sailed along behind the taxi driver's back in silence the rest of the way home, keeping our thoughts all to ourselves.

Desolation

So, now it's my turn with you. Just the two of us, my voice in your ears. Should I begin by trying to introduce myself? Probably not. Even if you were *that* interested, even if I could tell you who I really am, and you believed me, you wouldn't necessarily believe that any of the other things I'm going to tell you are true. Besides, you may be someone like me, who prefers not to be put in the position where right away you have to decide between fact and fiction.

In any case, what I'm anxious to tell you about involves myself only indirectly. It has to do with other people, two others mainly, who will probably seem more real to you than I could ever be: certainly they do to me. Here is some information about them to start with. If you like, you can check out its veracity.

First, the Births, Deaths, and Memorials page of the *Toronto Star* for 5 January, 1976. Look for a small item recording the death of Agnes Estelle Martin, "suddenly on 31 December at the age of 82." "Beloved sister," as the standard phrasing of the notice puts it — I've never seen anyone whose death is listed there who wasn't "beloved", which is a comforting commentary on human relations, no doubt — "beloved sister of Clarence Martin". A "private funeral," the newspaper goes on to say, was held in Aurora on 3 January, and (for the proper sense of finality), the body was cremated.

The other piece of information comes from the same newspaper (you see how easy I'm making it for everybody). "Robert and Reena Grosmann are proud to announce the birth of a son, 8 pounds 11 ounces (3978 grams) at Mount Sinai Hospital, 1 January. Proud great-grandparents Samuel and Phyllis Grosmann, proud grandparents Louis and Hindy Grosmann and Edward and Anne Greenwald. Sincere thanks to Dr. Sidney Baum and his staff."

Whatever the send-off given to Agnes Estelle Martin's remains by Clarence, friends or whoever chose to be at that private funeral in Aurora, the young Grosmann boy obviously had a cheerful family reception on his debut in Toronto.

That's about it as far as documentation is concerned. The rest comes out of experiences so intimate and personal and subjective that it's virtually impossible to verify, except of course by judgment and intuition. Just one more thing. The word "desolation" that I've placed in such a prominent position arises from the conversation I had (was to have or will have, perhaps I should say for the sake of immediacy) with Reena Grosmann on the afternoon of 31 December, 1975. I've always believed in the value of exactness, and so I find some satisfaction in the way the word is used. A dictionary search will show that underlying the large and vague suggestions of doom and misery aroused by the word is a clear core of meaning based on its etymological origins. Apparently it's from the Latin *solus,* meaning "alone", with the Latin prefix *de,* which serves as an intensive. There you have it. Desolation. *The condition of having been made to feel dreadfully alone.*

If you're such a confirmed and energetic truth-seeker that you've already leafed your way through the files of the *Toronto Star* looking for the issue of 5 January, 1976, you may have noticed (old newspapers are so strangely fascinating that once you begin to sail up or down their chaotic inconsequential rivers of the past, it's difficult to stop), you may have noticed, as I say, that 31 December, the day of the particular death and the eve of the particular birth I've singled out, was the occasion of a spectacular ice-storm in the Toronto region, causing a good deal of local disruption in traffic and services, temporary but inconvenient enough for some, even more serious for others.

Agnes Estelle Martin, on frail rather knobbly 82-year-old legs, would have been foolish to venture farther than the distance from her third-floor Toronto apartment, where she still dared to live all by herself, to the first-floor entrance to see if she has received any mail. She might then stand in the foyer of the small, four-storey, frequently renovated, 1920s-vintage apartment building just off Jarvis Street and look out the glass doors at the slippery road and sidewalks, a worried expression on her pale wrinkled brow beneath her netted white hair. Thinking, perhaps, of her 70-year-old brother Clarence, her only close living relation, who is due for afternoon tea, an annual Christmas-season occasion, after calling into his old law firm offices on University Avenue, but who on the other hand may still be making his way south on the treacherous highways from his home in Aurora 25 miles to the north.

Best that she not stand there for long, with those thin, trembling legs hardly protected from drafts by her loose-hanging calf-length floral dress and woolen-lined slippers, with people like me or you opening the doors and letting the icy wind rush in and along the musty-smelling corridor. She should step back at once into the manually operated elevator, with whoever else wishes to go up, try to remember not to talk to herself or click her false teeth, which she knows is a detestable habit, whether alone or in the presence of anyone who may ride up silently with her in the little, old-fashioned, rickety cubicle, and be sure to get out on the third floor, a belated Christmas card or two, some second-class mail, and her door key in hand, a cargo hardly worth her trip. Perhaps it's just as well that Agnes has lived all these years since her retirement from the nursing profession in such a dowdy — conservative would perhaps be a fairer word — such a conservative building. Now, as she opens the door of her apartment, a very small tap on the head with a blunt instrument from someone following her would crumple her small, bony body with ridiculous ease onto the old Oriental rug of her living-room and leave her 50- or 60- years' possessions readily available for a rough sorting through by any criminal who considered the effort worth his or her risk.

Agnes, a spinster, has lived this way most of her maturity after a brief, youthful, intimate sharing of living quarters with another slightly older nurse and after the awkward and painful adjustment when that woman married, opting in the end for a more natural family life. The fact that Agnes' brother is a lawyer might have given her some minimal sense of protection or support, even when he left the City twenty years ago and returned to the quieter rural life of their childhood. He did in fact deal with a difficult insurance agent for her once a decade ago, in the aftermath of the minor car accident that led her reluctantly to give up driving once and for all. And a couple of years later he got a quick capitulation from a negligent TV rental company with a letter he wrote on her behalf threatening action in the Small Claims Court. But on the whole her relation with her younger brother, though cordial enough, has long been limited to one or two social visits a year. These days, of course, Clarence is getting to the stage of life where he has few energies to spare for supporting anything else but his own declining years, even if he were in the least tempted to expend them more widely. Agnes would be right to worry about his trying to drive 25 miles through the worst storm of the season, and wrong to expect his support in any sudden extreme need she herself might have.

With Reena Grosmann, of course, the situation is entirely different. Why shouldn't she launch herself and her nine-months' embryo with gusto and confidence out the door of her fourth-floor apartment in that same building, and even stand in the main-floor entrance with the outside door ajar, instead of rushing back into the waiting elevator (which is just being entered by the shuffling Agnes Martin, whom Reena has smiled at and said hello to, though they've never met except in such passings), stand there and breathe the raw late-afternoon air deeply into her strong young lungs, swell her ripe breasts exuberantly against the embroidered corduroy of her tent-like maternity dress, and look down the street with cheerful anticipation of her husky, athletic young businessman husband's early return from work. She would even hold the door of the building open for anyone wanting to enter, and offer a friendly, warm, unsuspicious greeting to whomsoever it might be. Even Clarence Martin, wiry, slightly built, leather-cheeked, long-divorced old misogynist as he has sometimes been taken to be, could hardly avoid being charmed by such a fresh, hopeful, healthy example of pretty young wifehood and soon-to-be motherhood. And

Reena, of course, would have, figuratively speaking, embraced him in her warmth if it were they who happened to ascend in the elevator car together, her abundant love of life creating a zone of pleasure out of a six-by-six cube that might normally make his tired lawyer's mind think of prisons and solitary confinement, or possibly even mausoleums and ancestral tombs.

However, we have to suppose that Clarence is still somewhere between his simple Aurora bachelor's quarters and the City, the routes now all clogged with rush-hour traffic slowed almost to a standstill by the silvery gleam of rain turning to ice and magically coating everything it touches, roads, sidewalks, car windows, hydro lines, trees, lawns and shrubs, umbrellas and stray dogs and cats, from city core to suburbs. Perhaps, indeed, it would be best to picture him stranded somewhere to the north of the City, on the Second Concession of King Township, for example, at any rate, a place off the main highways on a slower, safer country road of the kind he prefers to travel, to avoid the dreariness of the unending metal flow the north-south routes have become since years ago Clarence first fled from Toronto back into the comparative peace of rural and small-town Ontario where he was born and grew up. To many, the disadvantages of the side-roads would be more evident than the pleasures on days like this. The sanding trucks leave them till the last, so that their surfaces can soon change from the gratifyingly tangible roughness of gravel to the giddy slickness of a country stream in mid-freeze.

So it's not an improbable picture: Clarence Martin, a prudent man who accepts the inevitability of ageing but who has decided to await a more or less natural termination of his shortening span, drawing off to the side of the concession road, near some battered rural mailbox from which the name has long ago faded, to sit with the motor keeping the car warm, looking out the unglazed lee windows at the bare, browny-white slopes of a last fall's harvested cornfield, or a whiter stretch of cattle-pasture fenced with split-cedar rails or nine-line wire, the faraway farmhouse's red-brick façade perhaps barely visible in its silvered wind-break trees, certainly not a human or animal in sight, even the farm dog refusing to come out to bark threateningly down the long lane at a strange car halted aimlessly in the distance beside the concession road culvert.

The bleakness of such a scene would certainly not offend Clarence Martin. In fact, it might chime in with his mood, arrested in his less than enthusiastic pilgrimage to a law firm office whose affairs ceased to interest him except financially twenty or more years ago and to an older sister, whose unswerving descent into decrepitude (physical though not yet so evidently mental) has not in itself been a grateful spectacle, quite apart from its secondary implications about his own route and journey. Life after a certain point, he might have conjectured, if his was a more philosophical cast of mind, looking unblinkingly on the skin of clear ice forming on top of the existing six-inch cover of snow, which in itself rests on brown rutted earth as hard and impervious as concrete, life is no longer seasonal. No happy everlasting cycle after all, but an ever-deepening of the one season: the one that is now ruthlessly crushing the landscape in its grip being only a cold metaphor for the more horrible reality, which has no hidden seeds waiting under the icy crust to break out into warm greenery.

Clarence could turn on his radio, which at this moment, if he leaves it set at his usual station, will be playing Mozart's Clarinet Concerto in A, K.622, the chief work in Bob Kerr's afternoon AM program for 31 December, or if he chooses to try other stations to pick up the weather forecasts, he might get the three o'clock news with the typical array of robberies, rapes and other standard features of the times. He may in fact prefer to sit in silence and stare at the blank winter landscape, waiting until it seems safer to drive back onto the road and perhaps head for a wayside telephone to inform Agnes that he won't be arriving for tea after all today. He personally does not relish family involvements and has obviously kept them, along with similar commitments, down to the minimum. He isn't unaware of the slightness of the threads that sometimes bind an old person to life. He could hardly help but feel uneasy about letting Agnes down, but what can he do? It's just this kind of painful dilemma that he has tried to avoid throughout his life. In any case, clearly he will not arrive on the downtown scene for the little 31 December drama, and he will have to glean what he can after it's over.

One other, shall we say, peripheral or off-stage figure must be quickly accounted for. Robert Grosmann is not so far away as Clarence Martin, merely over on Yonge Street, having left the movie theatre owned by his father and managed by the son as a step in his training for greater things, and having made his way homewards that far at an energetic and necessarily rather flamboyant walk — a walk filled, that is to say, with the many extravagant sudden gestures of an arm and leg in all directions that are required by the effort to negotiate the silvered pavements in a more or less upright position. Robert is not only closer, but is more determined and enthusiastic in his desire to make it to his destination as soon as possible. Moreover, he is in splendid physical condition, being the current men's champion of his downtown squash club and at this very moment standing (metaphorically speaking) undefeated in the third round of the inter-club tournament. He is hurrying, of course, because he must realize that his young wife, expecting her first baby within 24 hours, even in the course of a normal pregnancy, which hers most certainly is, may be a little concerned at his absence on such a foul day, and he is no doubt apprehensive that his robust embryonic son (he's certain it will be a son, and he has often listened to the miniature but powerful heartbeat throbbing to get out from under the distended skin of his wife's magnificent — how apt the word — and, to his eyes and touch, beautiful ripe belly), that his eager son may rush into the world without proper respect for the convenience of time and weather, ahead of schedule. Only this kind of explanation can account for the spectacularly galvanic performance the young man is putting on for watchers in Yonge Street doorways and windows and creeping cars and buses, most of whom in his bold slipping and sweeping progress he succeeds in leaving far behind, however comical and bizarre they may find him.

More the pity that Reena Grosmann, gazing for a last time out the front door of the apartment building and down the street, can't be pleased and reassured and no doubt amused by at least a glimpse of her acrobatic and ardent husband's imminent return. However, she has for the moment given up, and she turns in time to step back with measured pace into the elevator, which has gone up and come back down again and which is being held against its automatic instructions for a few seconds longer than expected to accommodate her belatedly signaled intentions. Courtesy also calls for the correct button to be pressed on her behalf, as the doors close.

"Thanks very much. Fourth floor for me, please."

The car jerks upward abruptly, but then continues so slowly, to the accompaniment of extraordinary creaks and rumbles, that the effect is soothing. There's a high flush in Reena Grosmann's cheeks from the fresh air and the exertion, and she's a little breathless, which gives her dark-haired rich-complexioned looks an accidental but delightful air of excitement. She clasps her hands in front of her as if to help hold up that handsome protuberance that is largely hidden in the full folds of her maternity dress, just the sort of gown indeed that many regal or aristocratic ladies centuries ago wore to veil the condition that so obviously pleases this modern young woman. The fact that she's not alone in the little cubicle is evidently not disturbing to her but enjoyable, promising a small social occasion. She is prepared to gaze candidly, smile cheerfully.

"Your floor?" she asks, as the elevator halts with a bump at the second floor, so roughly that nobody could keep balance easily, least of all an already precariously weighted female frame in the ninth month of pregnancy. No-one gets off or on. She laughs unconcernedly, however, as she holds the side railing and waits for the car to proceed upwards with another lurch.

"Isn't it terrible? This is the first time I haven't used the stairs in months," she says, standing once again with her hands folded in front of her, as the snail-like rise of the car continues. "Actually, I shouldn't really say so, since the building belongs to my own father, but this elevator is really something of a disgrace."

She's obviously more amused than bothered. She's looking across, expecting to have her sense of the fun, even the adventure, of the ascent reflected in another face, when abruptly, before she has time to focus, it is no longer possible to see another face, or indeed, in the words of the cliché, your hand in front of your face. Abruptly, as I say, without the slightest warning, the car halts and the lights simultaneously go out.

Restful as it may be in some ways to be spared the jiggle and lurch of the car's upward movement, there is an unavoidable impulse to share Reena's startled gasp and flare of fear at the sudden dark and the motionlessness and the silence. Fortunately, Reena has a reserve of confidence and resiliency. Her voice comes a little self-consciously to someone she has neglected to look at clearly until too late, a little strangely, perhaps even to her own ears, out of the sudden blackness, but with a rueful laugh.

"There, you see what I mean? I knew it would happen sooner or later. Now I wonder what we do?"

In a situation like this the full implications don't, of course, emerge at once. It will take a certain amount of time and of discussion, elliptical, disjointed, before it gradually becomes clear that the dead sounds, or relative lack of sound, in the building around the elevator shaft, doors instantly opening or closing and muted extremely faint voices, and especially the general darkness, that these are indications that it's not just a local mechanical failure to be blamed in part on Mr. Greenwald's sense of economy, but that more likely all the electrical equipment, lights, motors, alarums, and so forth, are deactivated and at least temporarily inert. The ice-storm has played its worst trick. The only question now is, will the invisible sustaining current of energy be denied for a minute, an hour or a day? At that point, an equally unanswerable question takes on a certain urgency: will Reena Grosmann's precious interior cargo continue to wait peacefully in its present location until a more suitable — I was going to say 'berth', when I reminded myself that this is no laughing matter — a more suitable dock is arranged for its unloading? One further question also becomes a matter of at least latent concern: what kind of company is Reena unexpectedly keeping in her now suddenly claustrophobic quarters?

Approximately one-half a floor above, Agnes Estelle Martin might be thought to be in altogether a more favourable situation. After all, she has only a few moments before vacated the very same elevator car and allowed it to descend at the main-floor call, and has thereby avoided being herself in Reena's predicament, at any rate, in as close duplication as her vastly different stage in life might allow. She has even managed to open her door and stand inside, in the little hallway, from which she can see the walnut table laid out with elegant china and tea-things in preparation for Clarence's arrival, the canary-cage by the window covered at the moment, so as not to waste the bird's song before Clarence's presence can be celebrated by the caroling, and the wicker basket in which her old Persian cat is now awake enough to commence washing the nearest portions of her anatomy without having to change her reclining position. Agnes might have been able to survey the entire room from her vantage point, taking in the somewhat incongruous television set among the antiques and bric-a-brac, the high shelf of books, mostly poetry in leather-bound editions, the water colours of rural scenes, the several photographs of a young woman in the garb of half-a-century ago who might have been Agnes' sister, daughter, aunt or mother, but is none of these, though for a time she may have filled a number of roles — photographs, pieces of furniture, the many other familiar features of Agnes' daily life observed as if through Clarence's eyes, since he is the one expected, and therefore viewed freshly, critically perhaps, but basically with calm acceptance.

However, Agnes has earlier fumbled a while at her outside door keyhole and at this point she too is due to be the victim of abruptly reduced perceptions. She too gasps at the suddenness with which for her the lights go out, and the at first rather alarming impact of a totally changed sensory environment. Another great difference, of course, between Agnes Martin and Reena Grosmann is that almost certainly the old lady's thoughts do not seriously and fervently wing out toward the somewhat less aged figure of her brother motionless behind the wheel of his automobile in a barren side-road twenty miles to the north, whereas just as certainly, Reena's whole mind and body emit a silent, passionate call toward that flailing, looping, gliding husband and lover who is hastening with all the power of his flourishing young tendons and tissues toward her, unaware of any real need but filled with vague (more delightful than troubling) premonitions of hazard and valiant rescue.

His strength and heroic spirit might be of use, if he were speedy enough and were heading for the third-floor apartment of Agnes Martin instead of the fourth-floor apartment of Mrs. Grosmann, Junior, but unfortunately he is not. Indeed Robert Grosmann has never even met the 82-year-old lady, though he, like Reena, would probably recognize her by sight from seeing her occasionally in the main-floor hallway or on the elevator. However, as Agnes lies slumped on the edge of her Oriental rug, conscious but unable to move more of her crumpled, chilled old body than her eyelids, it would never occur to her to think of either of her young neighbours from the floor above. Her mind, in fact, is having the greatest difficulty understanding her present position and the unaccustomed darkness, lit only by a greyer shade seeping through the taffeta curtains from the waning afternoon's hidden sun. She can spare a spasm of mental energy to realize that she is unlikely ever to see Clarence Martin step through the half-open door from the hallway. But it is more an impulse of subconscious association than a rational self-diagnosis and conclusion. The impulse sends flooding into vivid recall a picture of Clarence as he was before the first world war, a pale sombre boy of four or five in formal attire, listening with grave attention and holding back the tears barely visible in the corners of his eyes as his sister, a dozen years his senior, though still hardly more than a child herself, attempts to explain to him, while not entirely convinced to begin with, that they two will some day in the future once again be embraced by the warm arms of their mother, whose funeral, after a sudden mysterious fever struck her down in the prime of womanhood and motherhood, the uncomprehending children had just attended, and which both children viewed with more of a sense of finality than Agnes, the elder, felt she could reveal explicitly to the more tender-aged Clarence.

The memory would necessarily be coloured by its original tones and by its current context as well. In this case the two time periods reinforce each other, so that as Agnes' eyelids quiver with moisture rising almost sufficiently to overflow in a tear down her wrinkled cheek, or rather across it, given the position of her white-haired head resting on the rug, a tear of pain but primarily of grief, it might be seen as basically the same tear that trembled and refused to fall from the eyes of the young Clarence, whose mood was much the same, that is, one of profound loss, despondency and deprivation, as if the sun had gone and would never again warm the earth.

There's a small but not insignificant complication to the feelings of the old lady. Her angle of vision, restricted as it is, allows her to watch her cat's behaviour as the comfortable, well-spoiled creature becomes aware of the mistress's unusual posture and stillness. After some tentative circling and sniffing on the rug, the cat is satisfied that there is nothing further to interest her. She then casually leaps onto the television set to peer into the canary cage from this close but strictly forbidden perch. Agnes is unable to send her scurrying. In any case, after a futile reaching and clawing of air and measuring the distance she soon gives up, and drops with a solid lazy thud to the floor. Then she discovers the still half-open door into the corridor. A few moments seated just inside and peering out convince her that the exterior opportunities are more attractive than alarming, and she slips away into a hazardous life of long hallways and cold staircases and strange closed doors, gone forever from the helpless Agnes Martin's fading world. The canary huddles motionless and silent in its half-covered cage.

No-one experiences an occasional fleeting power-gap that dims the lights and cuts off the motors for a split second without a stir of apprehension not unlike the reaction to a missed heartbeat. But any longer delay in the return to normality, any sustained failure, especially in winter, brings strong reminders of the precariousness of technological civilization, the thin ice on which we forgetfully skate along through our ordinary urbanized days and nights. Reena Grosmann has no doubt found herself the most comfortable position possible in the elevator's dark cubicle, seated against the back wall, in a corner, with legs stretched out in front of her and hands protectively held over her belly. However, it's difficult to feel at ease, even without a distinct sense of the temperature falling as the furnace's residual heat fades, difficult when sitting on the floor in the dark with someone else perhaps moving about nearby, exploring the walls and floor for possible means of improving the situation, but with motions seemingly rather aimless and unpredictable, because the limitations are so obvious.

"It might be all right to try prying the doors, I suppose", Reena says upwards into the dark space above her head. "Just to be doing something, in case this thing is stuck here for hours....On the other hand, supposing it starts to move again all of a sudden."

There's a pause as the futility of any efforts at self-rescue becomes more apparent than ever. Then she goes on, with a higher note in her voice, a touch of strangeness if not uneasiness, at the dawning recognition of having to share this small dark space for an undefined period of time with someone who might not exist at all, for all she remembers from before the lights went out.

"You know, I don't think I've ever seen you here before....Do you live here, or are you just visiting?"

"Just visiting."

I can think of nothing else worth adding. It seems unlikely that anything could be said that would be genuinely reassuring. She's perfectly helpless, vulnerable, trapped in the little cage. If she's to be comforted, she must do it with the sound of her own voice.

"My husband's going to be so worried....He should be back from work by now. He'll be wondering where I've got to. It would never occur to him that I'd take the elevator. I just hope he doesn't find out and try to do anything silly like climbing into the elevator shaft. Do you mind my chattering? I must admit, I find all this a little scary."

Let her talk on, let her think about her family and friends. When you're most isolated, what a comfort to have those blood bonds, those deep relations to sustain you, to reassure you that you aren't really alone.

"He's going to be especially worried because ....I don't know whether you noticed, but I'm pregnant."

She laughs at what she's just said.

"Well of course you couldn't help but notice. But I mean I'm *very*, like would you believe tomorrow? Not just a bit, as my doctor said to me when I first went to him. Anyway, the little mischief has been very active in there. I just hope he's listening."

She laughs to herself again.

"It sounds silly, but my husband so much wants it all done properly. He's convinced it's going to be a boy, and we've already got it planned he's going to become a rabbi. We're Jewish you see, and there hasn't been a rabbi on either side of the family for four generations. Anyway, that would be very nice, though we don't really care whether it's a boy or a girl. My husband's got everybody convinced, he's so enthusiastic, but half the time he's joking. My parents and his parents and his grandfather and grandmother, they're all rooting for me to produce just the right specimen."

She's silent for a while, listening to sounds of hands roaming over the panels close by her and tugging at the doors.

"My non-Jewish friends think it's very funny," she goes on, sounding more self-absorbed than before, as if she's hypnotizing herself with her own voice, "I mean, how involved our family is in this. I've got three sisters and my husband has four brothers and a sister. My great grandfather was a wealthy man, and he had very strong feelings about family and the way things should be done, and he left money specifically for the proper Jewish education of all the grandchildren. It's amazing even for me, when we all get together as we often do, and there we are sitting around one big table or in the same room, 22 of us, everybody talking at once, knowing our Hebrew, and having the same kinds of background and upbringing and everything, though we're all very different too, of course, we're always arguing about something. It really is interesting."

Again there's a pause. And then quietly, firmly, against the darkness all around.

"I'd just love for my child to have my advantages."

There's a richness in the voice that vibrates in the air. But the air itself is growing colder still. There's something about that box suspended in space, that small, cramped chamber, that arouses associations. Somber, frightening associations. Now her voice comes again, the richness gone, embarrassed, nervous.

"This is terrible, but…I wonder how long it's going to be? I mean, I think it's because I'm so pregnant or maybe it's just my nerves. I feel terrible about it but…I don't think I can wait, I just have to go to the bathroom. What am I to do?"

The inescapable animal in us, the pathetic beast. It must be possible to pry the doors apart. Then if there's a space between the doors and the wall of the chute. For a man it would be easy. He could write his name on the wall. Make that futile little demonstration of defiance against his mere animality. For a woman, the ignominy of squatting, the humiliation, perhaps even the danger. Something has to be said.

"If you like, feel your way to the front. I'll hold the doors apart. Don't get any further out of the car than you have to."

Will she understand? Shouldn't it be put more explicitly? She mustn't place her buttocks, her bare ass so far out as to risk being crushed if the power comes on suddenly.

"I'm so sorry about this. I should be able to wait."

Her voice comes up from the gap between the doors. There is the unmistakable hiss, then far below a faint tinkle. Suddenly she giggles.

"Oh dear, somebody may be down there."

A slight pungency touches the nostrils. And after sounds of elastic and cloth being readjusted, the voice from the other side of the car, more calm and relaxed, dignity enough left still to be restored.

"Now it's your turn, please, if you're in the same boat."

"Thanks, I'm all right for now."

She sighs as she settles down on the floor again. At first there's energy in response to a crisis, and then it fades as the crisis stretches on. Now there's a new note in Reena's voice.

"I'm cold, I guess the furnace must be off."

"Here take my coat."

Quick to answer, upset at what she's provoked:

"Oh no, I couldn't, you keep it. It's just as cold for you as it is for me. Anyway I've got all this insulation."

Sounds of patting her stomach.

"I insist."

It wouldn't be wise to place it around her. Hands in the dark might alarm her more. Let her take it, lowered onto her legs by the collar. Let her adjust it around her shoulders or legs or wherever she feels the chill most. After a long while she says,

"Well, thank you. You tell me when you get cold. We'll pass it back and forth."

The forced intimacy has begun to have a strange effect on her mood. So buoyant, so self-centred in a charming sort of way, she's evidently turning her mind more and more to the other person present.

"Tell me, are you as scared as I am?"

"We'll be all right."

"Do you have someone who'll be worrying about you too?"

"Not really."

It might be possible to say more, but it would only depress her. What would be the point?

"What are you thinking?" she appeals abruptly against the silence.

It occurs to me that I could tell her. I could tell her what I'm thinking. It occurs to me that she's so confirmed in her attitudes and feelings that no messages from the opposite pole of creation where I exist would in the slightest degree affect her. I could tell her that I find her picture of family bonds, the great network of blood communications between young and old, the warm community life that she takes for granted, no, doesn't take for granted but rejoices in as a basic reality, that I find her nourishing and sustaining image an illusion, a rosy glow disguising the cold facts. I could tell her right now that the dark cell we share, that I share with this hopeful happy Jewish girl, arouses in me associations so dreadful I sicken into silence thinking of them. The cattle cars with their human freight jerking and lurching across Europe, crowded with frightened and suffering and helpless people reduced to their animal basis, stinking of excrement and urine and vomit, huddled together for the warmth and comfort of human society in an inhuman purgatory. Well, I *say* I have these associations, but to be truthful all that's so far from my own real experience that I have in my mind only a faint shadow, a mere sniff, a wisp of cloud from the billows of stifling black smoke given off by the vast furnaces that destroyed, once and for all, the hope, the dream that mankind can ever create a civilization in which the bestial is controlled and humanity is liberated and fulfilled.

So I don't reveal the depths of my mind. I don't ask Reena Grosmann angrily, "Why are you so happy? What makes you think I won't leap out of the shadows and kick you in the belly, little Jew, or rape you, or torture you, or rob you? What makes you think you, your family and your friends won't end up in some new nightmare of the Jews worse than the last? Why so excited about your baby, who may turn out to be a two-headed monster? Do you really think your husband can help you, I mean help you against disappointments and disillusionments and treachery and accidents and violence and bestiality and dreadful illnesses, and growing old and sooner or later, all alone, completely alone, in some dark corner like the one you're huddled in right now, meeting your death, going into nothingness?" It's pointless, of course, to try to get across what's basically a substructure of feeling and attitude to someone who's obviously built completely differently. So at last I answer:

"I'm thinking, you're very young."

"Meaning what?"

"Meaning you don't know what real fear is."

She is silent for a long while. It's almost as if, having sat there all that time in the dark, there just doesn't seem to be any hurry now, as if not just the clocks but time must be at a standstill as well. Finally she asks, quietly and broodingly:

"Maybe you're right, I never thought of it before. I've certainly been afraid lots of times. What do you mean by 'real fear'?"

"Real fear is when everything you've learned, everything you know, all the people you've ever met, all your experiences direct and indirect, the total meaning of life for you, adds up to one single state of mind. And you fear you'll fall into that state and never come out again."

"I see," Reena Grosmann whispers from the darkness, in the tone of somebody who doesn't really see but thinks she should and wants to very much. There's a hint in her voice that she's reluctant to go on, but has to follow the conversation through. "And what is that state of mind?"

"If I try to tell you, it won't mean anything to you. That's what I'm saying. You've never even caught a glimpse of it."

Now she sounds coaxing, almost tender in her desire to draw out the words, to offer the ease that she can, to woo the child back off the dangerous ledge, tempt the dog to drop the poisonous object he unwittingly holds in his mouth.

"Does it have a name?"

"I have name for it. I imagine everybody has his own name. Maybe for some it's nameless. I call it… 'desolation'."

"Ah", she sighs, as if she really knew it all along. "But you're wrong about me. You've just seen the one side. I've been very, very unhappy, often."

In the shadows, invisible, I shrug my shoulders, giving up. You can't communicate these things. But I have to say something to her.

"It's not the same. You? You're born happy. Bone happy. You have reserves, resources."

"Doesn't everyone?" she cries.

I go on, over-riding her ridiculous naivety.

"The world for you is full of people. People. Some not as nice as others, but always there are some you can rely on, you can love, be loved by. You're even willing to make a person of your own."

She's getting excited, animated, perhaps even exasperated listening to me. Certainly frustrated at what she takes as a kind of perversity. I can tell by her breathing and her false starts to interrupt me.

"But … but surely that's so for everybody. What kind of a world do *you* live in? Isn't that what the world really is? People?"

Well, what's to be done with such a charming little simpleton? I explain with calmness and patience.

"Incorrigible anthropomorphism. The world is so much more — and less. Animals, vegetables, minerals. Atoms and molecules. Trees, rocks, insects, bacteria. Ice-storms, snow. Mountains. And of course, stars, galaxies. People are one kind of animal, and animals are specks of dust in the universe."

I can hear her breathing still, but she says nothing. For a moment we seem to have lost each other in space. It's hardly the sort of thing to relish, but I have the feeling that at last I've got through to her. Then she surprises me, Her voice comes throbbing out of the darkness, charged to breaking with — with pity.

"You...you poor creature...I think that's so sad."

"Don't feel sorry for me," I say, perhaps a little more indignantly than I intended. "Feel sorry for yourself. That's the way things really are."

"I don't agree," she says, and I believe, unless it's my imagination, I can hear her dark hair swishing as she steadily shakes her head. "I just don't agree. It's a choice, that's what it is. It's a choice. You can see things that way if you want. But you don't have to. You can choose."

"Perhaps," I say. This is as far as my philosophy would allow me to go in accepting or refuting such an obviously irrational proposition. It's impossible to argue with anyone in those terms.

After a while in any sort of disaster people get restless again, tired of waiting to be rescued. Simply bored at best, at worst, increasingly alarmed to the point of desperately renewed effort. This can be a dangerous stage. The one area of the little cubicle that still needs exploration is the ceiling. It could be reached by someone with a lot less athletic agility than a Robert Grosmann, conceivably by a wiry old gentleman like Clarence Martin even, by making use of the hand-rails at one of the corners, and reaching for the light fixture located by feel high on the wall. Much groping, stretching and slipping might alarm Reena sufficiently to have her scramble back to her feet.

"What are you doing?"

"I think there may be a way out through the ceiling."

Reena is understandably doubtful, fearing both for what dangers would have to be run up there and perhaps also uneasy about the prospects of being left by herself after all this.

"What if it starts? You could get crushed. I've read about that."

"I'll be careful."

Some trial and error, one hand on the light fixture, both feet now a yard off the ground wedged into the hand-rail, a precarious position but fruitful in revealing to the other hand the presence of a crack outlining a trap door or removable panel in the ceiling. A firm push proves it to be the former. It falls back open to let in a gust of chillier air. For the moment it would be wiser to say nothing, but to explore silently. That high in the air, as far as Reena is concerned, is out of reach in any case, and she will be spared the alarming awareness of her unknown companion disappearing through the hole into a still higher dark space, perhaps never to be encountered again.

But Reena is no doubt listening intently, shrunk back as far as she can get into her corner of the cell. She will guess what's happening from the grunts and heavy breathing and soft thuds indicating degrees of effort and failure and success. Though she can see nothing, her eyes will be turned steadfastly upward. She will therefore get the fullest benefit of the sudden illumination that fills the car as the power surges back through the wires, and with a clanking and lurching the car abruptly begins its ascent. She cries out in a mixture of joy and alarm. Then, as if in answer to one part of her reaction, the light fades and the car jerks to a halt. But only for a moment. Again the power surges, the light goes on, the car continues its ascent, this time without further hesitation.

"Are you there? Are you all right?" Reena will cry again and again to the ceiling, but there is no black hole anymore, as if there never had been one, and there is no answer.

At the fourth floor she will rush out and along the corridor to fall into the arms of her strong young husband, her sisters, in-laws, uncles, cousins, nieces, nephews, aunts, her huge welcoming family, whose shrieks of mixed dismay and joy will fill the hallway and apartment, bringing neighbours smiling to their doors, and transforming the building into a synagogue of confused activity. Reena is trying to explain, pleading into his broad chest for her husband's attention, calling in the midst of embraces and the excited questioning, appealing to him to turn his concern to the elevator and her missing companion. Eventually they realize what she's saying. Relatives rush off to search the car and the shaft and the staircases and hallways. But no-one who can't be accounted for is to be found, and vice-versa.

Desolation

"But what about the coat?" Reena cries, looking back into the worried faces, feeling for it and not finding it over her shoulders, running her eyes around her own living-room, where she is being coddled and comforted until the doctor can come, much against her will, and give his professional opinion on her state. "The coat, it's what kept me from freezing in there."

Again a search reveals nothing. The coat like the person seems to have disappeared, both apparently ascended into thin air. Reena's thoughts are rapidly being taken over by present realities, her family are watching her carefully, concerned as much about her mental as her physical condition. The immediate past is fading for her. Robert is kneeling in front of her, rubbing her hands, pressed against her knees which he has covered in a quilt from their bed. He is talking non-stop.

"I never even thought," he groans, hitting his forehead with his palm again, "when have you last been on that elevator? I went all over the whole building, the caretaker's office, the laundry-room, the basement. I phoned everybody where you could have gone. It was just terrible, terrible. Are you sure you're all right, Reenie, some milk, have some milk, have some hot chocolate."

Reena is floating happily on a sea of attentions and good wishes. It's wonderful to be rescued. She strokes Robert's head and says again and again,

"Don't worry darling, I'm all right, the baby's all right. You feel, feel, he's moving, there...."

"Reenie, when I saw that ambulance," Robert goes on, repeating the story for the fourth or fifth time, "when I saw the stretcher coming in the front door...."

"Poor old lady," Reena murmurs, again trying to remember the look on Agnes Estelle Martin's wrinkled face a few hours earlier when they passed in the hall. Was she ailing then? Was she worried? Sad? In need? "Poor old lady."

The noise of the family around her continues, but whether from tiredness or an inexplicable reflex to some essence in the atmosphere, Reena seems to have withdrawn in spirit from the cheerful uproar.

Often in the centre of a joyful scene there is a moment of consciousness that's incompatible with everything around it. The thoughtful, even somber, certainly uncharacteristic expression on Reena's face may of course be the result of the recent strain at last showing itself, as the long day comes to an end. Or it could be caused by a faint image, shadowy, distracting, just off the periphery of her vision, that requires accommodation. An inaudible whisper from some dim corner of her mind. The dark seed of an alien memory that refuses to be simply discarded and forgotten, but that clutches at the soil of the familiar green planet she inhabits.

About the Author

F.W. Watt studied at the University of British Columbia, Oxford (as a Rhodes Scholar), and at the U. of Toronto, where he stayed as a professor in the English Department for 33 years. In the later stages of his career he dived into town and country life north of Toronto and became a commuter. Here were people in many ways different from those he knew in the ivory tower. He could see into their complicated and varied lives from close up as never before. And he was challenged to look more deeply into the ocean of his own intimate experiences, and those of many others he encountered daily. He felt driven to try to see below the surfaces. It became a compulsion to explore his visions in words and stories. He was not writing for others, but to satisfy his own need to be able to go back and relive moments of life which made him laugh and cry, and to try to understand them. Some of his visions he captured and published in poetry, others in short stories. The remaining mass of fiction, stories and novels, sat waiting during the quarter century of his retirement. Now, at 87 years, beyond the hopes and fears of young writers, but still wanting the fruits of sharing, he takes the ultimate test, the encounter with the minds and hearts of other readers. Go, little book. One of 8.

Printed in Canada